SKULLCRUSHER

CREATION ONEIROS

SKULLCRUSHER

SELECTED WEIRD FICTION

Volume One

ROBERT E HOWARD

ISBN 978-1-902197-39-5

Published 2012 by Creation Oneiros

www.creationbooks.com

All world rights reserved

Copyright © Creation Publishing 2012

Cover picture: Daniele Serra

Design by Atavistic Images

EDITOR'S INTRODUCTION

Skullcrusher is a two-volume anthology of 20 stories by Robert E Howard, written between the years 1927 and 1935 and, with a few exceptions, first published in *Weird Tales* magazine between 1929 and 1936, the year of Howard's suicide aged just 30. In presenting the stories I have decided to group them either thematically or according to main character, as opposed to a chronological format which seems less important when dealing with a body of work that appeared in such a relatively condensed time-span – although they do appear chronologically within each sub-group.

The book opens with four stories which feature either King Kull, or Bran Mak Morn, or both – two of Howard's earliest "barbarian" characters. "The Shadow Kingdom", written in 1927 and first published in *Weird Tales* in August 1929, was the first story to feature Kull – and, as such, is often cited as the first true story in the genre of "sword and sorcery". This is followed by "The Mirror Of Tuzun Thune" (first published in *Weird Tales* in September 1929) perhaps the most enigmatic Kull story of them all, and then by "Kings In The Night" (first published in *Weird Tales* in November 1930) which, as the title implies, features not only Kull but Howard's Pictish hero, Bran Mak Morn. Bran is also the hero of the next tale, "Worms Of The Earth", a Lovecraft-flavoured piece which remains one of Howard's very best weird tales, first published in the magazine of that name in November 1932.

The next group of stories feature as protagonist Solomon Kane, the puritan avenger who more often than not finds himself on the "dark continent", pitted against foes both human and supernatural. Kane debuted in "Red Shadows", written in 1927 and first published in *Weird Tales* in August 1928. This is followed by the epic "Moon Of Skulls" (first published in two parts in *Weird Tales* in June and July 1930) and "Wings In The Night", which first appeared in *Weird Tales* of July 1932. These tales are notable for, amongst other things, Howard's racial stereotyping and his portrayal of Africans as little more than sub-human, aspects which would not be tolerated today but which stand as testament to the attitudes of a different era.

Next comes a trilogy of "horror" tales, commencing with Howard's most famous (and most successfully realised) Lovecraftian entry, "The Black Stone" (first published in *Weird Tales* in November 1931). Here, Howard joins onto Lovecraft's *Cthulhu Mythos* cycle, producing a memorable character, the "mad poet" Justin Geoffrey, and also adding a new lexicon to the list of *Mythos* "necronomicons" in the form of the *Unaussprechlichen Kulten* (*Unspeakable Cults*) of Friedrich von Junzt. "Valley Of The Worm", first published in *Weird Tales* in February 1934, is also Lovecraft-tinged in its tale of James Allison (protagonist of several Howard stories), a modern man who regresses to a distant incarnation to face primal fear in the shape of an ancient, giant snake that rears from ruins graven with glyphs of "monstrous beings squatted loathsomely in inexplicable rituals rooted in the black dawn of the universe". These two stories bookend a tale of the American Deep South, "Black Canaan". First published in *Weird Tales* of June 1936, "Black Canaan" is a genuinely disturbing tale of voodoo and zombies, perhaps the most effective of Howard's horror tales in terms of unrelenting grotesquerie (and once again utilizing his customarily unflinching ethnic characterizations).

Skullcrusher Volume One ends with "Skullface", first published in *Weird Tales* in three parts (October, November and December 1929), and the only story included in the anthology to represent a relatively small section of Howard's work, that written in the genre of "weird detection". "Skullface" makes up for this in terms of length alone – it is by far the longest story in this collection. Obviously much influenced by Sax Rohmer, "Skullface" is a deranged tale of opium addiction and the hideous visions experienced by the user/ narrator as he is drawn into a web of macabre Oriental intrigue, culminating in a confrontation with an unspeakable, ancient evil in the labyrinthine drug-dens of old London.

Skullcrusher Volume Two opens with a section comprising four tales of extremely violent period adventure set roughly in and around the times of the Crusades, the first three featuring uncompromising heroes of Gaelic descent. First, Turlogh O'Brien features in "The Gods Of Bal-Sagoth", first published in *Weird Tales* in October 1931. O'Brien, *aka* Black Turlogh, is an Irish chieftain who in this story becomes king of an evil city even as it disintegrates around him in a barbaric apocalypse. Of the four stories in this section, "Gods Of Bal-Sogoth" is the only one to feature supernatural elements. In "Blood Of Belshazzar" (first published in *Oriental Stories*, Winter 1932 issue), the half-Irish knight Cormac Fitzgeoffrey – one of Howard's most hard-bitten characters – finds himself enmeshed in a death-struggle between rival bandits to acquire the fabulous jewel that gives the story its title. "The Sowers Of The Thunder", first published in *Oriental Stories*, Fall 1931 issue, stars Red Cahal, an exiled Irish prince who comes up against a ruthless adversary whom he is destined to slay at the instant of his own death. These disinherited, itinerant Gaelic mercenaries are amongst Howard's most nihilistic figures, wanderers in a world of epic carnage. The protagonist of "The Shadow Of The Vulture" (first published in *Magic Carpet* magazine in January 1934) is, by contrast, an ageing German knight caught up in the wars between Islam and the West (an aspect of this particular group of tales suddenly vitally relevant in the early 21st century). The story is perhaps more notable for another character, the Russian girl-warrior Red Sonja, prototype for the heroine much later introduced into Marvel's *Conan* comics series.

Which brings us to the final section of the anthology, comprising five of the very best stories featuring Howard's ultimate creation, Conan the Barbarian. "The Phoenix On The Sword", first published in *Weird Tales* of December 1932, is the one that started the whole Conan series, a rewrite of an old King Kull story, "By This Axe I Rule", with added supernatural flourishes, and the barbarian as King of Aquilonia; "The Scarlet Citadel", first published in *Weird Tales* of

January 1933, sees Conan in his period as King of Aquilonia once again; "Queen Of The Black Coast", first published in *Weird Tales* in May 1934, sees Conan as a river pirate, and is notable for its strong and sexy female character Bêlit, the bare-breasted pirate queen who becomes Conan's lover; this freebooter role is reprised in "Beyond The Black River" (first published in two parts *Weird Tales* of May and June 1935); and finally, comes the epic "Red Nails", first published in three parts in *Weird Tales* of July, August/September, and October of 1936, also featuring a strong female lead and much sex appeal in the form of the curvaceous swordswoman Valeria, in which Conan searches for lost treasure in an ancient, cursed city. Needing no more introduction, these stories reside at the core of Howard's literary legacy.

And so concludes **Skullcrusher**, after more than five hundred pulsating pages of weird horror, black magic, bloody carnage, dismemberment and death.

—James Havoc, editor, 2011

FOREWORD : "PRIMAL DREAMER"

"For certain sorts of writing are out in orbit monstrous, in the sense that one must be obsessed beyond normality even to set the words and the concepts onto the page. One must be dedicated, called, driven by one's peculiar god, by the creation of one's curious magic."

–Henry Treece (*Notes on Perception And Vision*, 1966)

Robert E Howard was certainly obsessed – probably beyond reason. Harlan Ellison described him as "madder than a bulldog". Never travelling physically more than twenty or thirty miles outside his Texas home, in his mind he voyaged through time and space to savage lands of fantasy. One would be tempted to write him off as an unreal daydreamer, a writer of puerile escapist fantasies – of escape into a simpler, more direct world of black and white morality ruled by muscle and sinew, where problems could be resolved by the simple swipe of a sword blade. But one could not write off that taste of authenticity, the throb of the primal in his writing. There is a pulse there as if he had connected with the archetypes and they possessed him and drove him like the voudon loas.

He was driven – unable to secure satisfactory employment. At odds with the mundane world around him, only content when parting the veil between what we call reality and that strange domain of violence and the sacred, where giant figures stalk through mist-shrouded landscapes propelled towards some unknown Ragnarok.

And what of his curious magic? Little refinement there. Narrow in scope. Blunt and at times, bludgeoning – like a punk-rock guitar riff or a Jerry Lee Lewis song expanded to the scale of a Wagnerian opera. His characters always variations on the same theme, renamed and transposed historically and spatially; each new scenario fabricated hastily from the remains of the previous one. A few new props scattered randomly. Doom, paranoia, hysterical violence.

Each Howard scenario comes complete with the same voice-over, meant to sound rousing or threatening – repeated until it becomes comforting, soothing. Same sketch of a plot. Historical notes and scholarly asides strewn randomly hither and yon as though as an afterthought. At times spurious. Sometimes shockingly accurate.

Dead – suicided – before his work saw publication in book form, Howard never got to create that novel he so wanted to write, set in the mist-haunted landscape of Roman Britain. Picts, Celts, Vikings – all somehow cut from the same cloth. Faced with problems that most of us would baulk at, his heroes would work up a black rage and hack, stamp and smash their way out. Frontiersmen all.

Even the most poorly written (technically speaking) of Howard's fiction is strong stuff. A weird mixture of gritty realism and bullshit. It grabs you like a pitbull and doesn't let go of you until you've turned the last page. What it lacks in subtlety and scope it makes up for in emotion.

Near the end of his short life he started to write tales of his native Texas. Stick to what you know, the man said. We'll never know if he could have developed further as a writer; stuck as he was below Faulkner and Steinbeck (quite a way below actually) but above Louis L'Amour and Sven Hassell (thankfully quite a way above!). All we have to go on is what has survived. Here is the very best of it.

Raw and bloody.

Still beating.

−D M Mitchell, 2011

THE SHADOW KINGDOM

I : A KING COMES RIDING

The blare of the trumpets grew louder, like a deep golden tide surge, like the soft booming of the even tides against the silver beaches of Valusia. The throng shouted, women flung roses from the roofs as the rhythmic chiming of silver hoofs came clearer and the first of the mighty array swung into view in the broad white street that curved round the golden-spired Tower of Splendor.

First came the trumpeters, slim youths, clad in scarlet, riding with a flourish of long, slender golden trumpets; next the bowmen, tall men from the mountains; and behind these the heavily armed footmen, their broad shields clashing in unison, their long spears swaying in perfect rhythm to their stride. Behind them came the mightiest soldiery in all the world, the Red Slayers, horsemen, splendidly mounted, armed in red from helmet to spur. Proudly they sat their steeds, looking neither to right nor to left, but aware of the shouting for all that. Like bronze statues they were, and there was never a waver in the forest of spears that reared above them.

Behind those proud and terrible ranks came the motley files of the mercenaries, fierce, wild-looking warriors, men of Mu and Kaa-u and of the hills of the east and the isles of the west. They bore spears and heavy swords, and a compact group that marched somewhat apart were the bowmen of Lemuria. Then came the light foot of the nation, and more trumpeters brought up the rear.

A brave sight, and a sight which aroused a fierce thrill in the soul of Kull, king of Valusia. Not on the Topaz Throne at the front of the regal Tower of Splendor sat Kull, but in the saddle, mounted on a great stallion, a true warrior king. His mighty arm swung up in reply to the salutes as the hosts passed. His fierce eyes passed the gorgeous trumpeters with a casual glance, rested longer on the following soldiery; they blazed with a ferocious light as the Red Slayers halted in front of him with a clang of arms and a rearing of steeds, and tendered him the crown salute. They narrowed slightly as the mercenaries strode by. They saluted no one, the mercenaries. They walked with shoulders flung back, eyeing Kull boldly and straightly, albeit with a certain appreciation; fierce eyes, unblinking; savage eyes, staring from beneath shaggy manes and heavy brows.

And Kull gave back a like stare. He granted much to brave men, and there were no braver in all the world, not even among the wild tribesmen who now disowned him. But Kull was too much the savage to have any great love for these. There were too many feuds. Many were age-old enemies of Kull's nation, and though the name of Kull was now a word accursed among the mountains and valleys of his people, and though Kull had put them from his mind, yet the old hates, the ancient passions still lingered. For Kull was no Valusian but an Atlantean.

The armies swung out of sight around the gem-blazing shoulders of the Tower of Splendor and Kull reined his stallion about and started toward the palace at an easy gait, discussing the review with the commanders that rode with him, using not many words, but saying much.

"The army is like a sword," said Kull, "and must not be allowed to rust." So down the street they rode, and Kull gave no heed to any of the whispers that reached his hearing from the throngs that still swarmed the streets.

"That is Kull, see! But what a king! And what a man! Look at his arms! His shoulders!"

And an undertone of more sinister whisperings: "Kull! Ha, accursed usurper from the pagan isles–"

"Aye, shame to Valusia that a barbarian sits on the Throne of Kings..."

Little did Kull heed. Heavy-handed had he seized the decaying throne of ancient Valusia and with a heavier hand did he hold it, a man against a nation.

After the council chamber, the social palace where Kull replied to the formal and laudatory phrases of the lords and ladies, with carefully hidden, grim amusement at such frivolities; then the lords and ladies took their formal departure and Kull leaned back upon the ermine throne and contemplated matters of state until an attendant requested permission from the great king to speak, and announced an emissary from the Pictish embassy.

Kull brought his mind back from the dim mazes of Valusian statecraft where it had been wandering, and gazed upon the Pict with little favor. The man gave back the gaze of the king without flinching. He was a lean-hipped, massive-chested warrior of middle height, dark, like all his race, and strongly built. From strong, immobile features gazed dauntless and inscrutable eyes.

"The chief of the Councilors, Ka-nu of the tribe, right hand of the king of Pictdom, sends greetings and says: There is a throne at the feast of the rising moon for Kull, king of kings, lord of lords, emperor of Valusia."

"Good," answered Kull, "Say to Ka-nu the Ancient, ambassador of the western isles, that the king of Valusia will quaff wine with him when the moon floats over the hills of Zalgara."

Still the Pict lingered. "I have a word for the king, not" – with a contemptuous flirt of his hand – "for these slaves."

Kull dismissed the attendants with a word, watching the Pict warily.

The man stepped nearer, and lowered his voice: "Come alone to feast tonight, lord king. Such was the word of my chief."

The king's eyes narrowed, gleaming like gray sword steel, coldly.

"Alone?"

"Aye."

They eyed each other silently, their mutual tribal enmity seething beneath their cloak of formality. Their mouths spoke the cultured speech, the conventional court phrases of a highly polished race, a race not their own, but from their eyes gleamed the primal traditions of the elemental savage. Kull might be the king of Valusia and the Pict might be an emissary to her courts, but there in the throne hall of kings, two tribesmen glowered at each other, fierce and wary, while ghosts of wild wars and world-ancient feuds whispered to each.

To the king was the advantage and he enjoyed it to its fullest extent. Jaw resting on hand, he eyed the Pict, who stood like an image of bronze, head flung back, eyes unflinching.

Across Kull's lips stole a smile that was more a sneer.

"And so I am to come – alone?" Civilization had taught him to speak by innuendo and the Pict's dark eyes glittered, though he made no reply. "How am I to know that you come from Ka-nu?"

"I have spoken," was the sullen response.

"And when did a Pict speak truth?" sneered Kull, fully aware that the Picts never lied, but using this means to enrage the man.

"I see your plan, king," the Pict answered imperturbably. "You wish to anger me. By Valka, you need go no further! I am angry enough. And I challenge you to meet me in single battle, spear, sword or dagger, mounted or afoot. Are you king or man?"

Kull's eyes glinted with the grudging admiration a warrior must needs give a bold foeman, but he did not fail to use the chance of further annoying his antagonist.

"A king does not accept the challenge of a nameless savage," he sneered, "nor does the emperor of Valusia break the Truce of Ambassadors. You have leave to go. Say to Ka-nu I will come alone."

The Pict's eyes flashed murderously. He fairly shook in the grasp of the primitive blood-lust; then, turning his back squarely upon the king of Valusia, he strode across the Hall of Society and vanished through the great door.

Again Kull leaned back upon the ermine throne and meditated.

So the chief of the Council of Picts wished him to come alone? But for what reason? Treachery? Grimly Kull touched the hilt of his great sword. But scarcely. The Picts valued too greatly the alliance with Valusia to break it for any feudal reason. Kull might be a warrior of Atlantis and hereditary enemy of all Picts, but too, he was king of Valusia, the most potent ally of the Men of the West.

Kull reflected long upon the strange state of affairs that made him ally of ancient foes and foe of ancient friends. He rose and paced restlessly across the hall, with the quick, noiseless tread of a lion. Chains of friendship, tribe and tradition had he broken to satisfy his ambition. And, by Valka, god of the sea and the land, he had realized that ambition! He was king of Valusia – a fading, degenerate Valusia, a Valusia living mostly in dreams of bygone glory, but still a mighty land and the greatest of the Seven Empires. Valusia – Land of Dreams, the tribesmen named it, and sometimes it seemed to Kull that he moved in a dream. Strange to him were the intrigues of court and palace, army and people. All was like a masquerade, where men and women hid their real thoughts with a smooth mask. Yet the seizing of the throne had been easy – a bold snatching of opportunity, the swift whirl of swords, the slaying of a tyrant of whom men had wearied unto death, short, crafty plotting with ambitious statesmen out of favor at court – and Kull, wandering adventurer, Atlantean exile, had swept up to the dizzy heights of his dreams: he was lord of Valusia, king of kings. Yet now it seemed that the seizing was far easier than the keeping. The sight of the Pict had brought back youthful associations to his mind, the free, wild savagery of his boyhood. And now a strange feeling of dim unrest, of unreality, stole over him as of late it had been doing. Who was he, a straightforward man of the seas and the mountain, to rule a race strangely and terribly wise with the mysticisms of antiquity? An ancient race—

"I am Kull!" said he, flinging back his head as a lion flings back his mane. "I am Kull!"

His falcon gaze swept the ancient hall. His self-confidence flowed back... And in a dim nook of the hall a tapestry moved – slightly.

II : THUS SPAKE THE SILENT HALLS OF VALUSIA

The moon had not risen, and the garden was lighted with torches aglow in silver cressets when Kull sat down on the throne before the table of Ka-nu, ambassador of the western isles. At his right hand sat the ancient Pict, as much unlike an emissary of the fierce race as a man could be. Ancient was Ka-nu and wise in statecraft, grown old in the game. There was no elemental hatred in the eyes that looked at Kull appraisingly; no tribal traditions hindered his judgments. Long associations with the statesmen of the civilized nations had swept away such cobwebs. Not: who and what is this man? was the question ever foremost in Ka-nu's mind, but: can I use this man, and how? Tribal prejudices he used only to further his own schemes.

And Kull watched Ka-nu, answering his conversation briefly, wondering if civilization would make of him a thing like the Pict. For Ka-nu was soft and paunchy. Many years had stridden across the sky-rim since Ka-nu had wielded a sword. True, he was old, but Kull had seen older than he in the forefront of battle. The Picts were a long-lived race. A beautiful girl stood at Ka-nu's elbow, refilling his goblet, and she was kept busy. Meanwhile Ka-nu kept up a running fire of jests and comments, and Kull, secretly contemptuous of his garrulity, nevertheless missed none of his shrewd humor.

At the banquet were Pictish chiefs and statesmen, the latter jovial and easy in their manner, the warriors formally courteous, but plainly hampered by their tribal affinities. Yet Kull, with a tinge of envy, was cognizant of the freedom and ease of the affair as contrasted with like affairs of the Valusian court. Such freedom prevailed in the rude camps of Atlantis – Kull shrugged his shoulders. After all, doubtless Ka-nu, who had seemed to have forgotten he was a Pict as far as time-hoary custom and prejudice went, was right and he, Kull, would better become a Valusian in mind as in name.

At last when the moon had reached her zenith, Ka-nu, having eaten and drunk as much as any three men there, leaned back upon his divan with a comfortable sigh and said, 'Now, get you gone, friends, for the king and I would converse on such matters as concern not children. Yes, you to my pretty; yet first let me kiss those ruby lips – so; now dance away, my rose-bloom."

Ka-nu's eyes twinkled above his white beard as he surveyed Kull, who sat erect, grim and uncompromising.

"You are thinking, Kull," said the old statesman, suddenly, "that Ka-nu is a useless old reprobate, fit for nothing except to guzzle wine and kiss wenches!"

In fact, this remark was so much in line with his actual thoughts, and so plainly put, that Kull was rather startled, though he gave no sign.

Ka-nu gurgled and his paunch shook with his mirth. "Wine is red and women are soft," he remarked tolerantly. "But – ha! ha! – think not old Ka-nu allows either to interfere with business."

Again he laughed, and Kull moved restlessly. This seemed much like being made sport of, and the king's scintillant eyes began to glow with a feline light.

Ka-nu reached for the wine-pitcher, filled his beaker and glanced questioningly at Kull, who shook his head irritably.

"Aye," said Ka-nu equably, "it takes an old head to stand strong drink. I am growing old, Kull, so why should you young men begrudge me such pleasures as we oldsters must find? Ah me, I grow ancient and withered, friendless and cheerless."

But his looks and expressions failed far of bearing out his words. His rubicund countenance fairly glowed, and his eyes sparkled, so that his white beard seemed incongruous. Indeed, he looked remarkably elfin, reflected Kull, who felt vaguely resentful. The old scoundrel had lost all of the primitive virtues of his race and of Kull's race, yet he seemed more pleased in his aged days than otherwise.

"Hark ye, Kull," said Ka-nu, raising an admonitory finger, "'tis a chancy thing to laud a young man, yet I must speak my true thoughts to gain your confidence."

"If you think to gain it by flattery–"

"Tush. Who spake of flattery? I flatter only to disguard."

There was a keen sparkle in Ka-nu's eyes, a cold glimmer that did not match his lazy smile. He knew men, and he knew that to gain his end he must smite straight with this tigerish barbarian, who, like a wolf scenting a snare, would scent out unerringly any falseness in the skein of his word-web.

"You have power, Kull," said he, choosing his words with more care than he did in the council rooms of the nation, "to make yourself mightiest of all kings, and restore some of the lost glories of Valusia. So. I care little Valusia – though the women and wine be excellent – save for the fact that the stronger Valusia is, the stronger is the Pict nation. More, with an Atlantean on the throne, eventually Atlantis will become united–"

Kull laughed in harsh mockery. Ka-nu had touched an old wound.

"Atlantis made my name accursed when I went to seek fame and fortune among the cities of the world. We – they – are age-old foes of the Seven Empires, as you should know."

Ka-nu tugged his beard and smiled enigmatically.

"Nay, nay. Let it pass. But I know whereof I speak. And then warfare will cease, wherein there is no gain; I see a world of peace and prosperity – man loving his fellow man – the good supreme. All this you can you accomplish – *if you live!*"

"Ha!" Kull's lean hand closed on his hilt and he half rose, with a sudden movement of such dynamic speed that Ka-nu, who fancied men as some men fancy blooded horses, felt his old blood leap with a sudden thrill. Valka, what a warrior! Nerves and sinews of steel and fire, bound together with the perfect coordination, the fighting instinct, that makes the terrible warrior.

But none of Ka-nu's enthusiasm showed in his mildly sarcastic tone.

"Tush. Be seated. Look about you. The gardens are empty, save for ourselves. You fear not *me*?"

Kull sank back, gazing about him warily.

"There speaks the savage," mused Ka-nu. "Think you if I planned treachery I would enact it here where suspicion would be sure to fall upon me? Tut. You young tribesmen have much to learn. There were my chiefs who were not at ease because you were born among the hills of Atlantis, and you despise me in your secret mind because I am a Pict. Tush. I see you as Kull, king of Valusia, not as Kull the reckless Atlantean, leader of the raiders who harried the western isles. So you should see in me, not a Pict but an international man, a figure of the world. Now to that figure, hark! If you were slain tomorrow, who would be king?"

"Kaanuub, baron of Blaal."

"Even so. I object to Kaanuub for many reasons, yet most of all for fact that he is but a figurehead."

"How so? He was my greatest opponent, but I did not know that he championed any cause but his own."

"The night can hear," answered Ka-nu obliquely. "There are worlds within worlds. But you may trust me and you may trust Brule, the Spear-Slayer. Look!" He drew from his robes a bracelet of gold representing a winged dragon coiled thrice, with three horns of ruby on the head.

"Examine it closely. Brule will wear it on his arm when he comes to you tomorrow night so that you may know him. Trust Brule as you trust yourself, and do what he tells you to. And in proof of trust, look ye!"

And with the speed of a striking hawk, the ancient snatched something from his robes, something that flung a weird green light over them, and which he replaced in an instant.

"The stolen gem!" exclaimed Kull, recoiling. "The green jewel from the Temple of the Serpent! Valka! You! And why do you show it to me?"

"To save your life. To prove my trust. If I betray your trust, deal with me likewise. You hold my life in your hands. Now I could not be false to you if I would, for a word from you would be my doom."

Yet for all his words the old scoundrel beamed merrily and seemed vastly pleased with himself.

"But why do you give me this hold over you?" asked Kull, becoming more bewildered each second.

"As I told you. Now, you see that I do not intend to deal you false, and tomorrow night when Brule comes to you, you will follow his advice without fear of treachery. Enough. An escort waits outside to ride to the palace with you, lord."

Kull rose. "But you have told me nothing."

"Tush. How impatient are youths!" Ka-nu looked more like a mischievous elf than ever. "Go you and dream of thrones and power and kingdoms, while I dream of wine and soft women and roses. And fortune ride with you, King Kull."

As he left the garden, Kull glanced back to see Ka-nu still reclining lazily in his seat, a merry ancient, beaming on all the world with jovial fellowship.

A mounted warrior waited for the king just without the garden and Kull was slightly surprised to see that it was the same that had brought Ka-nu's invitation. No word was spoken as Kull swung into the saddle nor as they clattered along the empty streets.

The color and the gaiety of the day had given way to the eerie stillness of night. The city's antiquity was more than ever apparent beneath the bent, silver moon. The huge pillars of the mansions and palaces towered up into the stars. The broad stairways, silent and deserted, seemed to climb endlessly until they vanished in the shadowy darkness of the upper realms. Stairs to the stars, thought Kull, his imaginative mind inspired by the weird grandeur of the scene.

Clang! clang! clang! sounded the silver hoofs on the broad, moon-flooded streets, but otherwise there was no sound. The age of the city, its incredible antiquity, was almost oppressive to the king; it was as if the great silent buildings laughed at him noiselessly, with unguessable mockery. And what secrets did they hold?

"You are young," said the palaces and the temples and the shrines, "but we are old. The world was wild with youth when we were reared. You and your tribe shall pass, but we are invincible, indestructible. We towered above a strange world, ere Atlantis and Lemuria rose from the sea; we still shall reign when the green waters sigh for many a restless fathom above the spires of Lemuria and the hills of Atlantis and when the isles of the Western Men are the mountains of a strange land.

"How many kings have we watched ride down these streets before Kull of Atlantis was even a dream in the mind of Ka, bird of Creation? Ride on, Kull of Atlantis; greater shall follow you; greater came before you. They are dust; they are forgotten; we stand; we know; we are. Ride, ride on, Kull of Atlantis; Kull the king, Kull the fool!"

And it seemed to Kull that the clashing hoofs took up the silent refrain to beat it into the night with hollow re-echoing mockery:

"Kull – the – king! Kull – the – fool!"

Glow, moon; you light a king's way! Gleam, stars; you are torches in the train of an emperor! And clang, silver-shod hoofs; you herald that Kull rides through Valusia.

Ho! Awakc, Valusia! It is Kull that rides, Kull the king!

"We have known many kings," said the silent halls of Valusia.

And so in a brooding mood Kull came to the palace, where his bodyguard, men of the Red Slayers, came to take the rein of the great stallion and escort Kull to his rest. There the Pict, still sullenly speechless, wheeled his steed with a savage wrench of the rein and fled away in the dark like phantom; Kull's heightened imagination pictured him speeding through the silent streets like a goblin out of the Elder World.

There was no sleep for Kull that night, for it was nearly dawn and he spent the rest of the night hours pacing the throne room, and pondering over what had passed. Ka-nu had told him nothing, yet he had put himself in Kull's complete power. At what had he hinted when he had said the baron of Blaal was naught but a figurehead? And who was this Brule who was to come to him by night, wearing the mystic armlet of the dragon? And why? Above all, why had Ka-nu shown him the green gem of terror, stolen long ago from the Temple of the Serpent, for which the world would rock in wars were it known to the weird and terrible keepers of that temple, and from whose vengeance not even Ka-nu's ferocious tribesmen might be able to save him? But Ka-nu knew he was safe, reflected Kull, for the statesman was too shrewd to expose himself to risk without profit. But was it to throw the king off his guard and pave the way to treachery? Would Ka-nu dare let him live now? Kull shrugged his shoulders.

III : THEY THAT WALK THE NIGHT

The moon had not risen when Kull, hand to hilt, stepped to a a window. The windows opened upon the great inner gardens of the royal palace, and the breezes of the night, bearing the scents of spice trees, blew the filmy curtains about. The king looked out. The walks and groves were deserted; carefully trimmed trees were bulky shadows; fountains near by flung their slender sheen of silver in the starlight and distant fountains rippled steadily. No guards walked those gardens, for so closely were the outer walls guarded that it seemed impossible for any invader to gain access to them.

Vines curled up the walls of the palace, and even as Kull mused upon the ease with which they might be climbed, a segment of shadow detached itself from the darkness below the window and a bare, brown arm curved up over the sill and into the room with the swift, easy motion of a climbing leopard.

"You are Brule?" asked Kull, and then stopped in surprise not unmingled with annoyance and suspicion; for the man was he whom Kull had taunted in the hall of Society; the same who had escorted him from the Pictish embassy.

"I am Brule, the Spear-Slayer," answered the Pict in a guarded voice; then swiftly, gazing closely in Kull's face, he said, barely above a whisper:

"Ka nama kaa lajerama!"

Kull started. "Ha! What mean you?"

"Know you not?"

"Nay, the words are unfamiliar; they are of no language I ever heard – and yet, by Valka! – somewhere – I have heard–"

"Aye," was the Pict's only comment. His eyes swept the room, the study room of the palace. Except for a few tables, a divan or two and great shelves of books of parchment, the room was barren compared to the grandeur of the rest of the palace.

"Tell me, king, who guards the door?"

"Eighteen of the Red Slayers. But how come you, stealing through the gardens by night and scaling the walls of the palace?"

Brule sneered. "The guards of Valusia are blind buffaloes. I could steal their girls from under their noses. I stole amid them and they saw me not nor heard me. And the walls – I could scale them without the aid of vines. I have hunted tigers on the foggy beaches when the sharp east breezes blew the mist in from seaward and I have climbed the steeps of the western sea mountain. But come – nay, touch this armlet."

He held out his arm and, as Kull complied wonderingly, gave an apparent sigh of relief.

"So. Now throw off those kingly robes; for there are ahead of you this night such deeds as no Atlantean ever dreamed of."

Brule himself was clad only in a scanty loin-cloth through which was thrust a short, curved sword.

"And who are you to give me orders?" asked Kull, slightly resentful.

"Did not Ka-nu bid you follow me in all things?" asked the Pict irritably, his eyes flashing momentarily. "I have no love for you, lord, but for the moment I have put the thought of feuds from my mind. Do you likewise. But come."

Walking noiselessly, he led the way across the room to the door. A slide door allowed a view of the outer corridor, unseen from without, and the Pict bade Kull look.

"What see you?"

"Naught but the eighteen guardsmen."

The Pict nodded, motioned Kull to follow him across the room. At a panel in the opposite wall Brule stopped and fumbled there a moment. Then with a light movement he stepped back, drawing his sword as he did so. Kull gave an exclamation as the panel swung silently open, revealing a dimly lighted passageway.

"A secret passage!" swore Kull softly. "And I knew nothing of it! By Valka, someone shall dance for this!"

"Silence!" hissed the Pict.

Brule was standing like a bronze statue as if straining every nerve for the slightest sound; something about his attitude made Kull's hair prickle slightly, not from fear but from some eerie anticipation. Then beckoning, Brule stepped through the secret doorway which stood open behind them. The passage was bare, but not dust-covered as should have been the case with an unused secret corridor. A vague, gray light filtered through somewhere, but the source of it was not apparent. Every few feet Kull saw doors, invisible as he knew, from the outside, but easily apparent from within.

"The palace is a very honeycomb," he muttered.

"Aye. Night and day you are watched, king, by many eyes."

The king was impressed by Brule's manner. The Pict slowly, warily, half crouching, blade held low and thrust forward. When he spoke it was in a whisper and he continually flung glances from side to side.

The corridor turned sharply, and Brule warily gazed past the turn.

"Look!" he whispered. "But remember! No word! No sound – on your life!"

Kull cautiously gazed past him. The corridor changed just at the bend to a flight of steps. And then Kull recoiled. At the foot of those stairs lay the eighteen Red Slayers who were that night stationed to watch the king's study room. Brule's grip upon his mighty arm and Brule's fierce whisper at his shoulder alone kept Kull from leaping down those stairs.

"Silent, Kull! Silent, in Valka's name!" hissed the Pict. "These corridors are empty now, but I risked much in showing you, that you might then believe what I had to say. Back now to the room of study." And he retraced his steps, Kull following; his mind in a turmoil of bewilderment

"This is treachery," muttered the king, his steel-gray eyes a-smolder, "foul and swift! Mere minutes have passed since those men stood at guard."

Again in the room of study Brule carefully closed the secret panel and motioned Kull to look again through the slit of the outer door. Kull gasped audibly. *For without stood the eighteen guardsmen!*

"This is sorcery!" he whispered, half-drawing his sword. "Do dead men guard the king?"

"*Aye!*" came Brule's scarcely audible reply; there was a strange expression in the Pict's scintillant eyes. They looked squarely into each other's eyes for an instant, Kull's brow wrinkled in a puzzled scowl as he strove to read the Pict's inscrutable face. Then Brule's lips, barely moving, formed the words:

"*The – snake – that – speaks!*"

"Silent!" whispered Kull, laying his hand over Brule's mouth. "That is death to speak! That is a name accursed!"

The Pict's fearless eyes regarded him steadily.

"Look again, King Kull. Perchance the guard was changed."

"Nay, those are the same men. In Valka's name, this is sorcery – this is insanity! I saw with my own eyes the bodies of those men, not eight minutes agone. Yet there they stand."

Brule stepped back, away from the door, Kull mechanically following.

"Kull, what know ye of the traditions of this race ye rule?"

"Much – and yet, little. Valusia is so old–"

"Aye," Brule's eyes lighted strangely, "we are but barbarians – infants compared to the Seven Empires. Not even they themselves know how old they are. Neither the memory of man nor the annals of the historians reach back far enough to tell us when the first men came up from the sea and built cities on the shore. But Kull, *men were not always ruled by men!*"

The king started. Their eyes met.

"Aye, there is a legend of my people–"

"And mine!" broke in Brule. "That was before we of the isles were allied with Valusia. Aye, in the reign of Lion-fang, seventh war chief of the Picts, so many years ago no man remembers how many. Across the sea we came, from the isles of the sunset, skirting the shores of Atlantis, and falling upon the beaches of Valusia with fire and sword. Aye, the long white beaches resounded with the clash of spears, and the night was like day from the flame of the burning castles. And the king, the king of Valusia, who died on the red sea sands that dim day–" His voice trailed off; the two stared at each other, neither speaking; then each nodded.

"Ancient is Valusia!" whispered Kull. "The hills of Atlantis and Mu were isles of the sea when Valusia was young."

The night breeze whispered through the open window. Not the free, sea air as Brule and Kull knew and reveled in, in their land, but a breath like a whisper from the past, laden with musk, scents of forgotten things, breathing secrets that were hoary when the world was young.

The tapestries rustled, and suddenly Kull felt like a naked child before the inscrutable wisdom of the mystic past. Again the sense of unreality swept upon him. At the back of his soul stole dim, gigantic phantoms, whispering monstrous things. He sensed that Brule experienced similar thoughts. The Pict's eyes were fixed upon his face with a fierce intensity. Their glances met. Kull felt warmly a sense of comradeship with this member of an enemy tribe. like rival leopards turning at bay against hunters, these two savages made common cause against the inhuman powers of antiquity.

Brule again led the way back to the secret door. Silently they entered and silently they proceeded down the dim corridor, taking the opposite direction from that in which they had previously traversed it. After a while the Pict stopped and pressed close to one of the secret doors, bidding Kull look with him through the hidden slot.

"This opens upon a little-used stair which leads to a corridor running past the study-room door."

They gazed, and presently, mounting the stair silently, came a silent shape.

"Tu! Chief councilor!" exclaimed Kull. "By night and with bared dagger! How, what means this, Brule?"

"Murder! And foulest treachery!" hissed Brule. "Nay" – as Kull would have flung the door aside and leaped forth – "we are lost if you meet him here, for more lurk at the foot of those stairs. Come!"

Half running, they darted back along the passage. Back through the secret door Brule led, shutting it carefully behind them, then across the chamber to an opening into a room seldom used. There he swept aside some tapestries in a dim corner nook and, drawing Kull with him, stepped behind them. Minutes dragged. Kull could hear the breeze in the other room blowing the window curtains about, and it seemed to him like the murmur of ghosts. Then through the door, stealthily, came Tu, chief councilor of the king. Evidently he had come through the study room and, finding it empty, sought his victim where he was most likely to be.

He came with upraised dagger, walking silently. A moment he halted, gazing about the apparently empty room, which was lighted dimly by a single candle. Then he advanced cautiously, apparently at a loss to understand the absence of the king. He stood before the hiding place – and–

"Slay!" hissed the Pict.

Kull with a single mighty leap hurled himself into the room. Tu spun but the blinding tigerish speed of the attack gave him no chance for defence or counter-attack. Sword steel flashed in the dim light and grated on bone as Tu toppled backward, Kull's sword standing out between his shoulders.

Kull leaned above him, teeth bared in the killer's snarl, heavy brows a scowl above eyes that were like the gray ice of the cold sea. Then he released the hilt and recoiled, shaken, dizzy, the hand of death at his spine.

For as he watched, Tu's face became strangely dim and unreal; the features mingled and merged in a seemingly impossible manner. Then, like a fading mask of fog, the face suddenly vanished and in its stead gaped and leered *a monstrous serpent's head!*

"Valka!" gasped Kull, sweat beading his forehead, and again: "Valka!"

Brule leaned forward, face immobile. Yet his glittering eyes mirrored something of Kull's horror.

"Regain your sword, lord king," said he. "There are yet deeds to be done."

Hesitantly Kull set his hand to the hilt. His flesh crawled as he set his foot upon the terror which lay at their feet, and as some jerk of muscular reaction caused the frightful mouth to gape suddenly, he recoiled, weak with nausea. Then, wrathful at himself, he plucked forth his sword and gazed more closely at the nameless thing that had been known as Tu, chief councilor. Save for the reptilian head, the thing was the exact counterpart of a man.

"A man with the head of a snake!" Kull murmured. 'This, then, is a priest of the serpent god?"

"Aye. Tu sleeps unknowing. These fiends can take any form they will. That is, they can, by a magic charm or the like, fling a web of sorcery about their faces, as an actor dons a mask, so that they resemble anyone they wish to."

"Then the old legends were true," mused the king; "the grim old tales few dare even whisper, lest they die as blasphemers, are no fantasies. By Valka, I had thought – I had guessed – but it seems beyond the bounds of reality. Ha! The guardsmen outside the door–"

"They too are snake-men. Hold! What would you do?"

"Slay them!" said Kull between his teeth.

"Strike at the skull if at all," said Brule. "Eighteen wait without the door and perhaps a score more in the corridors. Hark ye, king, Ka-nu learned of this plot. His spies have pierced the inmost fastnesses of the snake priests and they brought hints of a plot. Long ago he discovered the secret passageways of the palace, and at his command I studied the map thereof and came here by night to aid you, lest you die as other kings of Valusia have died. I came alone for the reason that to send more would have roused suspicion. Many could not steal into the palace as I did. Some of the foul conspiracy you have seen. Snake-men guard your door, and that one, as Tu, could pass anywhere else in the palace; in the morning, if the priests failed, the real guards would be holding their places again, nothing knowing, nothing remembering; there to take the blame if the priests succeeded. But stay you here while I dispose of this carrion."

So saying, the Pict shouldered the frightful thing stolidly and vanished with it through another secret panel. Kull stood alone, his mind a-whirl. Neophytes of the mighty Serpent, how many lurked among his cities? How might he tell the false from the true? Aye, how many of his trusted councilors, his generals, were men? He could be certain – of whom?

The secret panel swung inward and Brule entered.

"You were swift."

"Aye!" The warrior stepped forward, eyeing the floor. "There is gore upon the rug. See?"

Kull bent forward; from the corner of his eye he saw a blur of movement, a glint of steel. Like a loosened bow he whipped erect, thrusting upward. The warrior sagged upon the sword, his own clattering to the floor. Even at that instant Kull reflected grimly that it was appropriate that the traitor should meet death upon the sliding, upward thrust used so much by his race. Then, as Brule slid from the sword to sprawl motionless on the floor, the face began to merge and fade, and as Kull caught his breath, his hair a-prickle, the human features vanished and there the jaws of a great snake gaped hideously, the terrible beady eyes venomous even in death.

"He was a snake-priest all the time!" gasped the king. "Valka! What an elaborate plan to throw me off guard! Ka-nu there, is he a man? Was it Ka-nu to whom I talked in the gardens? Almighty Valka!" as his flesh crawled with a horrid thought: "are the people of Valusia men or are they all serpents?"

Undecided he stood, idly seeing that the thing named Brule no longer wore the dragon armlet. A sound made him wheel.

Brule was coming through the secret door.

"Hold!" upon the arm upthrown to halt the king's hovering sword gleamed the dragon armlet. "Valka!" The Pict stopped short. Then a grim smile curled his lips.

"By the gods of the seas! These demons are crafty past reckoning. For it must be that that one lurked in the corridors, and seeing me go carrying the carcass of that other, took my appearance. So. I have another to do away with."

"Hold!" there was the menace of death in Kull's voice; "I have seen two men turn to serpents before my eyes. How may I know if you are a true man?"

Brule laughed. "For two reasons, King Kull. No snake-man wears this" – he indicated the dragon armlet – "nor can say these words," and again Kull heard the strange phrase: *"Ka nama kaa lajerama."*

"Ka nama kaa lajerama," Kull repeated mechanically. "Now where, in Valka's name, have I heard that? I have not! And yet – and yet–"

"Aye, you remember, Kull," said Brule. "Through the dim corridors of memory those words lurk; though you never heard them in this life, yet in the bygone ages they were so terribly impressed upon the soul mind that never dies, that they will always strike dim chords in your memory, though you be reincarnated for a million years to come. For that phrase has come secretly down the grim and bloody eons, since when, uncounted centuries ago, those words were watch-words for the race of men who battled with the grisly beings of the Elder Universe. For none but a real man of men may speak them, whose jaws and mouth are shaped different from any other creature. Their meaning has been forgotten but not the words themselves."

"True," said Kull. "I remember the legends – Valka!" He stopped short, staring, for suddenly, like the silent swinging wide of a mystic door, misty, unfathomed reaches opened in the recesses of his unconsciousness and for an instant he seemed to gaze back through the vastness that spanned life and life; seeing through the vague and ghostly fogs dim shapes reliving dead centuries – men in combat with hideous monsters, vanquishing a planet of frightful terrors. Against a gray, ever-shifting background moved strange nightmare forms, fantasies of lunacy and fear; and man, the jest of the gods, the blind, wisdomless striver from dust to dust, following the long bloody trail of his destiny, knowing not why, bestial, blundering, like a great murderous child, yet feeling somewhere a spark of divine fire... Kull drew a hand across his brow, shaken; these sudden glimpses into the abysses of memory always startled him.

"They are gone," said Brule, as if scanning his secret mind; "the birdwomen, the harpies, the bat-men, the flying fiends, the wolf-people, the demons, the goblins – all save such as this being that lies at our feet, and a few of the wolf-men. Long and terrible was the war, lasting through the bloody centuries, since first the first men, risen from the mire of apedom, turned upon those who then ruled the world. And at last mankind conquered, so long ago that naught but dim legends came to us through the ages. The snake-people were the last to go, yet at last men conquered even them and drove them forth into the waste lands of the world, there to mate with true snakes until some day, say the sages, the horrid breed shall vanish utterly. Yet the Things returned in crafty guise as men grew soft and degenerate, forgetting ancient wars. Ah, that was a grim and secret war! Among the men of the Younger Earth stole the frightful monsters of the Elder Planet, safe-guarded by their horrid wisdom and mysticisms, taking all forms and shapes, doing deeds of horror secretly. No man knew who was true man and who false. No man could trust any man. Yet by means of their own craft they formed ways by which the false might be known from the true. Men took for a sign and a standard the figure of the flying dragon, the winged dinosaur, a monster of past ages, which was the greatest foe of the serpent. And men used those words which I spoke to you as a sign and symbol, for as I said, none but a true man can repeat them. So mankind triumphed. Yet again the fiends came after the years of forgetfulness had gone by – for man still an ape in that he forgets what is not ever before his eyes. As priests they came; and for that men in their luxury and might had by then lost faith in the old religions and worships, the snake-men, in the guise of teachers of a new and truer cult, built a monstrous religion about the worship of the serpent god. Such is their power that it is now death to repeat the old legends of the snake-people, and people bow again to the serpent god in new form; and blind fools that they are, the great hosts of men see no connection between this power and the power men overthrew eons ago. As priests the snake-men are content to rule – and yet–" He stopped.

Go on." Kull felt an unaccountable stirring of the short hair at the base of his scalp.

"Kings have reigned as true men in Valusia," the Pict whispered, "and yet, slain in battle, have died serpents – as died he who fell beneath the spear of Lion-fang on the red beaches when we of the isles harried the Seven Empires. And how can this be, Lord Kull? These kings were born of women and lived as men! This – the true kings died in secret – as you would have died tonight – and priests of the Serpent reigned in their stead, no man knowing."

Kull cursed between his teeth. "Aye, it must be. No one has ever seen a priest of the Serpent and lived, that is known. They live in utmost secrecy."

"The statecraft of the Seven Empires is a mazy, monstrous thing," said Brule. "There the true men know that among them glide the spies of the Serpent, and the men who are the Serpent's allies – such as Kaanuub, baron of Blaal – yet no man dares to seek to unmask a suspect lest vengeance befall him. No man trusts his fellow and the true statesmen dare not speak to each other what is in the minds of all. Could they be sure, could a snake-man or plot be unmasked before them all, then would the power of the Serpent be more than half broken; for all would then ally and make common cause, sifting out the traitors. Ka-nu alone is of sufficient shrewdness and courage to cope with them, and even Ka-nu learned only enough of their plot to tell me what would happen – what has happened up to this time. Thus far I was prepared; from now on we must trust to our luck and our craft. Here and now I think we are safe; those snake-men without the door dare not leave their post lest true men come here unexpectedly. But tomorrow they will try something else, you may be sure. Just what they will do, none can say, not even Ka-nu; but we must stay at each other's sides, King Kull, until we conquer or both be dead. Now come with me while I take this carcass to the hiding-place where I took the other being."

Kull followed the Pict with his grisly burden through the secret panel, and down the dim corridor. Their feet, trained to the silence of the wilderness, made no noise. Like phantoms they glided through the ghostly light, Kull wondering that the corridors should be deserted; at every turn he expected to run full upon some frightful apparition. Suspicion surged back upon him; was this Pict leading him into ambush? He fell back a pace or two behind Brule, his ready sword hovering at the Pict's unheeding back. Brule should die first if he meant treachery. But if the Pict was aware of the king's suspicion, he showed no sign. Stolidly he tramped along, until they came to a room, dusty and long unused, where moldy tapestries hung heavy. Brule drew aside some of these and concealed the corpse behind them.

Then they turned to retrace their steps, when suddenly Brule halted with such abruptness that he was closer to death than he knew; for Kull's nerves were on edge.

"Something is moving in the corridor," hissed the Pict. "Ka-nu said these ways would be empty, yet—"

He drew his sword and stole into the corridor, Kull following warily.

A short way down the corridor a strange, vague glow appeared that came toward them. Nerves a-leap, they waited, backs to the corridor wall; for what they knew not, but Kull heard Brule's breath hiss through his teeth and was reassured as to Brule's loyalty.

The glow merged into a shadowy form. A shape vaguely like a man it was, but misty and illusive, like a wisp of fog, that grew more tangible as it approached, but never fully material. A face looked at them, a pair of luminous great eyes, that seemed to hold all the tortures of a million centuries. There was no menace in that face, with its dim, worn features, but only a great pity – and that face – that face–

"Almighty gods!" breathed Kull, an icy hand at his soul; "Eallal, king of Valusia, who died a thousand years ago!"

Brule shrank back as far as he could, his narrow eyes widened in a blaze of pure horror, the sword shaking in his grip, unnerved for the first time that weird night. Erect and defiant stood Kull, instinctively holding his useless sword at the ready; flesh a-crawl, hair a-prickle, yet still a king of kings, as ready to challenge the powers of the unknown dead as the powers of the living.

The phantom came straight on, giving them no heed; Kull shrank back as it passed them, feeling an icy breath like a breeze from the arctic snow. Straight on went the shape with slow, silent footsteps, as if the chains of all the ages were upon those vague feet; vanishing about a bend of the corridor.

"Valka!" Kull shook his head wonderingly. "Did you not recognize the face? That was Eallal, who reigned in Valusia a thousand years ago and who was found hideously murdered in his throne room – the room now known as the Accursed Room. Have you not seen his statue in the Fame Room of Kings?"

"Yes, I remember the tale now. Gods, Kull! that is another sign of the frightful and foul power of the snake priests – that king was slain by snake-people and thus his soul became their slave, to do their bidding throughout eternity! For the sages have ever maintained that if a man is slain by a snake-man his ghost becomes their slave."

A shudder shook Kull's gigantic frame. "Valka! But what a fate! Hark—" his fingers closed upon Brule's sinewy arm like steel – "hark ye! If I am wounded unto death by these foul monsters, swear that ye will smite your sword through my breast lest my soul be enslaved."

"I swear," answered Brule, his fierce eyes lighting. "And do ye the same by me, Kull."

Their strong right hands met in a silent sealing of their bloody bargain.

IV : MASKS

Kull sat upon his throne and gazed broodingly upon the sea of faces turned toward him. A courtier was speaking in evenly modulated tones, but the king scarcely heard him. Close by, Tu, chief councilor, stood ready at Kull's command, and each time the king looked at him, Kull shuddered inwardly. The surface of court life was as the unrippled surface of the sea between tide and tide. To the musing king the affairs of the night before seemed as a dream, until his eyes dropped to the arm of his throne. A brown sinewy hand rested there, upon the wrist of which gleamed a dragon armlet; Brule stood beside his throne and ever the Pict's fierce secret whisper brought him back from the realm of unreality in which he moved.

No, that was no dream, that monstrous interlude. As he sat upon the throne in the Hall of Society and gazed upon the courtiers, the ladies, the lords, the statesmen, he seemed to see their faces as things of illusion, things unreal, existent only as shadows and mockeries of substance. Always he had seen their faces as masks, but before he had looked on them with contemptuous tolerance, thinking to see beneath the masks shallow, puny souls, avaricious, lustful, deceitful; now there was a grim undertone, a sinister meaning, a vague horror that lurked beneath the smooth masks. While he exchanged courtesies with some nobleman or councilor he seemed to see the smiling face fade like smoke and the frightful jaws of a serpent gaping there. How many of those he looked upon were horrid, inhuman monsters, plotting his death, beneath the smooth mesmeric illusion of a human face?

Valusia — land of dreams and nightmares — a kingdom of the shadows ruled by phantoms who glided back and forth behind the painted curtains, mocking the futile king who sat upon the throne — himself a shadow.

And like a comrade shadow Brule stood by his side, dark eyes glittering from immobile face. A real man, Brule! And Kull felt his friendship for the savage become a thing of reality and sensed that Brule felt a friendship for him beyond the mere necessity of statecraft.

And what, mused Kull, were the realities of life? Ambition, power, pride? The friendship of man, the love of women — which Kull had never known — battle, plunder, what? Was it the real Kull who sat upon the throne or was it the real Kull who had scaled the hills of Atlantis, harried the far isles of the sunset, and laughed upon the green roaring tides of the Atlantean sea? How could a man be so many different men in a lifetime? For Kull knew that there were many Kulls and he wondered which was the real Kull. After all, the priests of the Serpent merely went a step further in their magic, for all men wore masks, and many a different mask with each different man or woman; and Kull wondered if a serpent did not lurk under every mask.

So he sat and brooded in strange, mazy thought ways, and the courtiers came and went and the minor affairs of the day were completed, until at last the king and Brule sat alone in the Hall of Society save for the drowsy attendants.

Kull felt a weariness. Neither he nor Brule had slept the night before, nor had Kull slept the night before that, when in the gardens of Ka-nu he had had his first hint of the weird things to be. Last night nothing further had occurred after they had returned to the study room from the secret corridors, but they had neither dared nor cared to sleep. Kull, with the incredible vitality of a wolf, had aforetime gone for days upon days without sleep, in his wild savage days, but now his mind was edged from constant thinking and from the nerve-breaking eeriness of the past night. He needed sleep, but sleep was furthest from his mind.

And he would not have dared sleep if he had thought of it. Another thing that had shaken him was the fact that though he and Brule had kept a close watch to see if, or when, the study-room guard was changed, yet it was changed without their knowledge; for the next morning those who stood on guard were able to repeat the magic words of Brule, but they remembered nothing out of the ordinary. They thought that they had stood guard all night, as usual, and Kull said nothing to the contrary. He believed them true men, but Brule had advised absolute secrecy, and Kull also thought it best.

Now Brule leaned over the throne, lowering his voice so not even a lazy attendant could hear: "They will strike soon, I think, Kull. A while ago Ka-nu gave me a secret sign. The priests know that we know of their plot, of course, but they know not how much we know. We must be ready for any sort of action. Ka-nu and the Pictish chiefs will remain within hailing distance now until this is settled one way or another. Ha, Kull, if it comes to a pitched battle, the streets and the castles of Valusia will run red!"

Kull smiled grimly. He would greet any sort of action with a ferocious joy. This wandering in a labyrinth of illusion and magic was extremely irksome to his nature. He longed for the leap and clang of swords, for the joyous freedom of battle.

Then into the Hall of Society came Tu again, and the rest of the councilors.

"Lord king, the hour of the council is at hand and we stand ready to you to the council room."

Kull rose, and the councilors bent the knee as he passed through the way opened by them for his passage, rising behind him and following. Eyebrows were raised as the Pict strode defiantly behind the king, but no one dissented. Brule's challenging gaze swept the smooth faces of the councilors with the defiance of an intruding savage.

The group passed through the halls and came at last to the council chamber. The door was closed, as usual, and the councilors arranged themselves in the order of their rank before the dais upon which stood the king. Like a bronze statue Brule took up his stand behind Kull.

Kull swept the room with a swift stare. Surely no chance of treachery here. Seventeen councilors there were, all known to him; all of them espoused his cause when he ascended the throne.

"Men of Valusia—" he began in the conventional manner, then halted, perplexed. The councilors had risen as a man and were moving toward him. There was no hostility in their looks, but their actions were strange for council room. The foremost was close to him when Brule sprang forward, crouched like a leopard.

"*Ka nama kaa lajerama!*" his voice crackled through the sinister silence of the room and the foremost councilor recoiled, hand flashing to his robes, and like a spring released Brule moved and the man pitched headlong to the glint of his sword – headlong he pitched and lay still while his face faded and became the head of a mighty snake.

"Slay, Kull!" rasped the Pict's voice. "They be all serpent men!"

The rest was a scarlet maze. Kull saw the familiar faces dim like fading fog and in their places gaped horrid reptilian visages as the whole band rushed forward. His mind was dazed but his body faltered not.

The singing of his sword filled the room, and the onrushing flood broke into a red wave. But they surged forward again, seemingly willing to fling their lives away in order to drag down the king. Hideous jaws gaped at him; terrible eyes blazed into his unblinkingly; a frightful fetid scent pervaded the atmosphere – the serpent scent that Kull had known in southern jungles. Swords and daggers leaped at him and he was dimly aware that they wounded him. But Kull was in his element; never before had he faced such grim foes but it mattered little; they lived, their veins held blood that could be spilt and they died when his great sword cleft their skulls or drove through their bodies. Slash, thrust, thrust and swing. Yet had Kull died there but for the man who crouched at his side, parrying and thrusting. For the king was clear berserk, fighting in the terrible Atlantean way, that seeks death to deal death; he made no effort to avoid thrusts and slashes, standing straight up and ever plunging forward, no thought in his frenzied mind but to slay. Not often did Kull forget his fighting craft in his primitive fury, but now some chain had broken in his soul, flooding his mind with a red wave of slaughter-lust. He slew a foe at each blow, but they surged about him, and time and again Brule turned a thrust that would have slain, as he crouched beside Kull, parrying and warding with cold skill, slaying not as Kull slew with long slashes and plunges, but with short overhand blows and upward thrusts.

Kull laughed, a laugh of insanity. The frightful faces swirled about him in a scarlet blaze. He felt steel sink into his arm and dropped his sword in a flashing arc that cleft his foe to the breast-bone. Then the mists faded and the king saw that he and Brule stood alone above a sprawl of hideous crimson figures who lay still upon the floor.

"Valka! What a killing!" said Brule, shaking the blood from his eyes. "Kull, had these been warriors who knew how to use the steel, we had died here. These serpent priests know naught of swordcraft and die easier than any men I ever slew. Yet had there been a few more, I think the matter had ended otherwise."

Kull nodded. The wild berserker blaze had passed, leaving a mazed feeling of great weariness. Blood seeped from wounds on breast, shoulder, arm and leg. Brule, himself bleeding from a score of flesh wounds, glanced at him in some concern.

"Lord Kull, let us hasten to have your wounds dressed by the women."

Kull thrust him aside with a drunken sweep of his mighty arm.

"Nay, we'll see this through ere we cease. Go you, though, and have your wounds seen to – I command it."

The Pict laughed grimly. "Your wounds are more than mine, lord king–" he began, then stopped as a sudden thought struck him. "By Valka, Kull, this is not the council room!"

Kull looked about and suddenly other fogs seemed to fade. "Nay, this is the room where Eallal died a thousand years ago – since unused and named 'Accursed'."

"Then by the gods, they tricked us after all!" exclaimed Brule in a fury, kicking the corpses at their feet. "They caused us to walk like fools into their ambush! By their magic they changed the appearance of all–"

["hen there is further deviltry afoot," said Kull, "for if there be true men the councils of Valusia they should be in the real council room now. Come swiftly."

And leaving the room with its ghastly keepers they hastened through halls that seemed deserted until they came to the real council room. Then Kull halted with a ghastly shudder. *From the council room sounded a voice speaking, and the voice was his!*

With a hand that shook he parted the tapestries and gazed into the room. There sat the councilors, counterparts of the men he and Brule had slain, and upon the dais stood Kull, king of Valusia.

He stepped back, his mind reeling.

"This is insanity!" he whispered. "Am I Kull? Do I stand here or is that Kull yonder in very truth and am I but a shadow, a figment of thought?"

Brule's hand clutching his shoulder, shaking him fiercely, brought him to his senses.

"Valka's name, be not a fool! Can you yet be astounded after all we have seen? See you not that those are true men bewitched by a snake-man who has taken your form, as those others took their forms? By now you should have been slain and yon monster reigning in your stead, unknown by those who bowed to you. Leap and slay swiftly or else we are undone. The Red Slayers, true men, stand close on each hand and none but you can reach and slay him. Be swift!"

Kull shook off the onrushing dizziness, flung back his head in the old, defiant gesture. He took a long, deep breath as does a strong swimmer before diving into the sea; then, sweeping back the tapestries, made the dais in a single lion-like bound. Brule had spoken truly. There stood men of the Red Slayers, guardsmen trained to move quick as the striking leopard; any but Kull had died ere he could reach the usurper. But the sight of Kull, identical with the man upon the dais, held them in their tracks, their minds stunned for an instant, and that was long enough. He upon the dais snatched for his sword, but even as his fingers closed upon the hilt, Kull's sword stood out behind his shoulders and the thing that men had thought the king pitched forward from the dais to lie silent upon the floor.

"Hold!" Kull's lifted hand and kingly voice stopped the rush that had started, and while they stood astounded he pointed to the thing which lay before them – whose face was fading into that of a snake. They recoiled, and from one door came Brule and from another came Ka-nu.

These grasped the king's bloody hand and Ka-nu spoke: "Men of Valusia, you have seen with your own eyes. This is the true Kull, the mightiest king to whom Valusia has ever bowed. The power of the Serpent is broken and ye be all true men. King Kull, have you commands?"

"Lift that carrion," said Kull, and men of the guard took up the thing.

"Now, follow me," said the king, and he made his way to the Accursed Room. Brule, with a look of concern, offered the support of his arm but Kull shook him off.

The distance seemed endless to the bleeding king, but at last he stood at the door and laughed fiercely and grimly when he heard the horrified ejaculations of the councilors.

At his orders the guardsmen flung the corpse they carried beside the others, and motioning all from the room Kull stepped out last and closed the door.

A wave of dizziness left him shaken. The faces turned to him, palled and wonderingly, swirled and mingled in a ghostly fog. He felt the blood from his wounds trickling down his limbs and he knew that what he was to do, he must do quickly or not at all.

His sword rasped from its sheath.

"Brule, are you there?"

"Aye!" Brule's face looked at him through the mist, close to his shoulder, but Brule's voice sounded leagues and eons away.

"Remember our vow, Brule. And now, bid them stand back."

His left arm cleared a space as he flung up his sword. Then with all his waning power he drove it through the door into the jamb, driving the great sword to the hilt and sealing the room forever.

Legs braced wide, he swayed drunkenly, facing the horrified councilors. "Let this room be doubly accursed. And let those rotting skeletons lie there forever as a sign of the dying might of the Serpent. Here I swear that I shall hunt the serpent-men from land to land, from sea to sea, giving no rest until all be slain, that good triumph and the power of Hell be broken. This thing I swear – I – Kull – king – of – Valusia."

His knees buckled as the faces swayed and swirled. The councilors leaped forward, but ere they could reach him, Kull slumped to the floor, and lay still, face upward.

The councilors surged about the fallen king, chattering and shrieking. Ka-nu beat them back with his clenched fists, cursing savagely.

"Back, you fools! Would you stifle the little life that is yet in him? How,

Brule, is he dead or will he live?" – to the warrior who bent above the prostrate Kull.

"Dead?" sneered Brule irritably. "Such a man as this is not so easily killed. Lack of sleep and loss of blood have weakened him – by Valka, he has a score of deep wounds, but none of them mortal. Yet have those gibbering fools bring the court women here at once."

Brule's eyes lighted with a fierce, proud light.

"Valka, Ka-nu, but here is such a man as I knew not existed in these degenerate days. He will be in the saddle in a few scant days and then may the serpent-men of the world beware of Kull of Valusia. Valka! but that will he a rare hunt! Ah, I see long years of prosperity for the world with such a king upon the throne of Valusia."

THE MIRRORS OF
TUZUN THUNE

"A wild, weird clime that lieth sublime
Out of Space, out of Time."
—Poe

There comes, even to kings, the time of great weariness. Then the gold of the throne is brass, the silk of the palace becomes drab. The gems in the diadem sparkle drearily like the ice of the white seas; the speech of men is as the empty rattle of a jester's bell and the feel comes of things unreal; even the sun is copper in the sky, and the breath of the green ocean is no longer fresh.

Kull sat upon the throne of Valusia and the hour of weariness was upon him. They moved before him in an endless, meaningless panorama: men, women, priests, events and shadows of events; things seen and things to be attained. But like shadows they came and went, leaving no trace upon his consciousness, save that of a great mental fatigue. Yet Kull was not tired. There was a longing in him for things beyond himself and beyond the Valusian court. An unrest stirred in him, and strange, luminous dreams roamed his soul. At his bidding there came to him Brule the Spear-slayer, warrior of Pictland, from the islands beyond the West.

"Lord king, you are tired of the life of the court. Come with me upon my galley and let us roam the tides for a space."

"Nay." Kull rested his chin moodily upon his mighty hand. "I am weary beyond all these things. The cities hold no lure for me – and the borders are quiet. I hear no more the sea-songs I heard when I lay as a boy on the booming crags of Atlantis, and the night was alive with blazing stars. No more do the green woodlands beckon me as of old. There is a strangeness upon me and a longing beyond life's longings. Go!"

Brule went forth in a doubtful mood, leaving the king brooding upon his throne. Then to Kull stole a girl of the court and whispered:

"Great king, seek Tuzun Thune, the wizard. The secrets of life and death are his, and the stars in the sky and the lands beneath the seas."

Kull looked at the girl. Fine gold was her hair and her violet eyes were slanted strangely; she was beautiful, but her beauty meant little to Kull.

"Tuzun Thune," he repeated. "Who is he?"

"A wizard of the Elder Race. He lives here in Valusia, by the Lake of Visions in the House of a Thousand Mirrors. All things are known to him, lord king; he speaks with the dead and holds converse with the demons of the Lost Lands."

Kull arose.

"I will seek out this mummer; but no word of my going, do you hear?"

"I am your slave, my lord." And she sank to her knees meekly, but the smile of her scarlet mouth was cunning behind Kull's back and the gleam of her narrow eyes was crafty.

Kull came to the house of Tuzun Thune, beside the Lake of Visions. Wide and blue stretched the waters of the lake, and many a fine palace rose upon its banks; many swan-winged pleasure boats drifted lazily upon its hazy surface and evermore there came the sound of soft music.

Tall and spacious, but unpretentious, rose the House of a Thousand Mirrors. The great doors stood open, and Kull ascended the broad stair and entered, unannounced. There in a great chamber, whose walls were of mirrors, he came upon Tuzun Thune, the wizard. The man was ancient as the hills of Zalgara; like wrinkled leather was his skin, but his cold gray eyes were like sparks of sword steel.

"Kull of Valusia, my house is yours," said he, bowing with old-time courtliness and motioning Kull to a throne-like chair.

"You are a wizard, I have heard," said Kull bluntly, resting his chin upon his hand and fixing his sombre eyes upon the man's face. "Can you do wonders?"

The wizard stretched forth his hand; his fingers opened and closed like a bird's claws.

"Is that not a wonder – that this blind flesh obeys the thoughts of my mind? I walk, I breathe, I speak – are they not all wonders?"

Kull meditated awhile, then spoke. "Can you summon up demons?"

"Aye. I can summon up a demon more savage than any in ghostland – by smiting you in the face."

Kull started, then nodded. "But the dead, can you talk to the dead?"

"I talk with the dead always – as I am talking now. Death begins with birth, and each man begins to die when he is born; even now you are dead, King Kull, because you were born."

"But you, you are older than men become; do wizards never die?"

"Men die when their time comes. No later, no sooner. Mine has not come."

Kull turned these answers over in his mind.

"Then it would seem that the greatest wizard of Valusia is no more than an ordinary man, and I have been duped in coming here."

Tuzun Thune shook his head. "Men are but men, and the greatest men are they who soonest learn the simpler things. Nay, look into my mirrors, Kull."

The ceiling was a great many mirrors, and the walls were mirrors, perfectly joined, yet many mirrors of many sizes and shapes.

"Mirrors are the world, Kull," droned the wizard. "Gaze into my mirrors and be wise."

Kull chose one at random and looked into it intently. The mirrors upon the opposite wall were reflected there, reflecting others, so that he seemed to be gazing down a long, luminous corridor, formed by mirror behind mirror; and far down this corridor moved a tiny figure. Kull looked long ere he saw that the figure was the reflection of himself. He gazed and a queer feeling of pettiness came over him; it seemed that that tiny figure was the true Kull, representing the real proportions of himself. So he moved away and stood before another.

"Look closely, Kull. That is the mirror of the past," he heard the wizard say.

Gray fogs obscured the vision, great billows of mist, ever heaving and changing like the ghost of a great river; through these fogs Kull caught swift fleeting visions of horror and strangeness; beasts and men moved there and shapes neither men nor beasts; great exotic blossoms glowed through the grayness; tall tropic trees towered high over reeking swamps, where reptilian monsters wallowed and bellowed; the sky was ghastly with flying dragons, and the restless seas rocked and roared and beat endlessly along the muddy beaches. Man was not, yet man was the dream of the gods, and strange were the nightmare forms that glided through the noisome jungles. Battle and onslaught were there, and frightful love. Death was there, for Life and Death go hand in hand. Across the slimy beaches of the world sounded the bellowing of the monsters, and incredible shapes loomed through the steaming curtain of the incessant rain.

"This is of the future."

Kull looked in silence.

"See you – what?"

"A strange world," said Kull heavily. "The Seven Empires are crumbled to dust and are forgotten. The restless green waves roar for many a fathom above the eternal hills of Atlantis; the mountains of Lemuria of the West are the islands of an unknown sea. Strange savages roam the elder lands and new lands flung strangely from the deeps, defiling the elder shrines. Valusia is vanished and all the nations of today; they of tomorrow are strangers. They know us not."

"Time strides onward," said Tuzun Thune calmly. "We live today; what care we for tomorrow – or yesterday? The Wheel turns and nations rise and fall; the world changes, and times return to savagery to rise again through the long ages. Ere Atlantis was, Valusia was, and ere Valusia was, the Elder Nations were. Aye, we, too, trampled the shoulders of lost tribes in our advance. You, who have come from the green sea hills of Atlantis to seize the ancient crown of Valusia, you think my tribe is old, we who held these lands ere the Valusians came out of the East, in the days before there were men in the sea lands. But men were here when the Elder Tribes rode out of the waste lands, and men before men, tribe before tribe. The nations pass and are forgotten, for that is the destiny of man."

"Yes," said Kull. "Yet is it not a pity that the beauty and glory of men should fade like smoke on a summer sea?"

"For what reason, since that is their destiny? I brood not over the lost glories of my race, nor do I labor for races to come. Live now, Kull, live now. The dead are dead; the unborn are not. What matters men's forgetfulness of you when you have forgotten yourself in the silent worlds of death? Gaze in my mirrors and be wise."

Kull chose another mirror and gazed into it.

"That is the mirror of the deepest magic; what see ye, Kull?"

"Naught but myself."

"Look closely, Kull; is it in truth you?"

Kull stared into the great mirror, and the image that was his reflection returned his gaze.

"I come before this mirror," mused Kull, chin on fist, "and I bring this man to life. That is beyond my understanding, since first I saw him in the still waters of the lakes of Atlantis, till I saw him again in the gold-rimmed mirrors of Valusia. He is I, a shadow of myself, part of myself – I can bring him into being or slay him at my will; yet–" He halted, strange thoughts whispering through the vast dim recesses of his mind like shadowy bats flying through a great cavern, "yet where is he when I stand not in front of a mirror? May it be in man's power thus lightly to form and destroy a shadow of life and existence? How do I know that when I step back from the mirror he vanishes into the void of Naught?

"Nay, by Valka, am I the man or is he? Which of us is the ghost of the other? Mayhap these mirrors are but windows through which we look into another world. Does he think the same of me? Am I no more than a shadow, a reflection of himself to him, as he to me? And if I am the ghost, what sort of a world lives upon the other side of this mirror? What armies ride there and what kings rule? This world is all I know. Knowing naught of any other, how can I judge? Surely there are green hills there and booming seas and wide plains where men ride to battle. Tell me, wizard who is wiser than most men, tell me, are there worlds beyond our worlds?"

"A man has eyes, let him see," answered the wizard. "Who would see must first believe."

The hours drifted by, and Kull still sat before the mirrors of Tuzun Thune, gazing into that which depicted himself. Sometimes it seemed that he gazed upon hard shallowness; at other times gigantic depths seemed to loom before him. Like the surface of the sea was the mirror of Tuzun Thune; hard as the sea in the sun's slanting beams, in the darkness of the stars, when no eye can pierce her deeps; vast and mystic as the sea when the sun smites her in such way that the watcher's breath is caught at the glimpse of tremendous abysses. So was the mirror in which Kull gazed.

At last the king rose with a sigh and took his departure still wondering. And Kull came again to the House of a Thousand Mirrors; day after day he came and sat for hours before the mirror. The eyes looked out at him, identical with his; yet Kull seemed to sense a difference – a reality that was not of him. Hour upon hour he would stare with strange intensity into the mirror; hour after hour the image gave back his gaze.

The business of the palace and of the council went neglected. The people murmured; Kull's stallion stamped restlessly in his stable, and Kull's warrior's diced and argued aimlessly with one another. Kull heeded not. At times he seemed on the point of discovering some vast, unthinkable secret. He no longer thought of the image in the mirror as a shadow of himself; the thing, to him, was an entity, similar in outer appearance, yet basically as far from Kull himself as the poles are far apart. The image, it seemed to Kull, had an individuality apart from Kull's; he was no more dependent on Kull than Kull was dependent on him. And day by day Kull doubted in which world he really lived; was he the shadow, summoned at will by the other? Did he instead of the other live in a world of delusion, the shadow of the real world?

Kull began to wish that he might enter the personality beyond the mirror for a space, to see what might be seen; yet should he manage to go beyond that door, could he ever return? Would he find a world identical with the one in which he moved? A world, of which his was but a ghostly reflection? Which was reality and which illusion?

At times Kull halted to wonder how such thoughts and dreams had come to enter his mind, and at times he wondered if they came of his own volition or – here his thoughts would become mazed. His meditations were his own; no man ruled his thoughts, and he would summon them at his pleasure; yet could he? Were they not as bats, coming and going, not at his pleasure but at the bidding or ruling of – of whom? The gods? The Women who wove the webs of Fate? Kull could come to no conclusion, for at each mental step he became more and more bewildered in a hazy gray fog of illusory assertions and refutations. This much he knew: that strange visions entered his mind, like bats flying unbidden from the whispering void of non-existence; never had he thought these thoughts, but now they ruled his mind, sleeping and waking, so that he seemed to walk in a daze at times; and his sleep was fraught with strange, monstrous dreams.

"Tell me, wizard," he said, sitting before the mirror, eyes fixed intently upon his image, "how can I pass yon door? For of a truth, I am not sure that that is the real world and this the shadow; at least, that which I see must exist in some form."

"See and believe," droned the wizard. "Man must believe to accomplish. Form is shadow, substance is illusion, materiality is dream; man is because he believes he is; what is man but a dream of the gods? Yet man can be that which he wishes to be; form and substance, they are but shadows. The mind, the ego, the essence of the god-dream – that is real, that is immortal. See and believe, if you would accomplish, Kull."

The king did not fully understand; he never fully understood the enigmatical utterances of the wizard; yet they struck somewhere in his being a dim responsive chord. So day after day he sat before the mirrors of Tuzun Thune. Ever the wizard lurked behind him like a shadow.

Then came a day when Kull seemed to catch glimpses of strange lands; there flirted across his consciousness dim thoughts and recognitions. Day by day he had seemed to lose touch with the world; all things had seemed each succeeding day more ghostly and unreal; only the man in the mirror seemed like reality. Now Kull seemed to be close to the doors of some mightier worlds; giant vistas gleamed fleetingly; the fogs of unreality thinned; "form is shadow, substance is illusion; they are but shadows" sounded as if from some far country of his consciousness. He remembered the wizard's words and it seemed to him that now he almost understood – form and substance, could not he change himself at will, if he knew the master key that opened this door? What worlds within what worlds awaited the bold explorer?

The man in the mirror seemed smiling at him – closer, closer – a fog enwrapped all and the reflection dimmed suddenly – Kull knew a sensation of fading, of change, of merging...

"Kull!" the yell split the silence into a million vibratory fragments!

Mountains crashed and worlds tottered as Kull, hurled back by that frantic shout, made a superhuman effort, how or why he did not know.

A crash, and Kull stood in the room of Tuzun Thune before a shattered mirror, mazed and half blind with bewilderment. There before him lay the body of Tuzun Thune, whose time had come at last, and above him stood Brule the Spear-slayer, sword dripping red and eyes wide with a kind of horror.

"Valka!" swore the warrior. "Kull, it was time I came!"

"Aye, yet what happened?" The king groped for words.

"Ask this traitress," answered the Spear-slayer, indicating a girl who crouched in terror before the king; Kull saw that it was she who first sent him to Tuzun Thune. "As I came in I saw you fading into yon mirror as smoke fades into the sky, by Valka! Had I not seen I would not have believed – you had almost vanished when my shout brought you back."

"Aye," muttered Kull, "I had almost gone beyond the door that time."

"This fiend wrought most craftily," said Brule. "Kull, do you not now see how he spun and flung over you a web of magic? Kaanuub of Blaal plotted with this wizard to do away with you, and this wench, a girl of the Elder Race, put the thought in your mind so that you would come here. Ka-nu of the council learned of the plot today; I know not what you saw in that mirror, but with it Tuzun Thune enthralled your soul and almost by his witchery he changed your body to mist–"

"Aye." Kull was still mazed. "But being a wizard, having knowledge of all the ages and despising gold, glory, and position, what could Kaanuub offer Tuzun Thune that would make of him a foul traitor?"

"Gold, power, and position," grunted Brule. "The sooner you learn that men are men whether wizard, king, or thrall, the better you will rule, Kull. Now what of her?"

"Naught, Brule," as the girl whimpered and groveled at Kull's feet. "She was but a tool. Rise, child, and go your ways; none shall harm you."

Alone with Brule, Kull looked for the last time on the mirrors of Tuzun Thune.

"Mayhap he plotted and conjured, Brule; nay, I doubt you not, yet – was it his witchery that was changing me to thin mist, or had I stumbled on a secret? Had you not brought me back, had I faded in dissolution or had I found worlds beyond this?"

Brule stole a glance at the mirrors, and twitched his shoulders as if he shuddered. "Aye. Tuzun Thune stored the wisdom of all the hells here. Let us begone, Kull, ere they bewitch me, too."

"Let us go, then," answered Kull, and side by side they went forth from the House of a Thousand Mirrors – where, mayhap, are prisoned the souls of men.

None look now in the mirrors of Tuzun Thune. The pleasure boats shun the shore where stands the wizard's house, and no one goes in the house or to the room where Tuzun Thune's dried and withered carcass lies before the mirrors of illusion. The place is shunned as a place accursed, and though it stands for a thousand years to come, no footsteps shall echo there. Yet Kull upon his throne meditates often upon the strange wisdom and untold secrets hidden there, and wonders...

For there are worlds beyond worlds, as Kull knows, and whether the wizard bewitched him by words or by mesmerism, vistas did open to the king's gaze beyond that strange door, and Kull is less sure of reality since he gazed into the mirrors of Tuzun Thune.

KINGS OF THE NIGHT

I

"The Caesar lolled on his ivory throne
His iron legions came
To break a king in a land unknown,
And a race without a name."
−The Song of Bran

The dagger flashed downward. A sharp cry broke in a gasp. The form on the rough altar twitched convulsively and lay still. The jagged flint edge sawed at the crimsoned breast, and thin bony fingers, ghastly dyed, tore out the still twitching heart. Under matted white brows, sharp eyes gleamed with a ferocious intensity.

Besides the slayer, four men stood about the crude pile of stones that formed the altar of the God of Shadows. One was of medium height, lithely built, scantily clad, whose black hair was confined by a narrow iron band in the center of which gleamed a single red jewel. Of the others, two were dark like the first. But where he was lithe, they were stocky and misshapen, with knotted limbs, and tangled hair falling over sloping brows. His face denoted intelligence and implacable will; theirs merely a beast-like ferocity. The fourth man had little in common with the rest. Nearly a head taller, though his hair was black as theirs, his skin was comparatively light and he was gray-eyed. He eyed the proceedings with little favor.

And, in truth, Cormac of Connacht was little at ease. The Druids of his own isle of Erin had strange dark rites of worship, but nothing like this. Dark trees shut in this grim scene, lit by a single torch. Through the branches moaned an eery night-wind. Cormac was alone among men of a strange race and he had just seen the heart of a man ripped from his still pulsing body. Now the ancient priest, who looked scarcely human, was glaring at the throbbing thing. Cormac shuddered, glancing at him who wore the jewel. Did Bran Mak Morn, king of the Picts, believe that this white-bearded old butcher could foretell events by scanning a bleeding human heart? The dark eyes of the king were inscrutable. There were strange depths to the man that Cormac could not fathom, nor any other man.

"The portents are good!" exclaimed the priest wildly, speaking more to the two chieftains than to Bran. "Here from the pulsing heart of a captive Roman I read − defeat for the arms of Rome! Triumph for the sons of the heather!"

The two savages murmured beneath their breath, the fierce eyes smoldering.

"Go and prepare your clans for battle," said the king, and they lumbered away with the ape-like gait assumed by such stunted giants. Paying no

40

more heed to the priest who was examining the ghastly ruin on the altar, Bran beckoned to Cormac. The Gael followed him with alacrity. Once out of that grim grove, under the starlight, he breathed more freely. They stood on an eminence, looking out over long swelling undulations of gently waving heather. Near at hand a few fires twinkled, their fewness giving scant evidence of the hordes of tribesmen who lay close by. Beyond these were more fires and beyond these still more, which last marked the camp of Cormac's own men, hard-riding, hard-fighting Gaels, who were of that band which was just beginning to get a foothold on the western coast of Caledon – the nucleus of what was later to become the kingdom of Dalriadia. To the left of these, other fires gleamed.

And far away to the south were more fires – mere pin-points of light. But even at that distance the Pictish king and his Celtic ally could see that these fires were laid out in regular order.

"The fires of the legions," muttered Bran. "The fires that have lit a path around the world. The men who light those fires have trampled the races under their iron heels. And now – we of the heather have our backs at the wall. What will fall on the morrow?"

"Victory for us, says the priest," answered Cormac and made an impatient gesture. "Moonlight on the ocean. Wind in the fir tops. Do you think that I put faith in such mummery? Or that I enjoyed the butchery of a captive legionary? I must hearten my people; it was for Gron and Bocah that I let old Gonar read the portents. The warriors will fight better."

"And Gonar?"

Bran laughed. "Gonar is too old to believe – anything. He was high priest of the Shadows a score of years before I was born. He claims direct descent from that Gonar who was a wizard in the days of Brule, the Spear-slayer who was the first of my line. No man knows how old he is – sometimes I think he is the original Gonar himself!"

"At least," said a mocking voice, and Cormac started as a dim shape appeared at his side, "at least I have learned that in order to keep the faith and trust of the people, a wise man must appear to be a fool. I know secrets that would blast even your brain, Bran, should I speak them. But in order that the people may believe in me, I must descend to such things as they think proper magic – and prance and yell and rattle snakeskins, and dabble about in human blood and chicken livers."

Cormac looked at the ancient with new interest. The semi-madness of his appearance had vanished. He was no longer the charlatan, the spell-mumbling shaman. The starlight lent him a dignity which seemed to increase his very height, so that he stood like a white-bearded patriarch.

"Bran, your doubt lies there." The lean arm pointed to the fourth ring of fires.

"Aye," the king nodded gloomily. "Cormac – you know as well as I. Tomorrow's battle hinges upon the circle of the fires. With the chariots of the Britons and your own Western horsemen, our success would be certain, but surely the devil himself is in the heart of every Northman! And now that their chief, Rognar, is dead, they swear that they will be led only by a king of their own race! Else they will break their vow and go over to the Romans. Without them we are doomed, for we can not change our former plan."

"Take heart, Bran," said Gonar. "Touch the jewel in your iron crown. Mayhap it will bring you aid."

Bran laughed bitterly. "Now you talk as the people think. I am no fool to twist with empty words. What of the gem? It is a strange one, truth, and has brought me luck ere now. But I need now, no jewels, but the allegiance of three hundred fickle Northmen who are the only warriors among us who may stand the charge of the legions on foot."

"But the jewel, Bran, the jewel!" persisted Gonar.

"Well, the jewel!" cried Bran impatiently. "It is older than this world. It was old when Atlantis and Lemuria sank into the sea. It was given to Brule, the Spear-slayer, first of my line, by the Atlantean Kull, king of Valusia, in the days when the world was young. But shall that profit us now?"

"Who knows?" asked the wizard obliquely. "Time and space exist not. There was no past, and there shall be no future. NOW is all. All things that ever were, are, or ever will be, transpire *now*. Man is forever at the center of what we call time and space. I have gone into yesterday and tomorrow and both were as real as today – which is like the dreams of ghosts! But let me sleep and talk with Gonar. Mayhap he shall aid us."

"What means he?" asked Cormac, with a slight twitching of his shoulders, as the priest strode away in the shadows.

"He has ever said that the first Gonar comes to him in his dreams and talks with him," answered Bran. "I have seen him perform deeds that seemed beyond human ken. I know not. I am but an unknown king with an iron crown, trying to lift a race of savages out of the slime into which they have sunk. Let us look to the camps."

As they walked Cormac wondered. By what strange freak of fate had such a man risen among the race of savages, survivors of a darker, grimmer age? Surely he was an atavism, an original type of the days when the Picts ruled all Europe, before their primitive empire fell before the bronze swords of the Gauls. Cormac knew how Bran, rising by his own efforts from the negligent position of the son of a Wolf clan chief, had to an extent united the tribes of the heather and now claimed kingship over all Caledon. But his rule was loose and much remained before the Pictish clans would forget their feuds and present a solid front to foreign foes. On the battle of the morrow, the first pitched battle between the Picts under their king and the Romans, hinged the future of the rising Pictish kingdom.

Bran and his ally walked through the Pictish camp where the swart warriors lay sprawled about their small fires, sleeping or gnawing half-cooked food. Cormac was impressed by their silence. A thousand men camped here, yet the only sounds were occasional low guttural intonations. The silence of the Stone Age rested in the souls of these men.

They were all short – most of them crooked of limb. Giant dwarfs; Bran

Mak Morn was a tall man among them. Only the older men were bearded and they scantily, but their black hair fell about their eyes so that they peered fiercely from under the tangle. They were barefoot and clad scantily in wolfskins. Their arms consisted of short barbed swords of iron, heavy black bows, arrows tipped with flint, iron and copper, and stone-headed mallets. Defensive armor they had none, save for a crude shield of hide-covered wood; many had worked bits of metal into their tangled manes as a slight protection against sword-cuts. Some few, sons of long lines of chiefs, were smooth-limbed and lithe like Bran, but in the eyes of all gleamed the unquenchable savagery of the primeval.

These men are fully savages, thought Cormac, *worse than the Gauls, Britons and Germans. Can the old legends be true – that they reigned in a day when strange cities rose where now the sea rolls? And that they survived the flood that washed those gleaming empires under, sinking again into that savagery from which they once had risen?*

Close to the encampment of the tribesmen were the fires of a group of Britons – members of fierce tribes who lived south of the Roman Wall but who dwelt in the hills and forests to the west and defied the power of Rome. Powerfully built men they were, with blazing blue eyes and shocks of tousled yellow hair, such men as had thronged the Ceanntish beaches when Caesar brought the Eagles into the Isles. These men, like the Picts, wore no armor, and were clad scantily in coarse-worked cloth and deerskin sandals. They bore small round bucklets of hard wood, braced with bronze, to be worn on the left arm, and long heavy bronze swords with blunt points. Some had bows, though the Britons were indifferent archers. Their bows were shorter than the Picts' and effective only at close range. But ranged close by their fires were the weapons that had made the name Briton a word of terror to Pict, Roman and Norse raider alike. Within the circle of firelight stood fifty bronze chariots with long cruel blades curving out from the sides. One of these blades could dismember half a dozen men at once. Tethered close by under the vigilant eyes of their guards grazed the chariot horses – big, rangy steeds, swift and powerful.

"Would that we had more of them," mused Bran. "With a thousand chariots and my bowmen I could drive the legions into the sea."

"The free British tribes must eventually fall before Rome," said Cormac. "It would seem they would rush to join you in your war."

Bran made a helpless gesture. "The fickleness of the Celt. They cannot forget old feuds. Our ancient men have told us how they would not even unite against Caesar when the Romans first came. They will not make head against a common foe together. These men came to me because of some dispute with their chief, but I cannot depend on them when they are not actually fighting."

Cormac nodded. "I know; Caesar conquered Gaul by playing one tribe against another. My own people shift and change with the waxing and waning of the tides. But of all Celts, the Cymry are the most changeable, the least stable. Not many centuries ago my own Gaelic ancestors wrested Erin from the Cymric Danaans, because though they outnumbered us, they opposed us as separate tribes, rather than as a nation."

"And so these Cymric Britons face Rome," said Bran. "These will aid us on the morrow. Further I cannot say. But how shall I expect loyalty from alien tribes, who am not sure of my own people? Thousands lurk in the hills, holding aloof. I am king in name only. Let me win tomorrow and they will flock to my standard; if I lose, they will scatter like birds before a cold wind."

A chorus of rough welcome greeted the two leaders as they entered the camp of Cormac's Gaels. Five hundred in number they were, tall rangy men, black-haired and gray-eyed mainly, with the bearing of men who lived by war alone. While there was nothing like close discipline among them, there was an air of more system and practical order than existed in the lines of the Picts and Britons. These men were of the last Celtic race to invade the Isles and their barbaric civilization was of much higher order than that of their Cymric kin. The ancestors of the Gaels had learned the arts of war on the vast plains of Scythia and at the courts of the Pharaohs where they had fought as mercenaries of Egypt, and much of what they learned they brought into Ireland with them. Excelling in metal work, they were armed, not with clumsy bronze swords, but with high-grade weapons of iron.

They were clad in well-woven kilts and leathern sandals. Each wore a light shirt of chain mail and a vizorless helmet, but this was all of their defensive armor. Celts, Gaelic or Brythonic, were prone to judge a man's valor by the amount of armor he wore. The Britons who faced Caesar deemed the Romans cowards because they cased themselves in metal, and many centuries later the Irish clans thought the same of the mail-clad Northman knights of Strongbow.

Cormac's warriors were horsemen. They neither knew nor esteemed the use of the bow. They bore the inevitable round, metal-braced buckler, dirks, long straight swords and light single-handed axes. Their tethered horses grazed not far away – big boned animals, not so ponderous as those raised by the Britons, but swifter.

Bran's eyes lighted as the two strode through the camp. "These men are keen-beaked birds of war! See how they whet their axes and jest of the morrow! Would that the raiders in yon camp were as staunch as your men, Cormac, Then would I greet the legions with a laugh when they come up from the south tomorrow."

They were entering the circle of the Northmen fires.

Three hundred men sat about gambling, whetting their weapons and drinking deep of the heather ale furnished them by their Pictish allies. These gazed upon Bran and Cormac with no great friendliness. It was striking to note the difference between them and the Picts and Celts – the difference in their cold eyes, their strong moody faces, their very bearing. Here was ferocity, and savagery, but not of the wild, upbursting fury of the Celt. Here was fierceness backed by grim determination and stolid stubbornness. The charge of the British clans was terrible, overwhelming. But they had no patience; let them be balked of immediate victory and they were likely to lose heart and scatter or fall bickering among themselves. There was the patience of the cold blue North in these seafarers – a lasting determination that would keep them steadfast to the bitter end, once their face was set toward a definite goal.

As to personal stature, they were giants; massive yet rangy. That they did not share the ideas of the Celts regarding armor was shown by the fact that they were clad in heavy scale-mail shirts that reached below mid-thigh, heavy horned helmets and hardened hide leggings, reinforced, as were their shoes, with plates of iron. Their shields were huge oval affairs of hard wood, hide and brass. As to weapons, they had long iron-headed spears, heavy iron axes, and daggers. Some had long wide-bladed swords.

Cormac scarcely felt at ease with the cold magnetic eyes of these flaxen-haired men fixed upon him. He and they were hereditary foes, even though they did chance to be fighting on the same side at present – but were they?

A man came forward, a tall gaunt warrior on whose scarred, wolfish face the flickering firelight reflected deep shadows. With his wolfskin mantle flung carelessly about his wide shoulders, and the great horns on his helmet added to his height, he stood there in the swaying shadows, like some half-human thing, a brooding shape of the dark barbarism that was soon to engulf the world.

"Well, Wulfhere," said the Pictish king, "you have drunk the mead of council and have spoken about the fires – what is your decision?"

The Northman's eyes flashed in the gloom. "Give us a king of our own race to follow if you wish us to fight for you."

Bran flung out his hands. "Ask me to drag down the stars to gem your helmets! Will not your comrades follow you?"

"Not against the legions," answered Wulfhere sullenly. "A king led us on the Viking path – a king must lead us against the Romans. And Rognar is dead."

"I am a king," said Bran. "Will you fight for me if I stand at the tip of your fight wedge?"

"A king of our own race," said Wulfhere doggedly. "We are all picked men of the North. We fight for none but a king, and a king must lead us – against the legions."

Cormac sensed a subtle threat in this repeated phrase.

"Here is a prince of Erin," said Bran. "Will you fight for the Westerner?"

"We light under no Celt, West or East," growled the Viking, and a low rumble of approval rose from the onlookers. "It is enough to fight by their side."

The hot Gaelic blood rose in Cormac's brain and he pushed past Bran, his hand on his sword. "How mean you that, pirate?"

Before Wulfhere could reply Bran interposed: "Have done! Will you fools throw away the battle before it is fought, by your madness? What of your oath, Wulfhere?"

"We swore it under Rognar; when he died from a Roman arrow we were absolved of it. We will follow only a king – against the legions."

"But your comrades will follow you – against the heather people!" snapped Bran.

"Aye," the Northman's eyes met his brazenly. "Send a king or we join the Romans tomorrow."

Bran snarled. In his rage he dominated the scene, dwarfing the huge men who towered over him.

"Traitors! Liars! I hold your lives in my hand! Aye, draw your swords if you will– Cormac, keep your blade in its sheath. These wolves will not bite a king! Wulfhere – I spared your lives when I could have taken them.

"You came to raid the countries of the South, sweeping down from the northern sea in your galleys. You ravaged the coasts and the smoke of burning villages hung like a cloud over the shores of Caledon. I trapped you all when you were pillaging and burning – with the blood of my people on your hands. I burned your longships and ambushed you when you followed. With thrice your number of bowmen who burned for your lives hidden in the heathered hills about you, I spared you when we could have shot you down like trapped wolves. Because I spared you, you swore to come and fight for me."

"And shall we die because the Picts fight Rome?" rumbled a bearded raider.

"Your lives are forfeit to me; you came to ravage the South. I did not promise to send you all back to your homes in the North unharmed and loaded with loot. Your vow was to fight one battle against Rome under my standard. Then I will aid your survivors to build ships and you may go where you will, with a goodly share of the plunder we take from the legions. Rognar had kept his oath. But Rognar died in a skirmish with Roman scouts and now you, Wulfhere the Dissension-breeder, you stir up your comrades to dishonor themselves by that which a Northman hates – the breaking of the sword word."

"We break no oath," snarled the Viking, and the king sensed the basic Germanic stubbornness, far harder to combat than the fickleness of the fiery Celts. "Give us a king, neither Pict, Gael nor Briton, and we will die for you. If not – then we will fight tomorrow for the greatest of all kings – the emperor of Rome!"

For a moment Cormac thought that the Pictish king, in his black rage, would draw and strike the Northman dead. The concentrated fury that blazed in Bran's dark eyes caused Wulfhere to recoil and drop a hand to his belt.

"Fool!" said Mak Morn in a low voice that vibrated with passion. "I could sweep you from the earth before the Romans are near enough to hear your death howls. Choose – fight for me on the morrow – or die tonight under a black cloud of arrows, a red storm of swords, a dark wave of chariots!"

At the mention of the chariots, the only arm of war that had ever broken the Norse shield-wall, Wulfhere changed expression, but he held his ground.

"War be it," he said doggedly. "Or a king to lead us!"

The Northmen responded with a short deep roar and a clash of swords on shields. Bran, eyes blazing, was about to speak again when a white shape glided silently into the ring of firelight.

"Soft words, soft words," said old Gonar tranquilly. "King, say no more. Wulfhere, you and your fellows will fight for us if you have a king to lead you?"

"We have sworn."

"Then be at ease," quoth the wizard; "for ere battle joins on the morrow I will send you such a king as man on earth has followed for a hundred thousand years! A king neither Pict, Gael nor Briton, but one to whom the emperor of Rome is as but a village headman!"

While they stood undecided, Gonar took the arms of Cormac and Bran. "Come. And you, Northmen, remember your vow, and my promise which I have never broken. Sleep now, nor think to steal away in the darkness to the Roman camp, for if you escaped our shafts you would not escape either my curse or the suspicions of the legionaries."

So the three walked away and Cormac, looking back, saw Wulfhere standing by the fire, fingering his golden beard, with a look of puzzled anger on his lean face.

The three walked silently through the waving heather under the faraway stars while the weird night wind whispered ghostly secrets about them.

"Ages ago," said the wizard suddenly, "in the days when the world was young, great lands rose where now the ocean roars. On these lands thronged mighty nations and kingdoms. Greatest of all these was Valusia – Land of Enchantment. Rome is as a village compared to the splendor of the cities of Valusia. And the greatest king was Kull, who came from the land of Atlantis to wrest the crown of Valusia from a degenerate dynasty. The Picts who dwelt in the isles which now form the mountain peaks of a strange land upon the Western Ocean, were allies of Valusia, and the greatest of all the Pictish war-chiefs was Brule the Spear-slayer, first of the line men call Mak Morn.

"Kull gave to Brule the jewel which you now wear in your iron crown, oh king, after a strange battle in a dim land, and down the long ages it has come to us, ever a sign of the Mak Morn, a symbol of former greatness. When at last the sea rose and swallowed Valusia, Atlantis, and Lemuria, only the Picts survived and they were scattered and few. Yet they began again the slow climb upward, and though many of the arts of civilization were lost in the great flood, yet they progressed. The art of metal-working was lost, so they excelled in the working of flint. And they ruled all the new lands flung up by the sea and now called Europe, until down from the north came younger tribes who had scarce risen from the ape when Valusia reigned in her glory, and who, dwelling in the icy lands about the Pole, knew naught of the lost splendor of the Seven Empires and little of the flood that had swept away half a world.

"And still they have come – Aryans, Celts, Germans, swarming down from the great cradle of their race which lies near the Pole. So again was the growth of the Pictish nation checked and the race hurled into savagery. Erased from the earth, on the fringe of the world with our backs to the wall we fight. Here in Caledon is the last stand of a once mighty race. And we change. Our people have mixed with the savages of an elder age which we drove into the North when we came into the Isles, and now, save for their chieftains, such as thou, Bran, a Pict is strange and abhorrent to look upon."

"True, true," said the king impatiently, "but what has that to do—"

"Kull, king of Valusia," said the wizard imperturbably, "was a barbarian in his age as thou art in thine, though he ruled a mighty empire by the weight of his sword. Gonar, friend of Brule, your first ancestor, has been dead a hundred thousand years as we reckon time. Yet I talked with him a scant hour agone."

"You talked with his ghost—"

"Or he with mine? Did I go back a hundred thousand years, or did he come forward? If he came to me out of the past, it is not I who talked with a dead man, but he who talked with a man unborn. Past, present and future are one to a wise man. I talked to Gonar while he was alive; likewise was I alive. In a timeless, spaceless land we met and he told me many things."

The land was growing light with the birth of dawn. The heather waved and bent in long rows before the dawn wind as if bowing in worship of the rising sun.

"The jewel in your crown is a magnet that draws down the eons," said Gonar. "The sun is rising – and who comes out of the sunrise?"

Cormac and the king started. The sun was just lifting a red orb above the eastern hills. And full in the glow, etched boldly against the golden rim, a man suddenly appeared. They had not seen him come. Against the golden birth of day he loomed colossal; a gigantic god from the dawn of creation. Now as he strode toward them the waking hosts saw him and sent up a sudden shout of wonder.

"Who – or what – is it?" exclaimed Bran.

"Let us go to meet him, Bran," answered the wizard. "He is the king Gonar has sent to save the people of Brule."

II

"I have reached these lands but newly
From an ultimate dim Thule;
From a wild weird clime that lieth sublime
Out of Space – out of Time."
—Poe

The army fell silent as Bran, Cormac and Gonar went toward the stranger who approached in long swinging strides. As they neared him the illusion of monstrous size vanished, but they saw he was a man of great stature. At first Cormac thought him to be a Northman but a second glance told him that nowhere before had he seen such a man. He was built much like the Vikings, at once massive and lithe-tigerish. But his features were not as theirs, and his square-cut, lion-like mane of hair was as black as Bran's own. Under heavy brows glittered eyes gray as steel and cold as ice. His bronzed face, strong and inscrutable, was clean-shaven, and the broad forehead betokened a high intelligence just as the firm jaw and thin lips showed willpower and courage. But more than all, the bearing of him, the unconscious lion-like stateliness, marked him as a natural king, a ruler of men.

Sandals of curious make were on his feet and he wore a pliant coat of strangely meshed mail which came almost to his knees. A broad belt with a great golden buckle encircled his waist, supporting a long straight sword in a heavy leather scabbard. His hair was confined by a wide, heavy golden band about his head.

Such was the man who paused before the silent group. He seemed slightly puzzled, slightly amused. Recognition flickered in his eyes. He spoke in a strange archaic Pictish which Cormac scarcely understood. His voice was deep and resonant.

"Ha, Brule, Gonar did not tell me I would dream of you!"

For the first time in his life Cormac saw the Pictish king completely thrown off his balance. He gasped, speechless. The stranger continued:

"And wearing the gem I gave you, in a circlet on your head! Last night you wore it in a ring on your finger."

"Last night?" gasped Bran.

"Last night or a hundred thousand years ago – all one!" murmured Gonar in evident enjoyment of the situation.

"I am not Brule," said Bran. "Are you made to thus speak of a man dead a hundred thousand years? He was first of my line."

The stranger laughed unexpectedly. "Well, now I know I am dreaming! This will be a tale to tell Brule when I waken on the morrow! That I went into the future and saw men claiming descent from the Spear-slayer who is, as yet, not even married. No, you are not Brule, I see now, though you have his eyes and his bearing. But he is taller and broader in the shoulders. Yet you have his jewel – oh, well – anything can happen in a dream, so I will not quarrel with you. For a time I thought I had been transported to some other land in my sleep, and was in reality awake in a strange country, for this is the clearest dream I ever dreamed. Who are you?"

"I am Bran Mak Morn, king of the Caledonian Picts. An this ancient is Gonar, a wizard, of the line of Gonar. An this warrior is Cormac na Connacht, a prince of the isle of Erin."

The stranger slowly shook his lion-like head. "These words sound strangely to me, save Gonar – and that one is not Gonar, though he too is old. What land is this?"

"Caledon, or Alba, as the Gaels call it."

"And who are those squat ape-like warriors who watch us yonder, all agape?"

"They are the Picts who own my rule."

"How strangely distorted folk are in dreams!" muttered the stranger. "And who are those shock-headed men about the chariots?"

"They are Britons – Cymry from south of the Wall."

"What Wall?"

"The Wall built by Rome to keep the people of the heather out of Briton."

"Britain?" the tone was curious. "I have never heard of that land – and what is Rome?"

"What!" cried Bran. "You never have heard of Rome, the empire that rules the world?"

"No empire rules the world," answered the other haughtily. "The mightiest kingdom on earth is that wherein I reign."

"And who are you?"

"Kull of Atlantis, king of Valusia!"

Cormac felt a coldness trickle down his spine. The cold, gray eyes were unswerving – but this was incredible– monstrous – unnatural.

"Valusia!" cried Bran. "Why, man, the sea waves have rolled above the spires of Valusia for untold centuries!"

Kull laughed outright. "What a mad nightmare this is! When Gonar put on me the spell of deep sleep last night – or this night! – in the secret room of the inner palace, he told me I would dream strange things, but this is more fantastic than I reckoned. And the strangest thing is, I know I am dreaming!"

Gonar interposed as Bran would have spoken. "Question not the acts of the gods," muttered the wizard. "You are king because in the past you have seen and seized opportunities. The gods or the first Gonar have sent you this man. Let me deal with him."

Bran nodded, and while the silent army gaped in speechless wonder, just within earshot, Gonar spoke: "Oh great king, you dream, but is not all life a dream? How reckon you but that your former life is but a dream from which you have just awakened? Now we dream-folk have our wars and our peace, and just now a great host comes up from the south to destroy the people of Brule. Will you aid us?"

Kull grinned with pure zest. "Aye! I have fought battles in dreams ere now, have slain and been slain and was amazed when I woke from my visions. And at times, as now, dreaming I have known I dreamed. See, I pinch myself and feel it, but I know I dream for I have felt the pain of fierce wounds, in dreams. Yes, people of my dream, I will fight for you against the other dream-folk. Where are they?"

"And that you enjoy the dream more," said the wizard subtly, "forget that it is a dream and pretend that by the magic of the first Gonar, and the quality of the jewel you gave Brule, that now gleams on the crown of the Morni, you have in truth been transported forward into another, wilder age where the people of Brule fight for their life against a stronger foe."

For a moment the man who called himself king of Valusia seemed startled; a strange look of doubt, almost of fear, clouded his eyes. Then he laughed.

"Good! Lead on, wizard."

But now Bran took charge. He had recovered himself and was at ease. Whether he thought, like Cormac, that this was all a gigantic hoax arranged by

Gonar, he showed no sign.

"King Kull, see you those men yonder who lean on their long-shafted axes as they gaze upon you?"

"The tall men with the golden hair and beards?"

"Aye – our success in the coming battle hinges on them. They swear to go over to the enemy if we give them not a king to lead them – their own having been slain. Will you lead them to battle?"

Kull's eyes glowed with appreciation. "They are men such as my own Red Slayers, my picked regiment. I will lead them."

"Come then."

The small group made their way down the slope, through throngs of warriors who pushed forward eagerly to get a better view of the stranger, then pressed back as he approached. An undercurrent of tense whispering ran through the horde.

The Northmen stood apart in a compact group. Their cold eyes took in Kull and he gave back their stares, taking in every detail of their appearance.

"Wulfhere," said Bran, "we have brought you a king. I hold you to your oath."

"Let him speak to us," said the Viking harshly.

"He cannot speak your tongue," answered Bran, knowing that the Northmen knew nothing of the legends of his race. "He is a great king of the South–"

"He comes out of the past," broke in the wizard calmly. "He was the greatest of all kings, long ago."

"A dead man!" The Vikings moved uneasily and the rest of the horde pressed forward, drinking in every word. But Wulfhere scowled: "Shall a ghost lead living men? Ye bring us a man you say is dead. We will not follow a corpse."

"Wulfhere," said Bran in still passion, "you are a liar and a traitor. You set us this task, thinking it impossible. You yearn to fight under the Eagles of Rome. We have brought you a king neither Pict, Gael nor Briton and you deny your vow!"

"Let him fight me, then!" howled Wulfhere in uncontrollable wrath, swinging his axe about his head in a glittering arc. "If your dead man overcomes me – then my people will follow you. If I overcome him, you shall let us depart in peace to the camp of the legions!"

"Good!" said the wizard. "Do you agree, wolves of the North?"

A fierce yell and a brandishing of swords was the answer. Bran turned to Kull, who had stood silent, understanding nothing of what was said. But the Atlantean's eyes gleamed. Cormac felt that those cold eyes had looked on too many such scenes not to understand something of what had passed.

"This warrior says you must fight him for the leadership," said Bran, and Kull, eyes glittering with growling battle-joy, nodded: "I guessed as much. Give us space."

"A shield and a helmet!" shouted Bran, but Kull shook his head.

"I need none," he growled. "Back and give us room to swing our steel!"

Men pressed back on each side, forming a solid ring about the two men, who now approached each other warily. Kull had drawn his sword and the great blade shimmered like a live thing in his hand. Wulfhere, scarred by a hundred savage fights, flung aside his wolfskin mantle and came in cautiously, fierce eyes peering over the top of his out-thrust shield, axe half lifted in his right hand.

Suddenly when the warriors were still many feet apart Kull sprang. His attack brought a gasp from men used to deeds of prowess; for like a leaping tiger he shot through the air and his sword crashed on the quickly lifted shield. Sparks flew and Wulfhere's axe hacked in, but Kull was under its sweep and as it swished viciously above his head he thrust upward and sprang out again, cat-like. His motions had been too quick for the eye to follow. The upper edge of Wulfhere's shield showed a deep cut, and there was a long rent in his mail shirt where Kull's sword had barely missed the flesh beneath.

Cormac, trembling with the terrible thrill of the fight, wondered at this sword that could thus slice through scale-mail. And the blow that gashed the shield should have shattered the blade. Yet not a notch showed in the Valusian steel! Surely this blade was forged by another people in another age!

Now the two giants leaped again to the attack and like double strokes of lightning their weapons crashed. Wulfhere's shield fell from his arm in two pieces as the Atlantean's sword sheared clear through it, and Kull staggered as the Northman's axe, driven with all the force of his great body, descended on the golden circlet about his head. That blow should have sheared through the gold like butter to split the skull beneath, but the axe rebounded, showing a great notch in the edge. The next instant the Northman was overwhelmed by a whirlwind of steel – a storm of strokes delivered with such swiftness and power that he was borne back as on the crest of a wave, unable to launch an attack of his own. With all his tried skill he sought to parry the singing steel with his axe. But he could only avert his doom for a few seconds; could only for an instant turn the whistling blade that hewed off bits of his mail, so close fell the blows. One of the horns flew from his helmet; then the axe-head itself fell away, and the same blow that severed the handle, bit through the Viking's helmet into the scalp beneath. Wulfhere was dashed to his knees, a trickle of blood starting down his face.

Kill checked his second stroke, and tossing his sword to Cormac, faced the dazed Northman weaponless. The Atlantean's eyes were blazing with ferocious joy and he roared something in a strange tongue. Wulfhere gathered his legs under him and bounded up, snarling like a wolf, a dagger flashing into his hand. The watching horde gave tongue in a yell that ripped the skies as the two bodies clashed. Kull's clutching hand missed the Northman's wrist but the desperately lunging dagger snapped on the Atlantean's mail, and dropping the useless hilt, Wulfhere locked his arms about his foe in a bear-like grip that would have crushed the ribs of a lesser man. Kull grinned tigerishly and returned the grapple, and for a moment the two swayed on their feet. Slowly the black-haired warrior bent his foe backward until it seemed his spine would snap. With a howl that had nothing of the human in it, Wulfhere clawed frantically at Kull's face, trying to tear out his eyes, then turned his head and snapped his fang-like teeth into the Atlantean's arm. A yell went up as a trickle of blood started: "He bleeds! He bleeds! He is no ghost, after all, but a mortal man!"

Angered, Kull shifted his grip, shoving the frothing Wulfhere away from him, and smote him terrifically under the ear with his right hand. The Viking landed on his back a dozen feet away. Then, howling like a wild man, he leaped up with a stone in his hand and flung it. Only Kull's incredible quickness saved his face; as it was, the rough edge of the missile tore his cheek and inflamed him to madness. With a lion-like roar he bounded upon his foe, enveloped him in an irresistible blast of sheer fury, whirled him high above his head as if he were a child and cast him a dozen feet away. Wulfhere pitched on his head and lay still – broken and dead.

Dazed silence reigned for an instant; then from the Gaels went up a thundering roar, and the Britons and Picts took it up, howling like wolves, until the echoes of the shouts and the clangor of sword on shield reached the ears of the marching legionaries, miles to the south.

"Men of the gray North," shouted Bran, "will you hold by your oath now?"

The fierce souls of the Northmen were in their eyes as their spokesman answered. Primitive, superstitious, steeped in tribal lore of fighting gods and mythical heroes, they did not doubt that the black-haired fighting man was some supernatural being sent by the fierce gods of battle.

"Aye! Such a man as this we have never seen! Dead man, ghost, or devil, we will follow him, whether the trail lead to Rome or Valhalla!"

Kull understood the meaning, if not the words. Taking his sword from Cormac with a word of thanks, he turned to the waiting Northmen and silently held the blade toward them high above his head, in both hands, before he returned it to its scabbard. Without understanding, they appreciated the action. Bloodstained and disheveled, he was an impressive picture of stately, magnificent barbarism.

"Come," said Bran, touching the Atlantean's arm; "a host is marching on us and we have much to do. There is scant time to arrange our forces before they will be upon us. Come to the top of yonder slope."

There the Pict pointed. They were looking down into a valley which ran north and south, widening from a narrow gorge in the north until it debouched upon a plain to the south. The whole valley was less than a mile in length.

"Up this valley will our foes come," said the Pict, "because they have wagons loaded with supplies and on all sides of this vale the ground is too rough for such travel. Here we plan an ambush."

"I would have thought you would have had your men lying in wait long before now," said Kull. "What of the scouts the enemy is sure to send out?"

"The savages I lead would never have waited in ambush so long," said Bran with a touch of bitterness. "I could not post them until I was sure of the

Northmen. Even so I had not dared to post them ere now – even yet they may take panic from the drifting of a cloud or the blowing of a leaf, and scatter like birds before a cold wind. King Kull – the fate of the Pictish nation is at stake. I am called king of the Picts, but my rule as yet is but a hollow mockery. The hills are full of wild clans who refuse to fight for me. Of the thousand bowmen now at my command, more than half are of my own clan.

"Some eighteen hundred Romans are marching against us. It is not a real invasion, but much hinges upon it. It is the beginning of an attempt to extend their boundaries. They plan to build a fortress a day's march to the north of this valley. If they do, they will build other forts, drawing bands of steel about the heart of the free people. If I win this battle and wipe out this army, I will win a double victory. Then the tribes will flock to me and the next invasion will meet a solid wall of resistance. If I lose, the clans will scatter, fleeing to the north until they can no longer flee, fighting as separate clans rather than as one strong nation.

"I have a thousand archers, five hundred horsemen, fifty chariots with their drivers and swordsmen – one hundred and fifty men in all – and, thanks to you, three hundred heavily armed Northern pirates. How would you arrange your battle lines?"

"Well," said Kull, "I would have barricaded the north of the valley – no! That would suggest a trap. But I would block it with a band of desperate men, like those you have given me to lead. Three hundred could hold the gorge for a time against any number. Then, when the enemy was engaged with these men to the narrow part of the valley, I would have my archers shoot down into them until their ranks are broken, from both sides of the vale. Then, having my horsemen concealed behind the other, I would charge with both simultaneously and sweep the foe into a red ruin."

Bran's eyes glowed. "Exactly, king of Valusia. Such was my exact plan—"

"But what of the scouts?"

"My warriors are like panthers; they hide under the noses of the Romans. Those who ride into the valley will see only what we wish them to see. Those who ride over the ridge will not come back to report. An arrow is swift and silent.

"You see that the pivot of the whole thing depends on the men that hold the gorge. They must be men who can fight on foot and resist the charges of the heavy legionaries long enough for the trap to close. Outside these Northmen I had no such force of men. My naked warriors with their short swords could never stand such a charge for an instant. Nor is the armor of the Celts made for such work; moreover, they are not foot-fighters, and I need them elsewhere.

"So you see why I had such desperate need of the Northmen. Now will you stand in the gorge with them and hold back the Romans until I can spring the trap? Remember, most of you will die."

Kull smiled. "I have taken chances all my life, though Tu, chief councillor, would say my life belongs to Valusia and I have no right to so risk it—" His voice trailed off and a strange look flitted across his face. "By Valka," said he, laughing uncertainly, "sometimes I forget this is a dream! All seems so real. But it is – of course it is! Well, then, if I die I will but awaken as I have done in times past. Lead on, king of Caledon!"

Cormac, going to his warriors, wondered. Surely it was all a hoax; yet – he heard the arguments of the warriors all about him as they armed themselves and prepared to take their posts. The black-haired king was Neid himself, the Celtic war-god; he was an antediluvian king brought out of the past by Gonar; he was a mythical fighting man out of Valhalla. He was no man at all but a ghost! No, he was mortal, for he had bled. But the gods themselves bled, though they did not die. So the controversies raged. At least, thought Cormac, if it was all a hoax to inspire the warriors with the feeling of supernatural aid, it had succeeded. The belief that Kull was more than a mortal man had fired Celt, Pict, and Viking alike into a sort of inspired madness. And Cormac asked himself – what did he himself believe? This man was surely one from some far land – yet in his every look and action there was a vague hint of a greater difference than mere distance of space – a hint of alien Time, of misty abysses and gigantic gulfs of eons lying between the black-haired stranger and the men with whom he walked and talked. Clouds of bewilderment mazed Cormac's brain and he laughed in whimsical self-mockery.

III

"And the two wild peoples of the north
Stood fronting in the gloam,
And heard and knew each in his mind
A third great sound upon the wind,
The living walls that hedge mankind,
The walking walls of Rome."
—Chesterton

The sun slanted westward. Silence lay like an invisible mist over the valley. Cormac gathered the reins in his hand and glanced up at the ridges on both sides. The waving heather which grew rank on those steep slopes gave no evidence of the hundreds of savage warriors who lurked there. Here in the narrow gorge which widened gradually southward was the only sign of life. Between the steep walls three hundred Northmen were massed solidly in their wedge-shaped shield-wall, blocking the pass. At the tip, like the point of a spear, stood the man who called himself Kull, king of Valusia. He wore no helmet, only the great, strangely worked headband of hard gold, but he bore on his left arm the great shield borne by the dead Rognar; and in his right hand he held the heavy iron mace wielded by the sea-king. The Vikings eyed him in wonder and savage admiration. They could not understand his language, or he theirs. But no further orders were necessary. At Bran's directions they had bunched themselves in the gorge, and their only order was – hold the pass!

Bran Mak Morn stood just in front of Kull. So they faced each other, he whose kingdom was yet unborn, and he whose kingdom had been lost in the mists of Time for unguessed ages. Kings of darkness, thought Cormac, nameless kings of the night, whose realms are gulfs and shadows.

The hand of the Pictish king went out. "King Kull, you are more than king – you are a man. Both of us may fall within the next hour – but if we live, ask what you will of me."

Kull smiled, returning the firm grip. "You too are a man after my own heart, king of the shadows. Surely you are more than a figment of my sleeping imagination. Mayhap we will meet in waking life some day."

Bran shook his head in puzzlement, swung into the saddle and rode away, climbing the eastern slope and vanishing over the ridge. Cormac hesitated: "Strange man, are you in truth of flesh and blood, or are you a ghost?"

"When we dream, we are all flesh and blood – so long as we are dreaming," Kull answered. "This is the strangest nightmare I have ever known – but you, who will soon fade into sheer nothingness as I awaken, seem as real to me now, as Brule, or Kananu, or Tu, or Kelkor."

Cormac shook his head as Bran had done, and with a last salute, which Kull returned with barbaric stateliness, he turned and trotted away. At the top of the western ridge he paused. Away to the south a light cloud of dust rose and the head of the marching column was in sight. Already he believed he could feel the earth vibrate slightly to the measured tread of a thousand mailed feet beating in perfect unison. He dismounted, and one of his chieftains, Domnail, took his steed and led it down the slope away from the valley, where trees grew thickly. Only an occasional vague movement among them gave evidence of the five hundred men who stood there, each at his horse's head with a ready hand to check a chance nicker.

Oh, thought Cormac, *the gods themselves made this valley for Bran's ambush!* The floor of the valley was treeless and the inner slopes were bare save for the waist-high heather. But at the foot of each ridge on the side facing away from the vale, where the soil long washed from the rocky slopes had accumulated, there grew enough trees to hide five hundred horsemen or fifty chariots.

At the northern end of the valley stood Kull and his three hundred Vikings, in open view, flanked on each side by fifty Pictish bowmen. Hidden on the western side of the western ridge were the Gaels. Along the top of the slopes, concealed in the tall heather, lay a hundred Picts with their shafts on string. The rest of the Picts were hidden on the eastern slopes beyond which lay the Britons with their chariots in full readiness. Neither they nor the Gaels to the west could see what went on in the vale, but signals had been arranged.

Now the long column was entering the wide mouth of the valley and their scouts, light-armed men on swift horses, were spreading out between the slopes. They galloped almost within bowshot of the silent host that blocked the pass, then halted. Some whirled and raced back to the main force, while the others deployed and cantered up the slopes, seeking to see what lay beyond. This was the crucial moment. If they got any hint of the ambush, all was lost. Cormac, shrinking down into the heather, marveled at the ability of the Picts to efface themselves from view so completely. He saw a horseman pass within three feet of where he knew a bowman lay, yet the Roman saw nothing.

The scouts topped the ridges, gazed about; then most of them turned and trotted back down the slopes. Cormac wondered at their desultory manner of scouting. He had never fought Romans before, knew nothing of their arrogant self-confidence, of their incredible shrewdness in some ways, their incredible stupidity in others. These men were over-confident; a feeling radiating from their officers. It had been years since a force of Caledonians had stood before the legions. And most of these men were but newly come to Britain; part of a legion which had been quartered in Egypt. They despised their foes and suspected nothing.

But stay – three riders on the opposite ridge had turned and vanished on the other side. And now one, sitting his steed at the crest of the western ridge, not a hundred yards from where Cormac lay, looked long and narrowly down into the mass of trees at the foot of the slope. Cormac saw suspicion grow on his brown, hawk-like face. He half turned as though to call to his comrades, then instead reined his steed down the slope, leaning forward in his saddle. Cormac's heart pounded. Each moment he expected to see the man wheel and gallop back to raise the alarm. He resisted a mad impulse to leap up and charge the Roman on foot. Surely the man could feel the tenseness in the air – the hundreds of fierce eyes upon him. Now he was halfway down the slope, out of sight of the men in the valley. And now the twang of an unseen bow broke the painful stillness. With a strangled gasp the Roman flung his hands high, and as the steed reared, he pitched headlong, transfixed by a long black arrow that had flashed from the heather. A stocky dwarf sprang out of nowhere, seemingly, and seized the bridle, quieting the snorting horse and leading it down the slope. At the fall of the Roman, short crooked men rose like a sudden flight of birds from the grass and Cormac saw the flash of a knife. Then with unreal suddenness all had subsided. Slayers and slain were unseen and only the still waving heather marked the grim deed.

The Gael looked back into the valley. The three who had ridden over the eastern ridge had not come back and Cormac knew they never would. Evidently the other scouts had borne word that only a small band of warriors was ready to dispute the passage of the legionaries. Now the head of the column was almost below him and he thrilled at the sight of these men who were doomed, swinging along with their superb arrogance. And the sight of their splendid armor, their hawk-like faces and perfect discipline awed him as much as it is possible for a Gael to be awed.

Twelve hundred men in heavy armor who marched as one so that the ground shook to their tread! Most of them were of middle height, with powerful chests and shoulders and bronzed faces – hard-bitten veterans of a hundred campaigns: Cormac noted their javelins, short keen swords and heavy shields;

their gleaming armor and crested helmets, the eagles on the standards. These were the men beneath whose tread the world had shaken and empires crumbled! Not all were Latins; there were Romanized Britons among them, and one century or hundred was composed of huge yellow-haired men – Gauls and Germans, who fought for Rome as fiercely as did the native-born, and hated their wilder kinsmen more savagely.

On each side was a swarm of cavalry, outriders, and the column was flanked by archers and slingers. A number of lumbering wagons carried the supplies of the army. Cormac saw the commander riding in his place – a tall man with a lean, imperious face, evident even at that distance. Marcus Sulius – the Gael knew him by repute.

A deep-throated roar rose from the legionaries as they approached their foes. Evidently they intended to slice their way through and continue without a pause, for the column moved implacably on. Whom the gods destroy they first make mad – Cormac had never heard the phrase but it came to him that the great Sulius was a fool. Roman arrogance! Marcus was used to lashing the cringing peoples of a decadent East; little he guessed of the iron in these western races.

A group of cavalry detached itself and raced into the mouth of the gorge, but it was only a gesture. With loud jeering shouts they wheeled three spears-length away and cast their javelins, which rattled harmlessly on the overlapping shields of the silent Northmen. But their leader dared too much; swinging in, he leaned from his saddle and thrust at Kull's face. The great shield turned the lance and Kull struck back as a snake strikes; the ponderous mace crushed helmet and head like an eggshell, and the very steed went to its knees from the shock of that terrible blow. From the Northmen went up a short fierce roar, and the Picts beside them howled exultantly and loosed their arrows among the retreating horsemen. First blood for the people of the heather! The oncoming Romans shouted vengefully and quickened their pace as the frightened horse raced by, a ghastly travesty of a man, foot caught in the stirrup, trailing beneath the pounding hoofs.

Now the first line of the legionaries, compressed because of the narrowness of the gorge, crashed against the solid wall of shields – crashed and recoiled upon itself. The shield-wall had not shaken an inch. This was the first time the Roman legions had met with that unbreakable formation – that oldest of all Aryan battle lines – the ancestor of the Spartan regiment – the Theban phalanx – the Macedonian formation – the English square.

Shield crashed on shield and the short Roman sword sought for an opening in that iron wall. Viking spears, bristling in solid ranks above, thrust and reddened; heavy axes chopped down, shearing through iron, flesh and bone. Cormac saw Kull, looming above the stocky Romans in the forefront of the fray, dealing blows, like thunderbolts. A burly centurion rushed in, shield held high, stabbing upward. The iron mace crashed terribly, shivering the sword, rending the shield apart, shattering the helmet, crushing the skull down between the shoulders – in a single blow.

The front line of the Romans bent like a steel bar about the wedge, as the legionaries sought to struggle through the gorge on each side and surround their opposers. But the pass was too narrow; crouching close against the steep walls the Picts drove their black arrows in a hail of death. At this range the heavy shafts tore through shield and corselet, transfixing the armored men. The front line of battle rolled back, red and broken, and the Northmen trod their few dead under foot to close the gaps their fall had made. Stretched the full width of their front lay a thin line of shattered forms – the red spray of the tide which had broken upon them in vain.

Cormac had leaped to his feet, waving his arms. Domnail and his men broke cover at the signal and came galloping up the slope, lining the ridge. Cormac mounted the horse brought him and glanced impatiently across the narrow vale. No sign of life appeared on the eastern ridge. Where was Bran – and the Britons?

Down in the valley, the legions, angered at the unexpected opposition of the paltry force in front of them, but not suspicious, were forming in more compact body. The wagons which had halted were lumbering on again and the whole column was once more in motion as if it intended to crash through by sheer weight. With the Gaulish century in the forefront, the legionaries were advancing again in the attack. This time, with the full force of twelve hundred men behind, the charge would batter down the resistance of Kull's warriors like a heavy ram; would stamp them down, sweep over their red ruins. Cormac's men trembled in impatience. Suddenly Marcus Sulius turned and gazed westward, where the line of horsemen was etched against the sky. Even at that distance Cormac saw his face pale. The Roman at last realized the mettle of the men he faced, and that he had walked into a trap. Surely in that moment there flashed a chaotic picture through his brain – defeat – disgrace – red ruin!

It was too late to retreat – too late to form into a defensive square with the wagons for barricade. There was but one possible way out, and Marcus, a crafty general in spite of his recent blunder, took it. Cormac heard his voice cut like a clarion through the din, and though he did not understand the words, he knew that the Roman was shouting for his men to smite that knot of Northmen like a blast – to hack their way through and out of the trap before it could close!

Now the legionaries, aware of their desperate plight, flung themselves headlong and terribly on their foes. The shield-wall rocked, but it gave not an inch. The wild faces of the Gauls and the hard brown Italian faces glared over locked shields into the blazing eyes of the North. Shields touching, they smote and slew and died in a red storm of slaughter, where crimsoned axes rose and fell and dripping spears broke on notched swords.

Where in God's name was Bran with his chariots? A few minutes more would spell the doom of every man who held that pass. Already they were falling fast, though they locked their ranks closer and held like iron. Those wild men of the North were dying in their tracks; and looming among their gold heads the black lion-mane of Kull shone like a symbol of slaughter, and his reddened mace showered a ghastly rain as it splashed brains and blood like water.

Something snapped in Cormac's brain.

"These men will die while we wait for Bran's signal!" he shouted. "On! Follow me into Hell, sons of Gael!"

A wild roar answered him, and loosing rein he shot down the slope with five hundred yelling riders plunging headlong after him. And even at that moment a storm of arrows swept the valley from either side like a dark cloud and the terrible clamor of the Picts split the skies. And over the eastern ridge, like a sudden burst of rolling thunder on Judgment Day, rushed the war-chariots. Headlong down the slope they roared, foam flying from the horses' distended nostrils, frantic feet scarcely seeming to touch the ground, making naught of the tall heather. In the foremost chariot, with his dark eyes blazing, crouched Bran Mak Morn, and in all of them the naked Britons were screaming and lashing as if possessed by demons. Behind the flying chariots came the Picts, howling like wolves and loosing their arrows as they ran. The heather belched them forth from all sides in a dark wave.

So much Cormac saw in chaotic glimpses during the wild ride down the slopes. A wave of cavalry swept between him and the main line of the column. Three long leaps ahead of his men, the Gaelic prince met the spears of the Roman riders. The first lance turned on his buckler, and rising in his stirrups he smote downward, cleaving his man from shoulders to breastbone. The next Roman flung a javelin that killed Domnail, but at that instant Cormac's steed crashed into his, breast to breast, and the lighter horse rolled headlong under the shock, flinging his rider beneath the pounding hoofs.

Then the whole blast of the Gaelic charge smote the Roman cavalry, shattering it, crashing and rolling it down and under. Over its red ruins Cormac's yelling demons struck the heavy Roman infantry, and the whole line reeled at the shock. Swords and axes flashed up and down and the force of their rush carried them deep into the massed ranks. Here, checked, they swayed and strove. Javelins thrust, swords flashed upward bringing down horse and rider, and greatly outnumbered, leaguered on every side, the Gaels had perished among their foe, but at that moment, from the other side the crashing chariots smote the Roman ranks. In one long line they struck almost simultaneously, and at the moment of impact the charioteers wheeled their horses sidelong and raced parallel down the ranks, shearing men down like the mowing of wheat. Hundreds died on those curving blades in that moment, and leaping from the chariots, screaming like blood-mad wildcats, the British swordsmen flung themselves upon the spears of the legionaries, hacking madly with their two-handed swords. Crouching, the Picts drove their arrows point-blank and then sprang in to slash and thrust. Maddened with the sight of victory, these wild peoples were like wounded tigers, feeling no wounds, and dying on their feet with their last gasp a snarl of fury.

But the battle was not over yet. Dazed, shattered, their formation broken and nearly half their number down already, the Romans fought back with desperate fury. Hemmed in on all sides they slashed and smote singly, or in small clumps, fought back to back, archers, slingers, horsemen and heavy legionaries mingled into a chaotic mass. The confusion was complete, but not the victory.

Those bottled in the gorge still hurled themselves upon the red axes that barred their way, while the massed and serried battle thundered behind them. From one side Cormac's Gaels raged and slashed; from the other chariots swept back and forth, retiring and returning like iron whirlwinds. There was no retreat, for the Picts had flung a cordon across the way they had come, and having cut the throats of the camp followers and possessed themselves of the wagons, they sent their shafts in a storm of death into the rear of the shattered column. Those long black arrows pierced armor and bone, nailing men together. Yet the slaughter was not all on one side. Picts died beneath the lightning thrust of javelin and shortsword, Gaels pinned beneath their falling horses were hewed to pieces, and chariots, cut loose from their horses, were deluged with the blood of the charioteers.

And at the narrow head of the valley still the battle surged and eddied. *Great gods* – thought Cormac, glancing between lightning-like blows – *do these men still hold the gorge?* Aye! They held it! A tenth of their original number, dying on their feet, they still held back the frantic charges of the dwindling legionaries.

Over all the field went up the roar and the clash of arms, and birds of prey, swift-flying out of the sunset, circled above. Cormac, striving to reach Marcus Sulius through the press, saw the Roman's horse sink under him, and the rider rise alone in a waste of foes. He saw the Roman sword flash thrice, dealing a death at each blow; then from the thickest of the fray bounded a terrible figure. It was Bran Mak Morn, stained from head to foot. He cast away his broken sword as he ran, drawing a dirk. The Roman struck, but the Pictish king was under the thrust, and gripping the sword-wrist, he drove the dirk again and again through the gleaming armor.

A mighty roar went up as Marcus died, and Cormac, with a shout, rallied the remnants of his force about him and, striking in the spurs, burst through the shattered lines and rode full speed for the other end of the valley.

But as he approached he saw that he was too late. As they had lived, so had they died, those fierce sea-wolves, with their faces to the foe and their broken weapons red in their hands. In a grim and silent band they lay, even in death preserving some of the shield-wall formation. Among them, in front of them and all about them lay high-heaped the bodies of those who had sought to break them, in vain. *They had not given back a foot!* To the last man, they had died in their tracks. Nor were there any left to stride over their torn shapes; those Romans who had escaped the Viking axes had been struck down by the shafts of the Picts and swords of the Gaels from behind.

Yet this part of the battle was not over. High up on the steep western slope Cormac saw the ending of that drama. A group of Gauls in the armor of Rome pressed upon a single man – a black-haired giant on whose head gleamed a golden crown. There was iron in these men, as well as in the man who had held them to their fate. They were doomed – their comrades were being slaughtered behind them – but before their turn came they would at least have the life of the black-haired chief who had led the golden-haired men of the North.

Pressing upon him from three sides they had forced him slowly back up the steep gorge wall, and the crumpled bodies that stretched along his retreat showed how fiercely every foot of the way had been contested. Here on this steep it was task enough to keep one's footing alone; yet these men at once climbed and fought. Kull's shield and the huge mace were gone, and the great sword in his right hand was dyed crimson. His mail, wrought with a forgotten art, now hung in shreds, and blood streamed from a hundred wounds on limbs, head and body. But his eyes still blazed with the battle-joy and his wearied arm still drove the mighty blade in strokes of death.

But Cormac saw that the end would come before they could reach him. Now at the very crest of the steep, a hedge of points menaced the strange king's life, and even his iron strength was ebbing. Now he split the skull of a huge warrior and the backstroke shore through the neck-cords of another; reeling under a very rain of swords he struck again and his victim dropped at his feet, cleft to the breastbone. Then, even as a dozen swords rose above the staggering Atlantean for the death stroke, a strange thing happened. The sun was sinking into the western sea; all the heather swam red like an ocean of blood. Etched in the dying sun, as he had first appeared, Kull stood, and then, like a mist lifting, a mighty vista opened behind the reeling king. Cormac's astounded eyes caught a fleeting gigantic glimpse of other climes and spheres – as if mirrored in summer clouds he saw, instead of the heather hills stretching away to sea, a dim and mighty land of blue mountains and gleaming quiet lakes – the golden, purple and sapphirean spires and towering walls of a mighty city such as the earth has not known for many a drifting age.

Then like the fading of a mirage it was gone, but the Gauls on the high slope had dropped their weapons and stared like men dazed – *For the man called Kull had vanished and there was no trace of his going!*

As if in a daze Cormac turned his steed and rode back across the trampled field. His horse's hoofs splashed in lakes of blood and against the helmets of dead men. Across the valley the shout of victory was thundering. Yet all seemed shadowy and strange. A shape was striding across the torn corpses and Cormac was dully aware that it was Bran. The Gael swung from his horse and fronted the king. Bran was weaponless and gory; blood trickled from gashes on brow, breast and limb; what armor he had worn was clean hacked away and a cut had shorn halfway through his iron crown. But the red jewel still gleamed unblemished like a star of slaughter.

"It is in my mind to slay you," said the Gael heavily and like a man speaking in a daze, "for the blood of brave men is on your head. Had you given the signal to charge sooner, some would have lived."

Bran folded his arms; his eyes were haunted. "Strike if you will; I am sick of slaughter. It is a cold mead, this kinging it. A king must gamble with men's lives and naked swords. The lives of all my people were at stake; I sacrificed the Northmen – yes; and my heart is sore within me, for they were men! But had I given the order when you would have sired, all might have gone awry. The Romans were not yet massed in the narrow mouth of the gorge, and might have had time and space to form their ranks again and beat us off. I waited until the last moment – and the rovers died. A king belongs to his people, and cannot let either his own feelings or the lives of men influence him. Now my people are saved; but my heart is cold in my breast."

Cormac wearily dropped his sword-point to the ground. 'You are a born king of men, Bran," said the Gaelic prince.

Bran's eyes roved the field. A mist of blood hovered over where the victorious barbarians were looting the dead, while those Romans who had escaped slaughter by throwing down their swords, and now stood under guard, looked on with hot smoldering eyes.

"My kingdom – my people – are saved," said Bran wearily. They will come from the heather by the thousands and when Rome moves against us again, she will meet a solid nation. But I am weary. What of Kull?"

"My eyes and brain were mazed with battle," answered cormac. "I thought to see him vanish like a ghost into the sunset. I will seek his body."

"Seek not for him," said Bran. "Out of the sunrise he came – into the sunset he has gone. Out of the mists of the ages he came to us, and back into the mists of the eons has he returned – to his own kingdom."

Cormac turned away; night was gathering. Gonar stood like a white specter before him. "To his own kingdom," echoed the wizard. "Time and Space are naught. Kull has returned to his own kingdom – his own crown – his own age."

"Then he was a ghost?"

"Did you not feel the grip of his solid hand? Did you not hear his voice – see him eat and drink, laugh and slay and bleed?"

Still Cormac stood like one in a trance.

"Then if it be possible for a man to pass from one age into one yet unborn, or come forth from a century dead and forgotten, whichever you will, with his flesh-and-blood body and his arms – then he is as mortal as he was in his own day. Is Kull dead, then?"

"He died a hundred thousand years ago, as men reckon time," answered the wizard, "but in his own age. He died not from the swords of the Gauls of this age. Have we not heard in legends how the king of Valusia travelled into a strange, timeless land of the misty future ages, and there fought in a great battle? Why, so he did! A hundred thousand years ago, or today!

"And a hundred thousand years ago – or a moment agone! – Kull, king of Valusia, roused himself on the silken couch in his secret chamber and laughing, spoke to the first Gonar, saying: 'Ha, wizard, I have in truth dreamed strangely, for I went into a far clime and a far time in my visions, and fought for the king of a strange shadow-people!' And the great sorcerer smiled and pointed silently at the red, notched sword, and the torn mail and the many wounds that the king carried. And Kull, fully woken from his 'vision' and feeling the sting and the weakness of these yet bleeding wounds, fell silent and mazed, and all life and time and space seemed like a dream of ghosts to him, and he wondered thereat all the rest of his life. For the wisdom of the Eternities is denied even unto princes and Kull could no more understand what Gonar told him than you can understand my words."

"And then Kull lived despite his many wounds," said Cormac, "and has returned to the mists of silence and the centuries. Well – he thought us a dream; we thought him a ghost. And sure, life is but a web spun of ghosts and dreams and illusion, and it is in my mind that the kingdom which has this day been born of swords and slaughter in this howling valley is a thing no more solid than the foam of the bright sea."

WORMS OF THE EARTH

I

"Strike in the nails, soldiers, and let our guest see the reality of our good Roman justice!"

The speaker wrapped his purple cloak closer about his powerful frame and settled back into his official chair, much as he might have settled back in his seat at the Circus Maximus to enjoy the clash of gladiatorial swords. Realization of power colored his every move. Whetted pride was necessary to Roman satisfaction, and Titus Sulla was justly proud; for he was military governor of Ebbracum and answerable only to the emperor of Rome. He was a strongly built man of medium height, with the hawk-like features of the pure-bred Roman. Now a mocking smile curved his full lips, increasing the arrogance of his haughty aspect. Distinctly military in appearance, he wore the golden-scaled corselet and chased breastplate of his rank, with the, short stabbing sword at his belt, and he held on his knee the silvered helmet with its plumed crest. Behind him stood a clump of impassive soldiers with shield and spear – blond titans from the Rhineland.

Before him was taking place the scene which apparently gave him so much real gratification – a scene common enough wherever stretched the far-flung boundaries of Rome. A rude cross lay flat upon the barren earth and on it was bound a man – half naked, wild of aspect with his corded limbs, glaring eyes and shock of tangled hair. His executioners were Roman soldiers, and with heavy hammers they prepared to pin the victim's hands and feet to the wood with iron spikes.

Only a small group of men watched this ghastly scene, in the dread place of execution beyond the city walls: the governor and his watchful guards; a few young Roman officers; the man to whom Sulla had referred as "guest" and who stood like a bronze image, unspeaking. Beside the gleaming splendor of the Roman, the quiet garb of this man seemed drab, almost somber. He was dark, but did not resemble the Latins around him. There was about him none of the warm, almost Oriental sensuality of the Mediterranean which colored their features. The blond barbarians behind Sulla's chair were less unlike the man in facial outline than were the Romans. Not his were the full curving red lips, nor the rich waving locks suggestive of the Greek. Nor was his dark complexion the rich olive of the south; rather it was the bleak darkness of the north. The whole aspect of the man vaguely suggested the shadowed mists, the gloom, the cold and the icy winds of the naked northern lands. Even his black eyes were savagely cold, like black fires burning through fathoms of ice. His height was only medium but there was something about him which transcended mere physical bulk – a certain fierce innate vitality, comparable only to that of a wolf or a panther. In every line of his supple, compact body, as well as in his coarse straight hair and thin lips, this was evident – in the hawk-like set of the head on the corded neck, in the broad square shoulders, in the deep chest, the lean loins, the narrow feet. Built with the savage economy of a panther, he was an image of dynamic potentialities, pent in with iron self-control, At his feet crouched one like him in complexion – but there the resemblance ended. This other was a stunted giant, with gnarly limbs, thick body, a low sloping brow and an expression of dull ferocity, now clearly mixed with fear. If the man on the cross resembled, in a tribal way, the man Titus Sulla called guest, he far more resembled the stunted crouching giant.

"Well, Partha Mac Othna," said the governor with studied effrontery, "when you return to your tribe, you will have a tale to tell of the justice of Rome, who rules the south."

"I will have a tale," answered the other in a voice which betrayed no emotion, just as his dark face, schooled to immobility, showed no evidence of the maelstrom in his soul.

"Justice to all under the rule of Rome," said Sulla. "Pax Romana! Reward for virtue, punishment for wrong!" He laughed inwardly at his own black hypocrisy, then continued: "You see, emissary of Pictland, how swiftly Rome punishes the transgressor."

"I see," answered the Pict in a voice which strongly-curbed anger made deep with menace, "that the subject of a foreign king is dealt with as though he were a Roman slave."

"He has been tried and condemned in an unbiased court," retorted Sulla.

"Aye! and the accuser was a Roman, the witnesses Roman, the judge Roman! He committed murder? In a moment of fury he struck down a Roman merchant who cheated, tricked and robbed him, and to injury added insult – aye, and a blow! Is his king but a dog, that Rome crucifies his subjects at will, condemned by Roman courts? Is his king too weak or foolish to do justice, were he informed and formal charges brought against the offender?"

"Well," said Sulla cynically, "you may inform Bran Mak Morn yourself. Rome, my friend, makes no account of her actions to barbarian kings. When savages come among us, let them act with discretion or suffer the consequences."

The Pict shut his iron jaws with a snap that told Sulla further badgering would elicit no reply. The Roman made a gesture to the executioners. One of them seized a spike and placing it against the thick wrist of the victim, smote heavily. The iron point sank deep through the flesh, crunching against the bones. The lips of the man on the cross writhed, though no moan escaped him. As a trapped wolf fights against his cage, the bound victim instinctively wrenched and struggled. The veins swelled in his temples, sweat beaded his low forehead, the muscles in arms and legs writhed and knotted. The hammers fell in inexorable strokes, driving the cruel points deeper and deeper, through wrist. and ankles; blood flowed in a black river over the hands that held the spikes, staining the wood of the cross, and the splintering of bones was distinctly heard. Yet the sufferer made no outcry, though his blackened lips writhed back until the gums were visible, and his shaggy head jerked involuntarily from side to side.

The man called Partha Mac Othna stood like an iron image, eyes burning from an inscrutable face, his whole body hard as iron from the tension of his control. At his feet crouched his misshapen servant, hiding his face from the grim sight, his arms locked about his master's knees. Those arms gripped like steel and under his breath the fellow mumbled ceaselessly as if in invocation.

The last stroke fell; the cords were cut from arm and leg, so that the man would hang supported by the nails alone. He had ceased his struggling that only twisted the spikes in his agonizing wounds. His bright black eyes, unglazed, had hot left the face of the man called Partha Mac Othna; in them lingered a desperate shadow of hope. Now the solders lifted the cross and set the end of it in the hole prepared, stamped the dirt about it to hold it erect. The Pict hung in midair, suspended by the nails in his flesh, but still no sound escaped his lips. His eyes still hung on the somber face of the emissary, but the shadow of hope was fading.

"He'll live for days," said Sulla cheerfully. "These Picts are harder than cats to kill; I'll keep a guard of ten soldiers watching night and day to see that no one takes him down before he dies. Ho, there, Valerius, in honor of our esteemed neighbour; King Bran Mak Morn, give him a cup of wine!"

With a laugh the young officer came forward, holding a brimming wine-cup, and rising on his toes, lifted it to the parched lips of the sufferer. In the black eyes flared a red wave of unquenchable hatred; writhing his head aside to avoid even touching the cup, he spat full into the young Roman's eyes. With a curse Valerius dashed the cup to the ground, and before any could halt him, wrenched out his word and sheathed it in the man's body.

Sulla rose with an imperious exclamation of anger; the man called Partha Mac Othna had started violently, but he bit his lip and said nothing. Valerius seemed somewhat surprised at him, as he sullenly cleansed his sword. The act had been instinctive, following the insult to Roman pride, the one thing unbearable.

"Give up your sword, young sir!" exclaimed Sulla. "Centurion Publius, place him under arrest. A few days in a cell with stale bread and water will teach you to curb your patrician pride, in matters dealing with the will of the empire. What, you young fool, do you not realize that you could not have made the dog a more kindly gift? Who would not rather desire a quick death on the sword than the slow agony on the cross? Take him away. And you, centurion, see that guards remain at the cross so that the body is not cut down until the ravens pick bare the bones. Partha Mac Othna, I go to a banquet at the house of Demetrius – will you not accompany me?"

II

The emissary shook his head, his eyes fixed on the limp form which sagged on the black-stained cross. He made no reply. Sulla smiled sardonically, then rose and strode away, followed by his secretary who bore the gilded chair ceremoniously, and by the stolid soldiers, with whom walked Valerius, head sunken.

The man called Partha Mac Othna flung a wide fold of his cloak about his shoulder, halted a moment to gaze at the grim cross with its burden, darkly etched against the crimson sky, where the clouds of night were gathering. Then he stalked away, followed by his silent servant.

In an inner chamber of Ebbracum, the man called Partha Mac Othna paced tigerishly to and fro. His sandalled feet made no sound on the marble tiles.

"Grom!" he turned to the gnarled servant, "well I know why you held my knees so tightly – why you muttered aid of the Moon-Woman – you feared i would lose my self-control and make a mad attempt to succor that poor wretch. By the gods, I believe that was what that dog Roman wished – his iron-cased watchdogs watched me narrowly, I know, and his baiting was harder to bear than ordinarily.

"Gods black and white, dark and light!" he shook his clenched fists above his head in the black gust of his passion. "That I should stand by and see a man of mine butchered on a Roman cross – without justice and with no more trial than that farce! Black gods of R'lyeh, even you would I invoke to the ruin and destruction of those butchers! I swear by the Nameless Ones, men shall die howling for that deed, and Rome shall cry out as a woman in the dark who treads upon an adder!"

"He knew you, master," said Grom.

The other dropped his head and covered his eyes with a gesture of savage pain.

"His eyes will haunt me when I lie dying. Aye, he knew me, and almost until the last, I read in his eyes the hope that I might aid him. Gods and devils, is Rome to butcher my people beneath my very eyes? Then I am not king but dog!"

"Not so loud, in the name of all the gods!" exclaimed Grom In affright. "Did these Romans suspect you were Bran Mak Morn, they'd nail you on a cross beside that other."

"They will know it ere long," grimly answered the king. "Too long I have lingered here in the guise of an emissary, spying upon mine enemies. They have thought to play with me, these Romans, masking their contempt and scorn only tinder polished satire. Rome is courteous to barbarian ambassadors, they give us fine houses to live in, offer us slaves, pander to our lusts with women and gold and wine and games, but all the while they laugh at us; their very courtesy is an insult, and sometimes – as today – their contempt discards all veneer. Bah! I've seen through their baitings – have remained imperturbably serene and swallowed their studied insults. But this – by the fiends of Hell, this is beyond human endurance! My people look to me; if I fail them – if I fail even one – even the lowest of my people, who will aid them? To whom shall they turn? By the gods, I'll answer the gibes of these Roman dogs with black shaft and trenchant steel!"

"And the chief with the plumes?" Grom meant the governor and his gutturals thrummed with the blood-lust. "He dies?" He flicked out a length of steel.

Bran scowled. "Easier said than done. He dies – but how may I reach him? By day his German guards keep at his back; by night they stand at door and window. He has many enemies, Romans as well as barbarians. Many a Briton would gladly slit his throat."

Grom seized Bran's garment, stammering as fierce eagerness broke the bonds of his inarticulate nature.

"Let me go, master! My life is worth nothing. I will cut him down in the midst of his warriors!"

Bran smiled fiercely and clapped his hand on the stunted giant's shoulder with a force that would have felled a lesser man.

"Nay, old war-dog. I have too much need of thee! You shall not throw your life away uselessly. Sulla would read the intent in your eyes, besides, and the javelins of his Teutons would be through you ere you could reach him. Not by dagger in the dark will we strike this Roman, not by the venom in the cup nor the shaft from the ambush."

The king turned and paced the floor a moment, his head bent in thought. Slowly his eyes grew murky with a thought so fearful he did not speak it aloud to the waiting warrior.

"I have become somewhat familiar with the maze of Roman politics during my stay in this accursed waste of mud and marble," said he. "During a war on the Wall, Titus Sulla, as governor of this province, is supposed to hasten thither with his centurions. But this Sulla does not do; he is no coward, but the bravest avoid certain things – to each man, however bold, his own particular fear. So he sends in his place Caius Camillus, who in times of peace patrols the fens of the west, lest the Britons break over the border. And Sulla takes his place in the Tower of Trajan. Ha!"

He whirled and gripped Grom with steely fingers.

"Grom, take the red stallion and ride north I Let no grass grow under the stallion's hoofs! Ride to Cormac na Connacht and tell him to sweep the frontier with sword and torch! Let his wild Gaels feast their fill of slaughter. After a time I will be with him. But for a time I have affairs in the west."

Grom's black eyes gleamed and he made a passionate gesture with his crooked hand – an instinctive move of savagery.

Bran drew a heavy bronze seal from beneath his tunic.

"This is my safe-conduct as an emissary to Roman courts," he said grimly. "It will open all gates between this house and Baal-dor. If any official questions you too closely – here!"

Lifting the lid of an iron-bound chest, Bran took out a small, heavy leather bag which he gave into the hands of the warrior.

"When all keys fail at a gate," said he, "try a golden key. Go now!"

There were no ceremonious farewells between the barbarian king and his barbarian vassal. Grom flung up his arm in a gesture of salute; then turning he hurried out.

Bran stepped to a barred window and gazed out into the moonlit streets.

"Wait until the moon sets," he muttered grimly. "Then I'll take the road to – Hell! But before I go I have a debt to pay."

The stealthy clink of a hoof an the flags reached him.

"With the safe-conduct and gold, not even Rome can hold a Pictish reaver," muttered the king. "Now I'll sleep until the moon sets."

With a snarl at the marble frieze-work and fluted columns, as symbols of Rome, he flung himself down on a couch, from which he had long impatiently torn the cushions and silk stuffs, as too soft for his hard body. Hate and the black passion of vengeance seethed in him, yet he went instantly to sleep. The first lesson he had learned in his bitter hard life was to snatch sleep any time he could, like a wolf that snatches sleep on the hunting trail. Generally his slumber was as light and dreamless as a panther's, but tonight it was otherwise.

He sank into fleecy gray fathoms of slumber and in a timeless, misty realm of shadows he met the tall, lean, white-bearded figure of old Gonar, the priest of the Moon, high counsellor to the king. And Bran stood aghast, for Gonar's face was white as driven snow and he shook as with ague. Well might Bran stand appalled, for in all the years of his life he had never before seen Gonar the Wise show any sign of fear.

"What now, old one?" asked the king. "Goes all well in Baal-dor?"

"All is well in Baal-dor where my body lies sleeping," answered old Gonar. "Across the void I have come to battle with you for your soul. King, are you mad, this thought you have thought in your brain?"

"Gonar," answered Bran somberly, "this day I stood still and watched a man of mine die on the cross of Rome. What his name or his rank, I do not know. I do not care. He might have been a faithful unknown warrior of mine, he might have been an outlaw. I only know that he was mine; the first scents he knew were the scents of the heather; the first light he saw was the sunrise on the Pictish hills. He belonged to me, not to Rome. If punishment was just, then none but me should have dealt it. If he were to be tried, none but me should have been his judge. The same blood in our veins; the same fire maddened our brains; in infancy we listened to the same old tales, and In youth we sang the same old songs. He was bound to my heart-strings, as every man and every woman and every child of Pictland is bound. It was mine to protect him; now it is mine to avenge him."

"But in the name of the gods, Bran," pleaded the wizard, "take your vengeance in another way! Return to the heather – mass your warriors – join with Cormac and his Gaels, and spread a sea of blood and flame the length of the great Wall!"

"All that I will do," grimly answered Bran. "But now – now – I will have a vengeance such as no Roman ever dreamed of! Ha, what do they know of the mysteries of this ancient Isle, which sheltered strange life long before Rome rose from the marshes of the Tiber?"

"Bran, there are weapons too foul to use, even against Rome!"

Bran barked short and sharp as a jackal.

"Ha! There are no weapons I would not use against Rome! My back is at the wall. By the blood of the fiends, has Rome fought me fair? Bah! I am a barbarian king with a wolfskin mantle and an iron crown, fighting with my handful of bows and broken pikes against the queen of the world. What have I? The heather hills, the wattle huts, the spears of my shock-headed tribesmen! And I fight Rome – with her armored legions, her broad fertile plains and rich seas – her mountains and her rivers and her gleaming cities – her wealth, her steel, her gold, her mastery and her wrath. By steel and fire I will fight her – and by subtlety and treachery – by the thorn in the foot, the adder in the path, the venom in the cup, the dagger in the dark; aye," his voice sank somberly, "and by the worms of the earth!"

"But it is madness!" cried Gonar. "You will perish in the attempt you plan – you will go down to Hell and you will not return! What of your people then?"

"If I can not serve them I had better die," growled the king.

"But you can not even reach the beings you seek," cried Gonar. "For untold centuries they have dwelt *apart*. There is no door by which you can come to them. Long ago they severed the bonds that bound them to the world we know."

"Long ago," answered Bran somberly, "you told me that nothing in the universe was separated from the stream of Life – a saying the truth of which I have often seen evident. No race, no form of life but is dose-knit somehow, by some manner, to the rest of Life and the world. Somewhere there is a thin link connecting those I seek to the world I know. Somewhere there is a Door. And somewhere among the bleak fens of the west I will find it."

Stark horror flooded Gonar's eyes and he gave back crying, "Woe! Woe! Woe! Woe! to Pictdom! Woe to the unborn kingdom! Woe, black woe to the sons of men! Woe, woe, woe, woe!"

Bran awoke to a shadowed room and the starlight on the window-bars. The moon had sunk from sight though its glow was still faint above the house tops. Memory of his dream shook him and he swore beneath his breath.

Rising, he flung off cloak and mantle, donning a light shirt of black meshmail, and girding on sword and dirk. Going again to the iron-bound chest he lifted several compact bags and emptied the clinking contents into the leathern pouch of his girdle. Then wrapping his wide cloak about him, he silently left the house. No servants there were o spy on him – he had impatiently refused the offer of slaves which it was Rome's policy to furnish her barbarian emissaries. Gnarled Grom had attended to all Bran's simple needs.

The stables fronted on the courtyard. A moment's groping in the dark and he placed his hand over a great stallion's nose, checking the nicker of recognition. Working without a light he swiftly bridled and saddled the great brute, and went through the courtyard into a shadowy side-street, leading him. The moon was setting, the border of floating shadows widening along the western wall. Silence lay on the marble palaces and mud hovels of Ebbracum under the cold stars.

Bran touched the pouch at his girdle, which was heavy with minted gold that bore the stamp of Rome. He had come to Ebbracum posing as an emissary of Pictdom, to act the spy. But being a barbarian, he had not been able to play his part in aloof formality and sedate dignity. He retained a crowded memory of wild feasts where wine flowed in fountains; of white-bosomed Roman women, who, sated with civilized lovers, looked with something more than favor on a virile barbarian; of gladiatorial games; and of other games where dice clicked and spun and tall stacks of gold changed hands. He had drunk deeply and gambled recklessly, after the manner of barbarians, and he had had a remarkable run of luck, due possibly to the indifference with which he won or lost. Gold to the Pict was so much dust, flowing through his, fingers. In his land there was no need of it. But he had learned its power in the boundaries of civilization.

Almost under the shadow of the northwestern wall he saw ahead of him loom the great watch-tower which was connected with and reared above the outer wall. One corner of the castle-like fortress, farthest from the wall, served as a dungeon. Bran left his horse standing in a dark alley, with the reins hanging on the ground, and stole like a prowling wolf into the shadows of the fortress.

The young office Valerius was awakened from a light, unquiet sleep by a stealthy sound at the barred window. He sat up, cursing softly under his breath as the faint starlight which etched the window-bars fell across the bare stone floor and reminded him of his disgrace. Well, in a few days, he ruminated, he'd be well out of it; Sulla would not be too harsh on a man with such high connections; then let any man or woman gibe at him? Damn that insolent Pict! *But wait*, he thought suddenly, remembering: *what of the sound which had roused him?*

"Hsssst!" It was a voice from the window.

Why so much secrecy? It could hardly be a foe – yet, why should it be a friend? Valerius rose and crossed his cell, coming close to the window. Outside all was dim in the starlight and he made out but a shadowy form close to the window.

"Who are you?" he leaned close against the bars, straining his eyes into the gloom.

His answer was a snarl of wolfish laughter, a long flicker of steel in the starlight. Valerius reeled away from the window and crashed to the floor, clutching his throat, gurgling horribly as he tried to scream. Blood gushed through his fingers, forming about his twitching body a pool that reflected the dint starlight dully and redly.

Outside Bran glided away like a shadow, without pausing to peer into the cell. In another minute the guards would round the corner on their regular routine. Even now he heard the measured tramp of their iron-clad feet. Before they came in sight he had vanished and they clumped stolidly by the cell-windows with no intimation of the corpse that lay on the floor within.

Bran rode to the small gate in the western wall, unchallenged by the sleepy watch. What fear of foreign invasion in Ebbracum? – and certain well organized thieves and women-stealers made it profitable for the watchmen not to be too vigilant. But the single guardsman at the western gate – his fellows lay drunk in a nearby brothel – lifted his spear and bawled for Bran to halt and give an account of himself. Silently the Pict reined closer. Masked in the dark cloak, he seemed dim and indistinct to the Roman, who was only aware of the glitter of his cold eyes in the gloom. But Bran held up his hand against the starlight and the soldier caught the gleam of gold; in the other he saw a long sheen of steel. The soldier understood, and he did not hesitate between the choice of a golden bribe or a battle to the death with this unknown rider who apparently was a barbarian of some sort. With a grunt he lowered his spear and swung the gate open. Bran rode through, casting a handful of coins to the Roman. They fell about his feet in a golden shower, clinking against the flags. He bent in greedy haste to retrieve them and Bran Mak Morn rode westward like a flying ghost in the night.

Into the dim fens of the west came Bran Mak Morn. A cold wind breathed across the gloomy waste and against the gray sky a few herons flapped heavily. The long reeds and marsh-grass waved in broken undulations and out across the desolation of the wastes a few still meres reflected the dull light. Here and there rose curiously regular hillocks above the general levels, and gaunt against the somber sky Bran saw a marching line of upright monoliths – menhirs, reared by what nameless hands?

A faint blue line to the west lay the foothills that beyond the horizon grew to the wild mountains of Wales where dwelt still wild Celtic tribes – fierce blue-eyed men that knew not the yoke of Rome. A row of well-garrisoned watch-towers held them in check. Even now, far away across the moors, Bran glimpsed the unassailable keep men called the Tower of Trajan.

These barren wastes seemed the dreary accomplishment of desolation, yet human life was not utterly lacking. Bran met the silent men of the fen, reticent, dark of eye and hair; speaking a strange mixed tongue, whose long-blended elements had forgotten their pristine separate sources. Bran recognized a certain kinship in these people to himself, but he looked on them with the scorn of a pure-blooded patrician for men of mixed strains.

Not that the common people of Caledonia were altogether pure-blooded; they got their stocky bodies and massive limbs from a primitive Teutonic race which had found its way into the northern tip of the isle even before the Celtic conquest of Britain was completed, and had been absorbed by the Picts. But the chiefs of Bran's folk had kept their blood from foreign taint since the beginning of time, and he himself was a pure-bred Pict of the Old Race. But these fenmen, overrun repeatedly by British, Gaelic and Roman conquerors, had assimilated blood of each, and in the process almost forgotten their original language and lineage.

For Bran came of a race that was very old, which had spread over western Europe in one vast Dark Empire, before the coming of the Aryans, when the ancestors of the Celts, the Hellenes and the Germans were one primal people, before the days of tribal splitting-off and westward drift.

Only in Caledonia, Bran brooded, had his people resisted the flood of Aryan conquest. He had heard of a Pictish people called Basques, who in the crags of the Pyrenees called themselves an unconquered race; but he knew that they had paid tribute for centuries to the ancestors of the Gaels, before these Celtic conquerors abandoned their mountain-realm and set sail for Ireland. Only the Picts of Caledonia had remained free, and they had been scattered into small feuding tribes – he was the first acknowledged king in five hundred years – the beginning of a new dynasty under a new name. In the very teeth of Rome he dreamed his dreams of empire.

He wandered through the fens, seeking a Door. Of his quest he said nothing to the dark-eyed fenmen. They told him news that drifted from mouth to mouth – a tale of war in the north, the skin of war-pipes along the winding Wall, of gathering-fires in the heather, of flame and smoke and rapine and the glutting of Gaelic swords in the crimson sea of slaughter. The eagles of the legions were moving northward and the ancient road resounded to the measured tramp of the iron-clad feet. And Bran, in the fens of the west, laughed, well pleased.

In Ebbracum Titus Sulla gave secret word to seek out the Pictish emissary with the Gaelic name who had been under suspicion, and who had vanished the night young Valerius was found dead in his cell with his throat ripped out. Sulla felt that this sudden bursting flame of war on the Wall was connected closely with his execution of a condemned Pictish criminal, and he set his spy system to work, though he felt sure that Partha Mac Othna was by this time far beyond his reach. He prepared to march from Ebbracum, but he did not accompany the considerable force of legionaries which he sent north. Sulla was a brave man, but each man has his own dread, and Sulla's was Cormac na Connacht, the black-haired prince of the Gaels, who had sworn to cut out the governor's heart and eat it raw. So Sulla rode with his ever-present bodyguard, westward, where lay the Tower of Trajan with its war-like commander, Caius Camillus, who enjoyed nothing more than taking his superior's place when the red waves of war washed at the foot of the Wall. Devious politics, but the legate of Rome seldom visited this fair isle, and what with his wealth and intrigues, Titus Sulla was the highest power in Britain.

And Bran, knowing all this, patiently waited his coming, in the deserted hut in which he had taken up his abode.

One gray evening he strode on foot across the moors, a stark figure, blackly etched against the dim crimson fire of the sunset. He felt the incredible antiquity of the slumbering land, as he walked like the last man on the day after the end of the world. Yet at last he saw a token of human life – a drab hut of wattle and mud, set in the reedy breast of the fen.

A woman greeted him from the open door and Bran's somber eyes narrowed with a dark suspicion. The woman was not old, yet the evil wisdom of ages was in her eyes; her garments were ragged and scanty, her black locks tangled and unkempt, lending her an aspect of wildness well in keeping with her grim surroundings. Her red lips laughed but there was no mirth in her laughter, only a hint of mockery, and under the lips her teeth showed sharp and pointed like fangs.

"Enter, master," said she, "if you do not fear to share the roof of the witch-woman of Dagon-moor!"

Bran entered silently and sat him down on a broken bench while the woman busied herself with the scanty meal cooking over an open fire on the squalid hearth. He studied her lithe, almost serpentine motions, the ears which were almost pointed, the yellow eyes which slanted curiously.

"What do you seek in the fens, my lord?" she asked, turning toward him with a supple twist of her whole body.

"I seek a door," he answered, chin resting on his fist. "I have a song to sing to the worms of the earth!"

She started upright, a jar falling from her hands to shatter on the hearth.

"This is an ill saying, even spoken in chance," she stammered.

"I speak not by chance but by intent," he answered.

She shook her head. "I know not what you mean."

"Well you know," he returned. "Aye, you know well! My race is very old – they reigned in Britain before the nations of the Celts and the Hellenes were born out of the womb of peoples. But my people were not first in Britain. By the mottles on your skin, by the slanting of your eyes, by the taint in your veins, I speak with full knowledge and meaning."

A while she stood silent, her lips smiling but her face inscrutable.

"Man, are you mad," she asked, "that in your madness you come seeking that from which strong men fled screaming in old times?"

"I seek a vengeance," he answered, "that can be accomplished only by Them I seek."

She shook her head.

"You have listened to a bird singing; you have dreamed empty dreams."

"I have heard a viper hiss," he growled, "and I do not dream. Enough of this weaving of words. I came seeking a link between two worlds; I have found it."

"I need lie to you no more, man of the North," answered the woman. "They you seek still dwell beneath the sleeping hills. They have drawn apart, farther and farther from the world you know."

"But they still steal forth in the night to grip women straying on the moors," said he, his gaze on her slanted eyes.

She laughed wickedly.

"What would you of me?"

"That you bring me to Them."

She flung back her head with a scornful laugh. His left hand locked like iron in the breast of her scanty garment and his right closed on his hilt. She laughed in his face.

"Strike and be damned, my northern wolf! Do you think that such life as mine is so sweet that I could cling to it as a babe to the breast?"

His hand fell away.

"You are right. Threats are foolish. I will buy your aid."

"How?" the laughing voice hummed with mockery.

Bran opened his pouch and poured into his cupped palm a stream of gold.

"More wealth than the men of the fen ever dreamed of."

Again she laughed. "What is this rusty metal to me? Save it for some white-breasted Roman woman who will play the traitor for you!"

"Name me a price!" he urged. "The head of an enemy–"

"By the blood in my veins, with its heritage of ancient hate, who is mine enemy but thee?" she laughed and springing, struck cat-like. But her dagger splintered on the mail beneath his cloak and he flung her off with a loathsome flick of his wrist which tossed her sprawling across her grass-strewn bunk. Lying there she laughed up at him.

"I will name you a price, then, my wolf, and it may be in days to come you will curse the armor that broke Atla's dagger!" She rose and came close to him, her disquietingly long hands fastened fiercely into his cloak. "I will tell you, Black Bran, king of Caledon! Oh, I knew you when you came into my hut with your black hair and your cold eyes! I will lead you to the doors of Hell if you wish – and the price shall be the kisses of a king!

"What of my blasted and bitter life, I, whom mortal men loathe and fear? I have not known the love of men, the clasp of a strong arm, the sting of human kisses, I, Atla, the were-woman of the moors! What have I known but the lone winds of the fens, the dreary fire of cold sunsets, the whispering of the marsh grasses? – the faces that blink up at me in the waters of the meres, the foot-pad of night-things in the gloom, the glimmer of red eyes, the grisly murmur of nameless beIngs in the night!

"I am half-human, at least! Have I not known sorrow and yearning and crying wistfulness, and the drear ache of loneliness? Give to me, king – give me your fierce kisses and your hurtful barbarian's embrace. Then in the long dear years to come I shall not utterly eat out my heart in vain envy of the white-bosomed women of men; for I shall have a memory few of them can boast – the kisses of a king. One night of love, oh king, and I will guide you to the gates of Hell!"

Bran eyed her somberly; he reached forth and gripped her arm in his iron fingers. An involuntary shudder shook him at the feel of her sleek skin. He nodded slowly and drawing her close to him, forced his head down to meet her lifted lips.

III

The cold gray mists of dawn wrapped King Bran like a clammy cloak. He turned to the woman whose slanted eyes gleamed in the gray gloom.

"Make good your part of the contract," he said roughly. "I sought a link between worlds and in you I found it. I seek the one thing sacred to Them. It shall be the Key opening the Door that lies unseen between me and Them. Tell me how I can reach it."

"I will," the red lips smiled terribly. "Go to the mound men call Dagon's Barrow. Draw aside the stone that blocks the entrance and go under the dome of the mound. The floor of the chamber is made of seven great stones, six grouped about the seventh. Lift out the center stone – and you will see!"

"Will I find the Black Stone?" he asked.

"Dagon's Barrow is the Door to the Black Stone," she answered, "if you dare follow the Road."

"Will the symbol be well guarded?" He unconsciously loosened his blade in its sheath. The red lips curled mockingly.

"If you meet any on the Road you will die as no mortal man has died for long centuries. The Stone is not guarded, as men guard their treasures. Why should They guard what man has never sought? Perhaps They will be near, perhaps not. It is a chance you must take, if you wish the Stone. Beware, king of Pictdom! Remember it was your folk who, so long ago, cut the thread that bound Them to human life. They were almost human then – they overspread the land and knew the sunlight. Now they have drawn apart. They know not the sunlight and they shun the light of the moon. Even starlight they hate. Far, far apart have they drawn, who might have been men in time, but for the spears of your ancestors."

The sky was overcast with misty gray, through which the sun shone coldly yellow when Bran came to Dagon's Barrow, a round hillock overgrown with rank grass of a curious fungoid appearance. On the eastern side of the mound showed the entrance of a crudely built stone tunnel which evidently penetrated the barrow. One great stone blocked the entrance to the tomb. Bran laid hold of the sharp edges and exerted all his strength. It held fast. He drew his sword and worked the blade between the blocking stone and the sill. Using the sword as a lever, he worked carefully, and managed to loosen the great stone and wrench it out. A foul charnel-house scent flowed out of the aperture and the dim sunlight seemed less to illuminate the cavern-like opening than to be fouled by the rank darkness which clung there.

Sword in hand, ready for he knew not what, Bran groped his way into the tunnel, which was long and narrow, built up of heavy joined stones, and was too low for him to stand erect. Either his eyes became somewhat accustomed to the gloom, or the darkness was, after all, somewhat lightened by the sunlight filtering in through the entrance. At any rate he came into a round low chamber and was able to make out its general dome-like outline. Here, no doubt, in old times, had reposed the bones of him for whom the stones of the tomb had been joined and the earth heaped high above them; but now of those bones no vestige remained on the stone floor. And bending close and straining his eyes, Bran made out the strange, startlingly regular pattern of that floor: six well-cut slabs clustered about a seventh, six-sided stone.

He drove his sword-point into a crack and pried carefully. The edge of the central stone tilted slightly upward. A little work and he lifted it out and leaned it against the curving wall. Straining his eyes downward he saw only the gaping blackness of a dark well, with small, worn steps that led downward and out of sight. He did not hesitate. Though the skin between his shoulders crawled curiously, he swung himself into the abyss and felt the clinging blackness swallow him.

Groping downward, he felt his feet slip and stumble on steps too small for human feet. With one hand pressed hard against the side of the well he steadied himself, fearing a fall into unknown and unlighted depths. The steps were cut into solid rock, yet they were greatly worn away. The farther he progressed, the less like steps they became, mere bumps of worn stone. Then the direction of the shaft changed sharply. It still led down, but at a shallow slant down which he could walk, elbows braced against the hollowed sides, head bent low beneath the curved roof. The steps had ceased altogether and the stone felt slimy to the touch, like a serpent's lair. What beings, Bran wondered, had slithered up and down this slanting shaft, for how many centuries?

The tunnel narrowed until Bran found it rather difficult to shove through. He lay on his back and pushed himself along with his hands, feet first. Still he knew he was sinking deeper and deeper into the very guts of the earth; how far below the surface he was, he dared not contemplate. Then ahead a faint witch-fire gleam tinged the abysmal blackness. He grinned savagely and without mirth. If They he sought came suddenly upon him, how could he fight in that narrow shaft? But he had put the thought of personal fear behind him when he began this hellish quest. He crawled on, thoughtless of all else but his goal.

And he came at last into a vast space where he could stand upright. He could not see the roof of the place, but he got an impression of dizzying vastness. The blackness pressed in on all sides and behind him he could see the entrance to the shaft from which he had just emerged – a black well in the darkness. But in front of him a strange grisly radiance glowed about a grim altar built of human skulls. The source of that light he could not determine, but on the altar lay a sullen night-black object – the Black Stone!

Bran wasted no time in giving thanks that the guardians of the grim relic were nowhere near. He caught up the Stone, and gripping it under his left arm, crawled into the shaft. When a man turns his back on peril its clammy menace looms more grisly than when he advances upon it. So Bran, crawling back up the nighted shaft with his grisly prize, felt the darkness turn on him and slink behind him, grinning with dripping fangs. Clammy sweat beaded his flesh and he hastened to the best of his ability, ears strained for some stealthy sound to betray that fell shapes were at his heels. Strong shudders shook him, despite himself, and the short hair on his neck prickled as if a cold wind blew at his back.

When he reached the first of the tiny steps he felt as if he had attained to the outer boundaries of the mortal world. Up them he went, stumbling and slipping, and with a deep gasp of relief, came out into the tomb, whose spectral grayness seemed like the blaze of noon in comparison to the stygian depths he had just traversed. He replaced the central stone and strode into the light of the outer day, and never was the cold yellow light of the sun more grateful as it dispelled the shadows of black-winged nightmares of fear and madness that seemed to have ridden him up out of the black deeps. He shoved the great blocking stone back into place, and picking up the cloak he had left at the mouth of the tomb, he wrapped it about the Black Stone and hurried away, a strong revulsion and loathing shaking his soul and lending wings to his strides.

A gray silence brooded over the land. It was desolate as the blind side of the moon, yet Bran felt the potentialities of life – under his feet, in the brown earth – sleeping, but how soon to waken, and in what horrific fashion?

He came through the tall masking reeds to the still deep men called Dagon's Mere. No slightest ripple ruffled the cold blue water to give evidence of the grisly monster legend said dwelt beneath. Bran closely scanned the breathless landscape. He saw no hint of life, human or unhuman. He sought the instincts of his savage soul to know if any unseen eyes fixed their lethal gaze upon him, and found no response. He was alone as if he were the last man alive on earth.

Swiftly he unwrapped the Black Stone, and as it lay in his hands like a solid sullen block of darkness, he did not seek to learn the secret of its material nor scan the cryptic characters carved thereon. Weighing it in his hands and calculating the distance, he flung it far out, so that it fell almost exactly in the middle of the lake. A sullen splash and the waters closed over it. There was a moment of shimmering flashes on the bosom of the lake; then the blue surface stretched placid and unrippled again.

IV

The were-woman turned swiftly as Bran approached her door. Her slant eyes widened.

"You! And alive! And sane!"

"I have been into Hell and I have returned," he growled. "What is more, I have that which I sought."

"The Black Stone?" she cried. "You really dared steal it? Where is it?"

"No matter; but last night my stallion screamed in his stall and I heard something crunch beneath his thundering hoofs which was not the wall of the stable – and there was blood on his hoofs when I came to see, and blood on the floor of the stall. And I have heard stealthy sounds in the night, and noises beneath my dirt floor, as if worms burrowed deep in the earth. They know I have stolen their Stone. Have you betrayed me?"

She shook her head.

"I keep your secret; They do not need my word to know you. The farther They have retreated from the world of men, the greater have grown their powers in other uncanny ways. Some dawn your hut will stand empty and if men dare investigate they will find nothing – except crumbling bits of earth on the dirt floor."

Bran smiled terribly.

"I have not planned and toiled thus far to fall prey to the talons of vermin. If They strike me down in the night, They will never know what became of their idol – or whatever it be to Them. I would speak with Them."

"Dare you come with me and meet Them in the night?" she asked.

"Thunder of all gods!" he snarled. "Who are you to ask me if I dare? Lead me to Them and let me bargain for a vengeance this night. The hour of retribution draws nigh. This day I saw silvered helmets and bright shields gleam across the fens – the new commander has arrived at the Tower of Trajan and Caius Camillus has marched to the Wall."

That night the king went across the dark desolation of the moors with the silent were-woman. The night was thick and still as if the land lay in ancient slumber. The stars blinked vaguely, mere points of red struggling through the unbreathing gloom. Their gleam was dimmer than the glitter in the eyes of the woman who glided beside the king. Strange thoughts shook Bran, vague, titanic, primeval. Tonight ancestral linkings with these slumbering fens stirred in his soul and troubled him with the phantasmal, eon-veiled shapes of monstrous dreams. The vast age of his race was borne upon him: where now he walked an outlaw and an alien, dark-eyed kings in whose mold he was cast, had reigned in old times. The Celtic and Roman invaders were as strangers to this ancient isle beside his people. Yet his race likewise had been invaders, and there was an older race than his – a race whose beginnings lay lost and hidden back beyond the dark oblivion of antiquity.

Ahead of them loomed a low range of hills, which formed the easternmost extremity of those straying chains which far away climbed at last to the mountains of Wales. The woman led the way up what might have been a sheep-path, and halted before a wide black gaping cave.

"A door to those you seek, oh king!" her laughter rang hateful in the gloom. "Dare ye enter?"

His fingers closed in her tangled locks and he shook her viciously.

"Ask me but once more if I dare," he grated, "and your head and shoulders part company! Lead on."

Her laughter was like sweet deadly venom. They passed into the cave and Bran struck flint and steel. The flicker of the tinder showed him a wide dusty cavern, on the roof of which hung clusters of bats. Lighting a torch, he lifted it and scanned the shadowy recesses, seeing nothing but dust and emptiness.

"Where are They?" he growled.

She beckoned him to the back of the cave and leaned against the rough wall, as if casually. But the king's keen eyes caught the motion of her hand pressing hard against a projecting ledge. He recoiled as a round black well gaped suddenly at his feet. Again her laughter slashed him like a keen silver knife. He held the torch to the opening and again saw small worn steps leading down.

"They do not need those steps," said Atla. "Once They did, before your people drove Them into the darkness. But you will need them."

She thrust the torch into a niche above the well; it shed a faint red light into the darkness below. She gestured into the well and Bran loosened his sword and stepped into the shaft. As he went down into the mystery of the darkness, the light was blotted out above him, and he thought for an instant Atla had covered the opening again. Then he realized that she was descending after him.

The descent was not a long one. Abruptly Bran felt his feet on a solid floor. Atla swung down beside him and stood in the dim circle of light that drifted down the shaft. Bran could not see the limits of the place into which he had come.

"Many caves in these hills," said Atla, her voice sounding small and strangely brittle in the vastness, "are but doors to the greater caves which lie beneath, even as a man's words and deeds are but small indications of the dark caverns of murky thought lying behind and beneath."

And now Bran was aware of movement In the gloom. The darkness was filled with stealthy noises not like those made by any human foot. Abruptly spark began to flash and float in the blackness, like flickering fireflies. Closer they came until they girdled him in a wide half-moon. And beyond the ring gleamed other sparks,, a solid sea of them, fading away in the gloom until the farthest were mere tiny pin-points of light. And Bran knew they were the slanted eyes of the beings who had come upon him in such numbers that his brain reeled at the contemplation – and at the vastness of the cavern.

Now that he faced his ancient foes, Bran knew no fear. He felt the waves of terrible menace emanating from them, the grisly hate, the inhuman threat to body, mind and soul. More than a member of a less ancient race, he realized the horror of his position, but he did not fear, though he confronted the ultimate Horror of the dreams and legends of his race. His blood raced fiercely but it was with the hot excitement of the hazard, not the drive of terror.

"They know you have the Stone, oh king," said Atla, and though he knew she feared, though he felt her physical efforts to control her trembling limbs, there was no quiver of fright in her voice. "You are in deadly peril; they know your breed of old – oh, they remember the days when their ancestors were men! I can not save you; both of us will die as no human has died for ten centuries. Speak to them, if you will; they can understand your speech, though you may not understand theirs. But it will avail not – you are human – and a Pict."

Bran laughed and the closing ring of fire shrank back at the savagery in his laughter. Drawing his sword with a soul-chilling rasp of steel, he set his back against what he hoped was a solid stone wall. Facing the glittering eyes with his sword gripped in his right hand and his dirk in his left, he laughed as a blood-hungry wolf snarls.

"Aye," he growled, "I am a Pict, a son of those warriors who drove your brutish ancestors before them like chaff before the storm! – who flooded the land with your blood and heaped high your skulls for a sacrifice to the Moon-Woman! You who fled of old before my race, dare ye now snarl at your master? Roll on me like a flood, now, if ye dare! Before your viper fangs drink my life I will reap your multitudes like ripened barley – of your severed heads will I build a tower and of your mangled corpses will I rear up a wall! Dogs of the dark, vermin of Hell, worms of the earth, rush in and try my steel! When Death finds me in this dark cavern, your living will howl for the scores of your dead and your Black Stone will be lost to you forever – for only I know where it is hidden and not all the tortures of all the Hells can wring the secret from my lips!"

Then followed a tense silence; Bran faced the fire-lit darkness, tensed like a wolf at bay, waiting the charge; at his side the woman cowered, her eyes ablaze. Then from the silent ring that hovered beyond the dim torchlight rose a vague abhorrent murmur. Bran, prepared as he was for anything, started. Gods, was that the speech of creatures which had once been called men?

Atla straightened, listening intently. From her lips came the same hideous soft sibilances, and Bran, though he had already known the grisly secret of her being, knew that never again could he touch her save with soul-shaken loathing.

She turned to him, a strange smile curving her red lips dimly in the ghostly light.

"They fear you, oh king! By the black secrets of R'lyeh, who are you that Hell itself quails before you? Not your steel, but the stark ferocity of your soul has driven unused fear into Their strange minds. They will buy back the Black Stone at any price."

"Good," Bran sheathed his weapons. "They shall promise not to molest you because of your aid of me. And," his voice hummed like the purr of a hunting tiger, "they shall deliver into my hands Titus Sulla, governor of Ebbracum, now commanding the Tower of Trajan. This They can do – how, I know not. But I know that in the old days, when my people warred with these Children of the Night, babes disappeared from guarded huts and none saw the stealers come or go. Do They understand?"

Again rose the low frightful sounds and Bran, who feared not their wrath; shuddered at their voices.

"They understand" said Atla. "Bring the Black Stone to Dagon's Ring tomorrow night when the earth is veiled with the blackness that foreruns the dawn. Lay the Stone on the altar. There They will bring Titus Sulla to you. Trust Them; They have not interfered in human affairs for many centuries, but They will keep their word." Bran nodded and turning, climbed up the stair with Atla close behind him. At the top he turned and looked down once more. As far as he could see floated a glittering ocean of slanted yellow eyes upturned. But the owners of those eyes kept carefully beyond the dim circle of torchlight and of their bodies he could see nothing. Their low hissing speech floated up to him and he shuddered as his imagination visualized, not a throng of biped creatures, but a swarming, swaying myriad of serpents, gazing up at him with their glittering unwinking eyes.

He swung into the upper cave and Atla thrust the blocking stone back in place. It fitted into the entrance of the well with uncanny precision; Bran was unable to discern any crack in the apparently solid floor of the cavern. Atla made a motion to extinguish the torch, but the king stayed her.

"Keep it so until we are out of the cave," he grunted. "We might tread on an adder in the dark."

Atla's sweetly hateful laughter rose maddeningly in the flickering gloom.

V

It was not long before sunset when Bran came again to the reed-grown marge of Dagon's Mere. Casting cloak and sword-belt on the ground, he stripped himself of his short leathern breeches. Then gripping his naked dirk in his teeth, he went into the water with the smooth ease of a diving seal. Swimming strongly, he gained the center of the small lake, and turning, drove himself downward.

The mere was deeper than he had thought. It seemed he would never reach the bottom, and when he did, his groping hands failed to find what he sought. A roaring in his ears warned him and he swam to the surface.

Gulping deep of the refreshing air, he dived again, and again his quest was fruitless. A third time he sought the depth, and this time his groping hands met a familiar object in the silt of the bottom. Grasping it, he swam up to the surface.

The Stone was not particularly bulky, but it was heavy. He swam leisurely, and suddenly was aware of a curious stir in the waters about him which was not caused by his own exertions. Thrusting his face below the surface, he tried to pierce the blue depths with his eyes and thought to see a dim gigantic shadow hovering there.

He swam faster, not frightened, but wary. His feet struck the shallows and he waded up on the shelving shore. Looking back he saw the waters swirl and subside. He shook his head, swearing. He had discounted the ancient legend which made Dagon's Mere the lair of a nameless water-monster, but now he had a feeling as if his escape had been narrow. The time-worn myths of the ancient land were taking form and coming to life before his eyes. What primeval shape lurked below the surface of that treacherous mere, Bran could not guess, but he felt that the fenmen had good reason for shunning the spot, after all.

Bran donned his garments, mounted the black stallion and rode, not to his hut, but to the west, in the direction of the afterglow, with the Black Stone wrapped in his cloak. He rode, not to his hut, but to the west, in the direction of the Tower of Trajan and the Ring of Dagon. As he covered the miles that lay between, the red stars winked out. Midnight passed him in the moonless night and still Bran rode on. His heart was hot for his meeting with Titus Sulla. Atla had gloated over the anticipation of watching the Roman writhe under torture, but no such thought was in the Pict's mind. The governor should have his chance with weapons – with Bran's own sword he should face the Pictish king's dirk, and live or die according to his prowess. And though Sulla was famed throughout the provinces as a swordsman, Bran felt no doubt as to the outcome.

Dagon's Ring lay some distance from the Tower – a sullen circle of tall gaunt stones planted uptight, with a rough-hewn stone altar in the center. The Romans looked on these menhirs with aversion; they thought the Druids had reared them; but the Celts supposed Bran's people, the Picts, had planted them – and Bran well knew what hands reared those grim monoliths in lost ages, though for what reasons, he but dimly guessed.

The king did not tide straight to the Ring. He was consumed with curiosity as to how his grim allies intended carrying out their promise. That They could snatch Titus Sulla from the very midst of his men, he felt sure, and he believed he knew how They would do it. He felt the gnawings of a strange misgiving as if he had tampered with powers of unknown breadth and depth, and had loosed forces which he could not control. Each time he remembered that reptilian murmur, those slanted eyes of the night before, a cold breath passed over him. They had been abhorrent enough when his people drove Them into the caverns under the hills, ages ago, what had long centuries of retrogression made of Them? In their nighted, subterranean life, had They retained any of the attributes of humanity at all?

Some instinct prompted him to ride toward the Tower. He knew he was near; but for the thick darkness he could have plainly seen its dark outline tusking the horizon. Even now he should be able to make it out dimly. An obscure, shuddersome premonition shook him and he spurred the stallion into swift canter.

And suddenly Bran staggered in his saddle as from a physical impact, so stunning was the surprise of what met his gaze. The impregnable Tower of Trajan was no more! Bran's astounded gaze rested on a gigantic pile of ruins of shattered stone and crumbled granite, from which jutted the jagged and splintered ends of broken beams. At one corner of the tumbled heap one tower rose out of the waste of crumpled masonry, and it leaned drunkenly as if its foundations had been half cut away.

Bran dismounted and walked forward, dazed by bewilderment. The moat was filled in places by fallen stones and broken pieces of mortared wall. lie crossed over and came among the ruins. Where, he knew, only a few hours before the flags had resounded to the martial tramp of iron-clad feet, and the walls had echoed to the clang of shields and the blast of the loud-throated trumpets, an horrific silence reigned.

Almost under Bran's feet, a broken shape writhed and groaned. The king bent down to the legionary who lay in a sticky red pool of his own blood. A single glance showed the Pict that the man, horribly crushed and shattered, was dying.

Lifting the bloody head, Bran placed his flask to the pulped lips and the Roman instinctively drank deep, gulping through splintered teeth. In the dim starlight Bran saw his glazed eyes roll.

"The walls fell," muttered the dying man. "They crashed down like the skies falling on the day of doom. Ah Jove, the skies rained shards of granite and hailstones of marble!"

"I have felt no earthquake shock," Bran scowled, puzzled.

"It was no earthquake," muttered the Roman. "Before last dawn it began, the faint dim scratching and clawing far below the earth. We of the guard heard it – like rats burrowing, or like worms hollowing out the earth. Titus laughed at us, but all day long we heard it. Then at midnight the Tower quivered and seemed to settle – as if the foundations were being dug away–"

A shudder shook Bran Mak Morn. The worms of the earth! Thousands of vermin digging like moles far below the castle, burrowing away the foundations – gods, the land must be honeycombed with tunnels and caverns – these creatures were even less human than he had thought – what ghastly shapes of darkness had he invoked to his aid?

"What of Thus Sulla?" he asked, again holding the flask to the legionary's lips; In that moment the dying Roman seemed to him almost like a brother.

"Even As the Tower shuddered we heard a fearful scream from the governor's chamber," muttered the soldier. "We rushed there – as we broke down the door we heard his shrieks – they seemed to recede – *into the bowels of the earth!* We rushed in; the chamber was empty. His bloodstained sword lay on the floor; In the stone flags of the floor a black hole gaped. Then – the – towers – reeled – the – roof – broke; – through – a – storm – of – crashing – walls – I – crawled–"

A strong convulsion shook the broken figure.

"Lay me down, friend," whispered the Roman. "I die."

He had ceased to breathe before Bran could comply. The Pict rose, mechanically cleansing his hands. He hastened from the spot, and as he galloped over the darkened fens, the weight of the accursed Black Stone under his cloak was as the weight of a foul nightmare on a mortal breast.

As he approached the Ring, he saw an eery glow within, so that the gaunt stones stood etched like the ribs of a skeleton in which a witch-fire burns. The stallion snorted and reared as Bran tied him to one of the menhirs. Carrying the Stone he strode into the grisly circle and saw Atla standing beside the altar, one hand on her hip, her sinuous body swaying in a serpentine manner. The altar glowed all over with ghastly light and Bran knew someone, probably Atla, had rubbed it with phosphorus from some dank swamp or quagmire.

He strode forward and whipping his cloak from about the Stone; flung the accursed thing on to the altar.

"I have fulfilled my part of the contract," he growled.

"And They, Theirs," she retorted. "Look! – They come!"

He wheeled, his hand instinctively dropping to his sword. Outside the Ring the great stallion screamed savagely and reared against his tether. The night wind moaned through the waving grass and an abhorrent soft hissing mingled with it. Between the menhirs flowed a dark tide of shadows, unstable and chaotic. The Ring filled with glittering eyes which hovered beyond the dim illusive circle of illumination cast by the phosphorescent altar. Somewhere in the darkness a human voice tittered and gibbered idiotically. Bran stiffened, the shadows of a horror clawing at his soul.

He strained his eyes, trying to make out the shapes of those who ringed him. But he glimpsed only billowing masses of shadow which heaved and writhed and squirmed with almost fluid consistency.

"Let them make good their bargain!" he exclaimed angrily.

"Then see, oh king!" cried Atla in a voice of piercing mockery.

There was a stir, a seething in the writhing shadows, and from the darkness crept, like a four-legged animal, a human shape that fell down and groveled at Bran's feet and writhed and mowed, and lifting a death's-head, howled like a dying dog. In the ghastly light, Bran, soul-shaken, saw the blank glassy eyes, the bloodless features, the loose, writhing, froth-covered lips of sheer lunacy – gods, was this Titus Sulla, the proud lord of life and death in Ebbracum's proud city?

Bran bared his sword.

"I had thought to give this stroke in vengeance," he said somberly. "I give it in mercy – *Vale Caesar!*"

The steel flashed in the eery light and Sulla's head rolled in the foot of the glowing altar, where it lay staring up at the shadowed sky.

"They harmed him not!" Atla's hateful laugh slashed the sick silence. "It was what he saw and came to know that broke his brain! Like all his heavy-footed race, he knew nothing of the secrets of this ancient land. This night he has been dragged through the deepest pits of Hell, where even you might have blenched!"

"Well for the Romans that they know not the secrets of this accursed land," Bran roared, maddened, "with its monster-haunted meres, its foul witch-women, and its lost caverns and subterranean realms where spawn in the darkness shapes of Hell!"

"Are they more foul than a mortal who seeks their aid?" cried Atla with a shriek of fearful mirth. "Give them their Black Stone!"

A cataclysmic loathing shook Bran's soul with red fury.

"Aye, take your cursed Stone!" he roared, snatching it from the altar and dashing it among the shadows with such savagery that bones snapped under its impact. A hurried babel of grisly tongues rose and the shadows heaved in turmoil. One segment of the mass detached itself for an instant and Bran cried out in fierce revulsion, though he caught only a fleeting glimpse of the thing, had only a brief impression of a broad strangely flattened head, pendulous writhing lips that bared curved pointed fangs, and a hideously. misshapen, dwarfish body that seemed *mottled* – all set off by those unwinking reptilian eyes. God! – the myths had prepared him for horror in human aspect, horror induced by bestial visage and stunted deformity – but this was the horror of nightmare and the night.

"Go back to Hell and take your idol with you!" he yelled, brandishing his clenched fists to the skies, as the thick shadows receded, flowing back and away from him like the foul waters of some black flood. "Your ancestors were men, though strange and monstrous – but gods, ye have become in ghastly fact what my people called ye in scorn! Worms of the earth, back into your holes and burrows! Ye foul the air and leave on the clean earth the slime of the serpents ye have become! Gonar was right – there are shapes too foul to use even against Rome!"

He sprang from the Ring as a man flees the touch of a coiling snake, and tore the stallion free. At his elbow Atla was shrieking with fearful laughter, all human attributes dropped from her like a cloak in the night.

"King of Pictland!" she cried, "King of fools! Do you blench at so small a thing? Stay and let me show you real fruits of the pits! Ha! ha! ha! Run, fool, run! But you are stained with the taint – you have called them forth and they will remember! And in their own time they will come to you again!"

He yelled a wordless curse and struck her savagely in the mouth with his open hand. She staggered, blood starting from her lips, but her fiendish laughter only rose higher.

Bran leaped into the saddle, wild for the clean heather and the cold blue hills of the north where he could plunge his sword into clean slaughter and his sickened soul into the red maelstrom of battle, and forget the horror which lurked below the fens of the west. He gave the frantic stallion the rein, and rode through the night like a hunted ghost, until the hellish laughter of the howling were-woman died out in the darkness behind.

RED SHADOWS

I : THE COMING OF SOLOMON

The moonlight shimmered hazily, making silvery mists of illusion among the shadowy trees. A faint breeze whispered down the valley, bearing a shadow that was not of the moon-mist. A faint scent of smoke was apparent.

The man whose long, swinging strides, unhurried yet unswerving, had carried him for many a mile since sunrise, stopped suddenly. A movement in the trees had caught his attention, and he moved silently toward the shadows, a hand resting lightly on the hilt of his long, slim rapier.

Warily he advanced, his eyes striving to pierce the darkness that brooded under the trees. This was a wild and menacing country; death might be lurking under those trees. Then his hand fell away from the hilt and he leaned forward. Death indeed was there, but not in such shape as might cause him fear.

"The fires of Hades!" he murmured. "A girl! What has harmed you, child? Be not afraid of me."

The girl looked up at him, her face like a dim white rose in the dark.

"You – who are – you?" her words came in gasps.

"Naught but a wanderer, a landless man, but a friend to all in need." The gentle voice sounded somehow incongruous, coming from the man.

The girl sought to prop herself up on her elbow, and instantly he knelt and raised her to a sitting position, her head resting against his shoulder. His hand touched her breast and came away red and wet.

"Tell me." His voice was soft, soothing, as one speaks to a babe.

"Le Loup," she gasped, her voice swiftly growing weaker. "He and his men – descended upon our village – a mile up the valley. They robbed – slew – burned–"

"That, then, was the smoke I scented," muttered the man. "Go on, child."

"I ran. He, the Wolf, pursued me – and – caught me–" The words died away in a shuddering silence.

"I understand, child. Then–?"

"Then – he – he stabbed me with his dagger – oh, blessed saints! – mercy –"

Suddenly the slim form went limp. The man eased her to the earth, and touched her brow lightly.

"Dead!" he muttered.

Slowly he rose, mechanically wiping his hands upon his cloak. A dark scowl had settled on his somber brow. Yet he made no wild, reckless vow, swore no oath by saints or devils.

"Men shall die for this," he said coldly.

II : THE LAIR OF THE WOLF

"You are a fool " The words came in a cold snarl that curdled the hearer's blood.

He who had just been named a fool lowered his eyes sullenly without answer.

"You and all the others I lead!" The speaker leaned forward, his fist pounding emphasis on the rude table between them. He was a tall, rangy-built man, supple as a leopard and with a lean, cruel, predatory face. His eyes danced and glittered with a kind of reckless mockery.

The fellow spoken to replied sullenly, "This Solomon Kane is a demon from hell, I tell you."

"Faugh! Dolt! He is a man – who will die from a pistol ball or a sword thrust."

"So thought Jean, Juan and La Costa," answered the other grimly. "Where are they? Ask the mountain wolves that tore the flesh from their dead bones. Where does this Kane hide? We have searched the mountains and the valleys for leagues, and we have found no trace. I tell you, Le Loup, he comes up from hell. I knew no good would come from hanging that friar a moon ago."

The Wolf strummed impatiently upon the table. His keen face, despite lines of wild living and dissipation, was the face of a thinker. The superstitions of his followers affected him not at all.

"Faugh! I say again. The fellow has found some cavern or secret vale of which we do not know where he hides in the day."

"And at night he sallies forth and slays us," gloomily commented the other. "He hunts us down as a wolf hunts deer – by God, Le Loup, you name yourself Wolf but I think you have met at last a fiercer and more crafty wolf than yourself! The first we know of this man is when we find Jean, the most desperate bandit unhung, nailed to a tree with his own dagger through his breast, and the letters S. L. K. carved upon his dead cheeks. "Then the Spaniard Juan is struck down, and after we find him he lives long enough to tell us that his slayer is an Englishman, Solomon Kane, who has sworn to destroy our entire band! What then? La Costa, a swordsman second only to yourself, goes forth swearing to meet this Kane. By the demons of perdition, it seems he met him! For we found his sword-pierced corpse upon a cliff. What now? Are we all to fall before this English fiend?"

"True, our best men have been done to death by him," mused the bandit chief. "Soon the rest return from that little trip to the hermit's; then we shall see. Kane can not hide forever. Then – ha, what was that?"

The two turned swiftly as a shadow fell across the table. Into the entrance of the cave that formed the bandit lair, a man staggered. His eyes were wide and staring; he reeled on buckling legs, and a dark red stain dyed his tunic. He came a few tottering steps forward, then pitched across the table, sliding off onto the floor.

"Hell's devils!" cursed the Wolf, hauling him upright and propping him in a chair. "Where are the rest, curse you?"

"Dead! All dead!"

"How? Satan's curses on you, speak!" The Wolf shook the man savagely, the other bandit gazing on in wide-eyed horror.

"We reached the hermit's hut just as the moon rose," the man muttered. "I stayed outside – to watch – the others went in – to torture the hermit – to make him reveal – the hiding-place – of his gold."

"Yes, yes! Then what?" The Wolf was raging with Impatience.

"Then the world turned red – the hut went up in a roar and a red rain flooded the valley – through it I saw – the hermit and a tall man clad all in black – coming from the trees–"

"Solomon Kane!" gasped the bandit. "I knew it!"

"Silence, fool!" snarled the chief. "Go on!"

"I fled – Kane pursued – wounded me – but I outran – him – got – here – first–"

The man slumped forward on the table.

"Saints and devils!" raged the Wolf. "What does he look like, this Kane?"

"Like – Satan–"

The voice trailed off in silence. The dead man slid from the table to lie in a red heap upon the floor.

"Like Satan!" babbled the other bandit. "I told you! 'Tis the Horned One himself! I tell you–"

He ceased as a frightened face peered in at the cave entrance.

"Kane?"

"Aye." The Wolf was too much at sea to lie. "Keep close watch, La Mon; in a moment the Rat and I will join you."

The face withdrew and Le Loup turned to the other.

"This ends the band," said he. "You, I, and that thief La Mon are all that are left. What would you suggest?"

The Rat's pallid lips barely formed the word: "Flight!'"

"You are right. Let us take the gems and gold from the chests and flee, using the secret passageway."

"And La Mon?"

"He can watch until we are ready to flee. Then – why divide the treasure three ways?"

A faint smile touched the Rat's malevolent features. Then a sudden thought smote him.

"He," indicating the corpse on the floor, "said, 'I got here first'. Does that mean Kane was pursuing him here?" And as the Wolf nodded impatiently the other turned to the chests with chattering haste.

The flickering candle on the rough table lighted up a strange and wild scene. The light, uncertain and dancing, gleamed redly in the slowly widening lake of blood in which the dead man lay; It danced upon the heaps of gems and coins emptied hastily upon the floor from the brass-bound chests that ranged the walls; and it glittered in the eyes of the Wolf with the same gleam which sparkled from his sheathed dagger.

The chests were empty, their treasure lying in a shimmering mass upon the blood-stained floor. The Wolf stopped and listened. Outside was silence. There was no moon, and Le Loup's keen imagination pictured the dark slayer, Solomon Kane, gliding through the blackness, a shadow among shadows. He grinned crookedly; this time the Englishman would be foiled.

"There is a chest yet unopened," said he, pointing.

The Rat, with a muttered exclamation of surprise, bent over the chest indicated. With a single, cat-like motion, the Wolf sprang upon him, sheathing his dagger to the hilt in the Rat's back, between the shoulders. The Rat sagged to the floor without a sound.

"Why divide the treasure two ways?" murmured Le Loup, wiping his blade upon the dead man's doublet. "Now for La Mon."

He stepped toward the door; then stopped and shrank back.

At first he thought it was the shadow of a man who stood in the entrance; then he saw that it was a man himself, though so dark and still he stood that a fantastic semblance of shadow was lent him by the glittering candle.

A tall man, as tall as Le Loup he was, clad in black from head to foot, in plain, close-fitting garments that somehow suited the somber face. Long arms and broad shoulders betokened the swordsman, as plainly as the long rapier in his hand. The features of the man were saturnine and gloomy. A kind of dark pallor lent him a ghostly appearance in the uncertain light, an effect heightened by the satanic darkness of his lowering brows.

Eyes, large, deep-set and unblinking, fixed their gaze upon the bandit, and looking into them, Le Loup was unable to decide what color they were. Strangely, the mephistophelean trend of the lower features was offset by a high, broad forehead, though this was partly hidden by a featherless hat.

That forehead marked the dreamer, the idealist, the introvert, just as the eyes and the thin, straight nose betrayed the fanatic. An observer would have been struck by the eyes of the two men who stood there, facing each other. Eyes of both betokened untold deeps of power, but there the resemblance ceased.

The eyes of the bandit were hard, almost opaque, with a curious scintillant shallowness that reflected a thousand changing lights and gleams, like some strange gem; there was mockery in those eyes, cruelty and recklessness.

The eyes of the man in black, on the other hand, deep-set and staring from under prominent brows, were cold but deep; gazing into them, one had the impression of looking into countless fathoms of ice.

Now the eyes clashed, and the Wolf, who was used to being feared, felt a strange coolness on his spine. The sensation was new to him – a new thrill to one who lived for thrills, and he laughed suddenly.

"You are Solomon Kane, I suppose?" he asked, managing to make his question sound politely incurious.

"I am Solomon Kane." The voice was resonant and powerful. "Are you prepared to meet your God?"

"Why, Monsieur," Le Loup answered, bowing, "I assure you I am as ready as I ever will be. I might ask Monsieur the same question."

"No doubt I stated my inquiry wrongly," Kane said grimly. "I will change it: Are you prepared to meet your master, the Devil?"

"As to that, Monsieur" – Le Loup examined his finger nails with elaborate unconcern – "I must say that I can at present render a most satisfactory account to his Horned Excellency, though really I have no intention of so doing – for a while at least."

Le Loup did not wonder as to the fate of La Mon; Kane's presence in the cave was sufficient answer that did not need the trace of blood on his rapier to verify it.

"What I wish to know, Monsieur," said the bandit, "is why in the Devil's name have you harassed my band as you have, and how did you destroy that last set of fools?"

"Your last question is easily answered, sir," Kane replied. "I myself had the tale spread that the hermit possessed a store of gold, knowing that would draw your scum as carrion draws vultures.

"For days and nights I have watched the hut, and tonight, when I saw your villains coming, I warned the hermit, and together we went among the trees back of the hut. Then, when the rogues were inside, I struck flint and steel to the train I had laid, and flame ran through the trees like a red snake until it reached the powder I had placed beneath the hut floor. Then the hut and thirteen sinners went to hell in a great roar of flame and smoke. True, one escaped, but him I had slain in the forest had not I stumbled and fallen upon a broken root, which gave him time to elude me."

'Monsieur,' said Le Loup with another low bow, "I grant you the admiration I must needs bestow on a brave and shrewd foeman. Yet tell me this: Why have you followed me as a wolf follows deer?"

"Some moons ago," said Kane, his frown becoming more menacing, "you and your fiends raided a small village down the valley. You know the details better than I. There was a girl there, a mere child, who, hoping to escape your lust, fled up the valley; but you, you jackal of hell, you caught her and left her, violated and dying. I found her there, and above her dead form I made up my mind to hunt you down and kill you."

"H'm," mused the Wolf. "Yes, I remember the wench. Mon Dieu, so the softer sentiments enter into the affair! Monsieur, I had not thought you an amorous man; be not jealous, good fellow, there are many more wenches."

"Le Loup, take care!" Kane exclaimed, a terrible menace in his voice. "I have never yet done a man to death by torture, but by God, sir, you tempt me!"

The tone, and more especially the unexpected oath, coming as it did from Kane, slightly sobered Le Loup; his eyes narrowed and his hand moved toward his rapier. The air was tense for an instant; then the Wolf relaxed elaborately.

"Who was the girl?" he asked idly, "Your wife?"

"I never saw her before," answered Kane.

"Nom d'un nom!" swore the bandit. "What sort of a man are you, Monsieur, who takes up a feud of this sort merely to avenge a wench unknown to you?"

"That, sir, is my own affair; It is sufficient that I do so."

Kane could not have explained, even to himself, nor did he ever seek an explanation within himself. A true fanatic, his promptings were reasons enough for his actions.

"You are right, Monsieur." Le Loup was sparring now for time; casually he edged backward inch by inch, with such consummate acting skill that he aroused no suspicion even in the hawk who watched him.

"Monsieur," said he, "possibly you will say that you are merely a noble cavalier, wandering about like a true Galahad, protecting the weaker; but you and I know different. There on the floor is the equivalent to an emperor's ransom. Let us divide it peaceably; then if you like not my company, why – nom d'un nom! – we can go our separate ways.'

Kane leaned forward, a terrible brooding threat growing in his cold eyes. He seemed like a great condor about to launch himself upon his victim.

"Sir, do you assume me to be as great a villain as yourself?"

Suddenly be Loup threw back his head, his eyes dancing and leaping with a mild mockery and a kind of insane recklessness. His shout of laughter sent the echoes flying.

"Gods of hell! No, you fool, I do not class you with myself! Mon Dieu, Monsieur Kane, you have a task indeed if you intend to avenge all the wenches who have known my favors!"

"Shades of death! Shall I waste time in parleying with this base scoundrel! " Kane snarled in a voice suddenly blood-thirsting, and his lean frame flashed forward like a bent bow suddenly released.

At the same instant Le Loup with a wild laugh bounded backward with a movement as swift as Kane's. His timing was perfect; his back-flung hands struck the table and hurled it aside, plunging the cave into darkness as the candle toppled and went out.

Kane's rapier sang like an arrow in the dark as he thrust blindly and ferociously.

"Adieu, Monsieur Galahad!" the taunt came from somewhere in front of him, but Kane, plunging toward the sound with the savage fury of baffled wrath, caromed against a blank wall that did not yield to his blow. From somewhere seemed to come an echo of a mocking laugh.

Kane whirled, eyes fixed on the dimly outlined entrance, thinking his foe would try to slip past him and out of the cave; but no form bulked there, and when his groping hands found the candle and lighted it, the cave was empty, save for himself and the dead men on the floor.

III : THE CHANT OF THE DRUMS

Across the dusky waters the whisper came: boom, boom, boom! – a sullen reiteration. Far away and more faintly sounded a whisper of different timbre: thrum, throom, thrum! Back and forth went the vibrations as the throbbing drums spoke to each other. What tales did they carry? What monstrous secrets whispered across the sullen, shadowy reaches of the unmapped jungle?

"This, you are sure, is the bay where the Spanish ship put in?"

"Yes, Senhor; the negro swears this is the bay where the white man left the ship alone and went into the jungle." Kane nodded grimly. "Then put me ashore here, alone. Wait seven days; then If I have not returned and if you have no word of me, set sail wherever you will."

"Yes, Senhor."

The waves slapped lazily against the sides of the boat that carried Kane ashore. The village that he sought was on the river bank but set back from the bay shore, the jungle hiding it from sight of the ship.

Kane had adopted what seemed the most hazardous course, that of going ashore by night, for the reason that he knew, if the man he sought were in the village, he would never reach it by day. As it was, he was taking a most desperate chance in daring the night-time jungle, but all his life he had been used to taking desperate chances. Now he gambled his life upon the slim chance of gaining the native village under cover of darkness and unknown to the villagers.

At the beach he left the boat with a few muttered commands, and as the rowers put back to the ship which lay anchored some distance out in the bay, he turned and engulfed himself in the blackness of the jungle. Sword in one hand, dagger in the other, he stole forward, seeking to keep pointed in the direction from which the drums still muttered and grumbled.

He went with the stealth and easy movement of a leopard, feeling his way cautiously, every nerve alert and straining, but the way was not easy.

Vines tripped him and slapped him in the face, impeding his progress; he was forced to grope his way between the huge boles of towering trees, and all through the underbrush about him sounded vague and menacing rustlings and shadows of movement. Thrice his foot touched something that moved beneath it and writhed away, and once he glimpsed the baleful glimmer of feline eyes among the trees. They vanished, however, as he advanced.

Thrum, thrum, thrum, came the ceaseless monotone of the drums: war and death (they said); blood and lust; human sacrifice and human feast! The soul of Africa (said the drums); the spirit of the jungle; the chant of the gods of outer darkness, the gods that roar and gibber, the gods men knew when dawns were young, beast-eyed, gaping-mouthed, huge-bellied, bloody-handed, the Black Gods (sang the drums).

All this and more the drums roared and bellowed to Kane as he worked his way through the forest. Somewhere in his soul a responsive chord was smitten and answered. You too are of the night (sang the drums); there is the strength of darkness, the strength of the primitive in you; come back down the ages; let us teach you, let us teach you (chanted the drums).

Kane stepped out of the thick jungle and came upon a plainly defined trail. Beyond, through the trees came the gleam of the village fires, flames glowing through the palisades. Kane walked down the trail swiftly.

He went silently and warily, sword extended in front of him, eyes straining to catch any hint of movement in the darkness ahead, for the trees loomed like sullen giants on each hand; sometimes their great branches intertwined above the trail and he could see only a slight way ahead of him.

Like a dark ghost he moved along the shadowed trail; alertly he stared and harkened; yet no warning came first to him, as a great, vague bulk rose up out of the shadows and struck him down, silently.

IV : THE BLACK GOD

Thrum, thrum, thrum! Somewhere, with deadening monotony, a cadence was repeated, over and over, bearing out the same theme: "Fool – fool – fool!" Now it was far away, now he could stretch out his hand and almost reach it. Now it merged with the throbbing in his head until the two vibrations were as one: "Fool – fool – fool – fool–"

The fogs faded and vanished. Kane sought to raise his hand to his head, but found that he was bound hand and foot. He lay on the floor of a hut – alone? He twisted about to view the place. No, two eyes glimmered at him from the darkness. Now a form took shape, and Kane, still mazed, believed that he looked on the man who had struck him unconscious. Yet no; this man could never strike such a blow. He was lean, withered and wrinkled. The only thing that seemed alive about him were his eyes, and they seemed like the eyes of a snake.

The man squatted on the floor of the hut, near the doorway, naked save for a loin-cloth and the usual paraphernalia of bracelets, anklets and armlets. Weird fetishes of ivory, bone and hide, animal and human, adorned his arms and legs.

Suddenly and unexpectedly he spoke in English.

"Ha, you wake? Why you come here, eh?"

Kane asked the inevitable question: "You speak my language – how is that?"

The black man grinned.

"I slave – long time, me boy. Me, N'Longa, ju-ju man, me, great fetish. No man like me! You – you hunt brother?"

Kane snarled. "I! Brother! I seek a man, yes."

The native nodded. "Maybe so you find um, eh?"

"He dies!"

Again the negro grinned. "Me pow'rful ju-ju man," he announced apropos of nothing. He bent closer. "White man you hunt, eyes like a leopard, eh? Yes? Ha! ha! ha! ha! Listen, white man: man-with-eyes of-a-leopard, he and Chief Songa make pow'rful palaver; they blood brothers now. Say nothing, I help you; you help me, eh?"

"Why should you help me?" asked Kane suspiciously.

The ju-ju man bent closer and whispered, "White man Songa's right-hand man; Songa more pow'rful than N'Longa. White man mighty ju-ju! N'Longa's white brother kill man-with-eyes-of-a-leopard, be blood brother to N'Longa. N'Longa be more pow'rful than Songa; palaver set."

And like a dusky ghost he floated out of the hut so swiftly that Kane was not sure but that the whole affair was a dream.

Without, Kane could see the flare of fires. The drums were still booming, but close at hand the tones merged and mingled, and the impulse-producing vibrations were lost. All seemed a barbaric clamor without rime or reason, yet there was an undertone of mockery there, savage and gloating.

"Lies," thought Kane, his mind still swimming, "jungle lies like jungle women that lure a man to his doom."

Two warriors entered the hut – black giants, hideous with paint and armed with crude spears. They lifted the Englishman and carried him out of the hut. They bore him across an open space, leaned him upright against a post and bound him there. About him, behind him and to the side, a great semi-circle of black faces leered and faded in the firelight as the flames leaped and sank. There in front of him loomed a shape hideous and obscene – a black, formless thing, a grotesque parody of the human. Still, brooding, blood-stained, like the formless soul of Africa, the horror, the Black God.

And in front and to each side, upon roughly carven thrones of teakwood, sat two men. He who sat upon the right was a black man; huge, ungainly, a gigantic and unlovely mass of flesh and muscles. Small, hog-like eyes blinked out over sin-marked cheeks; huge, flabby red lips pursed in fleshly haughtiness. The other–

"An, Monsieur, we meet again." The speaker was far from being the debonair villain who had taunted Kane in the cavern among the mountains. His clothes were rags; there were more lines in his face; he had sunk lower in the years that had passed. Yet his eyes still gleamed and danced with their old recklessness, and his voice held the same mocking timbre.

"The last time I heard that accursed voice," said Kane calmly, "was in a cave, in darkness, whence you fled like a hunted rat."

"Aye, under different conditions," answered Le Loup imperturbably. "What did you do after blundering about like an elephant in the dark!"

Kane hesitated, then: "I left the mountain–"

"By the front entrance? Yes? I might have known you were too stupid to find the secret door. Hoofs of the Devil, had you thrust against the chest with the golden lock, which stood against the wall, the door had opened to you and revealed the secret passageway through which I went."

"I traced you to the nearest port and there took ship and followed you to Italy, where I found you had gone," said Kane.

"Aye, by the saints, you nearly cornered me in Florence. Ho! ho! ho! I was climbing through a back window while Monsieur Galahad was battering down the front door of the tavern. And had your horse not gone lame, you would have caught up with me on the road to Rome. Again, the ship on which I left Spain had barely put out to sea when Monsieur Galahad rides up to the wharfs. Why have you followed me like this? I do not understand."

"Because you are a rogue whom it is my destiny to kill," answered Kane coldly. He did not understand. All his life he had roamed about the world aiding the weak and fighting oppression; he neither knew nor questioned why. That was his obsession, his driving force of life. Cruelty and tyranny to the weak sent a red blaze of fury, fierce and lasting, through his soul. When the full flame of his hatred was wakened and loosed, there was no rest for him until his vengeance had been fulfilled to the uttermost. If he thought of it at all, he considered himself a fulfiller of God's judgement, a vessel of wrath to be emptied upon the souls of the unrighteous. Yet in the full sense of the word Solomon Kane was not wholly a Puritan, though he thought of himself as such.

Le Loup shrugged his shoulders. "I could understand had I wronged you personally. Mon Dieu! I, too, would follow an enemy across the world, but, though I would have joyfully slain and robbed you, I never heard of you until you declared war on me."

Kane was silent, his still fury overcoming him. Though he did not realize it, the Wolf was more than merely an enemy to him; the bandit symbolized to Kane all the things against which the Puritan had fought all his life: cruelty, outrage, oppression and tyranny.

Le Loup broke in on his vengeful meditations.

"What did you do with the treasure, which – gods of Hades! – took me years to accumulate? Devil take it, I had time only to snatch a handful of coins and trinkets as I ran."

"I took such as I needed to hunt you down. The rest I gave to the villages which you had looted."

"Saints and the devil!" swore Le Loup. "Monsieur, you are the greatest fool I have yet met. To throw that vast treasure – by Satan, I rage to think of it in the hands of base peasants, vile villagers! Yet, ho! ho! ho! ho! they will steal and kill each other for it? That is human nature."

"Yes, damn you!" flamed Kane suddenly, showing that his conscience had not been at rest. "Doubtless they will, being fools. Yet what could I do? Had I left it there, people might have starved and gone naked for lack of it. More, it would have been found, and theft and slaughter would have followed anyway. You are to blame, for had this treasure been left with its rightful owners, no such trouble would have ensued."

The Wolf grinned without reply. Kane not being a profane man, his rare curses had double effect and always startled his hearers, no matter how vicious or hardened they might be.

It was Kane who spoke next. "Why have you fled from me across the world? You do not really fear me."

"No, you are right. Really I do not know; perhaps flight is a habit which is difficult to break. I made my mistake when I did not kill you that night in the mountains. I am sure I could kill you in a fair fight, yet I have never even, ere now, sought to ambush you. Somehow, I have not had a liking to meet you, Monsieur – a whim of mine, a mere whim. Then – mon Dieu! – mayhap I have enjoyed a new sensation – and I had thought that I had exhausted the thrills of life. And then, a man must either be the hunter or the hunted. Until now, Monsieur, I was the hunted, but I grew weary of the role – I thought I had thrown you off the trail."

"A negro slave, brought from this vicinity, told a Portugal ship captain of an Englishman who landed from a Spanish ship and went into the jungle. I heard of it and hired the ship, paying the captain to bring me here."

"Monsieur, I admire you for your attempt, but you must admire me, too! Alone I came into this village, and alone among savages and cannibals I – with some slight knowledge of the language learned from a slave aboard ship – I gained the confidence of King Songa and supplanted that mummer, N'Longa. I am a braver man than you, Monsieur, for had no ship to retreat to, and a ship is waiting for you."

"I admire your courage," said Kane, "but you are content to rule amongst cannibals – you the evilest soul of them all. I intend to return to my own people when I have slain you."

"Your confidence would be admirable were it not amusing. Ho, Gulka!"

A giant negro stalked into the space between them. He was the hugest man that Kane had ever seen, though he moved with cat-like ease and suppleness. His arms and legs were like trees, and the great, sinuous muscles rippled with each motion. His ape-like head was set squarely between gigantic shoulders. His great, dusky hands were like the talons of an ape, and his brow slanted back from above bestial eyes. Flat nose and great, thick red lips completed this picture of primitive, lustful savagery.

"That is Gulka, the gorilla-slayer," said Le Loup. "He it was who lay in wait beside the trail and smote you down. You are like a wolf, yourself, Monsieur Kane, but since your ship hove in sight you have been watched by many eyes, and had you had all the powers of a leopard, you had not seen Gulka nor heard him. He hunts the most terrible and crafty of all beasts, in their native forests, far to the north, the beasts-who-walk-like-men – as that one, whom he slew some days since."

Kane, following Le Loup's fingers, made out a curious, man-like thing, dangling from a roof-pole of a hut. A jagged end thrust through the thing's body held it there. Kane could scarcely distinguish its characteristics by the firelight, but there was a weird, human-like semblance about the hideous, hairy thing.

"A female gorilla that Gulka slew and brought to the village," said Le Loup. The giant slouched close to Kane and stared into the Englishman's eyes. Kane returned his gaze somberly, and presently the savage's eyes dropped sullenly and he slouched back a few paces. The look in the Puritan's grim eyes had pierced the primitive hazes of the gorilla-slayer's soul, and for the first time in his life he felt fear. To throw this off, he tossed a challenging look about; then with unexpected animalness, he struck his huge chest resoundingly, grinned cavernously and flexed his mighty arms. No one spoke. Primordial bestiality had the stage, and the more highly developed types looked on with various feelings of amusement, tolerance or contempt.

Gulka glanced furtively at Kane to see if the Englishman was watching him, then with a sudden beastly roar, plunged forward and dragged a man from the semi-circle. While the trembling victim screeched for mercy, the giant hurled him upon the crude altar before the shadowy idol. A spear rose and flashed, and the screeching ceased. The Black God looked on, his monstrous features seeming to leer in the flickering firelight. He had drunk; was the Black God pleased with the draft – with the sacrifice?

Gulka stalked back, and stopping before Kane, flourished the bloody spear before the white man's face.

Le Loup laughed. Then suddenly N'Longa appeared. He came from nowhere in particular; suddenly he was standing there, beside the post to which Kane was bound. A lifetime of study of the art of illusion had given the ju-ju man a highly technical knowledge of appearing and disappearing – which after all, consisted only in timing the audience's attention.

He waved Gulka aside with a grand gesture, and the gorilla-man slunk back, apparently to get out of N'Longa's gaze – then with incredible swiftness he turned and struck the ju-ju man a terrific blow upon the side of the head with his open hand. N'Longa went down like a felled ox, and in an instant he had been seized and bound to a post close to Kane. An uncertain murmuring rose from the tribesmen, which died out as King Songa stared angrily toward them.

Le Loup leaned back upon his throne and laughed uproariously.

"The trail ends here, Monsieur Galahad. That ancient fool thought I did not know of his plotting! I was hiding outside the hut and heard the interesting conversation you two had. Ha! ha! ha! ha! The Black God must drink, Monsieur, but I have persuaded Songa to have you two burnt; that will be much more enjoyable, though we shall have to forego the usual feast, I fear. For after the fires are lit about your feet the devil himself could not keep your carcasses from becoming charred frames of bone."

Songa shouted something imperiously, and the blacks came bearing wood, which they piled about the feet of N'Longa and Kane. The ju-ju man had recovered consciousness, and he now shouted something In his native language. Again the murmuring arose among the shadowy throng. Songa snarled something in reply.

Kane gazed at the scene almost impersonally. Again, somewhere in his soul, dim primal deeps were stirring, age-old thought memories, veiled in the fogs of lost eons. He had been here before, thought Kane; he knew all this of old the lurid flames beating back the sullen night, the bestial faces leering expectantly, and the god, the Black God, there in the shadows! Always the Black God, brooding back in the shadows. He had known the shouts, the frenzied chant of the worshippers, back there in the gray dawn of the world, the speech of the bellowing drums, the singing priests, the repellent, inflaming, all-pervading scent of freshly spilt blood. *All this have I known, somewhere, sometime,* thought Kane; *now I am the main actor–*

He became aware that someone was speaking to him through the roar of the drums; he had not realized that the drums had begun to boom again. The speaker was N'Longa:

"Me pow-rful ju-ju man! Watch now: I work mighty magic. Songa!" His voice rose in a screech that drowned out the wildly clamoring drums.

Songa grinned at the words N'Longa screamed at him. The chant of the drums now had dropped to a low, sinister monotone and Kane plainly heard Le Loup when he spoke:

"N'Longa says that he will now work that magic which it is death to speak, even. Never before has it been worked in the sight of living men; it is the nameless ju-ju magic. Watch closely, Monsieur; possibly we shall be further amused." The Wolf laughed lightly and sardonically.

A black man stooped, applying a torch to the wood about Kane's feet. Tiny jets of flame began to leap up and catch. Another bent to do the same with N'Longa, then hesitated. The ju-ju man sagged in his bonds; his head drooped upon his chest. He seemed dying. Le Loup leaned forward, cursing: "Feet of the Devil! Is the scoundrel about to cheat us of our pleasure of seeing him writhe in the flames?"

The warrior gingerly touched the wizard and said something in his own language. Le Loup laughed: "He died of fright. A great wizard, by the–æ

His voice trailed off suddenly. The drums stopped as if the drummers had fallen dead simultaneously. Silence dropped like a fog upon the village and in the stillness Kane heard only the sharp crackle of the flames whose heat he was beginning to feel.

All eyes were turned upon the dead man upon the altar, *for the corpse had begun to move!*

First a twitching of a hand, then an aimless motion of an arm, a motion which gradually spread over the body and limbs. Slowly, with blind, uncertain gestures, the dead man turned upon his side, the trailing limbs found the earth. Then, horribly like something being born, like some frightful reptilian thing bursting the shell of non-existence, the corpse tottered and reared upright, standing on legs wide apart and stiffly braced, arms still making useless, infantile motions. Utter silence, save somewhere a man's quick breath sounded loud in the stillness.

Kane stared, for the first time in his life smitten speechless and thoughtless. To his Puritan mind this was Satan's hand manifested.

Le Loup sat on his throne, eyes wide and staring, hand still half-raised in the careless gesture he was making when frozen into silence by the unbelievable sight. Songa sat beside him, mouth and eyes wide open, fingers making curious jerky motions upon the carved arms of the throne.

Now the corpse was upright, swaying on stilt-like legs, body tilting far back until the sightless eyes seemed to stare straight into the red moon that was just rising over the black jungle. The thing tottered uncertainly in a wide, erratic half-circle, arms flung out grotesquely as if in balance, then swaying about to face the two thrones – and the Black God. A burning twig at Kane's feet cracked like the crash of a cannon in the tense silence. The horror thrust forth a foot – it took a wavering step – another. Then with stiff, jerky and automaton-like steps, legs straddled far apart, the dead man came toward the two who sat in speechless horror to each side of the Black God.

"Ah-h-h!" from somewhere came the explosive sigh, from that shadowy semi-circle where crouched the terror-fascinated worshippers. Straight on stalked the grim specter. Now it was within three strides of the thrones, and Le Loup, faced by fear for the first time in his bloody life, cringed back in his chair; while Songa, with a superhuman effort breaking the chains of horror that held him helpless, shattered the night with a wild scream and, springing to his feet, lifted a spear, shrieking and gibbering in wild menace. Then as the ghastly thing halted not its frightful advance, he hurled the spear with all the power of his muscles, and the spear tore through the dead man's breast with a rending of flesh and bone. Not an instant halted the thing – for the dead die not – and Songa the king stood frozen, arms outstretched as if to fend off the terror.

An instant they stood so, leaping firelight and eery moonlight etching the scene forever in the minds of the beholders. The changeless staring eyes of the corpse looked full into the bulging eyes of Songa, where were reflected all the hells of horror. Then, with a jerky motion, the arms of the thing went out and up. The dead hands fell on Songa's shoulders. At the first touch, the king to seemed to shrink, and shrivel, and with a scream that was to haunt the dreams of every watcher through all the rest of time, Songa crumpled and fell, and the dead man reeled stiffly and fell with him. Motionless lay the two at the feet of the Black God, and to Kane's dazed mind it seemed that the idol's great, inhuman eyes were fixed upon them with terrible, still laughter.

At the instant of the king's fall, a great shout went up from the blacks, and Kane, with a clarity lent his subconscious mind by the depths of his hate, looked for Le Loup and saw him spring from his throne and vanish in the darkness. Then vision was blurred by a rush of figures who swept into the space before the god. Feet knocked aside the blazing brands whose heat Kane had forgotten, and quick hands freed him; others loosed the wizard's body and laid it upon the earth. Kane dimly understood that the blacks believed this thing to be the work of N' Longa, and that they connected the vengeance of the wizard with himself. He bent, laid a hand on the ju-ju man's shoulder. No doubt of it: he was dead, the flesh was already cold. He glanced at the other corpses. Songa was dead, too, and the thing that had slain him lay now without movement.

Kane started to rise, then halted. Was he dreaming, or did he really feel a sudden warmth in the dead flesh he touched? Mind reeling, he again bent over the wizard's body, and slowly he felt warmness steal over the limbs and the blood begin to flow sluggishly through the veins again.

Then N'Longa opened his eyes and stared up into Kane's, with the blank expression of a new-born babe. Kane watched, flesh crawling, and saw the knowing, reptilian glitter come back, saw the wizard's thick lips part in a wide grin. N'Longa sat up, and a strange chant arose from the negroes.

Kane looked about. The blacks were all kneeling, swaying their bodies to and fro, and in their shouts Kane caught the word, "N'Longa!" repeated over and over in a kind of fearsomely ecstatic refrain of terror and worship. As the wizard rose, they all fell prostrate.

N'Longa nodded, as if in satisfaction.

"Great ju-ju – great fetish, me!" he announced to Kane. "You see? My ghost go out – kill Songa – come back to me! Great magic! Great fetish, me!"

Kane glanced at the Black God looming back in the shadows, at N'Longa, who now flung out his arms toward the idol as if in invocation.

I am everlasting (Kane thought the Black God said); *I drink, no matter who rules; chiefs, slayers, wizards, they pass like the ghosts of dead men through the gray jungle; I stand, I rule; I am the soul of the jungle* (said the Black God).

Suddenly Kane came back from the illusory mists in which he had been wandering. "The white man! Which way did he flee?"

N'Longa shouted something. A score of hands pointed; from somewhere Kane's rapier was thrust out to him. The fogs faded and vanished; again he was the avenger, the scourge of the unrighteous; with the sudden volcanic speed of a tiger he snatched the sword and was gone.

V : THE END OF THE RED TRAIL

Limbs and vines slapped against Kane's face. The oppressive steam of the tropic night rose like mist about him. The moon, now floating high above the jungle, limned the black shadows in its white glow and patterned the jungle floor in grotesque designs. Kane knew not if the man he sought was ahead of him, but broken limbs and trampled underbrush showed that some man had gone that way, some man who fled in haste, nor halted to pick his way. Kane followed these signs unswervingly. Believing in the justice of his vengeance, he did not doubt that the dim beings who rule men's destinies would finally bring him face to face with Le Loup.

Behind him the drums boomed and muttered. What a tale they had to tell this night! of the triumph of N'Longa, the death of Songa the King, the overthrow of the man-with-eyes-like–a-leopard, and a more darksome tale, a tale to be whispered in low, muttering vibrations: the nameless ju-ju.

Was he dreaming? Kane wondered as he hurried on. Was all this part of some foul magic? He had seen a dead man rise and slay and die again; he had seen a man die and come to life again. Did N'Longa in truth send his ghost, his soul, his life essence forth into the void, dominating a corpse to do his will? Aye, N'Longa died a real death there, bound to the torture stake, and he who lay dead on the altar rose and did as N'Longa would have done had he been free. Then, the unseen force animating the dead man fading, N'Longa had lived again.

Yes, Kane thought, he must admit it as a fact. Somewhere in the darksome reaches of jungle and river, N'Longa had stumbled upon the Secret – the Secret of controlling life and death, of overcoming the shackles and limitations of the flesh. How had this dark wisdom, born in the black and blood-stained shadows of this grim land, been given to the wizard? What sacrifice had been so pleasing to the Black Gods, what ritual so monstrous, as to make them give up the knowledge of this magic? And what thoughtless, timeless journeys had N'Longa taken, when he chose to send his ego, his ghost, through the far, misty countries, reached only by death?

There is wisdom in the shadows (brooded the drums), wisdom and magic; go into the darkness for wisdom; ancient magic shuns the light; we remember the lost ages (whispered the drums), ere man became wise and foolish; we remember the beast gods – the serpent gods and the ape gods and the nameless, the Black Gods, they who drank blood and whose voices roared through the shadowy hills, who feasted and lusted. The secrets of life and of death are theirs; we remember, we remember (sang the drums).

Kane heard them as he hastened on. The tale they told to the feathered black warriors farther up the river, he could not translate; but they spoke to him in their own way, and that language was deeper, more basic.

The moon, high in the dark blue skies, lighted his way and gave him a clear vision as he came out at last into a glade and saw Le Loup standing there. The Wolf's naked blade was a long gleam of silver in the moon, and he stood with shoulders thrown back, the old, defiant smile still on his face.

"A long trail, Monsieur," said he. "It began in the mountains of France; it ends in an African jungle. I have wearied of the game at last, Monsieur – and you die. I had not fled from the village, even, save that – I admit it freely – that damnable witchcraft of N'Longa's shook my nerves. More, I saw that the whole tribe would turn against me."

Kane advanced warily, wondering what dim, forgotten tinge of chivalry in the bandit's soul had caused him thus to take his chance in the open. He half suspected treachery, but his keen eyes could detect no shadow of movement in the jungle on either side of the glade.

"Monsieur, on guard!" Le Loup's voice was crisp. "Time that we ended this fool's dance about the world. Here we are alone."

The men were now within reach of each other, and Le Loup, in the midst of his sentence, suddenly plunged forward with the speed of light, thrusting viciously. A slower man had died there, but Kane parried and sent his own blade in a silver streak that slit Le Loup's tunic as the Wolf bounded backward. Le Loup admitted the failure of his trick with a wild laugh and came in with the breath-taking speed and fury of a tiger, his blade making a white fan of steel about him.

Rapier clashed on rapier as the two swordsmen fought. They were fire and ice opposed. Le Loup fought wildly but craftily, leaving no openings, taking advantage of every opportunity. He was a living flame, bounding back, leaping in, feinting, thrusting, warding, striking – laughing like a wild man, taunting and cursing.

Kane's skill was cold, calculating, scintillant. He made no waste movement, no motion not absolutely necessary. He seemed to devote more time and effort toward defense than did Le Loup, yet there was no hesitancy in his attack, and when he thrust, his blade shot out with the speed of a striking snake.

There was little to choose between the men as to height, strength and reach. Le Loup was the swifter by a scant, flashing margin, but Kane's skill reached a finer point of perfection. The Wolf's fencing was fiery, dynamic, like the blast from a furnace. Kane was more steady – less the instinctive, more the thinking fighter, though he, too, was a born slayer, with the co-ordination that only a natural fighter possessed.

Thrust, parry, a feint, a sudden whirl of blades – "Ha!" the Wolf sent up a shout of ferocious laughter as the blood started from a cut on Kane's cheek. As if the sight drove him to further fury, he attacked like the beast men named him. Kane was forced back before that blood-lusting onslaught, but the Puritan's expression did not alter.

Minutes flew by; the clang and clash of steel did not diminish. Now they stood squarely in the center of the glade, Le Loup untouched, Kane's garments red with the blood that oozed from wounds on cheek, breast, arm and thigh. The Wolf grinned savagely and mockingly in the moonlight, but he had begun to doubt. His breath came hissing fast and his arm began to weary; who was this man of steel and ice who never seemed to weaken? Le Loup knew that the wounds he had inflicted on Kane were not deep, but even so, the steady flow of blood should have sapped some of the man's strength and speed by this time. But if Kane felt the ebb of his powers, it did not show. His brooding countenance did not change in expression, and he pressed the fight with as much cold fury as at the beginning.

Le Loup felt his might fading, and with one last desperate effort he rallied all his fury and strength into a single plunge. A sudden, unexpected attack too wild and swift for the eye to follow, a dynamic burst of speed and fury no man could have withstood, and Solomon Kane reeled for the first time as he felt cold steel tear through his body. He reeled back, and Le Loup with a wild shout, plunged after him, his reddened sword free, a gasping taunt on his lips.

Kane's sword, backed by the force of desperation, met Le Loup's in mid-air; met, held and wrenched. The Wolf's yell of triumph died on his lips as his sword flew singing from his hand.

For a fleeting instant he stopped short, arms flung wide as a crucifix, and Kane heard his wild, mocking laughter peal forth for the last time, as the Englishman's rapier made a silver line in the moonlight.

Far away came the mutter of the drums. Kane mechanically cleansed his sword on his tattered garments. The trail ended here, and Kane was conscious of a strange feeling of futility. He always felt that, after he had killed a foe. Somehow it always seemed that no real good had been wrought; as if the foe had, after all, escaped his just vengeance.

With a shrug of his shoulders Kane turned his attention to his bodily needs. Now that the heat of battle had passed, he began to feel weak and faint from the loss of blood. That last thrust had been close; had he not managed to avoid its full point by a twist of his body, the blade had transfixed him. As it was, the sword had struck glancingly, plowed along his ribs and sunk deep in the muscles beneath the shoulder-blade, inflicting a long and shallow wound.

Kane looked about him and saw that a small stream trickled through the glade at the far side. Here he made the only mistake of that kind that he ever made in his entire life. Mayhap he was dizzy from loss of blood and still mazed from the weird happenings of the night; be that as it may, he laid down his rapier and crossed, weaponless, to the stream. There he laved his wounds and bandaged them as best he could, with strips torn from his clothing. Then he rose and was about to retrace his steps when a motion among the trees on the side of the glade where he first entered, caught his eye. A huge figure stepped out of the jungle, and Kane saw, and recognized, his doom. The man was Gulka, the gorilla-slayer. Kane remembered that he had not seen the giant among those doing homage to N'Longa. How could he know the craft and hatred in that slanting skull that had led the savage fighter, escaping the vengeance of his tribesmen, to trail down the only man he had ever feared? The Black God had been kind to his neophyte; had led him upon his victim helpless and unarmed. Now Gulka could kill his man openly and slowly, as a leopard kills, not sniffing him down from ambush as he had planned, silently and suddenly.

A wide grin split the negro's face, and he moistened his lips. Kane, watching him, was coldly and deliberately weighing his chances. Gulka had already spied the rapiers. He was closer to them than was Kane. The Englishman knew that there was no chance of his winning in a sudden race for the swords.

A slow, deadly rage surged in him – the fury of helplessness. The blood churned in his temples and his eyes smoldered with a terrible light as he eyed the warrior. His fingers spread and closed like claws. They were strong, those hands; men had died in their clutch. Even Gulka's huge column of a neck might break like a rotten branch between them – a wave of weakness made the futility of these thoughts apparent to an extent that needed not the verification of the moonlight glimmering from the spear in Gulka's hand. Kane could not even have fled had he wished – and he had never fled from a single foe.

The gorilla-slayer moved out into the glade. Massive, terrible, he was the personification of the primitive, the Stone Age. His mouth yawned in a red cavern of a grin; he bore himself with the haughty arrogance of savage might.

Kane tensed himself for the struggle that could end but one way. He strove to rally his waning forces. Useless; he had lost too much blood. At least he would meet his death on his feet, and somehow he stiffened his buckling knees and held himself erect, though the glade shimmered before him in uncertain waves and the moonlight seemed to have become a red fog through which he dimly glimpsed the approaching man.

Kane stooped, though the effort nearly pitched him on his face; he dipped water in his cupped   hands and dashed it into his face. This revived him, and he straightened, hoping that Gulka would charge and get it over with before his weakness crumpled him to the earth.

Gulka was now about the center of the glade, moving with the slow, easy stride of a great cat   stalking a victim. He was not at all in a hurry to consummate his purpose. He wanted to toy with his victim, to see fear come into those grim eyes which had looked him down, even when the possessor of those eyes had been bound to the death stake. He wanted to slay, at last, slowly, glutting his tigerish blood-lust and torture-lust to the fullest extent.

Then suddenly he halted, turned swiftly, facing another side of the glade. Kane, wondering,   followed his glance.

At first it seemed like a blacker shadow among the jungle shadows. At first there was no motion, no sound, but Kane instinctively knew that some terrible menace lurked there in the darkness that masked and merged the silent trees. A sullen horror brooded there, and Kane felt as if, from that monstrous shadow, inhuman eyes seared his very soul. Yet simultaneously there came the fantastic sensation that these eyes were not directed on him. He looked at the gorilla-slayer.

The black man had apparently forgotten him; he stood, half crouching, spear lifted, eyes fixed upon that clump of blackness. Kane looked again. Now there was motion in the shadows; they merged fantastically and moved out into the glade, much as Gulka had done. Kane blinked: was this the illusion that precedes death? The shape he looked upon was such as he had visioned dimly in wild nightmares, when the wings of sleep bore him back through lost ages.

He thought at first it was some blasphemous mockery of a man, for it went erect and was tall as a tall man. But it was inhumanly broad and thick, and its gigantic arms hung nearly to its misshapen feet.

Then the moonlight smote full upon its bestial face, and Kane's mazed mind thought that the thing was the Black God coming out of the shadows, animated and blood-lusting. Then he saw that it was covered with hair, and he remembered the man-like thing dangling from the roofpole in the native village. He looked at Gulka.

The negro was facing the gorilla, spear at the charge. He was not afraid, but his sluggish mind was wondering over the miracle that brought this beast so far from his native jungles.

The mighty ape came out into the moonlight and there was a terrible majesty about his movements. He was nearer Kane than Gulka but he did not seem to he aware of the Puritan. His small, blazing eyes were fixed on the giant native with terrible intensity. He advanced with a curious swaying stride.

Far away the drums whispered through the night, like an accompaniment to this grim Stone Age drama. The savage crouched in the middle of the glade, but the primordial came out of the jungle with eyes bloodshot and blood-lusting. The warrior was face to face with a thing more primitive than he. Again ghosts of memories whispered to Kane: *you have seen such sights before* (they murmured), *back in the dim days, the dawn days, when beast and beast-man battled for supremacy.*

Gulka moved away from the ape in a half-circle, crouching, spear ready. With all his craft he was seeking to trick the gorilla, to make a swift kill, for he had never before met such a monster as this, and though he did not fear, he had begun to doubt. The ape made no attempt to stalk or circle; he strode straight forward toward Gulka.

The black man who faced him and the white man who watched could not know the brutish love, the brutish hate that had driven the monster down from the low, forest-covered hills of the north to follow for leagues the trail of him who was the scourge of his kind – the slayer of his mate, whose body now hung from the roof-pole of the native village.

The end came swiftly, almost like a sudden gesture. They were close, now, beast and beast-man; and suddenly, with an earth-shaking roar, the gorilla charged. A great hairy arm smote aside the thrusting spear, and the ape closed with the warrior. There was a shattering sound as of many branches breaking simultaneously, and Gulka slumped silently to the earth, to lie with arms, legs and body flung in strange, unnatural positions. The ape towered an instant above him, like a statue of the primordial triumphant.

Far away Kane heard the drums murmur. *The soul of the jungle, the soul of the jungle*: this phrase surged through his mind with monotonous reiteration.

The three who had stood in power before the Black God that night, where were they? Back in the village where the drums rustled lay Songa – King Songa, once lord of life and death, now a shriveled corpse with a face set in a mask of horror. Stretched on his back in the middle of the glade lay he whom Kane had followed many a league by land and sea. And Gulka the gorilla-slayer lay at the feet of his killer, broken at last by the savagery which had made him a true son of this grim land which had at last overwhelmed him.

Yet the Black God still reigned, thought Kane dizzily, brooding back in the shadows of this dark country, bestial, blood-lusting, caring naught who lived or died, so that he drank.

Kane watched the mighty ape, wondering how long it would be before the huge simian spied and charged him. But the gorilla gave no evidence of having even seen him. Some dim impulse of vengeance yet unglutted prompting him, he bent and raised the negro. Then he slouched toward the jungle, Gulka's limbs trailing limply and grotesquely. As he reached the trees, the ape halted, whirling the giant form high in the air with seemingly no effort, and dashed the dead man up among the branches. There was a rending sound as a broken projecting limb tore through the body hurled so powerfully against it, and the dead gorilla-slayer dangled there hideously.

A moment the clear moon limned the great ape in its glimmer, as he stood silently gazing up at his victim; then like a dark shadow he melted noiselessly into the jungle. Kane walked slowly to the middle of the glade and took up his rapier. The blood had ceased to flow from his wounds, and some of his strength was returning, enough, at least, for him to reach the coast where his ship awaited him. He halted at the edge of the glade for a backward glance at Le Loup's upturned face and still form, white in the moonlight, and at the dark shadow among the trees that was Gulka, left by some bestial whim, hanging as the she-gorilla hung in the village.

Afar the drums muttered: "The wisdom of our land is ancient; the wisdom of our land is dark; whom we serve, we destroy. Flee if you would live, but you will never forget our chant. Never, never," sang the drums.

Kane turned to the trail which led to the beach and the ship waiting there.

MOON OF SKULLS

I : A MAN COMES SEEKING

"The wise men know what wicked things
Are written in the sky;
They trim sad lamps, they touch sad strings
Hearing the heavy purple wings,
Where the forgotten Seraph kings
Still plot how God shall die."
–CHESTERTON

A great black shadow lay across the land, cleaving the red flame of the red sunset. To the man who toiled up the jungle trail it loomed like a symbol of death and horror, a menace brooding and terrible, like the shadow of a stealthy assassin flung upon some candle-lit wall.

Yet It was only the shadow of the great crag which reared up in front of him, the first outpost of the grim foothills which were his goal. He halted a moment at its foot, staring upward where it rose blackly limned against me dying sun. He could have sworn that he caught the hint of a movement at the top, as he stared, hand shielding his eyes, but the fading glare dazzled him and he could not be sure. Was it a man who darted to cover? A man, or–?

He shrugged his shoulders and fell to examining the rough trail which led up and over me brow of the crag. At first glance it seemed that only a mountain goat could scale it, but closer investigation showed numbers of finger holds drilled into the solid rock. It would be a task to try his powers to the utmost but he had not come a thousand miles to turn back now.

He dropped the large pouch he wore at his shoulder, and laid down the clumsy musket, retaining only his long rapier, dagger, and one of his pistols. These he strapped behind him, and without a backward glance over the darkening trail he had come, he started the long ascent. He was a tall man, long-armed and iron-muscled, yet again and again he was forced to halt in his upward climb and rest for a moment, clinging like an ant to the precipitous face of the cliff. Night fell swiftly and the crag above him was a shadowy blur in which he was forced to feel with his fingers, blindly, for the holes which served him as a precarious ladder. Below him, the night noises of the tropical jungle broke forth, yet it appeared to him that even these sounds were subdued and hushed as though the great black hills looming above threw a spell of silence and fear even over the jungle creatures.

On up he struggled, and now to make his way harder, the cliff bulged outward near its summit, and the strain on nerve and muscle became heart-breaking. Time and again a hold slipped and he escaped falling by a hair's breadth. But every fibre in his lean hard body was perfectly co-ordinated, and his fingers were like steel talons with the grip of a vice. His progress grew slower and slower but on he went until at last he saw the cliff's brow splitting the stars a scant twenty feet above him.

And even as he looked, a vague bulk heaved into view, toppled on the edge and hurtled down toward him with a great rush of air about it. Flesh crawling, he flattened himself against the cliff's face and felt a heavy blow against his shoulder, only a glancing blow. but even so it nearly tore him from his hold,and as he fought desperately to right himself, he heard a reverberating crash among the rocks far below. Cold sweat beading his brow, he looked up. Who – or what – had shoved that boulder over the cliff edge? He was brave, as the bones on many a battlefield could testify, but the thought of dying like a sheep, helpless and with no chance of resistance, turned his blood cold.

Then a wave of fury supplanted his fear and he renewed his climb with reckless speed. The expected second boulder did not come, however, and no living thing met his sight as he clambered up over the edge and leaped erect, sword flashing from its scabbard.

He stood upon a sort of plateau which debouched into a very broken hilly country some half mile to the west, The crag he had just mounted jutted out from the rest of the heights like a sullen promontory, looming above the sea of waving foliage below, now dark and mysterious in the tropic night.

Silence ruled here in absolute sovereignty. No breeze stirred the sombre depths below, and no footfall rustled amid the stunted bushes which cloaked the plateau, yet that boulder which had almost hurled the climber to his death had not fallen by chance. What beings moved among these grim hills? The tropical darkness fell about the lone wanderer like a heavy veil through which the yellow stars blinked evilly. The steams of the rotting jungle vegetation floated up to him as tangible as a thick fog, and making a wry face he strode away from the cliff, heading boldly across the plateau, sword in one hand and pistol in the other.

There was an uncomfortable feeling of being watched in the very air. The silence remained unbroken save for the soft swishing that marked the stranger's cat-like tread through the tall upland grass, yet the man sensed that living things glided before and behind him and on each side. Whether man or beast trailed him he knew not, nor did he care over-much, for he was prepared to fight human or devil who barred his way. Occasionally he halted and glanced challengingly about him, but nothing met his eye except the shrubs which crouched like short dark ghosts about his trail, blended and blurred in the thick, hot darkness through which the very stars seemed to struggle, redly.

At last he came to the place where the plateau broke into the higher slopes and there he saw a clump of trees blocked out solidly in the lesser shadows. He approached warily, then halted as his gaze, growing somewhat accustomed to the darkness, made out a vague form among the sombre trunks which was not a part of them. He hesitated. The figure neither advanced nor fled. A dim form of silent menace, it lurked as if in wait. A brooding horror hung over that still cluster of trees.

The stranger advanced warily, blade extended. Closer. Straining his eyes for some hint of threatening motion. He decided that the figure was human but he was puzzled at its lack of movement. Then the reason became apparent – it was the corpse of a black man that stood among those trees, held erect by spears through his body, nailing him to the boles. One arm was extended in front of him, held in place along a great branch by a dagger through the wrist, the index finger straight as if the corpse pointed stiffly – back along the way the stranger had come.

The meaning was obvious; that mute grim signpost could have but one significance – death lay beyond. The man who stood gazing upon that grisly warning rarely laughed, but now he allowed himself the luxury of a sardonic smile. A thousand miles of land and sea – ocean travel and jungle travel – and now they expected to turn him back with such mummery – whoever they were.

He resisted the temptation to salute the corpse, as an action wanting in decorum, and pushed on boldly through the grove, half expecting an attack from the rear or an ambush. Nothing of the sort occurred, however, and emerging from the trees, he found himself at the foot of a rugged incline, the first of a series of slopes. He strode stolidly upward in the night, nor did he even pause to reflect how unusual his actions must have appeared to a sensible man. The average man would have camped at the foot of the crag and waited for morning before even attempting to scale the cliffs. But this was no ordinary man. Once his objective was in sight, he followed the straightest line to it, without a thought of obstacles, whether day or night. What was to be done, must be done. He had reached the outposts of the kingdom of fear at dusk, and invading its inmost recesses by night seemed to follow as a matter of course.

As he went up the boulder-strewn slopes the moon rose, lending its air of illusion, and in its light the broken hills ahead loomed up like the black spires of wizards' castles. He kept his eyes fixed on the dim trail he was following, for he knew not when another boulder might come hurtling down the inclines. He expected an attack of any sort and, naturally, it was the unexpected which really happened.

Suddenly from behind a great rock stepped a black man; an ebony giant in the pale moonlight, a long spear blade gleaming silver in his hand, his headpiece of ostrich plumes floating above him like a white cloud. He lifted the spear in a ponderous salute, and spoke in the dialect of the river-tribes:

"This is not the white man's land. Who is my white brother in his own kraal and why does he come into the Land of Skulls?"

"My name is Solomon Kane," the white man answered in the same language. "I seek the vampire queen of Negari."

"Few seek. Fewer find. None return," answered the other cryptically.

"Will you lead me to her ? "

"You bear a long dagger in your right hand. There are no lions here."

"A serpent dislodged a boulder. I thought to find snakes in the bushes."

The giant acknowledged this interchange of subtleties with a grim smile and a brief silence fell.

"Your life," said the black man presently, "is in my hand."

Kane smiled thinly. "I carry the lives of many warriors in *my* hand."

The negro's gaze travelled uncertainly up and down the shimmery length of the Englishman's sword. Then he shrugged his mighty shoulders and let his spear point sink to the earth.

"You bear no gifts," said he; "but follow me and I will lead you to the Terrible One, the Mistress of Doom, The Red Woman, Nakari, who rules the land of Negari."

He stepped aside, and motioned Kane to precede him, but the Englishman, his mind on a spear-thrust in the back, shook his head.

"Who am I that I should walk in front of my brother? We be two chiefs – let us walk side by side."

In his heart Kane railed that he should be forced to use such unsavoury diplomacy with a savage warrior, but he showed no sign. The giant bowed with a certain barbaric majesty and together they went up the hill trail, unspeaking. Kane was aware that men were stepping from hiding places and falling in behind them, and a surreptitious glance over his shoulder showed him some two score warriors trailing out behind them in two wedge-shaped lines. The moonlight glittered on sleek bodies, on waving headgears and long, cruel spear blades.

"My brothers are like leopards," said Kane courteously; "they lie in the low bushes and no eyes see them; they steal through the high grass and no man hears their coming."

The black chief acknowledged the compliment with a courtly inclination of his lion-like head, that set the plumes whispering.

"The mountain leopard is our brother, oh chieftain. Our feet are like drifting smoke but our arms are like iron. When they strike, blood drips red and men die."

Kane sensed an undercurrent of menace in the tone. There was no actual hint of threat on which he might base his suspicions, but the sinister minor note was there. He said no more for a space and the strange band moved silently upward in the moonlight like a cavalcade of spectres.

The trail grew steeper and more rocky, winding in and out among crags and gigantic boulders. Suddenly a great chasm opened before them, spanned by a natural bridge of rock, at the foot of which the leader halted.

Kane stared at the abyss curiously. It was some forty feet wide, and looking down, his gaze was swallowed by impenetrable blackness, hundreds of feet deep, he knew. On the other side rose crags dark and forbidding.

"Here," said the chief, "begin the true borders of Nakari's realm."

Kane was aware that the warriors were casually closing in on him. His fingers instinctively tightened about the hilt of the rapier which he had not sheathed. The air was suddenly super-charged with tension.

"Here, too," the warrior chief said, "they who bring no gifts to Nakari – *die!*"

The last word was a shriek, as if the thought had transformed the speaker into a maniac, and as he screamed it, the great arm went back and then forward with a ripple of mighty muscles, and the long spear leaped at Kane's breast.

Only a born fighter could have avoided that thrust. Kane's instinctive action saved his life – the great blade grazed his ribs as he swayed aside and returned the blow with a flashing thrust that killed a warrior who jostled between him and the chief at that instant.

Spears flashed in the moonlight and Kane, parrying one and bending under the thrust of another, sprang out upon the narrow bridge where only one could come at him at a time.

None cared to be first. They stood upon the brink and thrust at him, crowding forward when he retreated, giving back when he pressed them. Their spears were longer than his rapier but he more than made up for the difference and the great odds by his scintillant skill and the cold ferocity of his attack.

They wavered back and forth and then suddenly a giant leaped from among his fellows and charged out upon the bridge like a wild buffalo, shoulders hunched, spear held low, eyes gleaming with a look not wholly sane. Kane leaped back before the onslaught, leaped back again, striving to avoid that stabbing spear and to find an opening for his point. He sprang to one side and found himself reeling on the edge of the bridge with eternity gaping beneath him. The warriors yelled in savage exultation as he swayed and fought for his balance, and the giant on the bridge roared and plunged at his rocking foe.

Kane parried with all his strength – a feat few swordsman could have accomplished, off balance as he was – saw the cruel spear blade flash by his cheek – felt himself falling backward into the abyss. A desperate effort, and he gripped the spear shaft, righted himself and ran the spearman through the body. The giant's great red cavern of a mouth spouted blood and with a dying effort he hurled himself blindly against his foe. Kane, with his heels over the bridge's edge, was unable to avoid him and they toppled over together, to disappear silently into the depths below.

So swiftly had it all happened that the warriors stood stunned. The giant's roar of triumph had scarcely died on his lips before the two were falling into the darkness. Now the rest of the natives came out on the bridge to peer down curiously. but no sound came up from the dark void.

II : THE PEOPLE OF THE STALKING DEATH

"Their gods were sadder than the sea,
Gods of a wandering will.
Who cried for blood like beasts at night
Sadly, from hill to hill."
–CHESTERTON

As Kane fell he followed his fighting instinct, twisting in mid-air so that when he struck, were it ten or a thousand feet below, he would land on top of the man who fell with him.

The end came suddenly – much more suddenly than the Englishman had thought for. He lay half stunned for an instant, then looking up, saw dimly the narrow bridge banding the sky above him, and the forms of the warriors, limned in the moonlight and grotesquely foreshortened as they leaned over the edge. He lay still, knowing that the beams of the moon did not pierce the deeps in which he was hidden, and that to those watchers he was invisible. Then when they vanished from view he began to review his present plight. The black man was dead, and only for the fact that his corpse had cushioned the fall, Kane would have been dead likewise, for they had fallen a considerable distance. As it was, the white man was stiff and bruised.

He drew his sword from the native's body, thankful that it had not been broken, and began to grope about in the darkness. His hand encountered the edge of what seemed a cliff. He had thought that he was on the bottom of the chasm and that its impression of great depth had been a delusion, but now he decided that he had fallen on a ledge, part of the way down. He dropped a small stone over the side, and after what seemed a very long time he heard the faint sound of its striking far below.

Somewhat at a loss as to how to proceed, he drew flint and steel from his belt and struck them to some tinder, warily shielding the light with his hands. The faint illumination showed a large ledge jutting out from the side of the cliff, that is, the side next the hills, to which he had been attempting to cross. He had fallen close to the edge and it was only by the narrowest margin that he had escaped sliding off it, not knowing his position.

Crouching there, his eyes seeking to accustom themselves to the abysmal gloom, he made out what seemed to be a darker shadow in the shadows of the wall. On closer examination he found it to be an opening large enough to admit his body standing erect. A cavern, he assumed, and though its appearance was dark and forbidding in the extreme, he entered, groping his way when the tinder burned out.

Where it led to, he naturally had no idea, but any action was preferable to sitting still until the mountain vultures plucked his bones. For a long way the cave floor tilted upward – solid rock beneath his feet – and Kane made his way with some difficulty up the rather steep slant, slipping and sliding now and then. The cavern seemed a large one, for at no time after entering it could he touch the roof, nor could he, with a hand on one wall, reach the other.

At last the floor became level and Kane sensed that the cave was much larger there. The air seemed better, though the darkness was just as impenetrable. Suddenly he stopped dead in his tracks. From somewhere in front of him there came a strange indescribable rustling. Without warning something smote him in the face and slashed wildly. All about him sounded the eerie murmurings of many small wings and suddenly Kane smiled crookedly, amused, relieved and chagrined. Bats, of course. The cave was swarming with them. Still, it was a shaky experience, and as he went on and the wings whispered through the vast emptiness of the great cavern, Kane's mind found space to dally with a bizarre thought – had he wandered into Hell by some strange means, and were these in truth bats, or were they lost souls winging through everlasting night?

Then, thought Solomon Kane, I will soon confront Satan himself – and even as he thought this, his nostrils were assailed by a horrid scent, fetid and repellent. The scent grew as he went slowly on, and Kane swore softly, though he was not a profane man. He sensed that the smell betokened some hidden threat, some unseen malevolence, inhuman and deathly, and his sombre mind sprang at supernatural conclusions. However, he felt perfect confidence in his ability to cope with any fiend or demon, armoured as he was in unshakable faith of creed and the knowledge of the rightness of his cause.

What followed happened suddenly. He was groping his way along when in front of him two narrow yellow eyes leaped up in the darkness – eyes that were cold and expressionless, too hideously close-set for human eyes and too high for any four-legged beast. What horror had thus reared itself up in front of him ?

This is Satan, thought Kane as the eyes swayed above him, and the next instant he was battling for his life with the darkness that seemed to have taken tangible form and thrown itself about his body and limbs in great slimy coils. Those coils lapped his sword arm and rendered it useless; with the other hand he groped for dagger or pistol, flesh crawling as his fingers slipped from slick scales, while the hissing of the monster filled the cavern with a cold paean of terror.

There in the black dark to the accompaniment of the bats' leathery rustlings, Kane fought like a rat in the grip of a mouse-snake, and he could feel his ribs giving and his breath going before his frantic left hand closed on his dagger hilt.

Then with a volcanic twist and wrench of his steel-thewed body he tore his left arm partly free and plunged the keen blade again and again to the hilt in the sinuous writhing terror which enveloped him, feeling at last the quivering coils loosen and slide from his limbs to lie about his feet like huge cables.

The mighty serpent lashed wildly in its death struggles, and Kane, avoiding its bone-shattering blows, reeled away in the darkness, laboring for breath, If his antagonist had not been Satan himself, it had been Satan's nearest earthly satellite, thought Solomon, hoping devoutly that he would not be called upon to battle another in the darkness there.

It seemed to him that he had been walking through the blackness for ages and he began to wonder if there were any end to the cave when a glimmer of light pierced the darkness. He thought it to be an outer entrance a great way off, and started forward swiftly, but to his astonishment, he brought up short against a blank wall after taking a few strides.

Then he perceived that the light came through a narrow crack in the wall, and feeling over this wall he found it to be of different material from the rest of the cave, consisting, apparently, of regular blocks of stone joined together with mortar of some sort – an indubitably man-built wall. The light streamed between two of these stones where the mortar had crumbled away. Kane ran his hands over the surface with an interest beyond his present needs. The work seemed very old and very much superior to what might be expected of a tribe of ignorant negroes.

He felt the thrill of the explorer and discoverer. Certainly no white man had ever seen this place and lived to tell of it, for when he had landed on the dank West Coast some months before, preparing to plunge into the interior, he had had no hint of such a country as this. The few white men who knew anything at all of Africa with whom he had talked, had never even mentioned the Land of Skulls, or the she-fiend who ruled it.

Kane thrust against the wall cautiously. The structure seemed weakened from age – a vigorous shove and it gave perceptibly. He hurled himself against it with all his weight – and a whole section of wall gave way with a crash, precipitating him into a dimly lighted corridor amid a heap of stone, dust and mortar.

He sprang up and looked about, expecting the noise to bring a horde of wild spearmen. Utter silence reigned. The corridor in which he now stood was much like a long narrow cave itself, save that it was the work of man. It was several feet wide and the roof was many feet above his head. Dust lay ankle-deep on the floor as if no foot had trod there for countless centuries, and the dim light, Kane decided, filtered in somehow through the roof or ceiling, for nowhere did he see any doors or windows. At last he decided the source was the ceiling itself, which was of a peculiar phosphorescent quality.

He set off down the corridor, feeling uncomfortably like a grey ghost moving along the grey halls of death and decay. The evident antiquity of his surroundings depressed him, making him sense vaguely the fleeting and futile existence of mankind. That he was now on top of the earth he believed, since light of a sort came in, but where, he could not even offer a conjecture. This was a land of enchantment – a land of horror and fearful mysteries, the jungle and river natives had said, and he had gotten whispered hints of its terrors ever since he had set his back to the Slave Coast and ventured into the hinterlands alone.

Now and then he caught a low indistinct murmur which seemed to come through one of the walls, and he at last came to the conclusion that he had stumbled onto a secret passage in some castle or house. The natives who had dared speak to him of Negari, had whispered of a ju-ju city built of stone, set high amid the grim black crags of the fetish hills.

Then, thought Kane, it may be that I have blundered upon the very thing I sought and am in the midst of that city of terror. He halted, and choosing a place at random, began to loosen the mortar with his dagger. As he worked he again heard that low murmur, increasing in volume as he bored through the wall, and presently the point pierced through, and looking through the aperture it had made, he saw a strange and fantastic scene.

He was looking into a great chamber, whose walls and floors were of stone, and whose mighty roof was upheld by gigantic stone columns, strangely carved. Ranks of feathered black warriors lined the walls and a double column of them stood like statues before a throne set between two stone dragons which were larger than elephants. These men he recognized, by their bearing and general appearance, to be tribesmen of the warriors he had fought at the chasm. But his gaze was drawn irresistibly to the great, grotesquely ornamented throne. There, dwarfed by the ponderous splendour about her, a woman reclined. A black woman she was, young and of a tigerish comeliness. She was naked except for a beplumed helmet, armbands, anklets and a girdle of coloured ostrich feathers, and she sprawled upon the silken cushions with her limbs thrown about in voluptuous abandon.

Even at that distance Kane could make out that her features were regal yet barbaric, haughty and imperious, yet sensual, and with a touch of ruthless cruelty about the curl of her full red lips. Kane felt his pulse quicken. This could be no other than she whose crimes had become almost mythical – Nakari of Negari, demon queen of a demon city, whose monstrous lust for blood had set half a continent shivering. At least she seemed human enough; the tales of the fearful river tribes had lent her a supernatural aspect. Kane had half expected to see a loathsome semi-human monster out of some past and demoniacal age.

The Englishman gazed, fascinated though repelled. Not even in the courts of Europe had he seen such grandeur. The chamber and all its accoutrements, from the carven serpents twined about the bases of the pillars to the dimly seen dragons on the shadowy ceiling, were fashioned on a gigantic scale. The splendour was awesome – elephantine – inhumanly oversized, and almost numbing to the mind which sought to measure and conceive the magnitude thereof. To Kane it seemed that these things must have been the work of gods rather than men, for this chamber alone would dwarf most of the castles he had known in Europe. .

The black people who thronged that mighty room seemed grotesquely incongruous. They no more suited their surroundings than a band of monkeys would have seemed at home in the council chambers of the English king. As Kane realized this the sinister importance of Queen Nakari dwindled. Sprawled on that august throne in the midst of the terrific glory of another age, she seemed to assume her true proportions, a spoiled, petulant child engaged in a game of make-believe and using for her sport a toy discarded by her elders. And at the same time a thought entered Kane's mind – *who were these elders?*

Still, the child could become deadly in her game, as the Englishman soon saw.

A tall and massive black came through the ranks fronting the throne, and after prostrating himself four times before it, remained on his knees, evidently waiting permission to speak. The queen's air of lazy indifference fell from her and she straightened with a quick lithe motion that reminded Kane of a leopardess springing erect. She spoke, and the words came faintly to him as he strained his faculties to hear. She spoke in a language very similar to that of the river tribes.

"Speak!"

"Great and Terrible One," said the kneeling warrior, and Kane recognized him as the chief who had first accosted him on the plateau – the chief of the guards on the cliffs, "let not the fire of your fury consume your slave."

The young woman's eyes narrowed viciously.

"You know why you were summoned, son of a vulture?"

"Fire of Beauty, the stranger brought no gifts."

"No gifts?" she spat out the words. "What have I to do with gifts? I bade you slay all black men who come empty-handed – did I tell you to slay white men?"

"Gazelle of Negari, he came climbing the crags in the night like an assassin, with a dagger as long as a man's arm in his hand. The boulder we hurled down missed him, and we met him upon the plateau and took him to the Bridge-Across-the-Sky, where, as is the custom, we thought to slay him; for it was your word that you were weary of men who came wooing you."

"Fool," she snarled. "Fool!"

"Your slave did not know, Queen of Beauty. The white man fought like a mountain leopard. Two men he slew and fell with the last one into the chasm, and so he perished, Star of Negari."

"Aye," the queen's tone was venomous. "The first white man who ever came to Negari! One who might have – rise, fool"

The man got to his feet.

"Mighty Lioness, might not this one have come seeking–"

The sentence was never completed. Even as he straightened, Nakari made a swift gesture with her hand. Two warriors plunged from the silent ranks and two spears crossed in the chief's body before he could turn. A gurgling scream burst from his lips, blood spurted high in the air and the corpse fell flatly at the foot of the great throne.

The ranks never wavered, but Kane caught the sidelong flash of strangely red eyes and the involuntary wetting of thick lips. Nakari had half risen as the spears flashed, and now she sank back, an expression of cruel satisfaction on her beautiful face and a strange brooding gleam in her scintillant eyes.

An indifferent wave of her hand and the corpse was dragged away by the heels, the dead arms trailing limply in the wide smear of blood left by the passage of the body. Kane could see other wide stains crossing the stone floor, some almost indistinct, others less dim. How many wild scenes of blood and cruel frenzy had the great stone throne-dragons looked upon with their carven eyes ?

He did not doubt, now, the tales told him by the river tribes. These people were bred in rapine and horror. Their prowess had burst their brains. They lived, like some terrible beast, only to destroy. There were strange gleams behind their eyes which at times lit those eyes with up-leading flames and shadows of Hell. What had the river tribes said of these mountain people who had ravaged them for countless centuries? *That they were henchmen of death, who stalked among them, and whom they worshipped.*

Still the thought hovered in Kane's mind as he watched – who built this place, and why were these negroes evidently in possession? He knew this was the work of a higher race. No black tribe had ever reached such a stage of culture as evidenced by these carvings. Yet the river tribes had spoken of no other men than those upon which he now looked.

The Englishman tore himself away from the fascination of the barbaric scene with an effort. He had no time to waste; as long as they thought him dead, he had more chance of eluding possible guards and seeking what he had come to find. He turned and set off down the dim corridor. No plan of action offered itself to his mind and one direction was as good as another. The passage did not run straight; it turned and twisted, following the line of the walls, Kane supposed, and found time to wonder at the evident enormous thickness of those walls. He expected at any moment to meet some guard or slave, but as the corridors continued to stretch empty before him, with the dusty floors unmarked by any footprint, he decided that either the passages were unknown to the people of Negari or else for some reason were never used.

He kept a close lookout for secret doors, and at last found one, made fast on the inner side with a rusty bolt set in a groove of the wall. This he manipulated cautiously, and presently with a creaking which seemed terrifically loud in the stillness the door swung inward. Looking out he saw no one, and stepping warily through the opening, he drew the door to behind him, noting that it assumed the part of a fantastic picture painted on the wall. He scraped a mark with his dagger at the point where he believed the hidden spring to be on the outer side, for he knew not when he might need to use the passage again.

He was in a great hall, through which ran a maze of giant pillars much like those of the throne chamber. Among them he felt like a child in some great forest, yet they gave him some slight sense of security since he believed that, gliding among them like a ghost through a jungle, he could elude the black people in spite of their craft.

He set off, choosing his direction at random and going carefully. Once he heard a mutter of voices, and leaping upon the base of a column, clung there while two black women passed directly beneath him, but besides these he encountered no one. It was an uncanny sensation, passing through this vast hall which seemed empty of human life, but in some other part of which Kane knew there might be throngs of people, hidden from sight by the pillars.

At last, after what seemed an eternity of following these monstrous mazes, he came upon a huge wall which seemed to be either a side of the hall, or a partition, and continuing along this, he saw in front of him a doorway before which two spearmen stood like black statues.

Kane, peering about the corner of a column base, made out two windows high in the wall, one on each side of me door, and noting the ornate carvings which covered the walls, determined on a desperate plan. He felt it imperative that he should see what lay within that room. The fact that it was guarded suggested that the room beyond the door was either a treasure chamber or a dungeon, and he felt sure that his ultimate goal would prove to be a dungeon.

Kane retreated to a point out of sight of the blacks and began to scale the wall, using the deep carvings for hand and foot holds. It proved even easier than he had hoped, and having climbed to a point level with the windows, he crawled cautiously along a horizontal line, feeling like an ant on a wall.

The guards far below him never looked up, and finally he reached the nearer window and drew himself up over the sill. He looked down into a large room, empty of life, but equipped in a manner sensuous and barbaric. Silken couches and velvet cushions dotted the floor in profusion, and tapestries heavy with gold work hung upon tile walls. The ceiling too was worked in gold.

Strangely incongruous, crude trinkets of ivory and ironwood, unmistakably negroid in workmanship, littered the place, symbolic enough of this strange kingdom where signs of barbarism vied with a strange culture. The outer door was shut and in the wall opposite was another door, also closed.

Kane descended from the window, sliding down the edge of a tapestry as a sailor slides down a sail-rope, and crossed the room. His feet sank noiselessly into the deep fabric of the rug which covered the floor, and which, like all the other furnishings, seemed ancient to the point of decay.

At the door he hesitated. To step into the next room might be a desperately hazardous thing to do; should it prove to be filled with black men, his escape was cut off by the spearman outside the other door. Still, he was used to taking all sorts of wild chances, and now, sword in hand, he flung the door open with a suddenness intended to numb with surprise for an instant any foe who might be on the other side.

Kane took a swift step within, ready for anything – then halted suddenly, struck speechless and motionless for a second. He had come thousands of miles in search of something, and there before him lay the object of his search.

III : LILITH

"Lady of mystery, what is thy history?"
–VIERECK

A couch stood in the middle of the room, and its silken surface lay a woman – a woman whose skin was fair and whose reddish gold hair fell about her bare shoulders. She now sprang erect, fright flooding her fine grey eyes, lips parted to utter a cry which she as suddenly checked.

"You!" she exclaimed. "How did you–?"

Solomon Kane closed the door behind him and came toward her, a rare smile on his dark face.

"You remember me, do you not, Marylin?"

The fear had already faded from her eyes even before he spoke, to be replaced by a look of incredible wonder and dazed bewilderment.

"Captain Kane! I can not understand – it seemed no one would ever come–"

She drew a small hand wearily across her brow, swaying suddenly.

Kane caught her in his arms – she was only a child – and laid her gently on the couch. There, chafing her wrists gently, he talked in a low hurried monotone, keeping an eye on the door all the time – which door, by the way, seemed to be the only entrance or egress from the room. While he talked he mechanically took in the chamber, noting that it was almost a duplicate of the outer room as regards hangings and general furnishings.

"First," said he, "before we go into any other matters, tell me, are you closely guarded?"

"Very closely, sir," she murmured hopelessly, "I know not how you came here, but we can never escape."

"Let me tell you swiftly how I came to be here, and mayhap you will be more hopeful when I tell you of the difficulties already overcome. Lie still now, Marylin, and I will tell you how I came to seek an English heiress in the devil city of Negari.

"I killed Sir John Taferel in a duel. As to the reason, 'tis neither here nor there, but slander and a black lie lay behind it. Ere he died he confessed that he had committed a foul crime some years agone. You remember, of course, the affection cherished for you by your cousin, old Lord Hildred Taferal, Sir John's uncle? Sir John feared that the old lord, dying without issue, might leave the great Taferal estates to you.

"Years ago you disappeared and Sir John spread the rumour that you had drowned. Yet when he lay dying with my rapier through his body, he gasped out that he had kidnapped you and sold you to a Barbary rover, whom he named – a bloody pirate whose name has not been unknown on England's coasts aforetime. So I came seeking you, and a long weary trail it has been, stretching into long leagues and bitter years.

"First I sailed the seas searching for El Gar, the Barbary corsair named by Sir John. I found him in the crash and roar of an ocean battle; he died, but even as he lay dying he told me that he had sold you in turn to a merchant out of Stamboul. So to the Levant I went and there by chance came upon a Greek sailor whom the Moors had crucified on the shore for piracy. I cut him down and asked him the question I asked all men – if he had in his wanderings seen a captive English girl-child with yellow curls. I learned that he had been one of the crew of the Stamboul merchants, and that she had, on her homeward voyage, been set upon by a Portuguese slaver and sunk – this renegade Greek and the child being among the few who were taken aboard the slaver.

"This slaver then, cruising south for black ivory, had been ambushed in a small bay on the African West Coast, and of your further fate the Greek knew nothing, for he had escaped the general massacre, and taking to sea in an open boat, had been taken up by a ship of Genoese freebooters.

"To the West Coast, then, I came, on the slim chance that you still lived, and there heard among the natives that some years ago a white child had been taken from a ship whose crew had been slain, and sent inland as a part of the tribute the shore tribes paid to the upper river chiefs.

"Then all traces ceased. For months I wandered without a clue as to your whereabouts, nay, without a hint that you even lived. Then I chanced to hear among the river tribes of the demon city Negari and the black queen who kept a foreign woman for a slave. I came here."

Kane's matter-of-fact tone, his unfurbished narration, gave no hint of the full meaning of that tale – of what lay behind those calm and measured words – the sea-fights and the land fights – the years of privation and heart-breaking toil, the ceaseless danger, the everlasting wandering through hostile and unknown lands, the tedious and deadening labor of ferreting out the information he wished from ignorant, sullen and unfriendly savages, black and white.

"I came here," said Kane simply, but what a world of courage and effort was symbolized by that phrase! A long red trail, black shadows and crimson shadows weaving a devil's dance – marked by flashing swords and the smoke of battle – by faltering words falling like drops of blood from the lips of dying men.

Not a consciously dramatic man, certainly, was Solomon Kane. He told his tale in the same manner in which he had overcome terrific obstacles – coldly, briefly and without heroics.

"You see, Marylin," he concluded gently, "I have not come this far and done this much, to now meet with defeat. Take heart, child. We will find a way out of this fearful place."

"Sir John took me on his. saddlebow." the girl said dazedly, and speaking slowly as if her native language came strangely to her from years of unuse, as she framed in halting words an English evening of long ago: "He carried me to the seashore where a galley's boat waited, filled with fierce men, dark and moustached and having scimitars, and great rings to the fingers. The captain, a Moslem with a face like a hawk, took me, I a-weeping with fear, and bore me to his galley. Yet he was kind to me in his way, I being little more than a baby, and at last sold me to a Turkish merchant, as he told you. This merchant he met off the southern coast of France, after many days of sea travel.

"This man did not use me badly, yet I feared him, for he was a man of cruel countenance and made me understand that I was to be sold to a black sultan of the Moors. However, in the Gates of Hercules his ship was set upon by a Cadiz slaver and things came about as you have said.

"The captain of the slaver believed me to be the child of some wealthy English family and intended holding me for ransom, but in a grim darksome bay on the African coast he perished with all his men except the Greek you have mentioned, and I was taken captive by a black chieftain.

"I was terribly afraid and thought he would slay me, but he did me no harm and sent me up-country with an escort, who also bore much loot taken from the ship. This loot, together with myself, was, as you know, intended for a powerful king of the river peoples. But it never reached him, for a roving band of Negari fell upon the beach warriors and slew them all. Then I was taken to this city, and have since remained, slave to Queen Nakari.

"How I have lived through all those terrible scenes of battle and cruelty and murder, I know not."

"A providence has watched over you, child,' said Kane, "the power which doth care for weak women and helpless children; which led me to you in spite of all hindrances, and which shall yet lead us forth from this place, God willing."

"My people!" she exclaimed suddenly like one awaking from a dream; "what of them ?"

"All in good health and fortune, child, save that they have sorrowed for you through the long years. Nay, old Sir Hildred hath the gout and doth so swear thereat that I fear for his soul at times. Yet methinks that the sight of you, little Marylin, would mend him."

"Still, Captain Kane," said the girl, "I can not understand why you came alone."

"Your brothers would have come with me, child, but it was not sure that you lived, and I was loth that any other Taferal should die in a land far from good English soil. I rid the country of an evil Taferal – 'twas but just I should restore in his place a good Taferal, if so be she still lived – I, and I alone."

This explanation Kane himself believed. He never sought to analyse his motives and he never wavered once his mind was made up. Though he always acted on impulse, he firmly believed that all his actions were governed by cold and logical reasonings. He was a man born out of his time – a strange blending of Puritan and Cavalier, with a touch of the ancient philosopher, and more than a touch of the pagan, though the last assertion would have shocked him unspeakably. An atavist of the days of blind chivalry he was, a knight errant in the sombre clothes of a fanatic. A hunger in his soul drove him on and on, an urge to right all wrongs, protect all weaker things, avenge all crimes against right and justice. Wayward and restless as the wind, he was consistent in only one respect – he was true to his ideals of justice and right. Such was Solomon Kane.

"Marylin," he now said kindly, taking her small hands In his sword-calloused fingers, "methinks you have changed greatly in the years. You were a rosy and chubby little maid when I used to dandle you on my knee in old England. Now you seem drawn and pale of face, though you are beautiful as the nymphs of the heathen books. There are haunting ghosts in your eyes, child – do they misuse you here?"

She lay back on the couch and the blood drained slowly from her already pallid features until she was deathly white. Kane bent over her, startled. Her voice came in a whisper.

"Ask me not. There are deeds better hidden in the darkness of night and forgetfulness. There are sights which blast the eyes and leave their burning mark forever on the brain. The walls of ancient cities, recked not of by men, have looked upon scenes not to be spoken of, even in whispers."

Her eyes closed wearily and Kane's troubled, sombre eyes unconsciously traced the thin blue lines of her veins, prominent against the unnatural whiteness of her skin.

"Here is some demoniacal thing," he muttered. "A mystery–"

"Aye," murmured the girl, "a mystery that was old when Egypt was young! And nameless evil more ancient than dark Babylon – that spawned in terrible black cities when the world was young and strange."

Kane frowned, troubled. At the girl's strange words he felt an eery crawling fear at the back of his brain, as if dim racial memories stirred in the eon-deep gulfs, conjuring up grim chaotic visions, illusive and nightmarish.

Suddenly Marylin sat erect, her eyes flaring wide with fright. Kane heard a door open somewhere.

"Nakari!" whispered the girl urgently.

"Swift! She must not find you here! Hide quickly, and" – as Kane turned – "keep silent, whatever may chance!"

She lay back on the couch, feigning slumber as Kane crossed the room and concealed himself behind some tapestries which, hanging upon the wall, hid a niche that might have once held a statue of some sort.

He had scarcely done so when the single door of the room opened and a strange barbaric figure stood framed in it. Nakari, queen of Negari, had come to her slave.

The black woman was clad as she had been when he had seen her on the throne, and the coloured armlets and anklets clanked as she closed the door behind her and came into the room. She moved with the easy sinuousness of a she-leopard and in spite of himself the watcher was struck with admiration for her lithe beauty. Yet at the same time a shudder of repulsion shook him, for her eyes gleamed with vibrant and magnetic evil, older than the world.

"Lilith!" thought Kane. "She is beautiful and terrible as Purgatory. She is Lilith – that foul, lovely woman of ancient legend."

Nakari halted by the couch, stood looking down upon her captive for a moment, then with an enigmatic smile, bent and shook her. Marylin opened her eyes, sat up, then slipped from her couch and knelt before her savage mistress – an act which caused Kane to curse beneath his breath. The queen laughed and seating herself upon the couch, motioned the girl to rise, and then put an arm about her waist and drew her upon her lap. Kane watched, puzzled, while Nakari caressed the girl in a lazy, amused manner. This might be affection, but to Kane it seemed more like a sated leopard teasing its victim. There was an air of mockery and studied cruelty about the whole affair.

"You are very soft and pretty, Mara," Nakari murmured lazily, "much prettier than the black girls who serve me. The time approaches, little one, for your nuptial. And a fairer bride has never been borne up the Black Stairs."

Marylin began to tremble and Kane thought she was going to faint. Nakari's eyes gleamed strangely beneath her long-lashed drooping lids, and her full red lips curved in a faint tantalizing smile. Her ever, action seemed fraught with some sinister meaning. Kane began to sweat profusely.

"Mara," said the black queen, "you are honoured above all other girls, and yet you are not content. Think how the girls of Negari will envy you, Mara, when the priests sing the nuptial song and the Moon of Skulls looks over the black crest of the Tower of Death. Think, little bride-of-the-Master, how many girls have given their lives to be his bride!"

And Nakari laughed in her hateful, musical way as at a rare jest. And then suddenly she stopped short. Her eyes narrowed to slits as they swept the room, and her whole body tensed. Her hand went to her girdle and came away with a long thin dagger. Kane sighted along the barrel of his pistol, finger against the trigger. Only a natural hesitancy against shooting a woman kept him from sending death into the black heart of Nakari, for he believed that she was about to murder the girl.

Then, with a lithe, cat-like motion, she thrust the girl from her knees and bounded back across the room, her eyes fixed with blazing intensity on the tapestry behind which Kane stood. Had those keen eyes discovered him? He quickly learned.

"Who is there?" she rapped out fiercely.

"Who hides behind those hangings? I do not see you nor hear you, but I know someone is there!"

Kane remained silent. Nakari's wild beast instinct had betrayed him, and he was uncertain as to what course to follow. His next actions depended on the queen.

"Mara!" Nakari's voice slashed like a whip, "who is behind those hangings ? Answer me! Shall I give you a taste of the whip again?"

The girl seemed incapable of speech. She cowered where she had fallen, her beautiful eyes full of terror. Nakari, her blazing gaze never wavering, reached behind her with her free hand and gripped a cord hanging from the wall. She jerked viciously. Kane felt the tapestries whip back on either side of him and he stood revealed.

For a moment the strange tableau held – the gaunt adventurer in his blood-stained, tattered garments, the long pistol gripped in his right hand – across the room the black queen in her barbaric finery, one arm still lifted to the cord, the other hand holding the dagger in front of her – the white girl cowering on the floor.

Then Kane spoke: "Keep silent, Nakari. or you die!"

The queen seemed numbed and struck speechless by the sudden apparition. Kane stepped from among the tapestries and slowly approached her.

"You!" she found her voice at last. "You must be he of whom the guardsmen spake! There are not two other white men in Negari! They said you fell to your death! How then–"

"Silence!" Kane's voice cut in harshly on her amazed babblings; he knew that the pistol meant nothing to her, but she sensed the threat of the long blade in his left hand. "Marylin," still unconsciously speaking in the river tribes' language, "take cords from the hangings and bind her–"

He was about the middle of the chamber now. Nakari's face had lost much of its helpless bewilderment and into her blazing eyes stole a crafty gleam. She deliberately let her dagger fall as in token of surrender, then suddenly her hands shot high above her head and gripped another thick cord. Kane heard Marylin scream, but before he could pull the trigger or even think, the floor fell beneath his feet and he shot down into abysmal blackness. He did not fall far and he landed on his feet; but the force of the fall sent him to his knees and even as he went down, sensing a presence in the darkness beside him, something crashed against his skull and he dropped into a yet blacker abyss of unconsciousness.

IV : DREAMS OF EMPIRE

"For Rome was given to rule the world
And gat of it little joy—
But we, we shall enjoy the world,
The whole huge world a toy."
—CHESTERTON

Slowly Kane drifted back from the dim realms where the unseen assailant's bludgeon had hurled him. Something hindered the motion of his hands, and there was a metallic clanking when he sought to raise them to his aching, throbbing head. He lay in utter darkness, but he could not determine whether this was absence of light, or whether he was still blinded by the blow. He dazedly collected his scattered faculties and realized that he was lying on a damp stone floor, shackled by wrist and ankle with heavy iron chains which were rough and rusty to the touch.

How long he lay there, he never knew. The silence was broken only by the drumming pulse in his own aching head and the scamper and chattering of rats. At last a red glow sprang up in the darkness and grew before his eyes. Framed in the grisly radiance rose the sinister and sardonic face of Nakari. Kane shook his head, striving to rid himself of the illusion. But the light grew and as his eyes accustomed themselves to it, he saw that it emanated from a torch borne in the hand of the queen.

In the illumination he now saw that he lay in a small dank cell whose walls, ceiling and floor were of stone. The heavy chains which held him captive were made fast to metal rings set deep in the wall. There was but one door, which was apparently of bronze.

Nakari set the torch in a niche near the door, and coming forward, stood over her captive, gazing down at him in a manner rather speculating than mocking.

"You are he who fought the men on the cliff." The remark was an assertion rather than a question. "They said you fell into the abyss – did they lie? Did you bribe them to lie? Or how did you escape? Are you a magician and did you fly to the bottom of the chasm and then fly to my palace? Speak!"

Kane remained silent. Nakari cursed.

"Speak or I will have your eyes torn out! I will cut your fingers off and burn your feet!"

She kicked him viciously, but Kane lay silent, his deep sombre eyes boring up into her face, until the feral gleam faded from her eyes to be replaced by an avid interest and wonder.

She seated herself on a stone bench, resting her elbows on her knees and her chin on her hands.

"I never saw a white man before," she said. "Are all white men like you?

Bah! That cannot be! Most men are fools, black or white. I know most black men are fools, and white men are not gods, as the river tribes say – they are only men. I, who know all the ancient mysteries, say they are only men.

"But white men have strange mysteries too, they tell me – the wanderers of the river tribes, and Mara. They have war clubs that make a noise like thunder and kill afar off – that thing which you held in your right hand, was that one of those clubs?"

Kane permitted himself a grim smile.

"Nakari, if you know all mysteries, how can I tell you aught that you know not already?"

"How deep and cold and strange your eyes are!" the queen said as if he had not spoken. "How strange your whole appearance is – and you have the bearing of a king! You do not fear me – I never met a man who neither loved nor feared me. You would never fear me, but you could learn to love me. Look at me, bold one – am I not beautiful?"

"You are beautiful," answered Kane.

Nakari smiled and then frowned. "The way you say that it is no compliment. You hate me, do you not?"

"As a man hates a serpent," Kane replied bluntly.

Nakari's eyes blazed with almost insane fury. Her hands clenched until the long nails sank into the palms; then as quickly as her anger had arisen, it ebbed away.

"You have the heart of a king." she said calmly, "else you would fear me. Are you a king in your land?"

"I am only a landless wanderer."

"You might be a king here," Nakari said slowly.

Kane laughed grimly. "Do you offer me my life?"

"I offer you more than that!"

Kane's eyes narrowed as the queen leaned toward him, vibrant with suppressed excitement. "White man, what is it that you want more than anything else in the world ? "

"To take the white girl you call Mara, and go."

Nakari sank back with an impatient exclamation.

"You can not have her; she is he promised bride of the Master. Even I could not save her, even if I wished. Forget her. I will help you forget her. Listen, listen to the words of Nakari, queen of Negari! You say you are a landless man – I will make you a king! I will give you the world for a toy!

"No, no keep silent until I have finished." she rushed on, her words tumbling over each other in her eagerness. Her eyes blazed, her whole body quivered with dynamic intensity. "I have talked to travellers, to captives and slaves, men from far countries. I know that this land of mountains and rivers and jungle is not all the world. There are far-off nations and cities, and kings and queens to be crushed and broken.

"Negari is fading, her might is crumbling, but a strong man beside her queen might build it up again – might restore all her vanishing glory. Listen, white man! Sit by me on the throne of Negari! Send afar to your people for the thunder-clubs to arm my warriors! My nation is still lord of central Africa; together we will band the conquered tribes – call back the days when the realm of ancient Negari spanned the land from sea to sea! We will subjugate all the tribes of the river, the plain and the sea-shore, and instead of slaying them all, we will make one mighty army of them! And then, when all Africa is under our heel, we will sweep forth upon the world like a hungry lion to rend and tear and destroy!"

Solomon's brain reeled. Perhaps it was the woman's fierce magnetic personality, the dynamic power she instilled in her fiery words, but at the moment her wild plan seemed not at all wild and impossible. Lurid and chaotic visions flamed through the Puritan's brain – Europe torn by civil and religious strife, divided against herself, betrayed by her rulers, tottering – aye, Europe was in desperate straits now, and might prove an easy victim for some strong savage race of conquerors. What man can say truthfully that in his heart there lurks not a yearning for power and conquest? For a moment the Devil sorely tempted Solomon Kane. Then before his mind's eye rose the wistful, sad face of Marylin Taferal, and Solomon cursed.

"Out on ye, daughter of Satan! Avaunt! Am I a beast of the forest to lead your black devils against mine own people? Nay, no beast ever did so. Begone! If you wish my friendship, set me free and let me go with the girl."

Nakari leaped like a tiger-cat to her feet, her eyes flaming now with passionate fury. A dagger gleamed in her hand and she raised it high above Kane's breast with a feline scream of hate. A moment she hovered like a shadow of death above him; then her arm sank and she laughed.

"Freedom? She will find her freedom when the Moon of Skulls leers down on the black altar. As for you, you shall rot in this dungeon. You are a fool; Africa's greatest queen has offered you her love and the empire of the world – and you revile her! You love the slave girl, perhaps? Until the Moon of Skulls she is mine and I leave you to think about this: that she shall be punished as I have punished her before – hung up by her wrists, naked, and whipped until she swoons!"

Nakari laughed as Kane tore savagely at his shackles. She crossed to the door, opened it, then hesitated and turned back for another word.

"This is a foul place, white man, and maybe you hate me the more for chaining you here. Maybe in Nakari's beautiful throne room, with wealth and luxury spread before you, you will look upon her with more favour. Very soon I shall send for you, but first I will leave you here awhile to reflect. Remember – love Nakari and the kingdom of the world is yours; hate her – this cell is your realm."

The bronze door clanged sullenly, but more hateful to the imprisoned Englishman was the venomous, silvery laugh of Nakari.

Time passed slowly in the darkness. After what seemed a long time the door opened again, this time to admit a huge black who brought food and a sort of thin wine. Kane ate and drank ravenously and afterward slept. The strain of the last few days had worn him greatly, mentally and physically, but when he awoke he felt fresh and strong,

Again the door opened and two great black warriors entered. In the light of the torches they bore, Kane saw that they were giants, clad in loin-cloths and ostrich plume headgear, and bearing long spears in their hands.

"Nakari wishes you to come to her, white man," was all they said, as they took off his shackles. He arose, exultant in even brief freedom, his keen brain working fiercely for a way of escape.

Evidently the fame of his prowess had spread, for the two warriors showed great respect for him. They motioned him to precede them, and walked carefully behind him, the points of their spears boring into his back. Though they were two to one, and he was unarmed, they were taking no chances. The gazes they directed at him were full of awe and suspicion.

Down a long, dark corridor they went, his captors guiding him with light prods of their spears, up a narrow winding stair, down another passageway, up another stair, and then they emerged into the vast maze of gigantic pillars into which Kane had first come. As they started down this huge hall, Kane's eyes suddenly fell on a strange and fantastic picture painted on the wall ahead of him. His heart gave a sudden leap as he recognized it. It was some distance in front of him and he edged imperceptibly toward the wall until he and his guards were walking along very close to it. Now he was almost abreast of the picture and could even make out the mark his dagger had made upon it.

The warriors following Kane were amazed to hear him gasp suddenly like a man struck by a spear. He wavered in his stride and began clutching at the air for support. They eyed each other doubtfully and prodded him, but he cried out like a dying man and slowly crumpled to the floor, where he lay in a strange, unnatural position, one leg doubled back under him and one arm half supporting his lolling body.

The blacks looked at him fearfully. To all appearances he was dying, but there was no wound upon him. They threatened him with their spears, but he paid no heed. Then they lowered their weapons uncertainly and one of them bent over him.

Then it happened. The instant the guard stooped forward, Kane came up like a steel spring released. His right fist following his motion curved up from the hip in a whistling half-circle and crashed against the black giant's jaw. Delivered with all the power of arm and shoulder, propelled by the upthrust of the powerful legs as Kane straightened, the blow was like that of a sling-shot. The negro slumped to the floor, unconscious before his knees gave way.

The other warrior plunged forward with a bellow, but even as his victim fell, Kane twisted aside and his frantic hand found the secret spring in the painting and pressed. All happened in the breath of a second. Quick as the warrior was, Kane was quicker, for he. moved with the dynamic speed of a famished wolf. For an instant the falling body of the senseless black hindered the other warrior's thrust, and in that instant Kane felt the hidden door give way.

From the corner of his eye he saw a long gleam of steel shooting for his heart. He twisted about and hurled himself against the door, vanishing through it even as the stabbing spear slit the skin on his shoulder.

To the dazed and bewildered warrior, who stood with weapon upraised for another thrust, it seemed as if the white man had simply vanished through a solid wall, for only a fantastic picture met his gaze and this did not give to his efforts.

V : "FOR A THOUSAND YEARS–"

"The blind gods roar and rave and dream
Of all cities under the sea."
–CHESTERTON

Kane slammed the hidden door shut behind him, jammed down the spring and for a moment leaned against it, every muscle tensed, expecting to hold it against the efforts of a horde of spearmen. But nothing of the sort materialized. He heard the black warrior fumbling outside for a time; then that sound, too, ceased. It seemed impossible that these people should have lived in this palace as long as they had without discovering the secret doors and passages, but it was a conclusion which forced itself upon Kane's mind.

At last he decided that he was safe from pursuit for the time being, and turning, started down the long, narrow corridor with its eon-old dust and its dim grey light. He felt baffled and furious, though he was free from Nakari's shackles. He had no idea how long he had been in the palace; it seemed ages. It must be day now, for it was light in the outer halls, and he had seen no torches after they had left the subterranean dungeons. He wondered if Nakari had carried out her threat of vengeance on the helpless girl, and swore passionately. Free for the time being, yes; but unarmed and hunted through this infernal palace like a rat. How could he aid either himself or Marylin? But his confidence never faltered. He was in the right and some way would present itself.

Suddenly a narrow stairway branched off the main passageway, and up this he went, the light growing stronger and stronger until he stood in the full glare of the African sunlight. The stair terminated in a sort of small landing directly in front of which was a tiny window, heavily barred. Through this he saw the blue sky tinted gold with the blazing sunlight. The sight was like wine to him and he drew in deep breaths of fresh, untainted air, breathing deep as if to rid his lungs of the aura of dust and decayed grandeur through which he had been passing.

He was looking out over a weird and bizarre landscape. Far to the right and the left loomed up great black crags and beneath them there reared castles and towers of stone, of strange architecture – it was as if giants from some other planet had thrown them up in a wild and chaotic debauch of creation. These buildings were backed solidly against the cliffs, and Kane knew that Nakari's palace also must be built into the wall of the crag behind it. He seemed to be in the front of that palace in a sort of minaret built on the outer wall. But there was only one window in it and his view was limited. Far below him through the winding and narrow streets of that strange city, swarms of black people went to and fro, seeming like black ants to the watcher above. East, north and south, the cliffs formed a natural bulwark; only to the west was a built wall.

The sun was sinking west. Kane turned reluctantly from the barred window and went down the stairs again. Again he paced down the narrow grey corridor, aimlessly and planlessly, for what seemed miles and miles. He descended lower and lower into passages that lay below passages. The light grew dimmer, and a dank slime appeared on the walls. Then Kane halted, a faint sound from beyond the wall arresting him. What was that? A faint rattle – the rattle of chains.

Kane leaned close to the wall, and in the semi-darkness his hand encountered a rusty spring. He worked at it cautiously and presently felt the hidden door it betokened swing inward. He gazed out warily.

He was looking into a cell, the counterpart of the one in which he had been confined. A smoldering torch was thrust into a niche on the wall, and by its lurid and flickering light he made out a form on the floor, shackled wrist and ankle as he had been shackled. A man; at first Kane thought him to be a negro, but a second glance made him doubt. The hair was too straight, the features too regular. Negroid, yes, but some alien blood in his veins had sharpened those features and given the man that high, magnificent forehead, and those hard vibrant eyes which stared at Kane so intensely. The skin was dark, but not black.

The man spoke in an unfamiliar dialect, one which was strangely distinct and clear-cut in contrast to the guttural jargon of the black people with whom Kane was familiar. The Englishman spoke in English, and then in the language of the river tribes.

"You who come through the ancient door," said the other in the latter dialect, "who are you? You are no black man – at first I thought you one of the Old Race, but now I see you are not as they. Whence come you?"

"I am Solomon Kane," said the Puritan, "a prisoner in this devil-city. I come from far across the blue salt sea."

The man's eyes lighted at the word.

"The sea! The ancient and everlasting! The sea which I never saw but which cradled the glory of my ancestors! Tell me, stranger, have you, like they, sailed across the breast of the great blue monster, and have your eyes looked on the golden spires of Atlantis and the crimson walls of Mu?"

"Truly," answered Solomon uncertainly. "I have sailed the seas, even to Hindostan and Cathay, but of the countries you mention I know nothing."

"Nay," the other sighed. "I dream – I dream. Already the shadow of the great night falls across my brain and my words wander. Stranger, there have been times when these cold walls and floor have seemed to melt into green, surging deeps and my soul was filled with the deep booming of the everlasting sea. I who have never seen the sea!"

Kane shuddered involuntarily. Surely this man was insane. Suddenly the other shot out a withered, claw-like hand and gripped his arm, despite the hampering chain,

"You whose skin is so strangely white! Have you seen Nakari, the she-fiend who rules this crumbling city?"

"I have seen her," said Kane grimly, "and now I flee like a hunted rat from her murderers."

"You hate her!" the other cried. "Ha, I know! You seek Mara, the white girl who is her slave?"

"Aye."

"Listen," the shackled one spoke with strange solemnity; "I am dying. Nakari's rack has done its work. I die and with me dies the shadow of the glory that was my nation's. For I am the last of my race. In all the world there is none like me. Hark now, to the voice of a dying race."

And Kane leaning there in the flickering semi-darkness of the cell heard the strangest tale to which man has ever listened, brought out of the mist of the dim dawn ages by the lips of delirium. Clear and distinct the words fell from the dying man and Kane alternately burned and froze as vista after gigantic vista of time and space swept up before him.

"Long eons ago – ages, ages ago – the empire of my race rose proudly above the waves. So long ago was it that no man remembers an ancestor who remembered it. In a great land to the west our cities rose. Our golden spires split the stars; our purple-prowed galleys broke the waves around the world, looting the sunset for its treasure and the sunrise for its wealth.

"Our legions swept forth to the north and to the south, to the west and the east, and none could stand before them. Our cities banded the world; we sent our colonies to all lands to subdue all savages, red, white or black, and enslave them. They toiled for us in the mines and at the galley's oars. All over the world the brown people of Atlantis reigned supreme. We were a sea-people, and we delved the deeps of all the oceans. The mysteries were known to us, and the secret things of land and sea and sky. We read the stars and were wise. Sons of the sea, we exalted him above all others.

"We worshipped Valka and Hotah, Honen and Golgor. Many virgins, many strong youths, died on their altars and the smoke of the shrines blotted out the sun. Then the sea rose and shook himself. He thundered from his abyss and the thrones of the world fell before him! New lands rose from the deep and Atlantis and Mu were swallowed up by the gulf. The green sea roared through the fanes and the castles, and the sea-weed encrusted the golden spires and the topaz towers. The empire of Atlantis vanished and was forgotten, passing into the everlasting gulf of time and oblivion. Likewise the colony cities in barbaric lands, cut off from their mother kingdom, perished. The black savages and the white savages rose and burned and destroyed until in all the world only the colony city of Negari remained as a symbol of the lost empire.

"Here my ancestors ruled as kings, and the ancestors of Nakari – the she-cat! – bent the knee of slavery to them. Years passed, stretching into centuries. The empire of Negari dwindled. Tribe after tribe rose and flung off the chains. pressing the lines back from the sea, until at last the sons of Atlantis gave way entirely and retreated into the city itself – the last stronghold of the race. Conquerors no longer, hemmed in by ferocious tribes, yet they held those tribes at bay for a thousand years. Negari was invincible from without; her walls held firm; but within evil influences were at work.

"The sons of Atlantis had brought their slaves into the city with them. The rulers were warriors, scholars, priests, artisans; they did no menial work. For that they depended upon the slaves. There were more of these slaves than there were masters. And they increased while the sons of Atlantis dwindled.

"They mixed with each other more and more as the race degenerated until at last only the priestcraft was free of the taint of black blood. Rulers sat on the throne of Negari who were nearly purely negro, and these allowed more and more wild tribesmen to enter the city in the guise of servants, mercenaries and friends.

"Then came a day when these fierce slaves revolted and slew all who bore a trace of brown blood, except the priests and their families. These they imprisoned as 'fetish people'. For a thousand years black men have ruled in Negari, their kings guided by the captive brown priests, who though prisoners, were yet the masters of kings."

Kane listened enthralled. To his imaginative mind, the tale burned and lived with strange fire from cosmic time and space.

"After all the sons of Atlantis, save the priests, were dead, there rose a great king to the defiled throne of ancient Negari. He was a tiger and his warriors were like leopards. They called themselves Negari, ravishing even the name of their former masters, and none could stand before them. They swept the land from sea to sea, and the smoke of destruction put out the stars. The great river ran red and the black lords of Negari strode above the corpses of their black foes. Then the great king died and the black empire crumbled, even as the brown kingdom of Negari had crumbled. They were skilled in war. The dead sons of Atlantis, their former masters, had trained them in the ways of battle, and against the wild tribesmen they were invincible. But only the ways of war had they learned, and the empire was torn with civil strife. Murder and intrigue stalked red-handed through the palaces and the streets, and the boundaries of the empire dwindled and dwindled. All the while, black kings with red, frenzied brains sat on the throne, and behind the curtains, unseen but greatly feared, the brown priests guided the nation, holding it together, keeping it from absolute destruction.

"Prisoners in the city were we, for there was nowhere else in the world to go. We moved like ghosts through the secret passages in the walls and under the earth, spying on intrigue and doing secret magic. We upheld the cause of the royal family – the descendants of that tiger-like king of long ago – against all plotting chiefs, and grim are the tales which these silent walls could tell. For these black people are not as other negroes. A latent insanity lurks in the brains of every one. They have tasted so deeply and so long of slaughter and victory that they are as human leopards, forever thirsting for blood. On their myriad wretched slaves they have sated all lusts and desires until they have become foul and terrible beasts, forever seeking some new sensation, forever quenching their fearful thirsts in blood.

"Like a lion have they lurked in these crags for a thousand years, to rush forth and ravage the jungle and river people, enslaving and destroying. They are still invincible from without, though their possessions have dwindled to the very walls of this city, and their former great conquests and invasions have dwindled to raids for slaves.

"But as they faded, so too faded their secret masters, the brown priests. One by one they died, until only I remained. In the last century they too have mixed with their rulers and slaves, and now—oh, black the shame upon me! — I, the last son of Atlantis, bear in my veins the taint of negro blood. They died; I remained, doing magic and guiding the black kings, I the last brown man of Negari. Then the she-fiend, Nakari, arose."

Kane leaned forward with quickened interest. New life surged into the tale as it touched upon his own time.

"Nakari!" the name was spat as a snake hisses; "slave and the daughter of a slave! Yet she prevailed when her hour came and all the royal family died.

"And me, the last son of Atlantis, me she prisoned and chained. She feared not the silent brown priests, for she was the daughter of a Satellite — one of the lesser priests, black men who did the menial work of the brown masters — performing the lesser sacrifices, divining from the livers of fowls and serpents and keeping the holy fires for ever burning. Much she knew of us and our ways, and evil ambition burned in her.

"As a child she danced in the March of the New Moon, and as a young girl she was one of the Star-maidens. Much of the lesser mysteries was known to her, and more she learned, spying upon the secret rites of the priests who enacted hidden rituals that were old when the earth was young. For the remnants of Atlantis secretly kept alive the old worships of Valka and Hotah, Honen and Golgor, long forgotten and not to be understood by these black people whose ancestors died screaming on their altars. Alone of all the black Negari, she feared us not. Nakari not only overthrew the king and set herself on the throne, but she dominated the priests — the black Satellites and the few brown masters who were left. All these last, save me, died beneath the daggers of her assassins or on her racks. She alone of all the myriad black thousands who have lived and died between these walls guessed at the hidden passages and subterranean corridors, secrets which we of the priestcraft had guarded jealously from the people for a thousand years.

"Ha! Ha! Blind, black fools! To pass an ageless age in this city, yet never to learn of the secrets thereof! Black apes — fools! Not even the lesser black priests know of the long grey corridors, lit by phosphorescent ceilings, through which in bygone ages strange forms have glided silently. For our ancestors built Negari as they built Atlantis — on a mighty scale and with an unknown art. Not for men alone did we build, but for the gods who moved unseen among us. And deep the secrets these ancient walls hold!

"Torture could not wring these secrets from our lips, but shackled in her dungeons, we trod our hidden corridors no more. For years the dust has gathered there, untouched by human foot, while we, and finally I alone, lay chained in these foul cells. And among the temples and the dark, mysterious shrines of old, move vile black Satellites, elevated by Nakari to glories that were once mine – for I am the last Atlantean high priest. Black be their doom, and red their ruin! Valka and Golgor, gods lost and forgotten, whose memory shall die with me, strike down their walls and humble them unto the dust! Break the altars of their blind pagan gods–"

Kane realized that the man was wandering in his mind. The keen brain had begun to crumble at last.

"Tell me," said he; "you mentioned the fair girl. Mara. What do you know of her?"

"She was brought to Negari years ago by raiders," the other answered, "only a few years after the rise of the black queen, whose slave she is. Little of her I know, for shortly after her arrival. Nakari turned on me – and the years that lie between have been grim dark years, shot red with torture and agony. Here I have lain, hampered by my chains from escape which lay in that door through which you entered – and for the knowledge of which Nakari has torn me on racks and suspended me over slow fires."

Kane shuddered. "You know not if they have so misused the white girl? Her eyes are haunted. and she has wasted away."

"She has danced with the Star-maidens at Nakari's command, and has looked on the bloody and terrible rites of me Black Temple. She has lived for years among a people with whom blood is cheaper than water, who delight in slaughter and foul torture, and such sights as she has looked upon would blast the eyes and wither the flesh of strong men. She has seen the victims of Nakura die amid horrid torments, and the sight is burned forever in the brain of the beholder. The rites of the Atlanteans the blacks took whereby to honour their own crude gods, and though the essence of those rites is lost in the wasting years, yet even as Nakari's black apes perform them, they are not such as men can look on, unshaken."

Kane was thinking: *A fair day for the world when this Atlantis sank, for most certainly it bred a race of strange and unknown evil.* Aloud he said; "Who is this Master of whom Nakari spake, and what meant she by calling Mara his bride?"

"Nakura – Nakura. The skull of evil, the symbol of Death that they worship. What know these savages of the gods of sea-girt Atlantis? What know they of the dread and unseen gods whom their masters worshipped with majestic and mysterious rites ? They understand not of the unseen essence, the invisible deity that reigns in the air and the elements; they must worship a material object, endowed with human shape. Nakura was the last great wizard of Atlantean Negari. A brown renegade he was, who conspired against his own people and aided the revolt of the black beasts. In life they followed him and in death they deified him. High in the Tower of Death his fleshless skull is set, and on that skull hinge the brains of all the people of Negari. Nay, we of Atlantis worshipped Death, but we likewise worshipped Life. These people worship only Death and call themselves Sons of Death. And the skull of Nakura has been to them for a thousand years the symbol of their power, the evidence of their greatness.

"Do you mean," Kane broke in impatiently on these ramblings, "that they will sacrifice the girl to their god?"

"In the Moon of Skulls she will die on the Black Altar."

"What in God's name is this Moon of Skulls?" Kane cried passionately.

"The full moon. At the full of each moon, which we name the Moon of Skulls, a virgin dies on the Black Altar before the Tower of Death, where centuries ago, virgins died in honour of Golgor, the god of Atlantis. Now from the face of the tower that once housed the glory of Golgor, leers down the skull of the renegade wizard, and the people believe that his brain still lives therein to guide the star of the city. For look ye, stranger, when the full moon gleams over the rim of the tower and the chant of the priests falls silent, then from the skull of Nakura thunders a great voice, raised in an ancient Atlantean chant, and the people fall on their faces before it.

"But hark, there is a secret way, a stair leading up to a hidden niche behind the skull, and there a priest lurks and chants. In days gone by one of the sons of Atlantis had this office, and by all rights of men and gods it should be mine this day. For though we sons of Atlantis worshipped our ancient gods in secret, the black people would have none of them. To hold our power we were devotees to their foul gods and we sang and sacrificed to him whose memory we cursed.

"But Nakari discovered the secret, known before only to the brown priests, and now one of her black Satellites mounts the hidden stair and yammers forth the strange and terrible chant which is but meaningless gibberish to him, as to those who hear it. I, and only I, know it's grim and fearful meaning."

Kane's brain whirled in his efforts to formulate some plan of action. For the first time during the whole search for the girl, he felt himself against a blank wall. The palace was a labyrinth, a maze in which he could decide no direction. The corridors seemed to run without plan or purpose, and how could he find Marylin, prisoned as she doubtless was in one of the myriad chambers or cells? Or had she already passed over the borderline of life, or succumbed to the brutal torture-lust of Nakari ?

He scarcely heard me ravings and mutterings of the dying man.

"Stranger, do you indeed live or are you but one of the ghosts which have haunted me of late, stealing through the darkness of my cell? Nay, you are flesh and blood – but you are a white savage, even as Nakari's race are black savages. Eons ago when your ancestors were defending their caves against the tiger and the mammoth, with crude spears of flint, the gold spires of my people split the stars! They are gone and forgotten, and the world is a waste of barbarians, white and black. Let me, too, pass as a dream that is forgotten in the mists of the ages–"

Kane rose and paced the cell. His fingers closed like steel talons as on a sword hilt and a blind red wave of fury surged through his brain. Oh God! to get his foes before the keen blade that had been taken from him – to face the whole city, one man against them all–

Kane pressed his hands against his temples.

"The moon was nearly full when last I saw it. But I know not how long ago that was. I know not how long I have been in this accursed palace, or how long I lay in that dungeon where Nakari threw me. The time of full moon may be past, and – oh merciful God! – Marylin may be dead already."

"Tonight is the Moon of Skulls," muttered the other; "I heard one of my jailers speak of it."

Kane gripped the dying man's shoulder with unconscious force.

"If you hate Nakari or love mankind, in God's name tell me how to save the child."

"Love mankind?" the priest laughed insanely.

"What has a son of Atlantis and a priest of forgotten Golgor to do with love ? What are mortals but food for the jaws of the gods ? Softer girls than your Mara have died screaming beneath these hands and my heart was as iron to their cries . Yet hate" – the strange eyes flamed with fearful light – "for hate I will tell you what you wish to know!

"Go to the Tower of Death when the moon is risen. Slay the black priest who lurks behind the skull of Nakura, and then when the chanting of the worshippers below ceases, and the masked slayer beside the Black Altar raises the sacrificial dagger, speak in a loud voice that the people can understand, bidding them set free the victim and offer up instead, Nakari, queen of Negari!

"As for the rest, afterward you must rely on your own craft and prowess if you come free."

Kane shook him.

"Swift! Tell me how I am to reach this tower!"

"Go back through the door whence you came." The man was sinking fast, his words dropped to whispers. "Turn to the left and go a hundred paces. Mount the stair you come to, as high as it goes. In the corridor where it ceases go straight for another hundred paces, and when you come to what seems a blank wall, feel over it until you find a projecting spring. Press this and enter the door which will open. You will then be out of the palace and in the cliffs against which it is built, and in the only one of the secret corridors known to the people of Negari. Turn to your right and go straight down the passage for five hundred paces. There you will come to a stair, which leads up to the niche behind the skull. The Tower of Death is built into the cliff and projects above it. There are two stairs – "

Suddenly the voice trailed out. Kane leaned forward and shook the man but he suddenly rose up with a great effort. His eyes blazed with a wild and unearthly light and he flung his shackled arms wide.

"The sea!" he cried in a great voice. "The golden spires of Atlantis and the sun on the deep blue waters! I come!"

And as Kane reached to lay him down again, he slumped back, dead.

VI : THE SHATTERING OF THE SKULL

"By thought a crawling ruin,
By life a leaping mire,
By a broken heart in the breast of the world,
And the end of the world's desire."
–CHESTERTON

Kane wiped the cold sweat from his pale brow as he hurried down the shadowy passage. Outside this horrible palace it must be night. Even now the full moon – the grim Moon of Skulls – might be rising above the horizon. He paced off a hundred paces and came upon the stair the dying priest had mentioned. This he mounted, and coming into the corridor above, he measured off another hundred paces and brought up short against what appeared to be a doorless wall. It seemed an age before his frantic fingers found a piece of projecting metal. There was a creak of rusty hinges as the hidden door swung open and Kane looked into a passageway darker than the one in which he stood.

He entered, and when the door shut behind him he turned to his right and groped his way along for five hundred paces. There the corridor was lighter; light sifted in from without, and Kane discerned a stairway. Up this he went for several steps, then halted, baffled. At a sort of landing the stairway became two, one leading away to the left, the other to the right. Kane cursed. He felt that he could not afford to make a mistake – time was too precious – but how was he to know which would lead him to the niche where the priest hid?

The Atlantean had been about to tell him of these stairs when struck by the delirium which precedes death, and Kane wished fervently that he had lived only a few moments longer.

At any rate, he had no time to waste; right or wrong, he must chance it. He chose the right hand stair and ran swiftly up it. No time for caution now.

He felt instinctively that the time of sacrifice was close at hand. He came into another passage and discerned by the change in masonry that he was out of the cliffs again and in some building – presumably the Tower of Death. He expected any moment to come upon another stair, and suddenly his expectations were realized – but instead of up, it led down. From somewhere in front of him Kane heard a vague, rhythmic murmur and a cold hand gripped his heart. The chanting of the worshippers before the Black Altar!

He raced forward recklessly, rounded a turn in the corridor, brought up short against a door and looked through a tiny aperture. His heart sank. He had chosen the wrong stair and had wandered into some other building adjoining the Tower of Death.

He looked upon a grim and terrible scene. In a wide open space before a great black tower whose spire rose above the crags behind it, two long lines of black dancers swayed and writhed. Their voices rose in a strange meaningless chant, and they did not move from their tracks. From their knees upward their bodies swayed in fantastic rhythmical motions, and in their hands torches tossed and whirled, shedding a lurid shifting red light over the scene. Behind them were ranged a vast concourse of people who stood silent. The dancing torchlight gleamed on a sea of glittering eyes and black faces, In front of the dancers rose the Tower of Death, gigantically tall, black and horrific. No door or window opened in its face, but high on the wall in a sort of ornamented frame there leered a grim symbol of death and decay. The skull of Nakura! A faint, eery glow surrounded it, lit somehow from within the tower, Kane knew, and wondered by what strange art the priests had kept the skull from decay and dissolution so long.

But it was neither the skull nor the tower which gripped the Puritan's horrified gaze and held it. Between the converging lines of yelling, swaying worshippers there rose a great black altar. On this altar lay a slim, white shape.

"Marylin!" the word burst from Kane's lips in a great sob.

For a moment he stood frozen, helpless, struck blind. No time now to retrace his steps and find the niche where the skull priest lurked. Even now a faint glow was apparent behind the spire of the tower, etching that spire blackly against me sky. The moon had risen. The chant of the dancers soared up to a frenzy of sound, and from the silent watchers behind them began a sinister low rumble of drums. To Kane's dazed mind it seemed that he looked on some red debauch of a lower Hell. What ghastly worship of past eons did these perverted and degenerate rites symbolize? Kane knew that these black people aped the rituals of their former masters in their crude way, and even in his despair he found time to shudder at the thought of what those original rites must have been.

Now a fearful shape rose up beside the altar where lay the silent girl. A tall black man, entirely naked save for a hideous painted mask on his face and a great head-dress of waving plumes. The drone of the chant sank low for an instant, then rose up again to wilder heights. Was it the vibrations of their song that made the floor quiver beneath Kane's feet?

Kane with shaking fingers began to unbar the door. Naught to do now but to rush out bare-handed and die beside the girl he could not save. Then his gaze was blocked by a giant form which shouldered in front of the door. A huge black man, a chief by his bearing and apparel, leaned idly against the wall as he watched the proceedings. Kane's heart gave a great leap. This was too good to be true! Thrust in the chief's girdle was the pistol that he himself had carried! He knew that his weapons must have been divided among his captors. This pistol meant nothing to the chief, but he must have been taken by its strange shape and was carrying it as savages will wear useless trinkets, or perhaps he thought it a sort of war-club. At any rate, there it was. And again floor and building seemed to tremble.

Kane pulled the door silently inward and crouched in the shadows behind his victim like a great brooding tiger.

His brain worked swiftly and formulated his plan of action. There was a dagger in the girdle beside the pistol; the black man's back was turned squarely to him and he must strike from the left to reach the heart and silence him quickly.

All this passed through Solomon's brain in a flash as he crouched.

The black man was not aware of his foe's presence until Kane's lean right hand shot across his shoulder and clamped on his mouth, jerking him backward. At the same instant the Puritan's left hand tore the dagger from the girdle and with one desperate plunge sank the keen blade home. The black man crumpled without a sound and in an instant Kane's pistol was in its owner's hand. A second's investigation showed that it was still loaded and the flint still in place.

No one had seen the swift murder. Those few who stood near the doorway were all facing the Black Altar, enwrapped in the drama, which was there unfolding. As Kane stepped across the corpse, the chanting of the dancers ceased abruptly. In the instant of silence which followed, Kane heard, above the pounding of his own pulse, the night wind rustle the death-like plumes of the masked horror beside the altar. A rim of the moon glowed above the spire.

Then, from high up on the face of the Tower of Death, a deep voice boomed out in a strange chant Mayhap the black priest who spoke behind the skull knew not what his words meant, but Kane believed that he at least mimicked the very intonation of those long-dead brown acolytes. Deep, mystic, resonant the voice sounded out, like the endless flowing of long tides on the broad white beaches.

The masked one beside the altar drew himself up to his great height and raised a long, glimmering blade. Kane recognized his own sword, even as he levelled his pistol and fired – not at the masked priest but full at the skull which gleamed in the face of the tower. For in one blinding flash of intuition he remembered the dying Atlantean's words: "Their brains hinge on the skull of Nakura!"

Simultaneously with the crack of the pistol came a shattering crash; the dry skull flew into a thousand pieces and vanished, and behind it the chant broke off short in a death shriek. The rapier fell from the hand of the masked priest and many of the dancers crumpled to the earth, the others halting short, spellbound. Through the deathly silence which reigned for an instant, Kane rushed toward the altar; then all Hell broke loose.

A babel of bestial screams rose to the shuddering stars. For centuries only their faith in the dead Nakura had held together the blood-drenched brains of the black Negari. Now their symbol had vanished, had been blasted into nothing before their eyes. It was to them as if the skies had split, the moon fallen and the world ended. All the red visions which lurked at the backs of their corroded brains leaped into fearful life, all the latent insanity which was their heritage rose to claim its own, and Kane looked upon a whole nation turned to bellowing maniacs.

Screaming and roaring they turned on each other, men and women, tearing with frenzied fingernails, stabbing with spears with daggers, beating each other with the flaming torches, while over all rose the roar of frantic human beasts. With clubbed pistol Kane battered his way through the surging, writhing ocean of flesh, to the foot of the altar stairs. Nails raked him, knives slashed at him, torches scorched his garments, but he paid no heed.

Then as he reached the altar, a terrible figure broke from the struggling mass and charged him. Nakari, queen of Negari, crazed as any of her subjects, rushed upon the Englishman with dagger bared and eyes horribly aflame.

"You shall not escape this time!" she was screaming, but before she reached him a great black giant, dripping blood and blind from a gash across his eyes, reeled across her path and lurched into her. She screamed like a wounded cat and struck her dagger into him, and then the groping hands closed on her. The blind giant whirled her on high with one dying effort, and her last scream knifed the din of battle as Nakari, last queen of Negari, crashed against the stones of the altar and fell shattered and dead at Kane's feet.

Kane sprang up the black steps, worn deep by the feet of myriad priests and victims, and as he came, the masked figure, who had stood like one turned to stone, came suddenly to life. He bent swiftly, caught up the sword he had dropped and thrust savagely at the charging white man. But the dynamic quickness of Solomon Kane was such as few men could match. A twist and sway of his steely body and he was inside the thrust, and as the blade slid harmlessly between arm and chest, he brought down the heavy pistol barrel among the waving plumes, crushing head-dress, mask and skull with one blow.

Then ere he turned to the fainting girl who lay bound on the altar, he flung aside the shattered pistol and snatched his stolen sword from the nerveless hand which still grasped it, feeling a fierce thrill of renewed confidence at the familiar feel of the hilt.

Marylin lay white and silent, her death-like face turned blindly to the light of the moon which shone calmly down on the frenzied scene. At first Kane thought her to be dead, but his searching fingers detected a faint flutter of pulse. He cut her bonds and lifted her tenderly – only to drop her again and whirl as a hideous, blood-stained figure of insanity came leaping and gibbering up the steps. Full upon Kane's out-thrust blade the creature ran, and toppled back into the red swirl below, clawing beast-like at its mortal wound.

Then beneath Kane's feet the altar rocked; a sudden tremor hurled him to his knees and his horrified eyes beheld the Tower of Death sway to and fro. Some horror of Nature was taking place, and this fact pierced the crumbling brains of the fiends who fought and screamed below. A new element entered into their shrieking, and then the Tower of Death swayed far out with a terrible and awesome majesty – broke from the rocking crags and gave way with a thunder of crashing worlds. Great stones and shards of masonry came raining down, bringing death and destruction to hundreds of screaming humans below. One of these stones crashed to pieces on the altar beside Kane, showering him with dust.

"Earthquake!" he gasped, and smitten by this new terror he caught up the senseless girl and plunged recklessly down the cracking steps, hacking and stabbing a way through the crimson whirlpools of bestial humanity that still tore and ravened.

The rest was a red nightmare in which Kane's dazed brain refused to record all its horrors. It seemed that for screaming crimson centuries he reeled through narrow winding streets where bellowing, screeching black demons battled and died, among titanic walls and black columns that rocked against the sky and crashed to ruin about him, while the earth heaved and trembled beneath his staggering feet and the thunder of crashing towers filled the world.

Gibbering fiends in human shape clutched and clawed at him, to fade before his flailing sword, and falling stones bruised and battered him. He crouched as he reeled along, covering the girl with his body as best he could, sheltering her alike from blind stone and blinder human. And at last, when it seemed mortal endurance had reached its limit, he saw the great black outer wall of the city loom before him, rent from earth to parapet and tottering for its fall. He dashed through a crevice, and gathering his efforts, made one last sprint. And scarce was he out of reach than the wall crashed, falling inward like a great black wave.

The night wind was in his face and behind him rose the clamour of the doomed city as Kane staggered down the hill path that trembled beneath his feet.

VII : THE FAITH OF SOLOMON

"The last lost giant, even God,
Is risen against the world."
–CHESTERTON

Dawn lay like a cool white hand on the brow of Solomon Kane. The nightmares faded from his soul as he breathed deep of the morning wind which blew up from the jungle far below his feet – a wind laden with the musk of decaying vegetation. Yet it was like the breath of life to him, for the scents were those of the clean natural disintegration of outdoor things, not the loathsome aura of decadent antiquity that lurks in the walls of eon-old cities – Kane shuddered involuntarily.

He bent over the sleeping girl who lay at his feet, arranged as comfortably as possible with the few soft tree branches he had been able to find for her bed. Now she opened her eyes and stared about wildly for an instant; then as her gaze met the face of Solomon, lighted by one of his rare smiles, she gave a little sob of thankfulness and clung to him.

"Oh. Captain Kane! Have we in truth escaped from yon fearful city? Now it seems all like a dream – after you fell through the secret door in my chamber Nakari later went to your dungeon – as she told me – and returned in vile humour. She said you were a fool, for she had offered you the kingdom of the world and you had but insulted her. She screamed and raved and cursed like one insane and swore that she would yet, alone, build a great empire of Negari. Then she turned on me and reviled me, saying that you held me – a slave – in more esteem than a queen and all her glory. And in spite of my pleas she took me across her knees and whipped me until I swooned.

"Afterward I lay half senseless for a long time, and was only dimly aware that men came to Nakari and said that you had escaped. They said you were a sorcerer, for you faded through a solid wall like a ghost. But Nakari killed the men who had brought you from the cell, and for hours she was like a wild beast.

"How long I lay thus I know not. In those terrible rooms and corridors where no natural sunlight ever entered, one lost all track of time. But from the time you were captured by Nakari and the time that I was placed on the altar, at least a day and a night and another day must have passed. It was only a few hours before the sacrifice that word came you had escaped.

"Nakari and her Star-maidens came to prepare me for the rite." At the bare memory of that fearful ordeal she whimpered and hid her face in her hands. "I must have been drugged – I only know that they clothed me in the white robe of the sacrifice and carried me into a great black chamber filled with horrid statues. There I lay for a space like one in a trance, while the women performed various strange and shameful rites according to their grim religion. Then I fell into a swoon, and when I emerged I was lying bound on the Black Altar – the torches were tossing and the devotees chanting – behind the Tower of Death the rising moon was beginning to glow – all this I knew faintly, as in a deep dream. And as in a dream I saw the glowing skull high on the tower – and the gaunt black naked priest holding a sword above my heart; then I knew no more. What happened? "

"At about that moment," Kane answered, "I emerged from a building wherein I had wandered by mistake, and blasted their hellish skull to atoms with a pistol ball. Whereupon, all these people, being cursed from birth by demons, and being likewise possessed of devils, fall to slaying one another, and in the midst of the tumult an earthquake cometh to pass which shakes the walls down. Then I snatch you up, and running at random, come upon a rent in the outer wall and thereby escape, carrying you, who seem in a swoon.

"Once only you awoke, after I had crossed the Bridge-Across-the-Sky, as the people of Negari called it, which was crumbling beneath our feet by reason of the earthquake. After I had come to these cliffs, but dared not descend them in the darkness, the moon being nigh to setting by that time, you awoke and screamed and clung to me, whereupon I soothed you as best I might, and after a time you fell into a natural sleep."

"And now what?" asked the girl.

"England!" Kane's deep eyes lighted at the word. "I find it hard to remain in the land of my birth for more than a month at a time; yet though I am cursed with the wanderlust, 'tis a name which ever rouses a glow in my bosom. And how of you, child?"

"Oh heaven!" she cried, clasping her small hands. "Home! Something of which to be dreamed – never attained, I fear. Oh Captain Kane, how shall we gain through all the vast leagues of jungle which lie between this place and the coast?"

"Marylin," said Kane gently, stroking her curly hair, "methinks you lack somewhat in faith, both in Providence and in me. Nay, alone I am a weak creature, having no strength or might in me; yet in times past hath God made me a great vessel of wrath and a sword of deliverance. And, I trust, shall do so again.

"Look you, little Marylin: in the last few hours as it were, we have seen the passing of an evil race and the fall of a foul black empire. Men died by thousands about us, and the earth rose beneath our feet. hurling down towers that broke the heavens; yea, death fell about us in a red rain, yet we escaped unscathed.

"Therein is more than the hand of man! Nay, a Power – the mightiest Power! That which guided me across the world, straight to that demon city – which led me to your chamber – which aided me to escape again and led me to the one man in all the city who would give the information I must have, the strange, evil priest of an elder race who lay dying in a subterranean cell – and which guided me to the outer wall, as I ran blindly and at random – for should I have come under the cliffs which formed the rest of the wall, we had surely perished. That same Power brought us safely out of the dying city, and safe across the rocking bridge – which shattered and sundered down into the chasm just as my feet touched solid earth!

"Think you that having led me this far, and accomplished such wonders, the Power will strike us down now? Nay! Evil flourishes and rules in the cities of men and the waste places of the world, but anon the great giant that is God rises and smites for the righteous, and they lay faith on him.

"I say this: this cliff shall we descend in safety, and yon dank jungle traverse in safety, and it is as sure that in old Devon your people shall clasp you again to their bosom, as that you stand here."

And now for the first time Marylin smiled, with the quick eagerness of a normal young girl, and Kane sighed in relief. Already the ghosts were fading from her haunted eyes, and Kane looked to the day when her horrible experiences should be as a dimming dream. One glance he flung behind him, where beyond the scowling hills the lost city of Negari lay shattered and silent, amid the ruins of her own walls and the fallen crags which had kept her invincible so long, but which had at last betrayed her to her doom. A momentary pang smote him as he thought of the myriad of crushed, still forms lying amid those ruins; then the blasting memory of their evil crimes surged over him and his eyes hardened.

"'And it shall come to pass, that he who fleeth from the noise of the fear shall fall into the pit; and he that cometh up out of the midst of the pit shall be taken in the snare; for the windows from on high are open, and the foundations of the earth do shake.

"For Thou hast made of a city an heap; of a defended city a ruin; a palace of strangers to be no city; it shall never be built.

"Moreover, the multitude of Thy strangers shall be like small dust and the multitude of the terrible ones shall be as chaff that passeth suddenly away; yea, it shall be at an instant suddenly.

"Stay yourselves and wonder; cry ye out and cry; they are drunken but not with wine; they stagger but not with strong drink.'

"Verily, Marylin," said Kane with a sigh, "with mine own eyes have I seen the prophecies of Isaiah come to pass. They were drunken but not with wine. Nay, blood was their drink and in that red flood they dipped deep and terribly."

Then taking the girl by the hand he started toward the edge of the cliff. At this very point had he ascended in the night – how long ago it seemed.

Kane's clothing hung in tatters about him. He was torn, scratched and bruised. But in his eyes shone the clear calm light of serenity as the sun came up, flooding cliffs and jungle with a golden light that was like a promise of joy and happiness.

WINGS IN THE NIGHT

I : THE HORROR ON THE STAKE

Solomon Kane leaned on his strangely carved staff and gazed in scowling perplexity at the mystery which spread silently before him. Many a deserted village Kane had seen in the months that had passed since he turned his face east from the Slave Coast and lost himself in the mazes of jungle and river, but never one like this. It was not famine that had driven away the inhabitants, for yonder the wild rice still grew rank and unkempt in the untilled fields. There were no Arab slave-raiders in this nameless land – it must have been a tribal war that devastated the village, Kane decided, as he gazed sombrely at the scattered bones and grinning skulls that littered the space among the rank weeds and grasses. These bones were shattered and splintered, and Kane saw jackals and a hyena furtively slinking among the ruined huts. But why had the slayers left the spoils? There lay war spears, their shafts crumbling before the attacks of the white ants. There lay shields, moldering in the rains and sun. There lay the cooking pots, and about the neck-bones of a shattered skeleton glistened a necklace of gaudily painted pebbles and shells – surely rare loot for any savage conqueror.

He gazed at the huts, wondering why the thatch roofs of so many were torn and rent, as if by taloned things seeking entrance. Then something made his cold eyes narrow in startled unbelief. Just outside the moldering mound that was once the village wall towered a gigantic baobab tree, branchless for sixty feet, its mighty bole too large to be gripped and scaled. Yet in the topmost branches dangled a skeleton, apparently impaled on a broken limb.

The cold hand of mystery touched the shoulder of Solomon Kane. How came those pitiful remains in that tree? Had some monstrous ogre's inhuman hand flung them there?

Kane shrugged his broad shoulders and his hand unconsciously touched the black butts of his heavy pistols, the hilt of his long rapier, and the dirk in his belt. Kane felt no fear as an ordinary man would feel, confronted with the Unknown and Nameless. Years of wandering in strange lands and warring with strange creatures had melted away from brain, soul, and body all that was not steel and whalebone. He was tall and spare, almost gaunt, built with the savage economy of the wolf. Broad-shouldered, long-armed, with nerves of ice and thews of spring steel, he was no less the natural killer than the born swordsman.

The brambles and thorns of the jungle had dealt hardly with him; his garments hung in tatters, his featherless slouch hat was torn and his boots of Cordovan leather were scratched and worn. The sun had baked his chest and limbs to a deep bronze, but his ascetically lean face was impervious to its rays. His complexion was still of that strange, dark pallor which gave him an almost corpse-like appearance, belied only by his cold, light eyes.

And now Kane, sweeping the village once more with his searching gaze, pulled his belt into a more comfortable position, shifted to his left hand the cat-headed stave N'Longa had given him, and took up his way again.

To the west lay a strip of thin forest, sloping downward to a broad belt of savannas, a waving sea of grass waist-deep and deeper. Beyond that rose another narrow strip of woodlands, deepening rapidly into dense jungle. Out of that jungle Kane had fled like a hunted wolf with pointed-toothed men hot on his trail. Even now a vagrant breeze brought faintly the throb of a savage drum which whispered its obscene tale of hate and blood-hunger and belly-lust across miles of jungle and grassland.

The memory of his flight and narrow escape was vivid in Kane's mind, for only the day before had he realized too late that he was in cannibal country, and all that afternoon in the reeking stench of the thick jungle, he had crept and run and hidden and doubled and twisted on his track with the fierce hunters ever close behind him, until night fell and he gained and crossed the grasslands under cover of darkness. Now in the late morning he had seen nothing, heard nothing of his pursuers, yet he had no reason to believe that they had abandoned the chase. They had been close on his heels when he took to the savannas.

So Kane surveyed the land in front of him. To the east, curving from north to south ran a straggling range of hills, for the most part dry and barren, rising in the south to a jagged black skyline that reminded Kane of the black hills of Negari. Between him and these hills stretched a broad expanse of gently rolling country, thickly treed, but nowhere approaching the density of a jungle. Kane got the impression of a vast upland plateau, bounded by the curving hills to the east and by the savannas to the west.

Kane set out for the hills with his long, swinging, tireless stride. Surely somewhere behind him the savage demons were stealing after him, and he had no desire to be driven to bay. A shot might send them flying in sudden terror, but on the other hand, so low they were in the scale of humanity, it might transmit no supernatural fear to their dull brains. And not even Solomon Kane, whom Sir Francis Drake had called Devon's king of swords, could win in a pitched battle with a whole tribe.

The silent village with its burden of death and mystery faded out behind him. Utter silence reigned among these mysterious uplands where no birds sang and only a silent macaw flitted among the great trees. The only sounds were Kane's cat-like tread, and the whisper of the drum-haunted breeze.

And then Kane caught a glimpse among the trees that made his heart leap with a sudden, nameless horror, and a few moments later he stood before Horror itself, stark and grisly. In a wide clearing, on a rather bold incline stood a grim stake, and to this stake was bound a thing that had once been a man. Kane had rowed, chained to the bench of a Turkish galley, and he had toiled in Barbary vineyards; he had battled red Indians in the New Lands and had languished in the dungeons of Spain's Inquisition. He knew much of the fiendishness of man's inhumanity, but now he shuddered and grew sick. Yet it was not so much the ghastliness of the mutilations, horrible as they were, that shook Kane's soul, but the knowledge that the wretch still lived.

For as he drew near, the gory head that lolled on the butchered breast lifted and tossed from side to side, spattering blood from the stumps of ears, while a bestial, rattling whimper drooled from the shredded lips.

Kane spoke to the ghastly thing and it screamed unbearably, writhing in incredible contortions. while its head jerked up and down with the jerking of mangled nerves, and the empty, gaping eye-sockets seemed striving to see from their emptiness. And moaning low and brain-shatteringly it huddled its outraged self against the stake where it was bound and lifted its head in a grisly attitude of listening, as if it expected something out of the skies.

"Listen," said Kane, in the dialect of the river tribes. "Do not fear me – I will not harm you and nothing else shall harm you any more. I am going to loose you."

Even as he spoke Kane was bitterly aware of the emptiness of his words. But his voice had filtered dimly into the crumbling, agony-shot brain of the man before him. From between splintered teeth fell words, faltering and uncertain, mixed and mingled with the slavering droolings of imbecility. He spoke a language akin to the dialects Kane had learned from friendly river folk on his wanderings, and Kane gathered that he had been bound to the stake for a long time – many moons, he whimpered in the delirium of approaching death; and all this time, inhuman, evil things had worked their monstrous will upon him. These things he mentioned by name, but Kane could make nothing of it for he used an unfamiliar term that sounded like *akaana*. But these things had not bound him to the stake, for the torn wretch slavered the name of Goru, who was a priest and who had drawn a cord too tight about his legs – and Kane wondered that the memory of this small pain should linger through the red mazes of agony that the dying man should whimper over it.

And to Kane's horror, the man spoke of his brother who had aided in the binding of him, and he wept with infantile sobs. Moisture formed in the empty sockets and made tears of blood. And he muttered of a spear broken long ago in some dim hunt, and while he muttered in his delirium, Kane gently cut his bonds and eased his broken body to the grass. But even at the Englishman's careful touch, the poor wretch writhed and howled like a dying dog, while blood started anew from a score of ghastly gashes, which, Kane noted, were more like the wounds made by fang and talon than by knife or spear. But at last it was done and the bloody, torn thing lay on the soft grass with Kane's old slouch hat beneath its death's-head, breathing in great, rattling gasps.

Kane poured water from his canteen between the mangled lips, and bending close, said: "Tell me more of these devils, for by the God of my people, this deed shall not go unavenged, though Satan himself bar my way."

It is doubtful if the dying man heard. But he heard something else. The macaw, with the curiosity of its breed, swept from a near-by grove and passed so close its great wings fanned Kane's hair. And at the sound of those wings, the butchered man heaved upright and screamed in a voice that haunted Kane's dreams to the day of his death: "'The wings! the wings! They come again! Ahhh,

148

mercy, *the wings!*"

And the blood burst in a torrent from his lips and so he died.

Kane rose and wiped the cold sweat from his forehead. The upland forest shimmered in the noonday heat. Silence lay over the land like an enchantment of dreams. Kane's brooding eyes ranged to the black, malevolent hills crouching in the distance and back to the far-away savannas. An ancient curse lay over that mysterious land and the shadow of it fell across the soul of Solomon Kane.

Tenderly he lifted the red ruin that had once pulsed with life and youth and vitality, and carried it to the edge of the glade, where arranging the cold limbs as best he might, and shuddering once again at the unnameable mutilations, he piled stones above it till even a prowling jackal would find it hard to get at the flesh below.

And he had scarcely finished when something jerked him back out of his sombre broodings to a realization of his own position. A slight sound – or his own wolf-like instinct – made him whirl. On the other side of the glade he caught a movement among the tall grasses – the glimpse of a hideous black face, with an ivory ring in the flat nose, thick lips parted to reveal teeth whose filed points were apparent even at that distance, beady eyes and a low slanting forehead topped by a mop of frizzly hair. Even as the face faded from view Kane leaped back into the shelter of the ring of trees which circled the glade, and ran like a deer-hound, flitting from tree to tree and expecting at each moment to hear the exultant clamour of the braves and to see them break cover at his back.

But soon he decided that they were content to hunt him down as certain beasts track their prey, slowly and inevitably. He hastened through the upland forest, taking advantage of every bit of cover, and he saw no more of his pursuers; yet he *knew*, as a hunted wolf knows, that they hovered close behind him, waiting their moment to strike him down without risk to their own hides.

Kane smiled bleakly and without mirth. If it was to be a test of endurance, he would see how savage thews compared with his own spring-steel resilience. Let night come and he might yet give them the slip. If not – Kane knew in his heart that the savage essence of his very being which chafed at his flight, would make him soon turn at bay, though his pursuers outnumbered him a hundred to one.

The sun sank westward. Kane was hungry, for he had not eaten since early morning when he wolfed down the last of his dried meat. An occasional spring had given him water, and once he thought he glimpsed the roof of a large hut far away through the trees. But he gave it a wide berth. It was hard to believe that this silent plateau was inhabited, but if it were, the natives were doubtless as ferocious as those hunting him. Ahead of him the land grew rougher, with broken boulders and steep slopes as he neared the lower reaches of the brooding hills. And still no sight of his hunters except for faint glimpses caught by wary backward glances – a drifting shadow, the bending of the grass, the sudden straightening of a trodden twig, a rustle of leaves. Why should they be so cautious? Why did they not close in and have it over?

Night fell and Kane reached the first long slopes which led upward to the foot of the hills which now brooded black and menacing above him. They were his goal, where he hoped to shake off his persistent foes at last, yet a nameless aversion warned him away from them. They were pregnant with hidden evil, repellent as the coil of a great sleeping serpent, glimpsed in the tall grass.

Darkness fell heavily. The stars winked redly in the thick heat of the tropic night. And Kane, halting for a moment in an unusually dense grove, beyond which the trees thinned out on the slopes, heard a stealthy movement that was not the night wind – for no breath of air stirred the heavy leaves. And even as he turned, there was a rush in the dark, under the trees.

A shadow that merged with the shadows flung itself on Kane with a bestial mouthing and a rattle of iron, and the Englishman, parrying by the gleam of the stars on the weapon, felt his assailant duck into close quarters and meet him chest to chest. Lean wiry arms locked about him, pointed teeth gnashed at him as Kane returned the fierce grapple. His tattered shirt ripped beneath a jagged edge, and by blind chance Kane found and pinioned the hand that held the iron knife, and drew his own dirk, flesh crawling in anticipation of a spear in the back.

But even as the Englishman wondered why the others did not come to their comrade's aid, he threw all of his iron muscles into the single combat. Close-clinched they swayed and writhed in the darkness, each striving to drive his blade into the other's flesh, and as the superior strength of the Puritan began to assert itself, the cannibal howled like a rabid dog, tore and bit. A convulsive spin-wheel of effort pivoted them out into the starlit glade where Kane saw the ivory nose-ring and the pointed teeth that snapped beast-like at his throat. And simultaneously he forced back and down the hand that gripped his knife-wrist, and drove the dirk deep into the black ribs. The warrior screamed, and the raw acrid scent of blood flooded the night air. And in that instant Kane was stunned by a sudden savage rush and beat of mighty wings that dashed him to earth, and the black man was torn from his grip and vanished with a scream of mortal agony. Kane leaped to his feet, shaken to his foundation. The dwindling scream of the wretched savage sounded faintly *and from above him.*

Straining his eyes into the skies he thought he caught a glimpse of a shapeless and horrific Thing crossing the dim stars – in which the writhing limbs of a human mingled namelessly with great wings and a shadowy shape – but so quickly it was gone, he could not be sure.

And now he wondered if it were not all a nightmare. But groping in the grove he found the ju-ju stave with which he had parried the short stabbing spear that lay beside it. And here, if more proof was needed, was his long dirk, still stained with blood.

Wings! Wings in the night! The skeleton in the village of torn roofs – the mutilated warrior whose wounds were not made with knife or spear and who died shrieking of wings. Surely those hills were the haunt of gigantic birds who made humanity their prey. Yet if birds, why had they not wholly devoured the torn man on the stake? And Kane knew in his heart that no true bird ever cast such a shadow as he had seen flit across the stars.

He shrugged his shoulders, bewildered. The night was silent. Where were the rest of the cannibals who had followed him from their distant jungle? Had the fate of their comrade frightened them into flight? Kane looked to his pistols. Cannibals or no, he went not up into those dark hills that night.

Now he must sleep, if all the devils of the Elder World were on his track. A deep roaring to the westward warned him that beasts of prey were aroam, and he walked rapidly down the rolling slopes until he came to a dense grove some distance from that in which he had fought the cannibal. He climbed high among the great branches until he found a thick crotch that would accommodate even his tall frame. The branches above would guard him from a sudden swoop of any winged thing, and if savages were lurking near, their clamber into the tree would warn him, for he slept lightly as a cat. As for serpents and leopards, they were chances he had taken a thousand times.

Solomon Kane slept and his dreams were vague, chaotic, haunted with a suggestion of pre-human evil and which at last merged into a vision vivid as a scene in waking life. Solomon dreamed he woke with a start, drawing a pistol – for so long had his life been that of the wolf, that reaching for a weapon was his natural reaction upon waking suddenly. His dream was that a strange, shadowy thing had perched upon a great branch close by and gazed at him with greedy, luminous yellow eyes that seared into his brain. The dream-thing was tall and lean and strangely misshapen, so blended with the shadows that it seemed a shadow itself, tangible only in the narrow yellow eyes. And Kane dreamed he waited, spellbound, while uncertainty came into those eyes and then the creature walked out on the limb as a man would walk, raised great shadowy wings, sprang into space and vanished.

Kane jerked upright, the mists of sleep fading. In the dim starlight, under the arching Gothic-like branches, the tree was empty save for himself. Then it had been a dream, after all – yet it had been so vivid, so fraught with inhuman foulness – even now a faint scent like that exuded by birds of prey seemed to linger in the air. Kane strained his ears. He heard the sighing of the night-wind, the whisper of the leaves, the far-away roaring of a lion, but naught else. Again Solomon slept – while high above him a shadow wheeled against the stars, circling again and again as a vulture circles a dying wolf.

II : THE BATTLE IN THE SKY

Dawn was spreading whitely over the eastern hills when Kane woke. The thought of his nightmare came to him and he wondered again at its vividness as he climbed down out of the tree. A nearby spring slaked his thirst and some fruit, rare in these highlands, eased his hunger.

Then he turned his face again to the hills. A finish fighter was Solomon Kane. Along that grim skyline dwelt some evil foe to the sons of men, and that mere fact was as much a challenge to the Puritan as had ever been a glove thrown in his face by some hot-headed gallant of Devon.

Refreshed by his night's sleep, he set out with his long easy stride, passing the grove that had witnessed the battle in the night, and coming into the region where the trees thinned at the foot of the slopes. Up these slopes he went, halting for a moment to gaze back over the way he had come. Now that he was above the plateau, he could easily make out a village in the distance – a cluster of mud-and-bamboo huts with one unusually large hut a short distance from me rest on a sort of low knoll.

And while he gazed, with a sudden rush of grisly wings the terror was upon him! Kane whirled, galvanized. All signs had pointed to the theory of a winged thing that hunted by night. He had not expected attack in broad daylight – but here a bat-like monster was swooping at him out of the very eye of the rising sun. Kane saw a spread of mighty wings, from which glared a horribly human face; then he drew and fired with unerring aim and the monster veered wildly in midair and came whirling and tumbling out of the sky to crash at his feet.

Kane leaned forward, pistol smoking in his hand, and gazed wide-eyed. Surely this thing was a demon out of the pits of hell, said the sombre mind of the Puritan; yet a leaden ball had slain it. Kane shrugged his shoulders, baffled; he had never seen aught to approach this, though all his life had fallen in strange ways.

The thing was like a man, inhumanly tall and inhumanly thin; the head was long, narrow, and hairless – the head of a predatory creature. The ears were small, close-set and queerly pointed. The eyes, set in death, were narrow, oblique and of a strange yellowish colour. The nose was thin and hooked, like the beak of a bird of prey, the mouth a wide cruel gash, whose thin lips, writhed in a death snarl and flecked with foam, disclosed wolfish fangs.

The creature, which was naked and hairless, was not unlike a human being in other ways. The shoulders were broad and powerful, the neck long and lean. The arms were long and muscular, the thumb being set beside the fingers after the manner of the great apes. Fingers and thumbs were armed with heavy hooked talons. The chest was curiously misshapen, the breast-bone Jutting out like the keel of a ship, the ribs curving back from it. The legs were long and wiry with huge, hand-like, prehensile feet, the great toe set opposite the rest like a man's thumb. The claws on the toes were merely long nails.

But the most curious feature of this curious creature was on its back. A pair of great wings, shaped much like the wings of a moth but with a bony frame and of leathery substance, grew from its shoulders, beginning at a point just back and above where the arms joined the shoulders, and extending half way to the narrow hips. These wings, Kane reckoned, would measure some eighteen feet from tip to tip.

He laid hold on the creature, involuntarily shuddering at the slick, hard leather-like feel of the skin, and half-lifted it. The weight was little more than half as much as it would have been in a man the same height – some six and a halt feet. Evidently the bones were of a peculiar bird-like structure and the flesh consisted almost entirely of stringy muscles.

Kane stepped back, surveying the thing again. Then his dream had been no dream after all – that foul thing or another like it had in grisly reality lighted in the tree beside him – a whir of mighty wings! A sudden rush through the sky! Even as Kane whirled he realized he had committed the jungle-farer's unpardonable crime – he had allowed his astonishment and curiosity to throw him off guard. Already a winged fiend was at his throat and there was no time to draw and fire his other pistol. Kane saw, in a maze of thrashing wings, a devilish, semi-human face – he felt those wings battering at him – he felt cruel talons sink deep into his breast; then he was dragged off his feet and felt empty space beneath him.

The winged man had wrapped his limbs about the Englishman's legs, and the talons he had driven into Kane's breast muscles held like fanged vices. The wolf-like fangs drove at Kane's throat, but the Puritan gripped the bony throat and thrust back the grisly head, while with his right hand he strove to draw his dirk. The birdman was mounting slowly and a fleeting glance showed Kane that they were already high above the trees. The Englishman did not hope to survive this battle in the sky, for even if he slew his foe, he would be dashed to death in the fall. But with the innate ferocity of the fighting man he set himself grimly to take his captor with him.

Holding those keen fangs at bay, Kane managed to draw his dirk, and he plunged it deep into the body of the monster. The bat-man veered wildly and a rasping, raucous screech burst from his half-throttled throat. He floundered wildly, beating frantically with his great wings, bowing his back and twisting his head fiercely in a vain effort to free it and sink home his deadly fangs. He sank the talons of one hand agonizingly deeper and deeper into Kane's breast muscles, while with the other he tore at his foe's head and body. But the Englishman, gashed and bleeding, with the silent and tenacious savagery of a bulldog, sank his fingers deeper into the lean neck and drove his dirk home again and again, while far below awed eyes watched the fiendish battle that was raging at that dizzy height.

They had drifted out over the plateau, and the fast-weakening wings of the bat-man barely supported their weight. They were sinking earthward swiftly, but Kane, blinded with blood and battle fury, knew nothing of this. With a great piece of his scalp hanging loose, his chest and shoulders cut and ripped, the world had become a blind, red thing in which he was aware of but one sensation – the bulldog urge to kill his foe.

Now the feeble and spasmodic beating of the dying monster's wings held them hovering for an instant above a thick grove of gigantic trees, while Kane felt the grip of claws and twining limbs grow weaker and the slashing of the talons become a futile flailing.

With a last burst of power he drove the reddened dirk straight through the breastbone and felt a convulsive tremor run through the creature's frame. The great wings fell limp – and victor and vanquished dropped headlong and plummet-like earthward.

Through a red wave Kane saw the waving branches rushing up to meet them – he felt them flail his face and tear at his clothing, as still locked in that death-clinch he rushed downward through leaves which eluded his vainly grasping hand; then his head crashed against a great limb, and an endless abyss of blackness engulfed him.

III : THE PEOPLE IN THE SHADOW

Through colossal, black basaltic corridors of night, Solomon Kane fled for a thousand years. Gigantic winged demons, horrific in the utter darkness, swept over him with a rush of great bat-like pinions and in the blackness he fought with them as a cornered rat fights a vampire bat, while fleshless jaws drooled fearful blasphemies and horrid secrets in his ears, and the skulls of men rolled under his groping feet.

Solomon Kane came back suddenly from the land of delirium and his first sight of sanity was that of a fat, kindly black face bending over him. Kane saw he was in a roomy, clean and well-ventilated hut, while from a cooking pot bubbling outside wafted savoury scents. Kane realized he was ravenously hungry. And he was strangely weak, and the hand he lifted to his bandaged head shook, and its bronze was dimmed.

The fat man and another, a tall, gaunt, grim-faced warrior, bent over him, and the fat man said: "He is awake, Kuroba, and of sound mind." The gaunt man nodded and called something which was answered from without.

"What is this place?" asked Kane in a language he had learned that was similar to the dialect just used. "How long have I lain here?"

"This is the last village of Bogonda." The fat man pressed him back with hands as gentle as a woman's. "We found you lying beneath the trees on the slopes, badly wounded and senseless. You have raved in delirium for many days. Now eat."

A lithe young warrior entered with a wooden bowl full of steaming food and Kane ate ravenously. "He is like a leopard, Kuroba," said the fat man admiringly. "Not one in a thousand would have lived with his wounds."

"Aye," returned the other. "And he slew the akaana that rent him, Goru."

Kane struggled to his elbows. "Goru?" he cried fiercely. "The priest who binds men to stakes for devils to eat?"

And he strove to rise so that he could strangle the fat man, but his weakness swept over him like a wave, the hut swam dizzily to his eyes and he sank back panting, where he soon fell into a sound, natural sleep.

Later he awoke and found a slim young girl, named Nayela, watching him. She fed him, and feeling much stronger, Kane asked questions which she answered shyly but intelligently.

This was Bogonda, ruled by Kuroba the chief and Goru the priest.

None in Bogonda had ever seen or heard of a white man before. She counted the days Kane had lain helpless, and he was amazed. But such a battle as he had been through was enough to kill an ordinary man. He wondered that no bones had been broken, but the girl said the branches had broken his fall and he had landed on the body of the akaana. He asked for Goru, and the fat priest came to him, bringing Kane's weapons.

"Some we found with you where you lay." said Goru, "some by the body of the akaana you slew with the weapon which speaks in fire and smoke. You must be a god – yet the gods bleed not and you have just all but died. Who are you?"

"I am no god," Kane answered, "but a man like yourself. I come from a far land amid the sea, which land, mind ye, is the fairest and noblest of all lands. My name is Solomon Kane and I am a landless wanderer. From the lips of a dying man I first heard your name. Yet your face seemeth kindly."

A shadow crossed the eyes of me shaman and he hung his head.

"Rest and grow strong, oh man, or god, or whatever you be," said he, "and in time you will learn of the ancient curse that rests upon this ancient land."

And in the days that followed, while Kane recovered and grew strong with the wild beast vitality that was his, Goru and Kuroba sat and spoke to him at length, telling him many curious things.

Their tribe was not aboriginal here, but had come upon the plateau a hundred and fifty years before, giving it the name of their former home. They had once been a powerful tribe in Old Bogonda, on a great river far to the south. But tribal wars broke their power, and at last before a concerted uprising, the whole tribe gave way, and Goru repeated legends of that great flight of a thousand miles through jungle and swampland, harried at every step by cruel foes.

At last, hacking their way through a country of ferocious cannibals, they found themselves safe from man's attack – but prisoners in a trap from which neither they nor their descendants could ever escape. They were in the horror-country of Akaana, and Goru said his ancestors came to understand the jeering laughter of the man-eaters who had hounded them to the very borders of the plateau.

The Bogondi found a fertile country with good water and plenty of game. There were numbers of goats and a species of wild pig that throve here in great abundance. At first the people ate these pigs, but later they spared them for a good reason. The grasslands between plateau and jungle swarmed with antelopes, buffaloes and the like, and there were many lions. Lions also roamed the plateau, but Bogonda meant "Lion-slayer" in their tongue and it was not many moons before the remnants of the great cats took to the lower levels. But it was not lions they had to fear, as Goru's ancestors soon learned.

Finding that the cannibals would not come past the savannas, they rested from their long trek and built two villages – Upper and Lower Bogonda. Kane was in Upper Bogonda; he had seen the ruins of the lower village. But soon they found that they had strayed into a country of nightmares with dripping fangs and talons. They heard the beat of mighty wings at night, and saw horrific shadows cross the stars and loom against the moon. Children began to disappear and at last a young hunter strayed off into the hills, where night overtook him. And in the grey light of dawn a mangled, half-devoured corpse fell from the skies into the village street and a whisper of ogreish laughter from high above froze the horrified on-lookers. Then a little later the full horror of their position burst upon the Bogondi.

At first the winged men were afraid of the newcomers. They hid themselves and ventured from their caverns only at night. Then they grew bolder. In the full daylight, a warrior shot one with an arrow, but the fiends had learned they could slay a human, and its death scream brought a score of the devils dropping from the skies, who tore the slayer to pieces in full sight of the tribe.

The Bogondi then prepared to leave that devil's country and a hundred warriors went up into the hills to find a pass. They found steep walls, up which a man must climb laboriously, and they found the cliffs honeycombed with caves where the winged men dwelt.

Then was fought the first pitched battle between men and bat-men, and it resulted in a crushing victory for the monsters. The bows and spears of the natives proved futile before the swoops of the taloned fiends, and of all that hundred that went up into the hills, not one survived; for the akaanas hunted down those that fled and dragged down the last one within bowshot of the upper village.

Then it was that the Bogondi, seeing they could not hope to win through the hills, sought to fight their way out again the way they had come. But a great horde of cannibals met them in the grasslands, and in a great battle that lasted nearly all day, hurled them back, broken and defeated. And Goru said while the battle raged, the skies were thronged with hideous shapes, circling above and laughing their fearful mirth to see men die wholesale.

So the survivors of those two battles, licking their wounds, bowed to the inevitable with the fatalistic philosophy of the savage. Some fifteen hundred men, women and children remained, and they built their huts, tilled the soil and lived stolidly in the shadow of the nightmare.

In those days there were many of the bird-people, and they might have wiped out the Bogondi utterly, had they wished. No one warrior could cope with an akaana, for he was stronger than a human, he struck as a hawk strikes, and if he missed, his wings carried him out of reach of a counterblow.

Here Kane interrupted to ask why the Bogondi did not make war on the demons with arrows. But Goru answered that it took a quick and accurate archer to strike an akaana in midair at all, and so tough were their hides that unless the arrow struck squarely it would not penetrate. Kane knew that the natives were very indifferent bowmen and that they pointed their shafts with chipped stone, bone, or hammered iron almost as soft as copper; he thought of Poitiers and Agincourt and wished grimly for a file of stout English archers – or a rank of musketeers.

But Goru said the akaanas did not seem to wish to destroy the Bogondi utterly. Their chief food consisted of the little pigs which then swarmed the plateau, and young goats. Sometimes they went out on the savannas for antelope, but they distrusted the open country and feared the lions. Nor did they haunt the jungles beyond, for the trees grew too close for the spread of their wings. They kept to the hills and the plateau – and what lay beyond those hills none in Bogonda knew.

The akaanas allowed the Bogondi to inhabit the plateau much as men allow wild animals to thrive, or stock lakes with fish – for their own pleasure. The bat-people, said Goru, had a strange and grisly sense of humour which was tickled by the sufferings of a howling human. Those grim hills had echoed to cries that turned men's hearts to ice.

But for many years, Goru said, once the Bogondi learned not to resist their masters, the akaanas were content to snatch up a baby from time to time, or devour a young girl strayed from the village or a youth whom night caught outside the walls. The bat-folk distrusted the village; they circled high above it but did not venture within. There the Bogondi were safe until late years.

Goru said that the akaanas were fast dying out; once there had been hope that the remnants of his race would outlast them – in which event, he said fatalistically, the cannibals would undoubtedly come up from the jungle and put the survivors in their cooking pots. Now he doubted if there were more than a hundred and fifty akaanas altogether. Kane asked him why did not the warriors then sally forth on a great hunt and destroy the devils utterly, and Goru smiled a bitter smile and repeated his remarks about the prowess of the bat-people in battle. Moreover, said he, the whole tribe of Bogonda numbered only about four hundred souls now, and the bat-people were their only protection against the cannibals to the west.

Goru said the tribe had thinned more in the past thirty years than in all the years previous. As the numbers of the akaanas dwindled, their hellish savagery increased. They seized more and more of the Bogondi to torture and devour in their grim black caves high up in the hills, and Goru spoke of sudden raids on hunting parties and toilers in the plantain fields, and of the nights made ghastly by horrible screams and gibberings from the dark hills, and blood-freezing laughter that was half-human; of dismembered limbs and gory grinning heads flung from the skies to fall in the shuddering village, and of grisly feasts among the stars.

Then came drouth, Goru said, and a great famine. Many of the springs dried up and the crops of rice and yams and plantains failed. The gnus, deer, and buffaloes which had formed the main part of Bogonda's meat diet withdrew to the jungle in quest of water, and the lions, their hunger overcoming their fear of man, ranged into the uplands. Many of the tribe died, and the rest were driven by hunger to eat the pigs which were the natural prey of the bat-people. This angered the akaanas and thinned the pigs. Famine, Bogondi, and the lions destroyed all the goats and half the pigs.

At last the famine was past, but the damage was done. Of all the great droves which once swarmed the plateau, only a remnant was left, and these were hard to catch. The Bogondi had eaten the pigs, so the akaanas ate the Bogondi. Life became a hell for the humans, and the lower village, numbering now only some hundred and fifty souls, rose in revolt. Driven to frenzy by repeated outrages, they turned on their masters. An akaana lighting in the .very streets to steal a child was set on and shot to death with arrows. And the people of Lower Bogonda drew into their huts and waited for their doom.

And in the night, said Goru, it came. The akaanas had overcome their distrust of the huts. The full flock of them swarmed down from the hills, and Upper Bogonda awoke to hear the fearful cataclysm of screams and blasphemies that marked the end of the other village. All night Goru's people had lain sweating in terror, not daring to move, harkening to the howling and gibbering that rent the night. At last these sounds ceased, Goru said, wiping the cold sweat from his brow, but sounds of grisly and obscene feasting still haunted the night with demon's mockery.

In the early dawn Goru's people saw the hell-flock winging back to their hills, like demons flying back to hell through the dawn. They flew slowly and heavily, like gorged vultures. Later the people dared to steal down to the accursed village, and what they found there sent them shrieking away; and to that day, Goru said, no man passed within three bow shots of that silent horror. And Kane nodded in understanding, his cold eyes more sombre man ever.

For many days after that, Goru said, the people waited in quaking fear. Finally in desperation of fear, which breeds unspeakable cruelty, the tribe cast lots and the loser was bound to a stake between the two villages, in hopes that the akaanas would recognize this as a token of submission so that the people of Bogonda might escape the fate of their kinsmen. The custom, said Goru, had been borrowed from the cannibals who in old times worshipped the akaanas and offered a human sacrifice at each moon. But chance had shown them that the akaanas could be killed, so they ceased to worship them – at least that was Goru's deduction, and he explained at much length that no mortal thing is worthy of real adoration, however evil or powerful it may be.

His own ancestors had made occasional sacrifices to placate the winged devils, but until lately it had not been a regular custom. Now it was necessary; the akaanas expected it, and each moon they chose from their waning numbers a strong young man or a girl whom they bound to the stake.

Kane watched Goru's face closely as he spoke of his sorrow for this unspeakable necessity, and the Englishman realized that the priest was sincere. Kane shuddered at the thought of a tribe of human beings thus passing slowly but surely into the maws of a race of monsters.

Kane spoke of the wretch he had seen, and Goru nodded, pain in his soft eyes. For a day and a night he had been hanging there, while the akaanas glutted their vile torture-lust on his quivering, agonized flesh. Thus far the sacrifices had kept doom from the village. The remaining pigs furnished sustenance for the dwindling akaanas, together with an occasional baby snatched up, and they were content to have their nameless sport with the single victim each moon.

A thought came to Kane. "The cannibals never come up into the plateau?"

Goru shook his head; safe in their jungle, they never raided past the savannas.

"But they hunted me to the very foot of the hills."

Again Goru shook his head. There was only one cannibal; they had found his footprints. Evidently a single warrior, bolder than the rest, had allowed his passion for the chase to overcome his fear of the grisly plateau and had paid the penalty. Kane's teeth came together with a vicious snap which ordinarily took the place of profanity with him. He was stung by the thought of fleeing so long from a single enemy. No wonder that enemy had followed so cautiously, waiting until dark to attack. But, asked Kane, why had the akaana seized the cannibal instead of himself – and why had be not been attacked by the bat-man who alighted in his tree that night?

The cannibal was bleeding, Goru answered. The scent called the bat-fiend to attack, for they scented raw blood as far as vultures. And they were very wary. They had never seen a man like Kane, who showed no fear. Surely they had decided to spy on him, take him off guard before they struck.

Who were these creatures? Kane asked. Goru shrugged his shoulders. They were there when his ancestors came, who had never heard of them before they saw them. There was no intercourse with the cannibals, so they could learn nothing from them. The akaanas lived in caves, naked like beasts; they knew nothing of fire and ate only fresh, raw meat. But they had a language of a sort and acknowledged a king among them. Many died in the great famine when the stronger ate the weaker. They were vanishing swiftly; of late years no females or young had been observed among them. When these males died at last, there would be no more akaanas; but Bogonda, observed Goru, was doomed already, unless – he looked strangely and wistfully at Kane. But the Puritan was deep in thought.

Among the swarm of native legends he had heard on his wanderings, one now stood out. Long, long ago, an old, old ju-ju man had told him, winged devils came flying out of the north and passed over his country, vanishing in the maze of the jungle-haunted south. And the ju-ju man related an old, old legend concerning these creatures – that once they had abode in myriad numbers far on a great lake of bitter water many moons to the north, and ages and ages ago a chieftain and his warriors fought them with bows and arrows and slew many, driving the rest into the south. The name of the chief was N'Yasunna and he owned a great war canoe with many oars driving it swiftly through the bitter water.

And now a cold wind blew suddenly on Solomon Kane, as if from a door opened suddenly on Outer gulfs of Time and Space. For now he realized the truth of that garbled myth, and the truth of an older, grimmer legend. For what was the great bitter lake but the Mediterranean Ocean and who was the chief N'Yasunna but the hero Jason, who conquered the harpies and drove them

– not alone into the Strophades Isles but into Africa as well? The old pagan tale was true then, Kane thought dizzily, shrinking aghast from the strange realm: of grisly possibilities this opened up. For if this myth of the harpies were a reality, what of the other legends – the Hydra, the centaurs, the chimera, Medusa, Pan, and the satyrs? All those myths of antiquity – behind them did there lie and lurk nightmare realities with slavering fangs and talons steeped in shuddersome evil? Africa, the Dark Continent, land of shadows and horror, of bewitchment and sorcery, into which all evil things had been banished before the growing light of the western world!

Kane came out of his reveries with a start. Goru was tugging gently and timidly at his sleeve.

"Save us from the akaanas!" said Goru. "If you be not a god, there is the power of a god in you! You bear in your hand the mighty ju-ju stave which has in times gone by been the sceptre of fallen empires and the staff of mighty priests. And you have weapons which speak death in fire and smoke – for our young men watched and saw you slay two akaanas. We will make you king – god – what you will! More than a moon has passed since you came into Bogonda and the time for the sacrifice is gone by, but the bloody stake stands bare. The akaanas shun the village where you lie; they steal no more babes from us. We have thrown off their yoke because our trust is in you!"

Kane clasped his temples with his hands. "You know not what you ask!" he cried. "God knoweth it is in my deepest heart to rid the land of this evil, but I am no god. With my pistols I can slay a few of the fiends, but I have but a little powder left. Had I great store of powder and ball, and the musket I shattered in the vampire-haunted Hills of the Dead, then indeed would there be a rare hunting. But even if I slew all those fiends, what of the cannibals?"

"They too will fear you!" cried old Kuroba, while the girl Nayela and the lad, Loga, who was to have been the next sacrifice, gazed at him with their souls in their eyes. Kane dropped his chin on his fist and sighed.

"Yet will I stay here in Bogonda all the rest of my life if ye think I be protection to the people."

So Solomon Kane stayed at the village of Bogonda of the Shadow. The people were a kindly folk, whose natural sprightliness and fun-loving spirits were subdued and saddened by long dwelling in the Shadow. But now they had taken new heart by the Englishman's coming, and it wrenched Kane's heart to note the pathetic trust they placed in him. Now they sang in the plantain fields and danced about the fire, and gazed at him with adoring faith in their eyes. But Kane, cursing his own helplessness, knew how futile would be his fancied protection if the winged fiends swept suddenly out of the skies.

But he stayed in Bogonda. In his dreams the gulls wheeled above the cliffs of old Devon carved in the clean, blue, wind-whipped skies, and in the day the call of the unknown lands beyond Bogonda clawed at his heart with fierce yearning. But he abode in Bogonda and racked his brains for a plan. He sat and gazed for hours at the ju-ju stave, hoping in desperation that black magic would aid him, where his mind failed. But N'Longa's ancient gift gave him no aid.

Once he had summoned the Slave Coast shaman to him across leagues of intervening space – but it was only when confronted with supernatural manifestations that N'Longa could come to him, and these harpies were not supernatural.

The germ of an idea began to grow at the back of Kane's mind, but he discarded it. It had to do with a great trap – and how could the akaanas be trapped? The roaring of lions played a grim accompaniment to his brooding meditations. As man dwindled on the plateau, the hunting beasts who feared only the spears of the hunters were beginning to gather. Kane laughed bitterly. It was not lions, that might be hunted down and slain singly, that he had to deal with.

At some little distance from the village stood the great hut of Goru, once a council hall. This hut was full of many strange fetishes, which Goru said with a helpless wave of his fat hands, were strong magic against evil spirits but scant protection against winged hellions of gristle and bone and flesh.

IV : THE MADNESS OF SOLOMON

Kane woke suddenly from a dreamless sleep. A hideous medley of screams burst horrific in his ears. Outside his hut, people were dying in the night, horribly, as cattle die in the shambles. He had slept, as always, with his weapons buckled on him. Now he bounded to the door, and something fell mouthing and slavering at his feet to grasp his knees in a convulsive grin and gibber incoherent pleas.

In the faint light of a smoldering fire near by, Kane in horror recognized the face of the youth Loga, now frightfully torn and drenched in blood, already freezing into a death mask. The night was full of fearful sounds, inhuman howling mingled with the whisper of mighty wings, the tearing of thatch and a ghastly demon-laughter. Kane freed himself from the locked dead arms and sprang to the dying fire. He could make out only a confused and vague maze of fleeing forms and darting shapes, the shift and blur of dark wings against the stars.

He snatched up a brand and thrust it against the thatch of his hut – and as the flame leaped up and showed him the scene he stood frozen and aghast. Red, howling doom had fallen on Bogonda. Winged monsters raced screaming through her streets, wheeled above the heads of the fleeing people, or tore apart the hut thatches to get at the gibbering victims within.

With a choked cry the Englishman woke from his trance of horror, drew and fired at a darting flame-eyed shadow which fell at his feet with a shattered skull. And Kane gave tongue to one deep, fierce roar and bounded into the melee, all the berserk fury of his heathen Saxon ancestors bursting into terrible being.

Dazed and bewildered by the sudden attack, cowed by long years of submission, the Bogondi were incapable of combined resistance and for the most part died like sheep. Some, maddened by desperation, fought back, but their arrows went wild or glanced from the tough wings while the devilish agility of the creatures made spear thrust and axe stroke uncertain. Leaping from the ground they avoided the blows of their victims and, sweeping down upon their shoulders, dashed them to earth where fang and talon did their crimson work.

Kane saw old Kuroba, gaunt and bloodstained, at bay against a hut wall with his foot on the neck of a monster who had not been quick enough. The grim-faced old chief wielded a two-handed axe in great sweeping blows that for the moment held back the screeching onset of half a dozen of the devils. Kane was leaping to his aid when a low, pitiful whimper checked him. The girl Nayela writhed weakly, prone in the bloody dust, while on her back a vulture-like thing crouched and tore. Her dulling eyes sought the face of the Englishman in anguished appeal. Kane ripped out a bitter oath and fired point blank. The winged devil pitched backward with an abhorrent screeching and a wild flutter of dying wings, and Kane bent to the dying girl. She whimpered and kissed his hands with uncertain lips as he cradled her head in his arms. Her eyes set.

Kane laid the body gently down, looking for Kuroba. He saw only a huddled cluster of grisly shapes that sucked and tore at something between them. And Kane went mad. With a scream that cut through the inferno he bounded up, slaying even as he rose. Even in the act of lunging up from bent knee he drew and thrust, transfixing a vulture-like throat. Then whipping out his rapier as the thing floundered and twitched in its death struggle, the raging Puritan charged forward seeking new victims.

On all sides of him the people of Bogonda were dying hideously. They fought futilely or they fled and the demons coursed them down as a hawk courses a hare. They ran into the huts and the fiends rent the thatch or burst the door, and what took place in those huts was mercifully hidden from Kane's eyes. And to the frantic Puritan's horror-distorted brain it seemed that he alone was responsible. The Bogondi had trusted him to save them. They had withheld the sacrifice and defied their grim masters. Now they were paying the horrible penalty and he was unable to save them. In the agony-dimmed eyes turned toward him, Kane quaffed the black dregs of the bitter cup. It was not anger or the vindictiveness of fear. It was hurt and a stunned reproach. He was their god and he had failed them.

Now he ravened through the massacre and the fiends avoided him, turning to the easy victims. But Kane was not to be denied. In a red haze that was not of the burning hut, he saw a culminating horror; a harpy gripped a writhing naked thing that had been a woman, and the wolfish fangs gorged deep. As Kane sprang, thrusting, the bat-man dropped his yammering, mowing prey and soared aloft. But Kane dropped his rapier and with the bound of a blood-mad panther caught the demon's throat and locked his iron legs about its lower body.

Once again he found himself battling in mid-air, but this time close above the hut roofs. Terror had entered the cold brain of the harpy. He did not fight to hold and slay; he wished only to be rid of this silent, clinging thing that stabbed so savagely for his life. He floundered wildly, screaming abhorrently and thrashing with his wings, then as Kane's dirk bit deeper, dipped suddenly sidewise and fell headlong.

The thatch of a hut broke their fall, and Kane and the dying harpy crashed through to land on a writhing mass on the hut floor. In the lurid flickering of the burning hut outside that vaguely lighted the hut into which he had fallen, Kane saw a deed of brain-shaking horror being enacted – red-dripping fangs in a yawning gash of a mouth, and a crimson travesty of a human form that still writhed with agonized life. Then, in the maze of madness that held him, his steel fingers closed on the fiend's throat in a grip that no tearing of talons or hammering of wings could loosen, until he felt the horrid life flow out from under his fingers and the bony neck hung broken.

Outside, the red madness of slaughter continued. Kane bounded up, his hand closing blindly on the haft of some weapon, and as he leaped from the hut a harpy soared from under his very feet. It was an axe that Kane had snatched up, and he dealt a stroke that spattered the demon's brains like water. He sprang forward, stumbling over bodies and parts of bodies, blood streaming from a dozen wounds, and then halted baffled and screaming with rage.

The bat-people were taking to the air. No longer would they face this strange madman who in his insanity was more terrible than they. But they went not alone into the upper regions. In their lustful talons they bore writhing, screaming forms, and Kane, raging to and fro with his dripping axe, found himself alone in a corpse-choked village.

He threw back his head to shriek his hate at the fiends above him and he felt warm, thick drops fall into his face, while the shadowy skies were filled with screams of agony and the laughter of monsters. And Kane's last vestige of reason snapped as the sounds of that ghastly feast in the skies filled the night and the blood that rained from the stars fell into his face. He gibbered to and fro, screaming chaotic blasphemies.

And was he not a symbol of Man, staggering among the tooth-marked bones and severed grinning heads of humans, brandishing a futile axe, and screaming incoherent hate at the grisly, winged shapes of Night that make him their prey, chuckling in demoniac triumph above him and dripping into his mad eyes the pitiful blood of their human victims?

V : THE WHITE-SKINNED CONQUEROR

A shuddering, white-faced dawn crept over the black hills to shiver above the red shambles that had been the village of Bogonda. The huts stood intact, except for the one which had sunk to smoldering coals, but the thatches of many were torn. Dismembered bones, half or wholly stripped of flesh, lay in the streets, and some were splintered as though they had been dropped from a great height.

It was a realm of the dead where was but one sign of life. Solomon Kane leaned on his blood-clotted axe and gazed upon the scene with dull, mad eyes. He was grimed and clotted with half-dried blood from long gashes on chest, face, and shoulders, but he paid no need to his hurts.

The people of Bogonda had not died alone. Seventeen harpies lay among the bones. Six of these Kane had slain. The rest had fallen before the frantic dying desperation of the Bogondi. But it was poor toll to take in return. Of the four hundred odd people of Upper Bogonda, not one had lived to see the dawn. And the harpies were gone – back to their caves in the black hills, gorged to repletion.

With slow, mechanical steps Kane went about gathering up his weapons. He found his sword, dirk, pistols, and the ju-ju stave. He left the main village and went up the slope to the great hut of Goru. And there he halted, stung by a new horror. The ghastly humor of the harpies had prompted a delicious jest. Above the hut door stared the severed head of Goru. The fat cheeks were shrunken, the lips lolled in an aspect of horrified idiocy, and the eyes stared like a hurt child. And in those dead eyes Kane saw wonder and reproach.

Kane looked at the shambles that had been Bogonda, and he looked at the death mask of Goru. And he lifted his clenched fists above his head, and with glaring eyes raised and writhing lips flecked with froth, he cursed the sky and the earth and the spheres above and below. He cursed the cold stars, the blazing sun, the mocking moon, and the whisper of the wind. He cursed all fates and destinies, all that he had loved or hated, the silent cities beneath the seas, the past ages and the future eons. In one soul-shaking burst of blasphemy he cursed the gods and devils who make mankind their sport, and he cursed Man who lives blindly on and blindly offers his back to the iron-hoofed feet of his gods.

Then as breath failed he halted, panting. From the lower reaches sounded the deep roaring of a lion and into the eyes of Solomon Kane came a crafty gleam. He stood long, as one frozen, and out of his madness grew a desperate plan. And he silently recanted his blasphemy, for if the brazen-hoofed gods made Man for their sport and play-thing, they also gave him a brain that holds craft and cruelty greater than any other living thing.

"There you shall bide," said Solomon Kane to the head of Goru. "The sun will wither you and the cold dews of night will shrivel you. But I will keep the kites from you and your eyes shall see the fall of your slayers. Aye, I could not save the people of Bogonda, but by the God of my race, I can avenge them. Man is the sport and sustenance of titanic beings of Night and Horror whose giant wings hover ever above him. But even evil things may come to an end –and watch ye, Goru."

In the days that followed Kane labored mightily, beginning with the first grey light of dawn and toiling on past sunset, into the white moonlight till he fell and slept the sleep of utter exhaustion. He snatched food as he worked and he gave his wounds absolutely no heed, scarcely being aware that they healed of themselves. He went down into the lower levels and cut bamboo, great stacks of long, tough stalks. He cut thick branches of trees, and tough vines to serve as ropes.

With this material he reinforced the walls and roof of Goru's hut. He set the bamboos deep in the earth, hard against the wall, and interwove and twined them, binding them fast with the vines that were pliant and tough as cords. The long branches he made fast along the thatch, binding them close together. When he had finished, an elephant could scarcely have burst through the walls.

The lions had come into the plateau in great numbers and the herds of little pigs dwindled fast. Those the lions spared, Kane slew, and tossed to the jackals. This racked Kane's heart, for he was a kindly man and this wholesale slaughter, even of pigs who would fall prey to hunting beasts anyhow, grieved him. But it was part of his plan of vengeance, and he steeled his heart.

The days stretched into weeks. Kane toiled by day and by night, and between his stints he talked to the shrivelled, mummied head of Goru, whose eyes, strangely enough, did not change in the blaze of the sun or the haunt of the moon, but retained their life-like expression. When the memory of those lunacy-haunted days had become only a vague nightmare, Kane wondered if, as it had seemed to him, Goru's dried lips had moved in answer, speaking strange and mysterious things.

Kane saw the akaanas wheeling against the sky at a distance, but they did not come near, even when he slept in the great hut, pistols at hand. They feared his power to deal death with smoke and thunder. At first he noted that they flew sluggishly, gorged with the flesh they had eaten on that red night, and the bodies they had borne to their caves. But as the weeks passed they appeared leaner and leaner and ranged far afield in search of food. And Kane laughed, deeply and madly. This plan of his would never have worked before, but now there were no humans to fill the bellies of the harpy-folk. And there were no more pigs. In all the plateau there were no creatures for the bat-people to eat. Why they did not range east of the hills, Kane thought he knew. That must be a region of thick jungle like the country to the west. He saw them fly into the grassland for antelopes and he saw the lions take toll of them. After all, the akaanas were weak beings among the hunters, strong enough only to slay pigs and deer – and humans.

At last they began to soar close to him at night, and he saw their greedy eyes glaring at him through the gloom. He judged the time was ripe. Huge buffaloes, too big and ferocious for the bat-people to slay, had strayed up into the plateau to ravage the deserted fields of the dead Bogondi. Kane cut one of these out of the herd and drove him, with shouts and volleys of stones, to the hut of Goru. It was a tedious, dangerous task, and time and again Kane barely escaped the surly bull's sudden charges, but persevered and at last shot the beast before the hut.

A strong west wind was blowing and Kane flung handfuls of blood into the air for the scent to waft to the harpies in the hills. He cut the bull to pieces and carried its quarters into the hut, then managed to drag the huge trunk itself inside. Then he retired into the thick trees nearby and waited.

He had not long to wait. The morning air filled suddenly with the beat of many wings, and a hideous flock alighted before the hut of Goru. All of the beasts – or men – seemed to be there, and Kane gazed in wonder at the tall, strange creatures, so like to humanity and yet so unlike – the veritable demons of priestly legend. They folded their wings like cloaks about them as they walked upright, and they talked to one another in a strident, crackling voice that had nothing of the human in it. No, Kane decided, these things were not men. They were the materialization of some ghastly jest of Nature – some travesty of the world's infancy when Creation was an experiment. Perhaps they were the offspring of a forbidden and obscene mating of man and beast; more likely they were a freakish offshoot on the branch of evolution – for Kane had long ago dimly sensed a truth in the heretical theories of the ancient philosophers, that Man is but a higher beast. And if Nature made many strange beasts in the past ages, why should she not have experimented with monstrous forms of mankind? Surely Man as Kane knew him was not the first of his breed to walk the earth, nor yet to be the last.

Now the harpies hesitated, with their natural distrust for a building, and some soared to the roof and tore at the thatch. But Kane had builded well. They returned to earth and at last, driven beyond endurance by the smell of raw blood and the sight of the flesh within, one of them ventured inside. In an instant all were crowded into the great hut, tearing ravenously at the meat, and when the last one was within, Kane reached out a hand and jerked a long vine which tripped the catch that held the door he had built. It fell with a crash, and the bar he had fashioned dropped into place. That door would hold against the charge of a wild bull.

Kane came from his cover and scanned the sky. Some hundred and forty harpies had entered the hut. He saw no more winging through the skies and believed it safe to suppose he had the whole flock trapped. Then with a cruel, brooding smile, Kane struck flint and steel to a pile of dead leaves next the wall. Within sounded an uneasy mumbling as the creatures realized that they were prisoners. A thin wisp of smoke curled upward and a flicker of red followed it; the whole heap burst into flame and the dry bamboo caught.

A few moments later the whole side of the wall was ablaze. The fiends inside scented the smoke and grew restless. Kane heard them cackling wildly and clawing at the walls. He grinned savagely, bleakly and without mirth. Now a veer of the wind drove the flames around the wall and up over the thatch – with a roar the whole hut caught and leaped into flame.

From within sounded a fearful pandemonium. Kane heard bodies crash against the walls, which shook to the impact but held. The horrid screams were music to his soul, and brandishing his arms, he answered them with screams of fearful, soul-shaking laughter. The cataclysm of horror rose unbearably, paling the tumult of the flames. Then it dwindled to a medley of strangled gibbering and gasps as the flames ate in and the smoke thickened. An intolerable scent of burning flesh pervaded the atmosphere, and had there been room in Kane's brain for aught else than insane triumph, he would have shuddered to realize that the scent was of that nauseating and indescribable odour that only human flesh emits when burning.

From the thick cloud of smoke, Kane saw a mowing, gibbering thing emerge through the shredding roof and flap slowly and agonizingly upward on fearfully burned wings. Calmly he aimed and fired, and the scorched and blinded thing tumbled back into the flaming mass just as the walls crashed in. To Kane it seemed that Goru's crumbling face, vanishing in the smoke, split suddenly in a wide grin and a sudden shout of exultant human laughter mingled eerily in the roar of the flames. But the smoke and insane brain plays queer tricks.

Kane stood with the ju-ju stave in one hand the smoking pistol in the other, above the smoldering ruins that hid forever from the sight of man the last of those terrible, semi-human monsters whom another white-skinned hero had banished from Europe in an unknown age. Kane stood, an unconscious statue of triumph – the ancient empires fall, the dark-skinned peoples fade and even the demons of antiquity gasp their last, but over all stands the Aryan barbarian, white-skinned, cold-eyed, dominant, the supreme fighting man of the earth, whether he be clad in wolf-hide and horned helmet, or boots and doublet – whether he bear in his hand battle-axe or rapier – whether he be called Dorian, Saxon, or Englishman – whether his name be Jason, Hengist – or Solomon Kane.

Kane stood and the smoke curled upward into the morning sky, the roaring of foraging lions shook the plateau, and slowly, like light breaking through mists, sanity returned to him.

"The light of God's morning enters even into dark and lonesome lands," said Solomon Kane sombrely. "Evil rules in the waste lands of the earth, but even evil may come to an end. Dawn follows midnight and even in this lost land the shadows shrink. Strange are Thy ways, oh God of my people, and who am I to question Thy wisdom? My feet have fallen in evil ways but Thou hast brought me forth scatheless and hast made me a scourge for the Powers of Evil. Over the souls of men spread the condor wings of colossal monsters and all manner of evil things prey upon the heart and soul and body of Man. Yet it may be in some far day the shadows shall fade and the Prince of Darkness be chained forever in his hell. And till then mankind can but stand up stoutly to the monsters in his own heart and without, and with the aid of God he may yet triumph."

And Solomon Kane looked up into the silent hills and felt the silent call of the hills and the unguessed distances beyond; and Solomon Kane shifted his belt, took his staff firmly in his hand and turned his face eastward.

THE BLACK STONE

"They say foul beings of Old Times still lurk
In dark forgotten corners of the world,
And Gates still gape to loose, on certain nights,
Shapes pent in Hell."
–JUSTIN GEOFFREY

I read of it first in the strange book of Von Junzt, the German eccentric who lived so curiously and died in such grisly and mysterious fashion. It was my fortune to have access to his *Nameless Cults* in the original edition, the so-called Black Book, published in Düsseldorf in 1839, shortly before a hounding doom overtook the author. Collectors of rare literature are familiar with *Nameless Cults* mainly through the cheap and faulty translation which was pirated in London by Bridewall in 1845. and the carefully expurgated edition put out by the Golden Goblin Press of New York in 1909. But the volume I stumbled upon was one of the unexpurgated German copies, with heavy leather covers and rusty iron hasps. I doubt if there are more than half a dozen such volumes in the entire world today, for the quantity issued was not great, and when the manner of the author's demise was bruited about, many possessors of the book burned their volumes in panic.

Von Junzt spent his entire life (1795-1840) delving into forbidden subjects; he travelled in all parts of the world, gained entrance into innumerable secret societies, and read countless little-known esoteric books and manuscripts in the original; and in, the chapters of the Black Book, which range from startling clarity of exposition to murky ambiguity, there are statements and hints to freeze the blood of a thinking man. Reading what Von Junzt dared put in print arouses uneasy speculations as to what it was that he dared not tell. What dark matters, for instance, were contained in those closely written pages that formed the unpublished manuscript on which he worked unceasingly for months before his death, and which lay torn and scattered all over the floor of the locked and bolted chamber in which Von Junzt was found dead with the marks of taloned fingers on his throat? It will never be known, for the author's closest friend, the Frenchman Alexis Ladeau, after having spent a whole night piecing the fragments together and reading what was written, burnt them to ashes and cut his own throat with a razor.

But the contents of the published matter are shuddersome enough, even if one accepts the general view that they but represent the ravings of a madman. There among many strange things I found mention of the Black Stone, that curious, sinister monolith that broods among the mountains of Hungary, and about which so many dark legends cluster. Von Junzt did not devote much space to it – the bulk of his grim work concerns cults and objects of dark worship which he maintained existed in his day, and it would seem that the Black Stone represents some order or being lost and forgotten centuries ago. But he spoke of it as one of the *keys* – a phrase used many times by him, in various relations, and constituting one of the obscurities of his work. And he hinted briefly at curious sights to be seen about the monolith on Midsummer's Night. He mentioned Otto Dostmann's theory that this monolith was a remnant of the Hunnish invasion and had been erected to commemorate a victory of Attila over the Goths. Von Junzt contradicted this assertion without giving any refutatory facts, merely remarking that to attribute the origin of the Black Stone to the Huns was as logical as assuming that William the Conqueror reared Stonehenge.

This implication of enormous antiquity piqued my interest immensely and after some difficulty I succeeded in locating a rat-eaten and moldering copy of Dostmann's *Remnant Of Lost Empires* (Berlin, 1809, 'Das Drachenhaus' Press). I was disappointed to find that Dostmann referred to the Black Stone even more briefly than had Von Junzt, dismissing it with a few lines as an artifact comparatively modern in contrast with the Greco-Roman ruins of Asia Minor which were his pet theme. He admitted his inability to make out the defaced characters on the monolith but pronounced them unmistakably Mongoloid. However, little as I learned from Dostmann, he did mention the name of the village adjacent to the Black Stone – Stregoicavar – an ominous name, meaning something like Witch-Town.

A close scrutiny of guide-books and travel articles gave me no further information – Stregoicavar, not on any map that I could find, lay in a wild, little-frequented region, out of the path of casual tourists. But I did find subject for thought in Dornly's *Magyar Folklore*. In his chapter on *Dream Myths* he mentions the Black Stone and tells of some curious superstitions regarding it – especially the belief that if any one sleeps in the vicinity of the monolith, that person will he haunted by monstrous nightmares for ever after and he cited tales of the peasants regarding too-curious people who ventured to visit the Stone on Midsummer's Night and who died raving mad because of something they saw there.

That was all I could glean from Dornly, but my interest was even more intensely roused as I sensed a distinctly sinister aura about the Stone. The suggestion of dark antiquity, the recurrent hint of unnatural events on Midsummer's Night, touched some slumbering instinct in my being, as one senses, rather than hears, the flowing of some dark subterraneous river in the night.

And I suddenly saw a connection between this stone and a certain weird and fantastic poem written by the mad poet, Justin Geoffrey: *The People of the Monolith*. Inquiries led to the information that Geoffrey had indeed written that poem while travelling in Hungary, and I could not doubt that the Black Stone was the very monolith to which he referred in his strange verse. Reading his stanzas again, I felt once more the strange dim stirrings of subconscious promptings that I had noticed when first reading of the Stone.

I had been casting about for a place to spend a short vacation and I made up my mind. I went to Stregoicavar. A train of obsolete style carried me from Temesvar to within striking distance, at least, of my objective, and a three days' ride in a jouncing coach brought me to the little village which lay in a fertile valley high up in the fir-clad mountains. The journey itself was uneventful, but during the first day we passed the old battlefield of Schomvaal where the brave Polish-Hungarian knight, Count Boris Vladinoff, made his gallant and futile stand against the victorious hosts of Suleiman the Magnificent, when the Grand Turk swept over eastern Europe in 1526.

The driver of the coach pointed out to me a great heap of crumbling stones on a hill near by, under which, he said, the bones of the brave Count lay. I remembered a passage from Larson's *Turkish Wars*: 'After the skirmish' (in which the Count with his small army had beaten back the Turkish advance-guard) 'the Count was standing beneath the half-ruined walls of the old castle on the hill, giving orders as to the disposition of his forces, when an aide brought to him a small lacquered case which had been taken from the body of the famous Turkish scribe and historian, Selim Bahadur, who had fallen in the fight. The Count took therefrom a roll of parchment and began to read, but he had not read far before he turned very pale and without saying a word, replaced the parchment in the case and thrust the case into his cloak. At that very instant a hidden Turkish battery suddenly opened fire, and the balls striking the old castle, the Hungarians were horrified to see the walls crash down in ruin, completely covering the brave Count. Without a leader the gallant little army was cut to pieces, and in the war-swept years which followed, the bones of the nobleman were never recovered. Today the natives point out a huge and moldering pile of ruins near Schomvaal beneath which, they say, still rests all that the centuries have left of Count Boris Vladinoff.'

I found the village of Stregoicavar a dreamy, drowsy little village that apparently belied its sinister cognomen – a forgotten back-eddy that Progress had passed by. The quaint houses and the quainter dress and manners of the people were those of an earlier century. They were friendly, mildly curious but not inquisitive, though visitors from the outside world were extremely rare.

'Ten years ago another American came here and stayed a few days in the village,' said the owner of the tavern where I had put up, 'a young fellow and queer-acting – mumbled to himself – a poet, I think.'

I knew he must mean Justin Geoffrey.

'Yes, he was a poet,' I answered,' and he wrote a poem about a bit of scenery near this very village.'

'Indeed?' mine host's interest was aroused. 'Then, since all great poets are strange in their speech and actions, he must have achieved great fame, for his actions and conversations were the strangest of any man I ever knew.'

'As is usual with artists,' I answered, 'most of his recognition has come since his death,'

'He is dead, then?'

'He died screaming in a madhouse five years ago.'

'Too had, too bad,' sighed mine host sympathetically. 'Poor lad – he looked too long at the Black Stone.'

My heart gave a leap, but I masked my keen interest and said casually : 'I have heard something of this Black Stone; somewhere near this village, is it not ?'

'Nearer than Christian folk wish,' he responded. 'Look!' He drew me to a latticed window and pointed up at the fir-clad slopes of the brooding blue mountains. 'There beyond where you see the bare face of that jutting cliff stands that accursed stone. Would that it were ground to powder and the powder flung into the Danube to be carried to the deepest ocean! Once men tried to destroy the tiring, but each man who laid hammer or maul against it came to an evil end. So now the people shun it.'

'What is there so evil about it?' I asked curiously.

'It is a demon-haunted thing,' he answered uneasily and with the suggestion of a shudder. 'In my childhood I knew a young man who came up from below arid laughed at our traditions – in his foolhardiness he went to the Stone one Midsummer Night and at dawn stumbled into the village, stricken dumb and mad. Something had shattered his brain and sealed his lips, for until the day of his death, which came soon after, he spoke only to utter terrible blasphemies or to slaver gibberish.

'My own nephew when very small was lost in the mountains and slept in the woods near the Stone, and now in his manhood he is tortured by foul dreams, so that at times he makes the night hideous with his screams and wakes with cold sweat upon him.

'But let us talk of something else, Herr; it is not good to dwell upon such things.'

I remarked on the evident age of the tavern and he answered with pride: 'The foundations are more than four hundred years old; the original house was the only one in the village which was not burned to the ground when Suleiman's devils swept through the mountains. Here, in the house that then stood on these same foundations, it is said the scribe Selim Bahadur had his headquarters while ravaging the country hereabouts.'

I learned then that the present inhabitants of Stregoicavar are not descendants of the people who dwelt there before the Turkish raid of 1526. The victorious Moslems left no living human in the village or the vicinity thereabouts when they passed over. Men, women and children they wiped out in one red holocaust of murder, leaving a vast stretch of country silent and utterly deserted. The present people of Stregoicavar are descended from hardy settlers from the lower valleys who came into the upper level and rebuilt the ruined village after the Turk was thrust back.

Mine host did not speak of the extermination of the original inhabitants with any great resentment and I learned that his ancestors in the lower levels had looked on the mountaineers with even more hatred and aversion than they regarded the Turks. He was rather vague regarding the causes of this feud, but said that the original inhabitants of Stregoicavar had been in the habit of making stealthy raids on the lowlands and stealing girls and children. Moreover, he said that they were not exactly of the same blood as his own people;

the sturdy, original Magyar-Slavic stock had mixed and intermarried with a degraded aboriginal race until the breeds had blended, producing an unsavory amalgamation. Who these aborigines were, he had not the slightest idea, but maintained that they were 'pagans' and had dwelt in the mountains since time immemorial, before the coming of the conquering peoples.

I attached little importance to this tale; seeing in it merely a parallel to the amalgamation of Celtic tribes with Mediterranean aborigines in the Galloway hills, with the resultant mixed race which, as Picts, has such an extensive part in Scotch legendry. Time has a curiously foreshortening effect on folklore, and just as tales of the Picts became intertwined with legends of an older Mongoloid race, so that eventually the Picts were ascribed the repulsive appearance of the squat primitives, whose individuality merged in the telling, into Pictish tales, and was forgotten; so, I felt, the supposed inhuman attributes of the first villagers of Stregoicavar could be traced to older, outworn myths with invading Huns and Mongols.

The morning after my arrival I received directions from my host, who gave them worriedly, and set out to find the Black Stone. A few hours' tramp up the fir-covered slopes brought me to the face of the rugged, solid stone cliff which jutted boldly from the mountainside. A narrow trail wound up it, and mounting this, I looked out over the peaceful valley of Stregoicavar, which seemed to drowse, guarded on either hand by the great blue mountains. No huts or any sign of human tenancy showed between the cliff whereon I stood and the village. I saw numbers of scattering farms in the valley but all lay on the other side of Stregoicavar, which itself seemed to shrink from the brooding slopes which masked the Black Stone.

The summit of the cliffs proved to be a sort of thickly wooded plateau. I made my way through the dense growth for a short distance and came to a wide glade: and in the center of the glade reared a gaunt figure of black stone.

It was octagonal in shape, some sixteen feet in height and about a foot and a half thick. It had once evidently been highly polished, but now the surface was thickly dinted as if savage efforts had been made to demolish it; but the hammers had done little more than to flake off small bits of stone and mutilate the characters which once had evidently marched in a spiraling line round and round the shaft to the top. Up to ten feet from the base these characters were almost completely blotted out, so that it was very difficult to trace their direction. Higher up they were plainer, and I managed to squirm part of the way up the shaft and scan them at close range. All were more or less defaced, but I was positive that they symbolized no language now remembered on the face of the earth. I am fairly familiar with all hieroglyphics known to researchers and philologists and I can say, with certainty, that those characters were like nothing of which I have ever read or heard. The nearest approach to them that I ever saw were some crude scratches on a gigantic and strangely symmetrical rock in a lost valley of Yucatan. I remember that when I pointed out these marks to the archeologist who was my companion, he maintained that they either represented natural weathering or the idle scratching of some Indian. To my theory that the rock was really the base of a long-vanished column, he merely laughed, calling my attention to the dimensions of it, which suggested, if it were built with any natural rules of architectural symmetry, a column a thousand feet high. But I was not convinced.

I will not say that the characters on the Black Stone were similar to those on that colossal rock in Yucatan; but one suggested the other. As to the substance of the monolith, again I was baffled. The stone of which it was composed was a dully gleaming black, whose surface, where it was not dinted and roughened, created a curious illusion of semi-transparency.

I spent most of the morning there and came away baffled. No connection of the Stone with any other artifact in the world suggested itself to me. It was as if the monolith had been reared by alien hands, in an age distant and apart from human ken.

I returned to the village with my interest in no way abated. Now that I had seen the curious things, my desire was still more keenly whetted to investigate the matter further and seek to learn by what strange hands and for what strange purpose the Black Stone had been reared in the long ago.

I sought out the tavern keeper's nephew and questioned him in regard to his dreams, but he was vague, though willing to oblige. He did not mind discussing them, but was unable to describe them with any clarity. Though he dreamed the same dreams repeatedly, and though they were hideously vivid at the time, they left no distinct impression on his waking mind. He remembered them only as chaotic nightmares through which huge whirling fires shot lurid tongues of flame and a black drum bellowed incessantly. One thing only he clearly remembered – in one dream he had seen the Black Stone, not on a mountain slope but set like a spire on a colossal black castle.

As for the rest of the villagers I found them not inclined to talk about the Stone, with the exception of the schoolmaster, a man of surprising education, who spent much more of his time out in the world than any of the rest.

He was much interested in what I told him of Von Junzt's remarks about the Stone. and warmly agreed with the German author in the alleged age of the monolith. He believed that a coven had once existed in the vicinity and that possibly all of the original villagers had been members of that fertility cult which once threatened to undermine European civilization and gave rise to the tales of witchcraft. He cited the very name of the village to prove his point, it had not been originally named Stregoicavar, he said: according to legends the builders had called it Xuthltan, which was the aboriginal name of the site on which the village had been built many centuries ago.

This fact roused again an indescribable feeling of uneasiness. The barbarous name did not suggest connection with any Scythic, Slavic or Mongolian race to which an aboriginal people of these mountains would, under natural circumstances, have belonged.

That the Magyars and Slavs of the lower valleys believed the original inhabitants of the village to be members of the witchcraft cult was evident, the schoolmaster said, by the name they gave it, which name continued to be used even after the older settlers had been massacred by the lurks, and the village rebuilt by a cleaner and more wholesome breed.

He did not believe that the members of the cult erected the monolith but he did believe that they used it as a center of their activities, and repeated vague legends which had been handed down since before the Turkish invasion, he advanced the theory that the degenerate villagers had used it as a sort of altar on which they offered human sacrifices, using as victims the girls and babies stolen from his own ancestors in the lower valleys.

He discounted the myths of weird events on Midsummer Night, as well as a curious legend of a strange deity which the witch-people of Xuthltan were said to have invoked with chants and wild rituals of flagellation and slaughter.

He had never visited the Stone on Midsummer Night, he said, but he would not fear to do so; whatever had existed or taken place there in the past, had been long engulfed in the mists of time and oblivion. The Black Stone had lost its meaning save as a link to a dead and dusty past.

It was while returning from a visit with this schoolmaster one night about a week after my arrival at Stregoicavar that a sudden recollection struck me – it was Midsummer Night! The very time that the legends linked with grisly implications to the Black Stone. I turned away from the tavern and strode swiftly through the village. Stregoicavar lay silent; the villagers retired early. I saw no one as I passed rapidly out of the village and up into the firs which masked the mountain slopes with whispering darkness. A broad silver moon hung above the valley, flooding the crags and slopes in a weird light and etching the shadows blackly. No wind blew through the firs, but a mysterious, intangible rustling and whispering was abroad. Surely on such nights in past centuries, my whimsical imagination told me, naked witches astride magic broomsticks had flown across this valley, pursued by jeering demoniac familiars.

I came to the cliffs and was somewhat disquieted to note that the illusive moonlight lent them a subtle appearance I had not noticed before – in the weird light they appeared less like natural cliffs and more like the ruins of cyclopean and Titan-reared battlements jutting from the mountain-slope.

Shaking off this hallucination with difficulty I came upon the plateau and hesitated a moment before I plunged into the brooding darkness of the woods. A sort of breathless tenseness hung over the shadows, like an unseen monster holding its breath lest it scare away its prey.

I shook off the sensation – a natural one, considering the eeriness of the place and its evil reputation – and made my way through the wood, experiencing a most unpleasant sensation that I was being followed, and halting once, sure that something clammy and unstable had brushed against my face in the darkness.

I came out into the glade and saw the tall monolith rearing its gaunt height above the sward. At the edge of the woods on the side toward the cliffs was a stone which formed a sort of natural seat. I sat down, reflecting that it was probably while there that the mad poet, Justin Geoffrey, had written his fantastic *People of the Monolith*. Mine host thought that it was the Stone which had caused

Geoffrey's insanity, but the seeds of madness had been sown in the poet's brain long before he ever came to Stregoicavar.

A glance at my watch showed that the hour of midnight was close at hand. I leaned back, waiting for whatever ghostly demonstration might appear. A thin night wind started up among the branches of the firs, with an uncanny suggestion of faint, unseen pipes whispering an eery and evil tune. The monotony of the sound and my steady gazing at the monolith produced a sort of self-hypnosis upon me; I grew drowsy. I fought this feeling, but sleep stole on me in spite of myself; the monolith seemed to sway and dance, strangely distorted to my gaze, and then I slept.

I opened my eyes and sought to rise, but lay still, as if an icy hand gripped me helpless. Cold terror stole over me. The glade was no longer deserted. It was thronged by a silent crowd of strange people, and my distended eyes took in strange barbaric details of costume which my reason told me were archaic and forgotten even in this backward land. Surely, I thought, these are villagers who have come here to hold some fantastic conclave – but another glance told me that these people were not of the folk of Stregoicavar. They were a shorter, more squat race, whose brows were lower, whose faces were broader and duller. Some had Slavic or Magyar features, but those features were degraded as from a mixture of some baser, alien strain I could not classify. Many wore the hides of wild beasts, and their whole appearance, both men and women, was one of sensual brutishness, They terrified and repelled me, but they gave me no heed. They formed in a vast half-circle in front of the monolith and began a sort of chant, flinging their arms in unison and weaving their bodies rhythmically from the waist upward. All eyes were fixed on the top of the Stone which they seemed to be invoking. But the strangest of all was the dimness of their voices; not fifty yards from me hundreds of men and women were unmistakably lifting their voices in a wild chant, yet those voices came to me as a faint indistinguishable murmur as if from across vast leagues of Space – or *Time.*

Before the monolith stood a sort of brazier from which a vile, nauseous yellow smoke billowed upward, culling curiously in an undulating spiral around the black shaft, like a vast unstable serpent.

On one side of this brazier lay two figures – a young girl, stark naked and bound hand and foot, and an infant, apparently only a few months old. On the other side of the brazier squatted a hideous old hag with a queer sort of black drum on her lap; this drum she beat with slow, light blows of her open palms, but I could not hear the sound.

The rhythm of the swaying bodies grew faster and into the space between the people and the monolith sprang a naked young woman, her eyes blazing, her long black hair flying loose. Spinning dizzily on her toes, she whirled across the open space and fell prostrate before the Stone, where she lay motionless. The next instant a fantastic figure followed her – a man from whose waist hung a goatskin, and whose features were entirely hidden by a sort of mask from a huge wolf's head, so that he looked like a monstrous, nightmare being, horribly compounded of elements both human and bestial. In his hand he held a bunch of long fir switches bound together at the larger ends, and the moonlight glinted on a chain of heavy gold looped about his neck. A smaller chain depending from it suggested a pendant of some sort, but this was missing.

The people tossed their arms violently and seemed to redouble their shouts as this grotesque creature loped across the open space with many a fantastic leap and caper. Coming to the woman who lay before the moonlight, he began to lash her with the switches he bore, and she leaped up and spun into the wild mazes of the most incredible dance I have ever seen. And her tormentor danced with her, keeping the wild rhythm, matching her every whirl and bound, while incessantly raining cruel blows on her naked body. And at every blow he shouted a single word, over and over, and all the people shouted it back. I could see the working of their lips, and now the faint far-off murmur of their voices merged and blended into one distant shout, repeated over and over with slobbering ecstasy. But what that one word was, I could not make out.

In dizzy whirls spun the wild dancers, while the lookers-on, standing still in their tracks, followed the rhythm of their dance with swaying bodies and weaving arms. Madness grew in the eyes of the capering votaress and was reflected in the eyes of the watchers. Wilder and more extravagant grew the whirling frenzy of that mad dance – it became a bestial and obscene thing, while the old hag howled and battered the drum like a crazy woman, and the switches cracked out a devil's tune.

Blood trickled down the dancer's limbs but she seemed not to feel the lashing save as a stimulus for further enormities of outrageous motion; bounding into the midst of the yellow smoke which now spread out tenuous tentacles to embrace both flying figures, she seemed to merge with that foul fog and veil herself with it. Then emerging into plain view, closely followed by the beast-thing that flogged her, she shot into an indescribable, explosive burst of dynamic mad motion, and on the very crest of that mad wave, she dropped suddenly to the sward, quivering and panting as if completely overcome by her frenzied exertions. The lashing continued with unabated violence and intensity and she began to wriggle toward the monolith on her belly. The priest – for such I will call him – followed, lashing her unprotected body with all the power of his arm as she writhed along, leaving a heavy track of blood on the trampled earth. She reached the monolith, and gasping and panting, flung both arms about it and covered the cold stone with fierce hot kisses, as in frenzied and unholy adoration.

The fantastic priest bounded high in the air, flinging away the red-dabbled switches, and the worshippers, howling and foaming at the mouths, turned on each other with tooth and nail, rending one another's garments and flesh in a blind passion of bestiality. The priest swept up the infant with a long arm, and shouting again that Name, whirled the wailing babe high in the air and dashed its brains out against the monolith, leaving a ghastly stain on the black surface. Cold with horror I saw him rip the tiny body open with his bare brutish fingers and fling handfuls of blood on the shaft, then toss the red and torn shape into the brazier, extinguishing flame and smoke in a crimson rain, while the maddened brutes behind him howled over and over that Name. Then suddenly they all fell prostrate, writhing like snakes, while the priest flung wide his gory hands as in triumph. I opened my mouth to scream my horror and loathing, but only a dry rattle sounded; a huge monstrous toad-like *thing* squatted on the top of the monolith!

I saw its bloated, repulsive and unstable outline against the moonlight, and set in what would have been the face of a natural creature, its huge, blinking eyes which reflected all the lust, abysmal greed, obscene cruelty and monstrous evil that has stalked the suns of men since their ancestors moved blind and hairless in the tree-tops. In those grisly eyes were mirrored all the unholy things and vile secrets that sleep in the cities under the sea, and that skulk from the light of day in the blackness of primordial caverns. And so that ghastly thing that the unhallowed ritual of cruelty and sadism and blood had evoked from the silence of the hills, leered and blinked down on its bestial worshippers, who grovelled in abhorrent abasement before it.

Now the beast-masked priest lifted the bound and weakly writhing girl in his brutish hands and held her up toward that horror on the monolith. And as that monstrosity sucked in its breath, lustfully and slobberingly, something snapped in my brain and I fell into a merciful faint.

I opened my eyes on a still white dawn. All the events of the night rushed back on me and I sprang up, then stared about me in amazement. The monolith brooded gaunt and silent above the sward which waved, green and untrampled, in the morning breeze. A few quick strides took me across the glade; here had the dancers leaped and bounded until the ground should have been trampled bare, and here had the votaress wriggled her painful way to the Stone, streaming blood on the earth. But no drop of crimson showed on the uncrushed sward. I looked, shudderingly, at the side of the monolith against which the bestial priest had brained the stolen baby – but no dark stain nor grisly clot showed there.

A dream! It had been a wild nightmare – or else – I shrugged my shoulders. What vivid clarity for a dream!

I returned quietly to the village and entered the inn without being seen. And there I sat meditating over the strange events of the night. More and more was I prone to discard the dream-theory. That what I had seen was illusion and without material substance, was evident. But I believed that I had looked on the mirrored shadow of a deed perpetrated in ghastly actuality in bygone days. But how was I to know? What proof to show that my vision had been a gathering of foul specters rather than a mere nightmare originating in my own brain.

As if for answer a name flashed into my mind – Selim Bahadurl According to legend this man, who had been a soldier as well as a scribe, had commanded that part of Suleiman's army which had devastated Stregoicavar; it seemed logical enough; and if so, he had gone straight from the blotted-out countryside to the bloody field of Schomvaal, and his doom. I sprang up with a sudden shout – that manuscript which was taken from the Turk's body, and which Count Boris shuddered over – might it not contain some narration of what the conquering Turks found in Stregoicavar? What else could have shaken the iron nerves of the Polish adventurer? And since the bones of the Count had never been recovered, what more certain than that the lacquered case, with its mysterious contents, still lay hidden beneath the ruins that covered Boris Vladinoff? I began packing my bag with fierce haste.

Three days later found me ensconced in a little village a few miles from the old battlefield, and when the moon rose I was working with savage intensity on the great pile of crumbling stone that crowned the hill. It was back-breaking toil – looking back now I can not see how I accomplished it, though I labored without a pause from moonrise to dawn. Just as the sun was coming up I tore aside the last tangle of stones and looked on all that was mortal of Count Boris Vladinoff – only a few pitiful fragments of crumbling bone – and among them, crushed out of all original shape, lay a case whose lacquered surface had kept it from complete decay through the centuries.

I seized it with frenzied eagerness, and piling back some of the stones on the bones I hurried away; for I did not dare to be discovered by the suspicious peasants in an act of apparent desecration.

Back in my tavern chamber I opened the case and found the parchment comparatively intact; and there was something else in the case – a small squat object wrapped in silk. I was wild to plumb the secrets of those yellowed pages, but weariness forbade me. Since leaving Stregoicavar I had hardly slept at all, and the terrific exertions of the previous night combined to overcome me. In spite of myself I was forced to stretch myself on my bed, nor did I awake until sundown.

I snatched a hasty supper, and then in the light of a flickering candle, I set myself to read the neat Turkish characters that covered the parchment. It was difficult work, for I am not deeply versed in the language and the archaic style of the narrative baffled me. But as I toiled through it a word or a phrase here and there leaped at me and a dimly growing horror shook me in its grip. I bent my energies fiercely to the task, and as the tale grew clearer and took more tangible form my blood chilled in my veins, my hair stood up and my tongue cleaved to my mouth. All external things partook of the grisly madness of that infernal manuscript until the night sounds of insects and creatures in the woods took the form of ghastly murmurings and stealthy treadings of ghoulish horrors and the sighing of the night wind changed to tittering obscene gloating of evil over the souls of men.

At last when gray dawn was stealing through the latticed window, I laid down the manuscript and took up and unwrapped the thing in the bit of silk. Staring at it with haggard eyes I knew the truth of the matter was clinched, even had it been possible to doubt the veracity of that terrible manuscript.

And I replaced both obscene things in the case, nor did I rest or sleep or eat until that case containing them had been weighted with stones and flung into the deepest current of the Danube which, God grant, carried them back into the Hell from which they came.

It was no dream I dreamed on Midsummer Midnight in the hills above

Stregoicavar. Well for Justin Geoffrey that he tarried there only in the sunlight and went his way, for had he gazed upon that ghastly conclave, his mad brain would have snapped before it did. How my own reason held, I do not know.

No – it was no dream – I gazed upon a foul rout of votaries long dead, come up from Hell to worship as of old; ghosts that bowed before a ghost. For Hell has long claimed their hideous god. Long, long he dwelt among the hills, a brain-shattering vestige of an outworn age, but no longer his obscene talons clutch for the souls of living men, and his kingdom is a dead kingdom, peopled only by the ghosts of those who served him in his lifetime and theirs.

By what foul alchemy or godless sorcery the Gates of Hell are opened on that one eery night I do not know, but mine own eyes have seen. And I know I looked on no living thing that night, for the manuscript written in the hand of Selim Bahadur narrated at length what he and his raiders found in the valley of Stregoicavar: and I read, set down in detail, the blasphemous obscenities that torture wrung from the lips of screaming worshippers; and I read, too, of the lost, grim black cavern high in the hills where the horrified Turks hemmed a monstrous, bloated, wallowing toad-like being and slew it with flame and ancient steel blessed in old times by Muhammad, and with incantations that were old when Arabia was young. And even staunch old Selim's hand shook as he recorded the cataclysmic, earth-shaking death-howls of the monstrosity, which died not alone; for a half-score of his slayers perished with him, in ways that Selim would not or could not describe.

And the squat idol carved of gold and wrapped was an image of *himself*, and Selim tore it from the chain that looped the neck of the slain high priest of the mask.

Well that the Turks swept that foul valley with torch and cleanly steel! Such sights as those brooding mountains have looked on belong to the darkness and abysses of lost eons. No – it is not fear of the toad-thing that makes me shudder in the night. He is made fast in Hell with his nauseous horde, freed only for an hour on the most weird night of the year, as I have seen. And of his worshippers, none remains.

But it is the realization that such things once crouched beast-like above the souls of men which brings cold sweat to my brow; and I fear to peer again into the leaves of Von Junzt's abomination. For now I understand his repeated phrase of *keys!* – aye! Keys to Outer Doors – links with an abhorrent past and – who knows? – of abhorrent spheres of the *present*. And I understand why the cliffs look like battlements in the moonlight and why the tavern-keeper's nightmare-haunted nephew saw in his dream the Black Stone like a spire on a cyclopean black castle. If men ever excavate among those mountains they may find incredible things below those masking slopes. For the cave wherein the Turks trapped the – *thing* – was not truly a cavern, and I shudder to contemplate the gigantic gulf of eons which must stretch between this age and the time when the earth shook herself and reared up, like a wave, those blue mountains that, rising, enveloped unthinkable things. May no man ever seek to uproot the ghastly spire men call the Black Stone!

A Key! Aye, it is a Key, symbol of a forgotten horror. That horror has faded into the limbo from which it crawled, loathsomely, in the black dawn of the earth. But what of the other fiendish possibilities hinted at by Von Junzt – what of the monstrous hand which strangled out his life? Since reading what Selim Bahadur wrote, I can no longer doubt anything in the Black Book. Man was not always master of the earth – *and is he now?*

And the thought recurs to me – if such a monstrous entity as the Master of the Monolith somehow survived its own speakably distant epoch so long – *What nameless shapes may even now lurk in the dark places of the world?*

BLACK CANAAN

I

"Trouble on Tularoosa Creek!" A warning to send cold fear along the spine of any man who was raised in that isolated back-country, called Canaan, that lies between Tularoosa and Black River – to send him racing back to that swamp-bordered region, wherever the word might reach him.

It was only a whisper from the withered lips of a shuffling black crone, who vanished among the throng before I could seize her; but it was enough. No need to seek confirmation; no need to inquire by what mysterious, black-folk way the word had come to her. No need to inquire what obscure forces worked to unseal those wrinkled lips to a Black River man. It was enough that the warning had been given – and understood.

Understood? How could any Black River man fail to understand that warning? It could have but one meaning – old hates seething again in the jungle-deeps of the swamplands, dark shadows slipping through the cypress, and massacre stalking out of the black, mysterious village that broods on the moss-festooned shore of sullen Tularoosa.

Within an hour New Orleans was falling further behind me with every turn of the churning wheel. To every man born in Canaan, there is always an invisible tie that draws him back whenever his homeland is imperiled by the murky shadow that has lurked in its jungled recesses for more than half a century.

The fastest boats I could get seemed maddeningly slow for that race up the big river, and up the smaller, more turbulent stream. I was burning with impatience when I stepped off on the Sharpsville landing, with the last fifteen miles of my journey yet to make. It was past midnight, but I hurried to the livery stable where, by tradition half a century old, there is always a Buckner horse, day or night.

As a sleepy black boy fastened the cinches, I turned to the owner of the stable, Joe Lafely, yawning and gaping in the light of the lantern he upheld. "There are rumors of trouble on Tularoosa?"

He paled in the lantern-light.

"I don't know. I've heard talk. But you people in Canaan are a shut-mouthed clan. No one *outside* knows what goes on in there—"

The night swallowed his lantern and his stammering voice as I headed west along the pike.

The moon set red through the black pines. Owls hooted away off in the woods, and somewhere a hound howled his ancient wistfulness to the night. In the darkness that foreruns dawn I crossed Nigger Head Creek, a streak of shining black fringed by walls of solid shadows. My horse's hooves splashed through the shallow water and clinked on the wet stones, startlingly loud in the stillness. Beyond Nigger Head Creek began the country men called Canaan.

Heading in the same swamp, miles to the north, that gives birth to Tularoosa, Nigger Head flows due south to join Black River a few miles west of Sharpsville, while the Tularoosa runs westward to meet the same river at a higher point. The trend of Black River is from northwest to southeast; so these three streams form the great irregular triangle known as Canaan.

In Canaan lived the sons and daughters of the white frontiersmen who first settled the country, and the sons and daughters of their slaves. Joe Lafely was right; we were an isolated, shut-mouthed breed, self-sufficient, jealous of our seclusion and independence.

Beyond Nigger Head the woods thickened, the road narrowed, winding through unfenced pinelands, broken by live-oaks and cypresses. There was no sound except the soft clop-clop of hoofs in the thin dust, the creak of the saddle. Then someone laughed throatily in the shadows.

I drew up and peered into the trees. The moon had set and dawn was not yet come, but a faint glow quivered among the trees, and by it I made out a dim figure under the moss-hung branches. My hand instinctively sought the butt of one of the dueling-pistols I wore, and the action brought another low, musical laugh, mocking yet seductive. I glimpsed a brown face, a pair of scintillant eyes, white teeth displayed in an insolent smile.

"Who the devil are you?" I demanded.

"Why do you ride so late, Kirby Buckner?" Taunting laughter bubbled in the voice. The accent was foreign and unfamiliar; a faintly negroid twang was there, but it was rich and sensuous as the rounded body of its owner. In the lustrous pile of dusky hair a great white blossom glimmered palely in the darkness.

"What are you doing here?" I demanded. "You're a long way from any darky cabin. And you're a stranger to me."

"I came to Canaan since you went away," she answered. "My cabin is on the Tularoosa. But now I've lost my way. And my poor brother has hurt his leg and cannot walk."

"Where is your brother?" I asked, uneasily. Her perfect English was disquieting to me, accustomed as I was to the dialect of the black folk.

"Back in the woods, there – far back!" She indicated the black depths with a swaying motion of her supple body rather than a gesture of her hand, smiling audaciously as she did so.

I knew there was no injured brother, and she knew I knew it, and laughed at me. But a strange turmoil of conflicting emotions stirred in me. I had never before paid any attention to a black or brown woman. But this quadroon girl was different from any I had ever seen. Her features were regular as a white woman's, and her speech was not that of a common wench. Yet she was barbaric, in the open lure of her smile, in the gleam of her eyes, in the shameless posturing of her voluptuous body. Every gesture, every motion she made set her apart from the ordinary run of women; her beauty was untamed and lawless, meant to madden rather than to soothe, to make a man blind and dizzy, to rouse in him all the unreined passions that are his heritage from his ape ancestors.

I hardly remember dismounting and tying my horse. My blood pounded suffocatingly through the veins in my temples as I scowled down at her, suspicious yet fascinated.

"How do you know my name? Who *are* you?"

With a provocative laugh, she seized my hand and drew me deeper into the shadows. Fascinated by the lights gleaming in her dark eyes, I was hardly aware of her action.

"Who does not know Kirby Buckner?" she laughed. "All the people of Canaan speak of you, white or black. Come! My poor brother longs to look upon you!" And she laughed with malicious triumph.

It was this brazen effrontery that brought me to my senses. Its cynical mockery broke the almost hypnotic spell in which I had fallen.

I stopped short, throwing her hand aside, snarling: "What devil's game are you up to, wench?"

Instantly the smiling siren was changed to a blood-mad jungle cat. Her eyes flamed murderously, her red lips writhed in a snarl as she leaped back, crying out shrilly. A rush of bare feet answered her call. The first faint light of dawn struck through the branches, revealing my assailants, three gaunt black giants. I saw the gleaming whites of their eyes, their bare glistening teeth, the sheen of naked steel in their hands.

My first bullet crashed through the head of the tallest man, knocking him dead in full stride. My second pistol snapped – the cap had somehow slipped from the nipple. I dashed it into a black face, and as the man fell, half stunned, I whipped out my bowie knife and closed with the other. I parried his stab and my counter-stroke ripped across the belly-muscles. He screamed like a swamp-panther and made a wild grab for my knife wrist, but I stuck him in the mouth with my clenched left fist, and felt his lips split and his teeth crumble under the impact as he reeled backward, his knife waving wildly. Before he could regain his balance I was after him, thrusting, and got home under his ribs. He groaned and slipped to the ground in a puddle of his own blood.

I wheeled about, looking for the other. He was just rising, blood streaming down his face and neck. As I started for him he sounded a panicky yell and plunged into the underbrush. The crashing of his blind flight came back to me, muffled with distance. The girl was gone.

II : THE STRANGER ON TULAROOSA

The curious glow that had first showed me the quadroon girl had vanished. In my confusion I had forgotten it. But I did not waste time on vain conjecture as to its source, as I groped my way back to the road. Mystery had come to the pinelands and a ghostly light that hovered among the trees was only part of it.

My horse snorted and pulled against his tether, frightened by the smell of blood that hung in the heavy damp air. Hoofs clattered down the road, forms bulked in the growing light. Voices challenged.

"Who's that? Step out and name yourself, before we shoot!"

"Hold on, Esau!" I called. "It's me – Kirby Buckner!"

"Kirby Buckner, by thunder!" ejaculated Esau McBride, lowering his pistol. The tall rangy forms of the other riders loomed behind him.

"We heard a shot," said McBride. "We was ridin' patrol on the roads around Grimesville like we've been ridin' every night for a week now – ever since they killed Ridge Jackson."

"Who killed Ridge Jackson?"

"The swamp niggers. That's all we know. Ridge come out of the woods early one mornin' and knocked at Cap'n Sorley's door. Cap'n says he was the color of ashes. He hollered for the Cap'n for God's sake to let him in, he had somethin' awful to tell him. Well, the Cap'n started down to open the door, but before he'd got down the stairs he heard an awful row among the dogs outside, and a man screamed he reckoned was Ridge. And when he got to the door, there wasn't nothin' but a dead dog layin' in the yard with his head knocked in, and the others all goin' crazy. They found Ridge later, out in the pines a few hundred yards from the house. From the way the ground and the bushes was tore up, he'd been dragged that far by four or five men. Maybe they got tired of haulin' him along. Anyway, they beat his head into a pulp and left him layin' there."

"I'll be damned!" I muttered. "Well, there's a couple of niggers lying back there in the brush. I want to see if you know them. I don't."

A moment later we were standing in the tiny glade, now white in the growing dawn. A black shape sprawled on the matted pine needles, his head in a pool of blood and brains. There were wide smears of blood on the ground and bushes on the other side of the little clearing, but the wounded black was gone.

McBride turned the carcass with his foot.

"One of them niggers that came in with Saul Stark," he muttered.

"Who the devil's that?" I demanded.

"Strange nigger that moved in since you went down the river last time. Come from South Carolina, he says. Lives in that old cabin in the Neck – you know, the shack where Colonel Reynolds' niggers used to live."

"Suppose you ride on to Grimesville with me, Esau," I said, "and tell me about this business as we ride. The rest of you might scout around and see if you can find a wounded nigger in the brush."

They agreed without question; the Buckners have always been tacitly considered leaders in Canaan, and it came natural for me to offer suggestions. Nobody gives orders to white men in Canaan.

"I reckoned you'd be showin' up soon," opined McBride, as we rode along the whitening road. "You usually manage to keep up with what's happenin' in Canaan."

"What *is* happening?" I inquired. "I don't know anything. An old black woman dropped me the word in New Orleans that there was trouble. Naturally I came home as fast as I could. Three strange niggers waylaid me—" I was curiously disinclined to mention the woman. "And now you tell me somebody killed Ridge Jackson. What's it all about?"

"The swamp niggers killed Ridge to shut his mouth," announced McBride. "That's the only way to figure it. They must have been close behind him when he knocked on Cap'n Sorley's door. Ridge worked for Cap'n Sorley most of his life; he thought a lot of the old man. Some kind of deviltry's bein' brewed up in the swamps, and Ridge wanted to warn the Cap'n. That's the way I figure it."

"Warn him about what?"

"We don't know," confessed McBride. "That's why we're all on edge. It must be an uprisin'."

That word was enough to strike chill fear into the heart of any Canaan-dweller. The blacks had risen in 1845, and the red terror of that revolt was not forgotten, nor the three lesser rebellions before it, when the slaves rose and spread fire and slaughter from Tularoosa to the shores of Black River. The fear of a black uprising lurked for ever in the depths of that forgotten back-country; the very children absorbed it in their cradles.

"What makes you think it might be an uprising?" I asked.

"The niggers have all quit the fields, for one thing. They've all got business in Goshen. I ain't seen a nigger nigh Grimesville for a week. *The town niggers have pulled out.*"

In Canaan we still draw a distinction born in antebellum days. "Town niggers" are descendants of the houseservants of the old days, and most of them live in or near Grimesville. There are not many, compared to the mass of "swamp niggers" who dwell on tiny farms along the creeks and the edge of the swamps, or in the black village of Goshen, on the Tularoosa. They are descendants of the field-hands of other days, and, untouched by the mellow civilization which refined the natures of the house-servants, they remain as primitive as their African ancestors.

"Where have the town niggers gone?" I asked.

"Nobody knows. They lit out a week ago. Probably hidin' down on Black River. If we win, they'll come back. If we don't, they'll take refuge in Sharpsville."

I found his matter-of-factness a bit ghastly, as if the actuality of the uprising were an assured fact.

"Well, what have you done?" I demanded.

"Ain't much we could do," he confessed. "The niggers ain't made no open move, outside of killin' Ridge Jackson; and we couldn't prove who done that, or why they done it.

"They ain't done nothin' but clear out. But that's mighty suspicious. We can't keep from thinkin' Saul Stark's behind it."

"Who is this fellow?" I asked.

"I told you all I know, already. He got permission to settle in that old deserted cabin on the Neck; a great big black devil that talks better English than I like to hear a nigger talk. But he was respectful enough. He had three or four big South Carolina bucks with him, and a brown wench which we don't know whether she's his daughter, sister, wife or what. He ain't been in to Grimesville but that one time, and a few weeks after he came to Canaan, the niggers begun actin' curious. Some of the boys wanted to ride over to Goshen and have a show-down, but that's takin' a desperate chance."

I knew he was thinking of a ghastly tale told us by our grandfathers of how a punitive expedition from Grimesville was once ambushed and butchered among the dense thickets that masked Goshen, then a rendezvous for runaway slaves, while another red-handed band devastated Grimesville, left defenseless by that reckless invasion.

"Might take all the men to get Saul Stark," said McBride. "And we don't dare leave the town unprotected. But we'll soon have to – hello, what's this?"

We had emerged from the trees and were just entering the village of Grimesville, the community center of the white population of Canaan. It was not pretentious. Log cabins, neat and whitewashed, were plentiful enough. Small cottages clustered about big, old-fashioned houses which sheltered the rude aristocracy of that backwoods democracy. All the "planter" families lived "in town". "The country" was occupied by their tenants, and by the small independent farmers, white and black.

A small log cabin stood near the point where the road wound out of the deep forest. Voices emanated from it, in accents of menace, and a tall lanky figure, rifle in hand, stood at the door.

"Howdy, Esau!" this man hailed us. "By golly, if it ain't Kirby Buckner! Glad to see you, Kirby."

"What's up, Dick?" asked McBride.

"Got a nigger in the shack, tryin' to make him talk. Bill Reynolds seen him sneakin' past the edge of town about daylight, and nabbed him."

"Who is it?" I asked.

"Tope Sorley. John Willoughby's gone after a blacksnake."

With a smothered oath I swung off my horse and strode in, followed by McBride. Half a dozen men in boots and gun-belts clustered about a pathetic figure cowering on an old broken bunk. Tope Sorley (his forebears had adopted the name of the family that owned them, in slave days) was a pitiable sight just then. His skin was ashy, his teeth chattered spasmodically, and his eyes seemed to be trying to roll back into his head.

"Here's Kirby!" ejaculated one of the men as pushed my way through the group. "I'll bet he'll make this coon talk!"

"Here comes John with the blacksnake!" shouted someone, and a tremor ran through Tope Sorley's shivering body.

I pushed aside the butt of the ugly whip thrust eagerly into my hand.

"Tope," I said, "you've worked one of my father's farms for years. Has any Buckner ever treated you any way but square?"

"Nossuh," came faintly.

"Then what are you afraid of? Why don't you speak up? Something's going on in the swamps. You know, and I want you to tell us why the town niggers have all run away, why Ridge Jackson was killed, why the swamp niggers

186

are acting so mysteriously."

"And what kind of devilment that cussed Saul Stark's cookin' up over on Tularoosa!" shouted one of the men.

Tope seemed to shrink into himself at the mention of Stark.

"I don't dast," he shuddered. "He'd put me in de swamp!"

"Who?" I demanded. "Stark? Is Stark a conjer man?"

Tope sank his head in his hands and did not answer. I laid my hand on his shoulder.

"Tope," I said, :you know if you'll talk, we'll protect you. If you don't talk, I don't think Stark can treat you much rougher than these men are likely to. Now spill it – what's it all about?"

He lifted desperate eyes.

"You-all got to lemme stay here," he shuddered. "And guard me, and gimme money to git away on when de trouble's over."

"We'll do all that," I agreed instantly. "You can stay right here in this cabin, until you're ready to leave for New Orleans or wherever you want to go."

He capitulated, collapsed, and words tumbled from his livid lips.

"Saul Stark's a conjer man. He come here because it's way off in back-country. He aim to kill all de white folks in Canaan–"

A growl rose from the group, such a growl as rises unbidden from the throat of the wolf-pack that scents peril.

"He aim to make hisself king of Canaan. He sent me to spy dis mornin' to see if Mistah Kirby got through. He sent men to waylay him on de road, cause he knowed Mistah Kirby was comin' back to Canaan. Niggers makin' voodoo on Tularoosa, for weeks now. Ridge Jackson was goin' to tell Cap'n Sorley; so Stark's niggers foller him and kill him. That make Stark mad. He ain't want to *kill* Ridge; he want to put him in de swamp with Tunk Bixby and de others."

"What are you talking about?" I demanded.

Far out in the woods rose a strange, shrill cry, like the cry of a bird. But no such bird ever called before in Canaan. Tope cried out as if in answer, and shriveled into himself. He sank down on the bunk in a veritable palsy of fear.

"That was a signal!" I snapped. "Some of you go out there."

Half a dozen men hastened to follow my suggestion, and I returned to the task of making Tope renew his revelations. It was useless. Some hideous fear had sealed his lips. He lay shuddering like a stricken animal, and did not even seem to hear our questions. No one suggested the use of the blacksnake. Anyone could see the Negro was paralyzed with terror.

Presently the searchers returned empty-handed. They had seen no one, and the thick carpet of pine needles showed no foot-prints. The men looked at me expectantly. As Colonel Buckner's son, leadership was expected of me.

"What about it, Kirby?" asked McBride. "Breckinridge and the others have just rode in. They couldn't find that nigger you cut up."

"There was another nigger I hit with a pistol," I said. "Maybe he came back and helped him." Still I could not bring myself to mention the brown girl. "Leave Tope alone. Maybe he'll get over his scare after a while. Better keep a guard in the cabin all the time. The swamp niggers may try to get him as they got Ridge Jackson. Better scour the roads around the town, Esau; there may be some of them hiding in the woods."

"I will. I reckon you'll want to be gettin' up to the house, now, and seein' your folks."

"Yes. And I want to swap these toys for a couple of .44s. Then I'm going to ride out and tell the country people to come into Grimesville. If it's to be an uprising, we don't know when it will commence."

You're not goin' alone!" protested McBride.

"I'll be all right," I answered impatiently. "All this may not amount to anything, but it's best to be on the safe side. That's why I'm going after the country folks. No, I don't want anybody to go with me. Just in case the niggers do get crazy enough to attack the town, you'll need every man you've got. But if I can get hold of some of the swamp niggers and talk to them, I don't think there'll be any attack."

"You won't get a glimpse of them," McBride predicted.

III : SHADOWS OVER CANAAN

It was not yet noon when I rode out of the village westward along the old road. Thick woods swallowed me quickly. Dense walls of pines marched with me on either hand, giving way occasionally to fields enclosed with straggling rail fences, with the log cabins of the tenants or owners close by, with the usual litters of tow-headed children and lank hound dogs.

Some of the cabins were empty. The occupants, if white, had already gone into Grimesville; if black they had gone into the swamps, or fled to the hidden refuge of the town niggers, according to their affiliations. In any event, the vacancy of their hovels was sinister in its suggestion.

A tense silence brooded over the pinelands, broken only by the occasional wailing call of a plowman. My progress was not swift, for from time to time I turned off the main road to give warning to some lonely cabin huddled on the bank of one of the many thicket-fringed creeks. Most of these farms were south of the road; the white settlements did not extend far to the north; for in that direction lay Tularoosa Creek with its jungle-grown marshes that stretched inlets southward like groping fingers.

The actual warning was brief; there was no need to argue or explain. I called from the saddle: "Get into town; trouble's brewing on Tularoosa." Faces paled, and people dropped whatever they were doing: the men to grab guns and jerk mules from the plow to hitch to the wagons, the women to bundle necessary belongings together and shrill the children in from their play. As I rode I heard the cow-horns blowing up and down the creeks, summoning men from distant fields – blowing as they had not blown for a generation, a warning and a defiance which I knew carried to such ears as might be listening in the edges of the swamplands. The country emptied itself behind me, flowing in thin but steady streams toward Grimesville.

The sun was swinging low among the topmost branches of the pines when I reached the Richardson cabin, the westernmost "white" cabin in Canaan. Beyond it lay the Neck, the angle formed by the junction of Tularoosa with Black River, a jungle-like expanse occupied only by scattered Negro huts.

Mrs. Richardson called to me anxiously from the cabin stoop.

"Well, Mr. Kirby, I'm glad to see you back in Canaan! We been hearin' the horns all evenin', Mr. Kirby. What's it mean? It – it ain't–"

"You and Joe better get the children and light out for Grimesville," I answered. "Nothing's happened yet, and may not, but it's best to be on the safe side. All the people are going."

"We'll go right now!" she gasped, paling, as she snatched off her apron. "Lord, Mr. Kirby, you reckon they'll cut us off before we can git to town?"

I shook my head. "They'll strike at night, if at all. We're just playing safe. Probably nothing will come of it."

"I bet you're wrong there," she predicted, scurrying about in desperate activity. "I been hearin' a drum beatin' off toward Saul Stark's cabin, off and on, for a week now. They beat drums back in the Big Uprisin'. My pappy's told me about it many's the time. The nigger skinned his brother alive. The horns was blowin' all up and down the creeks, and the drums was beatin' louder'n the horns could blow. You'll be ridin' back with us, won't you, Mr. Kirby?"

"No; I'm going to scout down along the trail apiece."

"Don't go too far. You're liable to run into old Saul Stark and his devils. Lord! *Where* is that man? Joe! *Joe!*"

As I rode down the trail her shrill voice followed me, thin-edged with fear.

Beyond the Richardson farm pines gave way to live oaks. The underbrush grew ranker. A scent of rotting vegetation impregnated the fitful breeze. Occasionally I sighted a nigger hut, half hidden under the trees, but always it stood silent and deserted. Empty nigger cabins meant but one thing: the blacks were collecting at Goshen, some miles to the east on the Tularoosa; and that gathering, too, could have but one meaning.

My goal was Saul Stark's hut. My intention had been formed when I heard Tope Sorley's incoherent tale. There could be no doubt that Saul Stark was the dominant figure in this web of mystery. With Saul Stark I meant to deal. That I might be risking my life was a chance any man must take who assumes the responsibility of leadership.

The sun slanted through the lower branches of the cypresses when I reached it – a log cabin set against a background of gloomy tropical jungle. A few steps beyond it began the uninhabitable swamp in which Tularoosa emptied its murky current into Black River. A reek of decay hung in the air; gray moss bearded the trees, and poisonous vines twisted in rank tangles.

I called: "Stark! Saul Stark! Come out here!"

There was no answer. A primitive silence hovered over the tiny clearing. I dismounted, tied my horse and approached the crude, heavy door.

Perhaps this cabin held a clue to the mystery of Saul Stark; at least it doubtless contained the implements and paraphernalia of his noisome craft. The faint breeze dropped suddenly. The stillness became so intense it was like a physical impact. I paused, startled; it was as if some inner instinct had shouted urgent warning.

As I stood there every fiber of me quivered in response to that subconscious warning; some obscure, deep-hidden instinct sensed peril, as a man senses the presence of the rattlesnake in the darkness, or the swamp-panther crouching in the bushes. I drew a pistol, sweeping the trees and bushes, but saw no shadow or movement to betray the ambush I feared. But my instinct was unerring; what I sensed was not lurking in the woods about me; it was inside the cabin – *waiting*. Trying to shake off the feeling, and irked by a vague half-memory that kept twitching at the back of my brain, I again advanced. And again I stopped short, with one foot on the tiny stoop, and a hand half advanced to pull open the door. A chill shivering swept over me, a sensation like that which shakes a man to whom a flicker of lightning has revealed the black abyss into which another blind step would have hurled him. For the first time in my life I knew the meaning of fear; I knew that black horror lurked in that sullen cabin under the moss-bearded cypresses – a horror against which every primitive instinct that was my heritage cried out in panic.

And that insistent half-memory woke suddenly. It was the memory of a story of how voodoo men leave their huts guarded in their absence by a powerful ju-ju spirit to deal madness and death to the intruder. White men ascribed such deaths to superstitious fright and hypnotic suggestion. But in that instant I understood my sense of lurking peril; I comprehended the horror that breathed like an invisible mist from that accursed hut. I sensed the reality of the ju-ju, of which the grotesque wooden images which voodoo men place in their huts are only a symbol.

Saul Stark was gone; but he had left a Presence to guard his hut.

I backed away, sweat beading the backs of my hands.

Not for a bag of gold would I have peered into the shuttered windows or touched that unbolted door. My pistol hung in my hand, useless I knew against the *Thing* in that cabin. What it was I could not know, but I knew it was some brutish, soulless entity drawn from the black swamps by the spells of voodoo. Man and the natural animals are.not the only sentient beings that haunt this planet. There are invisible *Things* – black spirits of the deep swamps and the slimes of the river beds – the Negroes know of them .

My horse was trembling like a leaf and he shouldered close to me as if seeking security in bodily contact. I mounted and reined away, fighting a panicky urge to strike in the spurs and bolt madly down the trail.

I breathed an involuntary sigh of relief as the somber clearing fell away behind me and was lost from sight. I did not, as soon as I was out of sight of the cabin, revile myself for a silly fool. My experience was too vivid in my mind. It was not cowardice that prompted my retreat from that empty hut; it was the natural instinct of self-preservation, such as keeps a squirrel from entering the lair of a rattlesnake.

My horse snorted and shied violently. A gun was in my hand before I saw what had startled me. Again a rich musical laugh taunted me.

She was leaning against a bent tree-trunk, her hands clasped behind her sleek head, insolently posing her sensuous figure. The barbaric fascination of her was not dispelled by daylight; if anything, the glow of the low-hanging sun enhanced it.

"Why did you not go into the ju-ju cabin, Kirby Buckner?" she mocked, lowering her arms and moving insolently out from the tree.

She was clad as I had never seen a swamp woman, or any other woman, dressed. Snakeskin sandals were on her feet, sewn with tiny sea-shells that were never gathered on this continent. A short silken skirt of flaming crimson molded her full hips, and was upheld by a broad bead-worked girdle. Barbaric anklets and armlets clashed as she moved, heavy ornaments of crudely hammered gold that were as African as her loftily piled coiffure. Nothing else she wore, and on her bosom, between her arching breasts, I glimpsed the faint lines of tattooing on her brown skin.

She posed derisively before me, not in allure, but in mockery. Triumphant malice blazed in her dark eyes; her red lips curled with cruel mirth. Looking at her then I found it easy to believe all the tales I had heard of torture and mutilations inflicted by the women of savage races on wounded enemies. She was alien, even in this primitive setting; she needed a grimmer, more bestial background, a background of steaming jungle, reeking black swamps, flaring fires and cannibal feasts, and the bloody altars of abysmal tribal gods.

"Kirby Buckner!" She seemed to caress the syllables with her red tongue, yet the very intonation was an obscene insult. "Why did you not enter Saul Stark's cabin? It was not locked! Did you fear what you might see there? Did you fear you might come out with your hair white like an old man's, and the drooling lips of an imbecile?"

"What's in that hut?" I demanded.

She laughed in my face, and snapped her fingers with a peculiar gesture.

"One of the ones which come oozing like black mist out of the night when Saul Stark beats the ju-ju drum and shrieks the black incantation to the gods that crawl on their bellies in the swamp."

"What is he doing here? The black folk were quiet until he came."

Her red lips curled disdainfully. "Those black dogs? They are his slaves. If they disobey he kills them, *or puts them in the swamp*. For long we have looked for a place to begin our rule. We have chosen Canaan. You whites must go. And since we know that white people can never be driven away from their land, we must kill you all."

It was my turn to laugh, grimly.

"They tried that, back in '45."

"They did not have Saul Stark to lead them, then," she answered calmly.

"Well, suppose they won? Do you think that would be the end of it? Other white men would come into Canaan and kill them all."

"They would have to cross water," she answered.

We can defend the rivers and creeks. Saul Stark will have many *servants in the swamps* to do his bidding. He will be king of black Canaan. No one can cross the waters to come against him. He will rule his tribe, as his fathers fled their tribes in the Ancient Land."

"Mad as a loon!" I muttered. Then curiosity impelled me to ask: "Who is this fool? What are you to him?"

"He is the son of a Kongo witch-finder, and he is the greatest voodoo priest out of the Ancient Land," she answered, laughing at me again. "I? You shall learn who I am, tonight in the swamp, in the House of Damballah."

"Yes?" I grunted. "What's to prevent me from taking you into Grimesville with me? You know the answers to questions I'd like to ask."

Her laughter was like the slash of a velvet whip.

"You drag me to the village of the whites? Not all death and hell could keep me from the Dance of the Skull, tonight in the House of Damballah. You are my captive, already." She laughed derisively as I started and glared into the shadows about me. "No-one is hiding there. I am alone, and you are the strongest man in Canaan. Even Saul Stark fears you, for he sent me with three men to kill you before you could reach the village. Yet you are my captive. I have but to beckon so – she crooked a contemptuous finger – and you will follow to the fires of Damballah and the knives of the torturers."

I laughed at her, but my mirth rang hollow. I could not deny the incredible magnetism of this brown enchantress; it fascinated and impelled, drawing me toward her, beating at my will power. I could not fail to recognize it any more than I could fail to recognize the peril in the ju-ju hut.

My agitation was apparent to her, for her eyes flashed with unholy triumph.

"Black men are fools, all but Saul Stark," she laughed. "White men are fools, too. I am the daughter of a white man, who lived in the hut of a black king and mated with his daughters. I know the strength of white men, and their weakness. I failed last night when I met you in the woods, but now I cannot fail!" Savage exultation thrummed in her voice. "By the blood in your veins I have snared you. The knife of the man you killed scratched your hand – seven drops of blood that fell on the pine needles have given me your soul! I took that blood, and Saul Stark gave me the man who ran away. Saul Stark hates cowards. With his hot, quivering heart, and seven drops of your blood, Kirby Buckner, deep in the swamps I have made such magic as none but the Bride of Damballah can make. Already you feel its urge! Oh, you are strong! The man you fought with the knife died less than an hour later. But you cannot fight me. Your blood makes you my slave. I have put a conjurement upon you."

By heaven, it was not mere madness she was mouthing! Hypnotism, magic, call it what you will, I felt its onslaught on my brain and will – a blind, senseless impulse that seemed to be rushing me against my will to the brink of some nameless abyss.

"I have made a charm you cannot resist!" she cried. "When I call you, you will come! Into the deep swamps you will follow me. You will see the Dance of the Skull and you will see the doom of a poor fool who sought to betray Saul Stark – who dreamed he could resist the Call of Damballah when it came. Into the swamp he goes tonight, with Tunk Bixby and the other four fools who opposed Saul Stark. You shall see that. You shall know and understand your own doom. And then you too shall go into the swamp, into darkness and silence deep as the darkness of nighted Africa! But before the darkness engulfs you there will be sharp knives, and little fires – oh, you will scream for death, even for the death that is beyond death!"

With a choking cry I whipped out a pistol and leveled it full at her breast. It was cocked and my finger was on the trigger. At that range I could not miss. But she looked full into the black muzzle and laughed – laughed – laughed, in wild peals that froze the blood in my veins.

And I sat there like an image pointing a pistol I could not fire! A frightful paralysis gripped me. I knew, with numbing certainty, that my life depended on the pull of that trigger, but I could not crook my finger – not though every muscle in my body quivered with the effort and sweat broke out on my face in clammy beads.

She ceased laughing, then, and stood looking at me in a manner indescribably sinister.

"You cannot shoot me, Kirby Buckner," she said quietly. "I have enslaved your soul. You cannot understand my power, but it has ensnared you. It is the Lure of the Bride of Damballah – the blood I have mixed with the mystic waters of Africa drawing the blood in your veins. Tonight you will come to me, in the House of Damballah."

"You lie!" My voice was an unnatural croak bursting from dry lips. "You've hypnotized me, you she-devil, so I can't pull this trigger. But you can't drag me across the swamps to you."

"It is you who lie," she returned calmly. "You know you lie. Ride back toward Grimesville or wherever you will, Kirby Buckner. But when the sun sets and the black shadows crawl out of the swamps, you will see me beckoning you, and you will follow me. Long I have planned your doom, Kirby Buckner, since first I heard the white men of Canaan talking to you. It was I who sent the word down the river that brought you back to Canaan. Not even Saul Stark knows of my plans for you.

"At dawn Grimesville shall go up in flames, and the heads of the white men will be tossed in the blood-running streets. But tonight is the Night of Damballah, and a white sacrifice shall be given to the black gods. Hidden among the trees you shall watch the Dance of the Skull – and then I shall call you forth – to die! And now, go fool! Run as far and as fast as you will. At sunset, wherever you are, you will turn your footsteps toward the House of Damballah!"

And with the spring of a panther she was gone into the thick brush, and as she vanished the strange paralysis dropped from me. With a gasped oath I fired blindly after her, but only a mocking laugh floated back to me.

Then in a panic I wrenched my horse about and spurred him down the trail. Reason and logic had momentarily vanished from my brain, leaving me in the grasp of blind primitive fear. I had confronted sorcery beyond my power to resist. I had felt my will mastered by the mesmerism in a brown woman's eyes. And now one driving urge overwhelmed me – a wild desire to cover as much distance as I could before that low-hanging sun dipped below the horizon and the black shadows came crawling from the swamps.

And yet I knew I could not outrun the grisly specter that menaced me. I was like a man fleeing in a nightmare, trying to escape from a monstrous phantom which kept pace with me despite my desperate speed.

I had not reached the Richardson cabin when above the drumming of my flight I heard the clop of hoofs ahead of me, and an instant later, sweeping around a kink in the trail, I almost rode down a tall, lanky man on an equally gaunt horse.

He yelped and dodged back as I jerked my horse to its haunches, my pistol presented at his breast.

"Look out, Kirby! It's me – Jim Braxton! My God, you look like you'd seen a ghost! What's chasin' you?"

"Where are you going?" I demanded, lowering my gun.

"Lookin' for you. Folks got worried as it got late and you didn't come in with the refugees. I 'lowed I'd light out and look for you. Miz Richardson said you rode into the Neck. Where in tarnation you been?"

"To Saul Stark's cabin."

"You takin' a big chance. What'd you find there?"

The sight of another white man had somewhat steadied my nerves. I opened my mouth to narrate my adventure, and was shocked to hear myself saying, instead: "Nothing. He wasn't there."

"Thought I heard a gun crack, a while ago," he remarked, glancing sharply at me sidewise.

"I shot at a copperhead," I answered, and shuddered. This reticence regarding the brown woman was compulsory; I could no more speak of her than I could pull the trigger of the pistol aimed at her. And I cannot describe the horror that beset me when I realized this. The conjer spells the black men feared were not lies, I realized sickly; demons in human form *did* exist who were able to enslave men's will and thoughts.

Braxton was eyeing me strangely.

"We're lucky the woods ain't full of black copperheads," he said. "Tope Sorley's pulled out."

"What do you mean?" By an effort I pulled myself together.

"Just that. Tom Breckinridge was in the cabin with him. Tope hadn't said a word since you talked to him. Just laid on that bunk and shivered. Then a kind of holler begun way out in the woods, and Tom went to the door with his rifle-gun, but couldn't see nothin'. Well, while he was standin' there he got a lick on the head from behind, and as he fell he seen that crazy nigger Tope jump over him and light out for the woods. Tom he taken a shot at him, but missed. Now what do you make of that?"

'The Call of Damballah!" I muttered, a chill perspiration beading my body. "God! The poor devil!"

"Huh? What's that?"

"For God's sake let's not stand here mouthing! The sun will soon be down!" In a frenzy of impatience I kicked my mount down the trail. Braxton followed me, obviously puzzled. With a terrific effort I got a grip on myself. How madly fantastic it was that Kirby Buckner should be shaking in the grip of unreasoning terror! It was so alien to my whole nature that it was no wonder Jim Braxton was unable to comprehend what ailed me.

"Tope didn't go of his own free will," I said. "That call was a summons he couldn't resist. Hypnotism, black magic, voodoo, whatever you want to call it, Saul Stark has some damnable power that enslaves men's will-power. The blacks are gathered somewhere in the swamp, for some kind of a devilish voodoo ceremony, which I have reason to believe will culminate in the murder of Tope Sorley. We've got to get to Grimesville if we can. I expect an attack at dawn."

Braxton was pale in the dimming light. He did not ask me where I got my knowledge.

"We'll lick 'em when they come; but it'll be slaughter."

I did not reply. My eyes were fixed with savage intensity on the sinking sun, and as it slid out of sight behind the trees I was shaken with an icy tremor. In vain I told myself that no occult power could draw me against my will. If she had been able to compel me, why had she not forced me to accompany her from the glade of the ju-ju hut? A grisly whisper seemed to tell me that she was but playing with me, as a cat allows a mouse almost to escape, only to be pounced upon again.

"Kirby, what's the matter with you?" I scarcely heard Braxton's anxious voice. "You're sweatin' and shakin' like you had the aggers. What – hey, what you stoppin' for?"

I had not consciously pulled on the rein, but my horse halted, and stood trembling and snorting, before the mouth of a narrow trail which meandered away at right angles from the road we were following – a trail that led north.

"Listen!" I hissed tensely.

"What is it?" Braxton drew a pistol. The brief twilight of the pinelands was deepening into dusk.

"Don't you hear it?" I muttered. "Drums! Drums beating in Goshen!"

"I don't hear nothin'," he mumbled uneasily. "If they was beatin' drums in Goshen you couldn't hear 'em this far away."

"Look there!" my sharp sudden cry made him start. I was pointing down the dim trail, at the figure which stood there in the dusk less than a hundred yards away. There in the dusk I saw her, even made out the gleam of her strange eyes, the mocking smile on her red lips. "Saul Stark's brown wench!" I raved, tearing at my scabbard.

195

"My God, man, are you stone-blind? Don't you see her?"

"I don't see nobody!" he whispered, livid. "What are you talkin' about, Kirby?"

With eyes glaring I fired down the trail, and fired again, and yet again. This time no paralysis gripped my arm. But the smiling face still mocked me from the shadows. A slender, rounded arm lifted, a finger beckoned imperiously; and then she was gone and I was spurring my horse down the narrow trail, blind, dead and dumb, with a sensation as of being caught in a black tide that was carrying me with it as it rushed on to a destination beyond my comprehension.

Dimly I heard Braxton's urgent yells, and then he drew up beside me with a clatter of hoofs, and grabbed my reins, setting my horse back on its haunches. I remember striking at him with my gun-barrel, without realizing what I was doing. All the black rivers of Africa were surging and foaming within my consciousness, roaring into a torrent that was sweeping me down to engulf me in an ocean of doom.

"Kirby, are you crazy? This trail leads to Goshen!"

I shook my head dazedly. The foam of the rushing waters swirled in my brain, and my voice sounded far away. "Go back! Ride for Grimesville! I'm going to Goshen."

"Kirby, you're mad!"

"Mad or sane, I'm going to Goshen this night," I answered dully. I was fully conscious. I knew what I was saying, and what I was doing. I realized the incredible folly of my action, and I realized my inability to help myself. Some shred of sanity impelled me to try to conceal the grisly truth from my companion, to offer a rational reason for my madness. "Saul Stark is in Goshen. He's the one who's responsible for all this trouble. I'm going to him. That will stop the uprising before it starts."

He was trembling like a man with the ague.

"Then I'm goin' with you."

"You must go on to Grimesville and warn the people," I insisted, holding to sanity, but feeling a strong urge begin to seize me, an irresistible urge to be in motion – to be riding in the direction toward which I was so horribly drawn.

"They'll be on their guard," he said stubbornly. "They won't need my warnin'. I'm goin' with you. I don't know what's got in you, but I ain't goin' to let you die alone among these black woods."

I did not argue. I could not. The blind rivers were sweeping me on – on – on! And down the trail, dim in the dusk, I glimpsed a supple figure, caught the gleam of uncanny eyes, the crook of a lifted finger... Then I was in motion, galloping down the trail, and I heard the drum of Braxton's horse's hoofs behind me.

IV : THE DWELLERS IN THE SWAMP

Night fell and the moon shone through the trees, blood-red behind the black branches. The horses were growing hard to manage.

"They got more sense'n us, Kirby," muttered Braxton.

"Panther, maybe," I replied absently, my eyes searching the gloom of the trail ahead.

"Naw, t'ain't. Closer we get to Goshen, the worse they git. And every time we swing nigh to a creek they shy and snort."

The trail had not yet crossed any of the narrow, muddy creeks that criss-crossed that end of Canaan, but several times it had swung so close to one of them that we glimpsed the black streak that was water glinting dully in the shadows of the thick growth. And each time, I remembered, the horses showed signs of fear.

But I had hardly noticed, wrestling as I was with the grisly compulsion that was driving me. Remember, I was not like a man in a hypnotic trance. I was fully aware, fully conscious. Even the daze in which I had seemed to hear the roar of black rivers had passed, leaving my mind clear, my thoughts lucid. And that was the sweating hell of it: to realize my folly clearly and poignantly, but to be unable to conquer it. Vividly I realized that I was riding to torture and death, and leading a faithful friend to the same end. But on I went. My efforts to break the spell that gripped me almost unseated my reason, but on I went. I cannot explain my compulsion, any more than I can explain why a sliver of steel is drawn to a magnet. It was a black power beyond the ring of white man's knowledge; a basic, elemental thing of which formal hypnotism is but scanty crumbs, spilled at random. A power beyond my control was drawing me to Goshen, and beyond; more I cannot explain, any more than the rabbit could explain why the eyes of the swaying serpent draw him into its gaping jaws.

We were not far from Goshen when Braxton's horse unseated its rider, and my own began snorting and plunging.

"They won't go no closer!" gasped Braxton, fighting at the reins.

I swung off, threw the reins over the saddle-horn.

"Go back, for God's sake, Jim! I'm going on afoot."

I heard him whimper an oath, then his horse was galloping after mine, and he was following me on foot. The thought that he must share my doom sickened me, but I could not dissuade him; and ahead of me a supple form was dancing in the shadows, luring me on – on – on.

I wasted no more bullets on that mocking shape. Braxton could not see it, and I knew it was part of my enchantment, no real woman of flesh and blood, but a hell-born will-o'-the-wisp, mocking me and leading me through the night to a hideous death. A "sending", the people of the Orient, who are wiser than we, call such a thing.

Braxton peered nervously at the black forest walls about us, and I knew his flesh was crawling with the fear of sawed-off shotguns blasting us suddenly from the shadows. But it was no ambush of lead or steel I feared as we emerged into the moonlit clearing that housed the cabins of Goshen.

The double line of log cabins faced each other across the dusty street. One line backed against the bank of Tularoosa Creek. The black stoops almost overhung the black waters. Nothing moved in the moonlight. No lights showed, no smoke oozed up from the stick-and-mud chimneys. It might have been a dead town, deserted and forgotten.

"It's a trap!" hissed Braxton, his eyes blazing slits. He bent forward like a skulking panther, a gun in each hand. "They're layin' for us in them huts!"

Then he cursed, but followed me as I strode down the street. I did not hail the silent huts. I *knew* Goshen was deserted. I felt its emptiness. Yet there was a contradictory sensation as of spying eyes fixed upon us. I did not try to reconcile these opposite convictions.

"They're gone," muttered Braxton, nervously. "I can't smell 'em. I can always smell niggers, if they're a lot of 'em, or if they're right close. You reckon they've gone to raid Grimesville?"

"No," I muttered. "They're in the House of Damballah."

He shot a quick glance at me.

"That's a neck of land in the Tularoosa about three miles west of here. My grandpap used to talk about it. The niggers held their heathen palavers there back in slave times. You ain't − Kirby − you−"

"Listen!" I wiped the icy sweat from my face.

"*Listen!*"

Through the black woodlands the faint throb of a drum whispered on the wind that glided up the shadowy reaches of the Tularoosa.

Braxton shivered. "It's them, all right. But for God's sake, Kirby − *look out!*"

With an oath he sprang toward the houses on the bank of the creek. I was after him just in time to glimpse a dark clumsy object scrambling or tumbling down the sloping bank into the water. Braxton threw up his long pistol, then lowered it, with a baffled curse. A faint splash marked the disappearance of the creature. The shiny black surface crinkled with spreading ripples.

"What was it?" I demanded.

"A nigger on his all-fours!" swore Braxton. His face was strangely pallid in the moonlight. "He was crouched between them cabins there, watchin' us!"

"It must have been an alligator. " What a mystery is the human mind! I was arguing for sanity and logic, I, the blind victim of a compulsion beyond sanity and logic. "A nigger would have to come up for air."

"He swum under the water and come up in the shadder of the bresh where we couldn't see him," maintained Braxton. "Now he'll go warn Saul Stark."

"Never mind!" The pulse was thrumming in my temples again, the roar of foaming water rising irresistibly in my brain. "I'm going straight through the swamp. For the last time, go back!"

"No! Sane or mad, I'm goin' with you!"

The pulse of the drum was fitful, growing more distinct as we advanced. We struggled through jungle-thick growth; tangled vines tripped us; our boots sank in scummy mire. We were entering the fringe of the swamp which grew deeper and denser until it culminated in the uninhabitable morass where the Tularoosa flowed into Black River, miles farther to the west.

The moon had not yet set, but the shadows were black under the interlacing branches with their mossy beards. We plunged into the first creek we must cross, one of the many muddy streams flowing into the Tularoosa. The water was only thigh-deep, the moss-clogged bottom fairly firm. My foot felt the edge of a sheer drop, and Î warned Braxton: "Look out for a deep hole; keep right behind me."

His answer was unintelligible. He was breathing heavily, crowding close behind me. Just as I reached the sloping bank and pulled myself up by the slimy, projecting roots, the water was violently agitated behind me. Braxton cried out incoherently, and hurled himself up the bank, almost upsetting me. I wheeled, gun in hand, but saw only the black water seething and whirling, after his thrashing rush through it.

"What the devil, Jim?"

"Somethin' grabbed me!" he panted. "Somethin' out of the deep hole. I tore loose and busted up the bank. I tell you, Kirby, something's follerin' us! Somethin' that swims under the water."

"Maybe it was that nigger you saw. These swamp people swim like fish. Maybe he swam up under the water to try to drown you."

He shook his head, staring at the black water, gun in hand.

"It *smelt* like a nigger, and the little I saw of it *looked* like a nigger. But it didn't *feel* like any kind of a human."

"Well, it was an alligator then," I muttered absently as I turned away. As always when I halted, even, for a moment, the roar of peremptory and imperious rivers shook the foundations of my reason.

He splashed after me without comment. Scummy puddles rose about our ankles, and we stumbled over moss-grown cypress knees. Ahead of us there loomed another, wider creek, and Braxton caught my arm.

"Don't do it, Kirby!" he gasped. "If we go into that water, it'll git us sure!"

"What?"

"I don't know. Whatever it was that flopped down that bank back there in Goshen. The same thing that grabbed me in that creek back yonder. Kirby, let's go back."

"Go back?" I laughed in bitter agony. "I wish to God I could! I've got to go on. Either Saul Stark or I must die before dawn."

He licked dry lips and whispered. "Go on, then; I'm with you, come heaven or hell." He thrust his pistol back into its scabbard, and drew a long keen knife from his boot. "Go ahead!"

I climbed down the sloping bank and splashed into the water that rose to my hips. The cypress branches bent a gloomy, moss-trailing arch over the creek. The water was black as midnight. Braxton was a blur, toiling behind me. I gained the first shelf of the opposite bank and paused, in water knee-deep, to turn and look back at him.

Everything happened at once, then. I saw Braxton halt short, staring at something on the bank behind me. He cried out, whipped out a gun and fired, just as I turned. In the flash of the gun I glimpsed a supple form reeling backward, a brown face fiendishly contorted. Then in the momentary blindness that followed the flash, I heard Jim Braxton scream.

Sight and brain cleared in time to show me a sudden swirl of the murky water, a round, black object breaking the surface behind Jim – and then Braxton gave a strangled cry and went under with a frantic thrashing and splashing. With an incoherent yell I sprang into the creek, stumbled and went to my knees, almost submerging myself. As I struggled up I saw Braxton's head, now streaming blood, break the surface for an instant, and I lunged toward it. It went under and another head appeared in its place, a shadowy black head. I stabbed at it ferociously, my knife cut only the blank water as the thing dipped of sight.

I staggered from the wasted force of the blow, and when I righted myself, the water lay unbroken about me. I called Jim's name, but there was no answer. Then panic laid a hand on me, and I splashed to the bank, sweating and trembling. With the water no higher than my knees I halted and waited, for I knew not what. But presently, down the creek a short distance, I made out a vague object lying in the shallow water near the shore.

I waded to it, through the clinging mud and crawling vines. It was Jim Braxton, and he was dead. It was not the wound in his head which had killed him. Probably he had struck a submerged rock when he was dragged under. But the marks of strangling fingers showed black on his throat. At the sight a nameless horror oozed out of that black swamp and coiled itself clammily about my soul; for no human fingers ever left such marks as those.

I had seen a head rise in the water, a head that looked like that of a Negro, though the features had been indistinct in the darkness. But no man, white or black, ever possessed the fingers that had crushed the life out of Jim Braxton. The distant drum grunted as if in mockery.

I dragged the body up on the bank and left it. I could not linger longer, for the madness was foaming in my brain again, driving me with white-hot spurs. But as I climbed the bank, I found blood on the bushes, and was shaken by the implication.

I remembered the figure I had seen staggering in the flash of Braxton's gun. *She* had been there, waiting for me on the bank, then – not a spectral illusion, but the woman herself, in flesh and blood! Braxton had fired at her, and wounded her. But the wound could not have been mortal; for no corpse lay among the bushes, and the grim hypnosis that dragged me onward was unweakened. Dizzily I wondered if she could be killed by mortal weapons.

The moon had set. The starlight scarcely penetrated the interwoven branches. No more creeks barred my way, only shallow streams, through which I splashed with sweating haste. Yet I did not expect to be attacked. Twice the dweller in the depths had passed me by to attack my companion. In icy despair I knew I was being saved for the grimmer fate. Each stream I crossed might be hiding the monster that killed Jim Braxton. Those creeks were all connected in a network of winding waterways. It could follow me easily. But my horror of it was less than the horror of the jungle-born magnetism that lurked in a witch-woman's eyes.

And as I stumbled through the tangled vegetation, I heard the drum rumbling ahead of me, louder and louder, a demoniacal mockery. Then a human voice mingled with its mutter, in a long-drawn cry of horror and agony that set every fiber of me quivering with sympathy. Sweat coursed down my clammy flesh; soon my own voice might be lifted like that, under unnamable torture. But on I went, my feet moving like automatons, apart from my body, motivated by a will not my own.

The drum grew loud, and a fire glowed among the black trees. Presently, crouching among the bushes, I stared across the stretch of black water that separated me from a nightmare scene. My halting there was as compulsory as the rest of my actions had been. Vaguely I knew the stage for horror had been set, but the time for my entry upon it was not yet. When the time had come, I would receive my summons.

A low, wooded island split the black creek, connected with the shore opposite me by a narrow neck of land. At its lower end the creek split into a network of channels threading their way among hummocks and rotting logs and moss-grown, vine-tangled clumps of trees. Directly across from my refuge the shore of the island was deeply indented by an arm of open, deep black water. Bearded trees walled a small clearing, and partly hid a hut. Between the hut and the shore burned a fire that sent up weird twisting snake-tongues of green flames. Scores of black people squatted under the shadows of the overhanging branches. When the green fire lit their faces it lent them the appearance of drowned corpses.

In the midst of the glade stood a giant Negro, an awesome statue in black marble. He was clad in ragged trousers, but on his head was a band of beaten gold set with a huge red jewel, and on his feet were barbaric sandals. His features reflected titanic vitality no less than his huge body. But he was all Negro – flaring nostrils, thick lips, ebony skin. I knew I looked upon Saul Stark, the conjure man.

He was regarding something that lay in the sand before him, something dark and bulky that moaned feebly. Presently, lifting his head, he rolled out a sonorous invocation across the black waters. From the blacks huddled under the trees there came a shuddering response, like a wind wailing through midnight branches. Both invocation and response were framed in an unknown tongue – a guttural, primitive language.

Again he called out, this time a curious high-pitched wail. A shuddering sigh swept the black people. All eyes were fixed on the dusky water. And presently an object rose slowly from the depths. A sudden trembling shook me. It looked like the head of a Negro. One after another it was followed by similar objects until five heads reared above the black, cypress-shadowed water. They might have been five Negroes submerged except for their heads – but I knew this was not so. There was something diabolical here. Their silence, motionlessness, their whole aspect was unnatural. From the trees came the hysterical sobbing of women, and someone whispered a man's name.

Then Saul Stark lifted his hands, and the five heads silently sank out of sight. Like a ghostly whisper I seemed to hear the voice of the African witch: *"He puts them in the swamp!"*

Stark's deep voice rolled out across the narrow water: "And now the Dance of the Skull, to make the conjer sure!"

What had the witch said? *"Hidden among the trees you shall watch the dance of the Skull!"*

The drum struck up again, growling and rumbling. The blacks swayed on their haunches, lifting a wordless chant. Saul Stark paced measuredly about the figure on the sand, his arms weaving cryptic patterns. Then he wheeled and faced toward the other end of the glade. By some sleight of hand he now grasped a grinning human skull, and this he cast upon the wet sand beyond the body. "Bride of Damballah!" he thundered. "The sacrifice awaits!"

There was an expectant pause; the chanting sank. All eyes were glued on the farther end of the glade. Stark stood waiting, and I saw him scowl as if puzzled. Then as he opened his mouth to repeat the call, a barbaric figure moved out of the shadows.

At the sight of her a chill shuddering shook me. For a moment she stood motionless, the firelight glinting on her gold ornaments, her head hanging on her breast. A tense silence reigned and I saw Saul Stark staring at her sharply. She seemed to be detached, somehow, standing aloof and withdrawn, head bent strangely.

Then, as if rousing herself, she began to sway with a jerky rhythm, and presently whirled into the mazes of a dance that was ancient when the ocean drowned the black kings of Atlantis. I cannot describe it. It was bestiality and diabolism set to motion, framed in a writhing, spinning whirl of posturing and gesturing that would have appalled a dancer of the Pharaohs. And that cursed skull danced with her; rattling and clashing on the sand, it bounded and spun like a live thing in time with her leaps and prancings.

But there was something amiss. I sensed it. Her arms hung limp, her drooping head swayed. Her legs bent and faltered, making her lurch drunkenly and out of time. A murmur rose from the people, and bewilderment etched Saul Stark's black countenance. For the domination of a conjure man is a thing hinged on a hair-trigger. Any trifling dislocation of formula or ritual may disrupt the whole web of his enchantment.

As for me, I felt the perspiration freeze on my flesh as I watched the grisly dance. The unseen shackles that bound me to that gyrating she-devil were strangling, crushing me. I knew she was approaching a climax, when she would summon me from my hiding-place, to wade through the black waters to the House of Damballah, to my doom.

Now she whirled to a floating stop, and when she halted, poised on her toes, she faced toward the spot where I lay hidden, and I knew that she could see me as plainly as if stood in the open; knew, too, somehow, that only she knew of my presence. I felt myself toppling on the edge of the abyss. She raised her head and I saw the flame of her eyes, even at that distance. Her face was lit with awful triumph. Slowly she raised her hand, and I felt my limbs begin to jerk in response to that terrible magnetism. She opened her mouth–

But from that open mouth sounded only a choking gurgle, and suddenly her lips were dyed crimson. And suddenly, without warning, her knees gave way and she pitched headlong into the sands.

And as she fell, so I too fell, sinking into the mire. Something burst in my brain with a shower of flame. And then I was crouching among the trees, weak and trembling, but with such a sense of freedom and lightness of limb as I never dreamed a man could experience. The black spell that gripped me was broken; the foul incubus lifted from my soul. It was as if light had burst upon a night blacker than African midnight.

At the fall of the girl a wild cry rose from the blacks, and they sprang up, trembling on the verge of panic. I saw their rolling white eyeballs, their bared teeth glistening in the firelight. Saul Stark had worked their primitive natures up to a pitch of madness, meaning to turn this frenzy, at the proper time, into a fury of battle. It could as easily turn into a hysteria of terror. Stark shouted sharply at them.

But just then the girl in a last convulsion, rolled over on the wet sand, and the firelight shone on a round hole between her breasts, which still oozed crimson. Jim Braxton's bullet had found its mark.

From the first I had felt that she was not wholly human; some black jungle spirit sired her, lending her the abysmal subhuman vitality that made her what she was. She had said that neither death nor hell could keep her from the Dance of the Skull. And, shot through the heart and dying, she had come through the swamp from the creek where she had received her death-wound to the House of Damballah. And the Dance of the Skull had been her death dance.

Dazed as a condemned man just granted a reprieve, at first I hardly grasped the meaning of the scene that now unfolded before me.

The blacks were in a frenzy. In the sudden, and to them inexplicable, death of the sorceress they saw a fearsome portent. They had no way of knowing that she was dying when she entered the glade. To them, their prophetess and priestess had been struck down under their very eyes, by an invisible death. This was magic blacker than Saul Stark's wizardry – and obviously hostile to them.

Like fear-maddened cattle they stampeded. Howling, screaming, tearing at one another they blundered through the trees, heading for the neck of land and the shore beyond. Saul Stark stood transfixed, heedless of them as he stared down at the brown girl, dead at last. And suddenly I came to myself, and with my awakened manhood came cold fury and the lust to kill. I drew a gun, and aiming in the uncertain firelight, pulled the trigger. Only a click answered me. The powder in the cap-and-ball pistols was wet.

Saul Stark lifted his head and licked his lips. The sounds of flight faded in the distance, and he stood alone in the glade. His eyes rolled whitely toward the black woods around him. He bent, grasped the man-like object that lay on the sand, and dragged it into the hut. The instant he vanished I started toward the island, wading through the narrow channels at the lower end. I had almost reached the shore when a mass of driftwood gave way with me and I slid into a deep hole.

Instantly the water swirled about me, and a head rose beside me; a dim face was close to mine – the face of a Negro – *the face of Tunk Bixby*. But now it was inhuman; as expressionless and soulless as that of a catfish; the face of a being no longer human, and no longer mindful of its human origin.

Slimy, misshapen fingers gripped my throat, and I drove my knife into the sagging mouth. The features vanished in a wave of blood; mutely the thing sank out of sight, and I hauled myself up the bank, under the thick bushes.

Stark had run from his hut, a pistol in his hand. He was staring wildly about, alarmed by the noise he had heard, but I knew he could not see me. His ashy skin glistened with perspiration. He who had ruled by fear was now ruled by fear. He feared the unknown hand that had slain his mistress; feared the Negroes who had fled him; feared the abysmal swamp which had sheltered him, and the monstrosities he had created. He lifted a weird call that quavered with panic. He called again as only four heads broke the water, but he called in vain.

But the four heads began to move toward the shore and the man who stood there. He shot them one after another. They made no effort to avoid the bullets. They came straight on, sinking one by one. He had fired six shots before the last head vanished. The shots drowned the sounds of my approach. I was close behind him when he turned at last.

I know he knew me; recognition flooded his face and fear went with it, at the knowledge that he had a human being to deal with. With a scream he hurled his empty pistol at me and rushed after it with a lifted knife.

I ducked, parried his lunge and countered with a thrust that bit deep into his ribs. He caught my wrist and I gripped his, and there we strained, breast to breast. His eyes were like a mad dog's in the starlight, his muscles like steel cords.

I ground my heel down on his bare foot, crushing the instep. He howled and lost balance, and I tore my knife hand free and stabbed him in the belly. Blood spurted and he dragged me down with him. I jerked loose and rose, just as he pulled himself up on his elbow and hurled his knife. It sang past my ear, and I stamped on his breast. His ribs caved in under my heel. In a red killing-haze I knelt, jerked back his head and cut his throat from ear to ear.

There was a pouch of dry powder in his belt. Before I moved further I reloaded my pistols. Then I went into the hut with a torch. And there I understood the doom the brown witch had meant for me. Tope Sorley lay moaning on a bunk. The transmutation that was to make him a mindless, soulless semi-human dweller in the water was not complete, but his mind was gone. Some of the physical changes had been made – by what godless sorcery out of Africa's black abyss I have no wish to know. His body was rounded and elongated, his legs dwarfed; his feet were flattened and broadened, his fingers horribly long, and webbed. His neck was inches longer than it should be. His features were not altered, but the expression was no more human than that of a great fish. And there, but for the loyalty of Jim Braxton, lay Kirby Buckner. I placed my pistol muzzle against Tope's head in grim mercy and pulled the trigger.

And so the nightmare closed, and I would not drag out the grisly narration. The white people of Canaan never found anything on the island except the bodies of Saul Stark and the brown woman. They think to this day that a swamp Negro killed Jim Braxton, after he had killed the brown woman, and that I broke up the threatened uprising by killing Saul Stark. I let them think it. They will never know the shapes the black water of Tularoosa hides. That is a secret I share with the cowed and terror-haunted black people of Goshen and of it neither they nor I have spoken.

THE VALLEY OF THE WORM

I will tell you of Niord and the Worm. You have heard the tale before in many guises wherein the hero was named Tyr, or Perseus, or Siegfried, or Beowulf, or Saint George. But it was Niord who met the loathly demoniac thing that crawled hideously up from hell, and from which meeting sprang the cycle of hero-tales that revolves down the ages until the very substance of the truth is lost and passes into the limbo of all forgotten legends. I know whereof I speak – for I was Niord.

As I lie here awaiting death, which creeps slowly upon me like a blind slug, my dreams are filled with glittering visions and the pageantry of glory. It is not of the drab, disease-racked life of James Allison I dream, but all the gleaming figures of the mighty pageantry that have passed before, and shall come after; for I have faintly glimpsed, not merely the shapes that trail out behind, but shapes that come after, as a man in a long parade glimpses, far ahead, the line of figures that precede him winding over a distant hill, etched shadow-like against the sky. I am one and all the pageantry of shapes and guises and masks which have been, are, and shall be the visible manifestations of that illusive, intangible, but vitally existent spirit now promenading under the brief and temporary name of James Allison.

Each man on earth, each woman, is part and all of a similar caravan of shapes and beings. But they can not remember – their minds can not bridge the brief, awful gulfs of blackness which lie between those unstable shapes, and which the spirit, soul or ego, in spanning, shakes off its fleshy masks. I remember. Why I can remember is the strangest tale of all; but as i lie here with death's black wings slowly unfolding over me, all the dim folds of my previous lives are shaken out before my eyes, and I see myself in many forms and guises – braggart, swaggering, fearful, loving, foolish, all that men have been or will be.

I have been Man in many lands and many conditions; yet – and here is another strange thing – my line of reincarnation runs straight down one unerring channel. I have never been any but a man of that restless race men once called Nordheimer and later Aryans, and today name by many names and designations. Their history is my history, from the first mewling wail of a hairless white ape cub in the wastes of the arctic, to the death-cry of the last degenerate product of ultimate civilization, in some dim and unguessed future age.

My name has been Hialmar, Tyr, Bragi, Bran, Horsa, Eric, and John. I strode red-handed through the deserted streets of Rome behind the yellow-maned Brennus; I wandered through the violated plantations with Alaric and his Goths when the flame of burning villas lit the land like day and an empire was gasping its last under our sandalled feet; I waded sword in hand through the foaming surf from Hengist's galley to lay the foundations of England in blood and pillage; when Leif the Lucky sighted the broad white beaches of an unguessed world, I stood beside him in the bows of the dragon-ship, my golden beard blowing in the wind; and when Godfrey of Bouillon led his Crusaders over the walls of Jerusalem, I was among them in steel cap and brigandine.

But it is of none of these things I would speak. I would take you back with me into an age beside which that of Brennus and Rome is as yesterday. I would take you back through, not merely centuries and millenniums, but epochs and dim ages unguessed by the wildest philosopher. Oh far, far and far will you fare into the nighted Past before you wind beyond the boundaries of my race, blue-eyed, yellow-haired, wanderers, slayers, lovers, mighty in rapine and wayfaring.

It is the adventure of Niord Worm's-bane of which I would speak – the root-stem of a whole cycle of hero-tales which has not yet reached its end, the grisly underlying reality that lurks behind time-distorted myths of dragons, fiends and monsters.

Yet it is not alone with the mouth of Niord that I will speak. I am James Allison no less than I was Niord, and as I unfold the tale, I will interpret some of his thoughts and dreams and deeds from the mouth of the modern I, so that the saga of Niord shall not be a meaningless chaos to you. His blood is your blood, who are sons of Aryan; but wide misty gulfs of eons lie horrifically between, and the deeds and dreams of Niord seem as alien to your deeds and dreams as the primordial and lion-haunted forest seems alien to the white-walled city street.

It was a strange world in which Niord lived and loved and fought, so long ago that even my eon-spanning memory can not recognize landmarks. Since then the surface of the earth has changed, not once but a score of times; continents have risen and sunk, seas have changed their beds and rivers their courses, glaciers have waxed and waned, and the very stars and constellations have altered and shifted.

It was so long ago that the cradle-land of my race was still in Nordheim. But the epic drifts of my people had already begun, and blue-eyed, yellow-maned tribes flowed eastward and southward and westward, on century-long treks that carried them around the world and left their bones and their traces in strange lands and wild waste places. On one of these drifts I grew from infancy to manhood. My knowledge of that northern homeland was dim memories, like half-remembered dreams, of blinding white snow plains and ice fields, of great fires roaring in the circle of hide tents, of yellow manes flying in great winds, and a sun setting in a lurid wallow of crimson clouds, blazing on trampled snow where still dark forms lay in pools that were redder than the sunset.

That last memory stands out clearer than the others. It was the field of Jotunheim, I was told in later years, whereon had just been fought that terrible battle which was the Armageddon of the Æsir-folk, the subject of a cycle of hero-songs for long ages, and which still lives today in dim dreams of Ragnarok and Goetterdämmerung. I looked on that battle as a mewling infant; so I must have lived about – but I will not name the age, for I would be called a madman, and historians and geologists alike would rise to dispute me.

But my memories of Nordheim were few and dim, paled by memories of that long, long trek upon which I had spent my life. We had not kept to a straight course, but our trend had been forever southward. Sometimes we had bided for a while in fertile upland valleys or rich river-traversed plains, but always we took up the trail again, and not always because of drouth or famine. Often we left countries teeming with game and wild grain to push into wastelands. On our trail we moved endlessly, driven only by our restless whim, yet blindly following a cosmic law, the workings of which we never guessed, any more than the wild geese guess in their flights around the world. So at last we came into the Country of the Worm.

I will take up the tale at the time when we came into jungle-clad hills reeking with rot and teeming with spawning life, where the tom-toms of a savage people pulsed incessantly through the hot breathless night. These people came forth to dispute our way – short, strongly built men, black-haired, painted, ferocious, but indisputably white men. We knew their breed of old. They were Picts, and of all alien races the fiercest. We had met their kind before in thick forests, and in upland valleys beside mountain lakes. But many moons had passed since those meetings.

I believe this particular tribe represented the easternmost drift of the race. They were the most primitive and ferocious of any I ever met. Already they were exhibiting hints of characteristics I have noted among black savages in jungle countries, though they had dwelt in these environs only a few generations. The abysmal jungle was engulfing them, was obliterating their pristine characteristics and shaping them in its own horrific mold. They were drifting into headhunting, and cannibalism was but a step which I believe they must have taken before they became extinct. These things are natural adjuncts to the jungle; the Picts did not learn them from the black people, for then there were no blacks among those hills. In later years they came up from the south, and the Picts first enslaved and then were absorbed by them. But with that my saga of Niord is not concerned.

We came into that brutish hill country, with its squalling abysms of savagery and black primitiveness. We were a whole tribe marching on foot, old men, wolfish with their long beards and gaunt limbs, giant warriors in their prime, naked children running along the line of march, women with tousled yellow locks carrying babies which never cried – unless it were to scream from pure rage. I do not remember our numbers, except that there were some five hundred fighting-men – and by fighting-men I mean all males, from the child just strong enough to lift a bow, to the oldest of the old men. In that madly ferocious age all were fighters. Our women fought, when brought to bay, like tigresses, and I have seen a babe, not yet old enough to stammer articulate words, twist its head and sink its teeth in the foot that stamped out its life.

Oh, we were fighters! Let me speak of Niord. I am proud of him, the more when I consider the paltry crippled body of James Allison, the unstable mask I now wear. Niord was tall, with great shoulders, lean hips and mighty limbs. His muscles were long and swelling, denoting endurance and speed as well as strength. He could run all day without tiring, and he possessed a co-ordination that made his movements a blur of blinding speed. If I told you his full strength, you would brand me a liar. But there is no man on earth today strong enough to bend the bow Niord handled with ease. The longest arrow-flight on record is that of a Turkish archer who sent a shaft 482 yards. There was not a stripling in my tribe who could not have bettered that flight.

As we entered the jungle country we heard the tom-toms booming across the mysterious valleys that slumbered between the brutish hills, and in a broad, open plateau we met our enemies. I do not believe these Picts knew us, even by legends, or they had never rushed so openly to the onset, though they outnumbered us. But there was no attempt at ambush. They swarmed out of the trees, dancing and singing their war-songs, yelling their barbarous threats. Our heads should hang in their idol-hut and our yellow-haired women should bear their sons. Ho! ho! ho! By Ymir, it was Niord who laughed then, not James Allison. Just so we of the Æsir laughed to hear their threats – deep thunderous laughter from broad and mighty chests. Our trail was laid in blood and embers through many lands. We were the slayers and ravishers, striding sword in hand across the world and that these folk threatened us woke our rugged humor.

We went to meet them, naked but for our wolf-hides, swinging our bronze swords, and our singing was like rolling thunder in the hills. They sent their arrows among us, and we gave back their fire. They could not match us in archery. Our arrows hissed in blinding clouds among them, dropping them like autumn leaves, until they howled and frothed like mad dogs and charged to hand-grips. And we, mad with the fighting joy, dropped our bows and ran to meet them, as a lover runs to his love.

By Ymir, it was a battle to madden and make drunken with the slaughter and the fury. The Picts were as ferocious as we, but ours was the superior physique, the keener wit, the more highly developed fighting-brain. We won because we were a superior race, but it was no easy victory. Corpses littered the blood-soaked earth; but at last they broke, and we cut them down as they ran, to the very edge of the trees. I tell of that fight in a few bald words. I can not paint the madness, the reek of sweat and blood, the panting, muscle-straining effort, the splintering of bones under mighty blows, the rending and hewing of quivering sentient flesh; above all the merciless abysmal savagery of the whole affair, in which there was neither rule nor order, each man fighting as he would or could. If I might do so, you would recoil in horror; even the modern I, cognizant of my close kinship with those times, stand aghast as I review that butchery. Mercy was yet unborn, save as some individual's whim, and rules of warfare were as yet undreamed of. It was an age in which each tribe and each human fought tooth and fang from birth to death, and neither gave nor expected mercy.

So we cut down the fleeing Picts, and our women came out on the field to brain the wounded enemies with stones, or cut their throats with copper knives. We did not torture. We were no more cruel than life demanded. The rule of life was ruthlessness, but there is more wanton cruelty today than ever we dreamed of. It was not wanton bloodthirstiness that made us butcher wounded and captive foes. It was because we knew our chances of survival increased with each enemy slain.

Yet there was occasionally a touch of individual mercy, and so it was in this fight. I had been occupied with a duel with an especially valiant enemy. His tousled thatch of black hair scarcely came above my chin, but he was a solid knot of steel-spring muscles, than which lightning scarcely moved faster. He had an iron sword and a hide-covered buckler. I had a knotty-headed bludgeon, That fight was one that glutted even my battle-lusting soul. I was bleeding from a score of flesh wounds before one of my terrible, lashing strokes smashed his shield like cardboard, and an instant later my bludgeon glanced from his unprotected head. Ymir! Even now I stop to laugh and marvel at the hardness of that Pict's skull. Men of that age were assuredly built on a rugged plan! That blow should have spattered his brains like water. It did lay his scalp open horribly, dashing him senseless to the earth, where I let him lie, supposing him to be dead, as I joined in the slaughter of the fleeing warriors.

When I returned reeking with sweat and blood, my club horribly clotted with blood and brains, I noticed that my antagonist was regaining consciousness, and that a naked tousle-headed girl was preparing to give him the finishing touch with a stone she could scarcely lift. A vagrant whim caused me to check the blow. I had enjoyed the fight, and I admired the adamantine quality of his skull.

We made camp a short distance away, burned our dead on a great pyre, and after looting the corpses of the enemy, we dragged them across the plateau and cast them down in a valley to make a feast for the hyenas, jackals and vultures which were already gathering. We kept close watch that night, but we were not attacked, though far away through the jungle we could make out the red gleam of fires, and could faintly hear, when the wind veered, the throb of tom-toms and demoniac screams and yells – keenings for the slain or mere animal squallings of fury.

Nor did they attack us in the days that followed. We bandaged our captive's wounds and quickly learned his primitive tongue, which, however, was so different from ours that I can not conceive of the two languages having ever had a common source.

His name was Grom, and he was a great hunter and fighter, he boasted. He talked freely and held no grudge, grinning broadly and showing tusk-like teeth, his beady eyes glittering from under the tangled black mane that fell over his low forehead. His limbs were almost ape-like in their thickness.

He was vastly interested in his captors, though he could never understand why he had been spared; to the end it remained an inexplicable mystery to him. The Picts obeyed the law of survival even more rigidly than did the Æsir. They were the more practical, as shown by their more settled habits. They never roamed as far or as blindly as we. Yet in every line we were the superior race.

Grom, impressed by our intelligence and fighting qualities, volunteered to go into the hills and make peace for us with his people. It was immaterial to us, but we let him go. Slavery had not yet been dreamed of.

So Grom went back to his people, and we forgot about him, except that

I went a trifle more cautiously about my hunting, expecting him to be lying in wait to put an arrow through my back. Then one day we heard a rattle of tom-toms, and Grom appeared at the edge of the jungle, his face split in his gorilla-grin, with the painted, skin-clad, feather-bedecked chiefs of the clans. Our ferocity had awed them, and our sparing of Grom further impressed them. They could not understand leniency; evidently we valued them too cheaply to bother about killing one when he was in our power.

So peace was made with much pow-wow, and sworn to with many strange oaths and rituals – we swore only by Ymir, and an Æsir never broke that vow. But they swore by the elements, by the idol which sat in the fetish-hut where fires burned for ever and a withered crone slapped a leather-covered drum all night long, and by another being too terrible to be named.

Then we all sat around the fires and gnawed meat-bones, and drank a fiery concoction they brewed from wild grain, and the wonder is that the feast did not end in a general massacre, for that liquor had devils in it and made maggots writhe in our brain. But no harm came of our vast drunkenness, and thereafter we dwelt at peace with our barbarous neighbours. They taught us many things, and learned many more from us. But they taught us iron-workings, into which they had been forced by the lack of copper in those hills, and we quickly excelled them.

We went freely among their villages – mud-walled clusters of huts in hilltop clearings overshadowed by giant trees – and we allowed them to come at will among our camps – straggling lines of hide tents on the plateau where the battle had been fought. Our young men cared not for their squat beady-eyed women, and our rangy clean-limbed girls with their tousled yellow heads were not drawn to the hairy-breasted savages. Familiarity over a period of years would have reduced the repulsion on either side, until the two races would have flowed together to form one hybrid people, but long before that time the Æsir rose and departed, vanishing into the mysterious hazes of the haunted south. But before that exodus there came to pass the horror of the Worm.

I hunted with Grom and he led me into brooding, uninhabited valleys and up into silence-haunted hills where no men had set foot before us. But there was one valley, off in the mazes of the southwest, into which he would not go. Stumps of shattered columns, relics of a forgotten civilization, stood among the trees on the valley floor. Grom showed them to me, as we stood on the cliffs that flanked the mysterious vale, but he would not go down into it, and he dissuaded me when I would have gone alone. He would not speak plainly of the danger that lurked there, but it was greater than that of serpent or tiger, or the trumpeting elephants which occasionally wandered up in devastating droves from the south.

Of all beasts, Grom told me in the gutturals of his tongue, the Picts feared only Satha, the great snake, and they shunned the jungle where he lived. But there was another thing they feared, and it was connected in some manner with the Valley of Broken Stones, as the Picts called the crumbling pillars. Long ago, when his ancestors had first come into the country, they had dared that grim vale, and a whole clan of them had perished, suddenly, horribly, and unexplainably. At least Grom did not explain. The horror had come up out of the earth, somehow, and it was not good to talk of it, since it was believed that it might be summoned by speaking of it – whatever it was.

But Grom was ready to hunt with me anywhere else; for he was the greatest hunter among the Picts, and many and fearful were our adventures. Once I killed, with the iron sword I had forged with my own hands, that most terrible of all beasts – old saber-tooth, which men today call a tiger because he was more like a tiger than anything else. In reality he was almost as much like a bear in build, save for his unmistakably feline head. Saber-tooth was massive-limbed, with a low-hung, great, heavy body, and he vanished from the earth because he was too terrible a fighter, even for that grim age. As his muscles and ferocity grew, his brain dwindled until at last even the instinct of self-preservation vanished. Nature, who maintains her balance in such things, destroyed him because, had his super-fighting powers been allied with an intelligent brain, he would have destroyed all other forms of life on earth. He was a freak on the road of evolution – organic-development gone mad and run to fangs and talons, to slaughter and destruction.

I killed saber-tooth in a battle that would make a saga in itself, and for months afterward I lay semi-delirious with ghastly wounds that made the toughest warriors shake their heads. The Picts said that never before had a man killed a saber-tooth single-handed. Yet I recovered, to the wonder of all.

While I lay at the doors of death there was a secession from the tribe. It was a peaceful secession, such as continually occurred and contributed greatly to the peopling of the world by yellow-haired tribes. Forty-five of the young men took themselves mates simultaneously and wandered off to found a clan of their own. There was no revolt; it was a racial custom which bore fruit in all the later ages, when tribes sprung from the same roots met, after centuries of separation, and cut one another's throats with joyous abandon. The tendency of the Aryan and the pre-Aryan was always towards disunity, clans splitting off the main stem, and scattering.

So these young men, led by one Bragi, my brother-in-arms, took their girls and venturing southwest, took up their abode in the Valley of Broken Stones. The Picts expostulated, hinting vaguely of a monstrous doom that haunted the vale, but the Æsir laughed. We had left our own demons and weirds in the icy wastes of the far blue north, and the devils of other races did not much impress us.

When my full strength was returned, and the grisly wounds were only scars, I girt on my weapons and strode over the plateau to visit Bragi's clan. Grom did not accompany me. He had not been in the Æsir camp for several days. But I knew the way. I remembered well the valley, from the cliffs of which I had looked down and seen the lake at the upper end, the trees thickening into forest at the lower extremity. The sides of the valley were high sheer cliffs, and a steep broad ridge at either end cut it off from the surrounding country. It was toward the lower or southwestern end that the valley-floor was dotted thickly with ruined columns, some towering high among the trees, some fallen into heaps of lichen-clad stones. What race reared them none knew. But Grom had hinted fearsomely of a hairy, apish monstrosity dancing loathsomely under the moon to a demoniac piping that induced, horror and madness.

I crossed the plateau whereon our camp was pitched, descended the slope, traversed a shallow vegetation-choked valley, climbed another slope, and plunged into the hills. A half-day's leisurely travel brought me to the ridge on the other side of which lay the valley of the pillars. For many miles I had seen no sign of human life. The settlements of the Picts all lay many miles to the east: I topped the ridge and looked down into the dreaming valley with its still blue lake, its brooding cliffs and its broken columns jutting among the trees. I looked for smoke. I saw none, but I saw vultures wheeling in the sky over a cluster of tents on the lake shore.

I came down the ridge warily and approached the silent camp. In it I halted, frozen with horror. I was not easily moved. I had seen death in many forms, and had fled from or taken part in red massacres that spilled blood like water and heaped the earth with corpses. But here I was confronted with an organic devastation that staggered and appalled me. Of Bragi's embryonic clan, not one remained alive, and not one corpse was whole. Some of the hide tents still stood erect. Others were mashed down and flattened out, as if crushed by some monstrous weight, so that at first I wondered if a drove of elephants had stampeded across the camp. But no elephants ever wrought such destruction as I saw strewn on the bloody ground. The camp was a shambles, littered with bits of flesh and fragments of bodies – hands, feet, heads, pieces of human debris. Weapons lay about, some of them stained with a greenish slime like that which spurts from a crushed caterpillar.

No human foe could have committed this ghastly atrocity. I looked at the lake, wondering if nameless amphibian monsters had crawled from the calm waters whose deep blue told of unfathomed depths. Then I saw a print left by the destroyer. It was a track such as a titanic worm might leave, yards broad, winding back down the valley. The grass lay flat where it ran, and bushes and small trees had been crushed down into the earth, all horribly smeared with blood and greenish slime.

With berserk fury in my soul I drew my sword and started to follow it, when a call attracted me. I wheeled, to see a stocky form approaching me from the ridge. It was Grom the Pict, and when I think of the courage it must have taken for him to have overcome all the instincts planted in him by traditional teachings and personal experience, I realize the full depths of his friendship for me.

Squatting on the lake shore, spear in his hand, his black eyes ever roving fearfully down the brooding tree-waving reaches of the valley, Grom told me of the horror that had come upon Bragi's clan under the moon. But first he told me of the Worm, as his sires had told the tale to him.

Long ago the Picts had drifted down from the northwest on a long, long trek, finally reaching these jungle-covered hills, where, because they were weary, and because the game and fruit were plentiful and there were no hostile tribes, they halted and built their mud-walled villages.

Some of them, a whole clan of that numerous tribe, took up their abode in the Valley of the Broken Stones. They found the columns and a great ruined temple back in the trees, and in that temple there was no shrine or altar, but the mouth of a shaft that vanished deep into the black earth, and in which there were no steps such as a human being would make and use. They built their village in the valley, and in the night, under the moon, horror came upon them and left only broken walls and bits of slime-smeared flesh. In those days the Picts feared nothing. The warriors of the other clans gathered and sang their war-songs and danced their war dances, and followed a broad track of blood and slime to the shaft-mouth in the temple. They howled defiance and hurled down boulders which were never heard to strike bottom. Then began a thin demoniac piping, and up from the well pranced a hideous anthropomorphic figure dancing to the weird trains of a pipe it held in its monstrous hands. The horror of its aspect froze the fierce Picts with amazement, and close behind it a vast white hulk heaved up from the subterranean darkness. Out of the shaft came a slavering mad nightmare which arrows pierced but could not check, which swords carved but could not slay. It fell slobbering upon the warriors, crushing them to crimson pulp, tearing them to bits as an octopus might tear small fishes, sucking their blood from their mangled limbs and devouring them even as they screamed and struggled. The survivors fled, pursued to the very ridge, up which, apparently, the monster could not propel its quaking mountainous bulk.

After that they did not dare the silent valley. But the dead came to their shamans and old men in dreams and told them strange and terrible secrets. They spoke of an ancient, ancient race of semi-human beings which once inhabited that valley and reared those columns for their own weird inexplicable purpose. The white monster in the pits was their god, summoned up from the nighted abysses of mid-earth uncounted fathoms below the black mold, by sorcery unknown to the sons of men. The hairy anthropomorphic being was its servant, created to serve the god, a formless elemental spirit drawn up from below and cased in flesh, organic but beyond the understanding of humanity. The Old Ones had long vanished into the limbo from whence they crawled in the black dawn of the universe, but their bestial god and his inhuman slave lived on. Yet both were organic after a fashion, and could be wounded, though no human weapon had been found potent enough to slay them.

Bragi and his clan had dwelt for weeks in the valley before the horror struck. Only the night before, Grom, hunting above the cliffs, and by that token daring greatly, had been paralyzed by a high-pitched demon piping, and then by a mad clamor of human screaming. Stretched face down in the dirt, hiding his head in a tangle of grass, he had not dared to move, even when the shrieks died away in the slobbering, repulsive sounds of a hideous feast. When dawn broke he had crept shuddering to the cliffs to look down into the valley, and the sight of the devastation, even when seen from afar, had driven him in yammering flight far into the hills. But it had occurred to him, finally, that he should warn the rest of the tribe, and returning, on his way to the camp on the plateau, he had seen me entering the valley.

So spoke Grom, while I sat and brooded darkly, my chin on my mighty fist. I can not frame in modern words the clan-feeling that in those days was a living vital part of every man and woman. In a world where talon and fang were lifted on every hand, and the hands of all men raised against an individual, except those of his own clan, tribal instinct was more than the phrase it is today. It was as much a part of a man as was his heart or his right hand. This was necessary, for only thus banded together in unbreakable groups could mankind have survived in the terrible environments of the primitive world. So now the personal grief I felt for Bragi and the clean-limbed young men and laughing white-skinned girls was drowned in a deeper sea of grief and fury that was cosmic in its depth and intensity. I sat grimly, while the Pict squatted anxiously beside me, his gaze roving from me to the menacing deeps of the valley where the accursed columns loomed like broken teeth of cackling hags among the waving leafy reaches.

I, Niord, was not one to use my brain over-much. I lived in a physical world, and there were the old men of the tribe to do my thinking. But I was one of a race destined to become dominant mentally as well as physically, and I was no mere muscular animal. So as I sat there there came dimly and then clearly a thought to me that brought a short fierce laugh from my lips.

Rising, I bade Grom aid me, and we built a pyre on the lake shore of dried wood, the ridgepoles of the tents, and the broken shafts of spears. Then we collected the grisly fragments that had been parts of Magi's band, and we laid them on the pile, and struck flint and steel to it.

The thick sad smoke crawled serpent-like into the sky, and turning to Grom, I made him guide me to the jungle where lurked that scaly horror, Satha. the great serpent. Grom gaped at me; not even the greatest hunters among the Picts sought out the mighty crawling one. But my will was like a wind that swept him along my course, and at last he led the way. We left the valley by the upper end, crossing the ridge, skirting the tall cliffs, and plunged into the fastnesses of the south, which was peopled only by the grim denizens of the jungle. Deep into the jungle we went, until we came to a low-lying expanse, dark and dank beneath the great creeper-festooned trees, where our feet sank deep into the spongy silt, carpeted by rotting vegetation, and slimy moisture oozed up beneath their pressure. This, Grom told me, was the realm haunted by Satha, the great serpent.

Let me speak of Satha. There is nothing like him on earth today, nor has there been for countless ages. Like the meat-eating dinosaur, like old saber-tooth, he was too terrible to exist. Even then he was a survival of a grimmer age when life and its forms were cruder and more hideous. There were not many of his kind then, though they may have existed in great numbers in the reeking ooze of the vast jungle-tangled swamps still farther south.He was larger than any python of modern ages, and his fangs dripped with poison a thousand times more deadly than that of a king cobra.

He was never worshipped by the pure-blood Picts, though the blacks that came later deified him, and that adoration persisted in the hybrid race that sprang from the Negroes and their white conquerors. But to other peoples he was the nadir of evil horror, and tales of him became twisted into demonology; so in later ages Satha became the veritable devil of the white races, and the Stygians first worshipped, and then, when they became Egyptians, abhorred him under the name of Set, the Old Serpent, while to the Semites he became Leviathan and Satan. He was terrible enough to be a god, for he was a crawling death. I had seen a bull elephant fall dead in his tracks from Satha's bite. I had seen him, had glimpsed him writhing his horrific way through the dense jungle, had seen him take his prey, but had never hunted him. He was too grim, even for the slayer of old saber-tooth.

But now I hunted him, plunging farther and farther into the hot, breathless reek of his jungle, even when friendship for me could not drive Grom farther. He urged me to paint my body and sing my death-song before I advanced farther, but I pushed on unheeding.

In a natural runway that wound between the shouldering trees, I set a trap. I found a large tree, soft and spongy of fiber, but thick-boled and heavy, and I hacked through its base close to the ground with my great sword, directing its fall so that when it toppled, its top crashed into the branches of a smaller tree, leaving it leaning across the runway, one end resting on the earth, the other caught in the small tree. Then I cut away the branches on the underside, and cutting a slim tough sapling I trimmed it and stuck it upright like a prop-pole under the leaning tree. Then, cutting away the tree which supported it, I left the great trunk poised precariously on the prop-pole, to which I fastened a long vine, as thick as my wrist.

Then I went alone through that primordial twilight jungle until an overpowering fetid odor assailed my nostrils, and from the rank vegetation in front of me, Satha reared up his hideous head, swaying lethally from side to side, while his forked tongue jetted in and out, and his great yellow terrible eyes burned icily on me with all the evil wisdom of the black elder world that was when man was not. I backed away, feeling no fear, only an icy sensation along my spine, and Satha came sinuously after me, his shining eighty-foot barrel rippling over the rotting vegetation in mesmeric silence. His wedge-shaped head was bigger than the head of the hugest stallion, his trunk was thicker than a man's body, and his scales shimmered with a thousand changing scintillations. I was to Satha as a mouse is to a king cobra, but I was fanged as no mouse ever was. Quick as I was, I knew I could not avoid the lightning stroke of that great triangular head; so I dared not let him come too close. Subtly I fled down the runway, and behind me the rush of the great supple body was like the sweep of wind through the grass.

He was not far behind me when I raced beneath the deadfall, and as the great shining length glided under the trap, I gripped the vine with both hands and jerked desperately. With a crash the great trunk fell across Satha's scaly back, some six feet back of his wedge-shaped head.

I had hoped to break his spine but I do not think it did, for the great body coiled and knotted, the mighty tail lashed and thrashed, mowing down the bushes as if with a giant flail. At the instant of the fall, the huge head had whipped about and struck the tree with terrific impact, the mighty fangs shearing through bark and wood like scimitars. Now, as if aware he fought an inanimate foe, Satha turned on me, standing out of his reach. The scaly neck writhed and arched, the mighty jaws gaped, disclosing fangs a foot in length, from which dripped venom that might have burned through solid stone.

I believe, what with his stupendous strength, that Satha would have writhed from under the trunk, but for a broken branch that had been driven deep into his side, holding him like a barb. The sound of his hissing filled the jungle and his eyes glared at me with such concentrated evil that I shook despite myself. Oh, he knew it was I who had trapped him! Now I came as close as I dared, and with a sudden powerful cast of my spear, transfixed his neck just below the gaping jaws, nailing him to the tree-trunk, Then I dared greatly, for he was far from dead, and I knew he would in an instant tear the spear from the wood and be free to strike. But in that instant I ran in, and swinging my sword with all my great power, I hewed off his terrible head.

The heavings and contortions of Satha's prisoned form in life were naught to the convulsions of his headless length in death. I retreated, dragging the gigantic head after me with a crooked pole, and a safe distance from the lashing, flying tail, I set to work. I worked with naked death then, and no man ever toiled more gingerly than did I. For I cut out the poison sacs at the base of the great fangs, and in the terrible venom I soaked the heads of eleven arrows, being careful that only the bronze points were in the liquid, which else had corroded away the wood of the tough shafts. While I was doing this, Grom, driven by comradeship and curiosity, came stealing nervously through the jungle, and his mouth gaped as he looked on the head of Satha.

For hours I steeped the arrowheads in the poison, until they were caked with a horrible green scum, and showed tiny flecks of corrosion where the venom had eaten into the solid bronze. I wrapped them carefully in broad, thick, rubber-like leaves, and then, though night had fallen and the hunting beasts were roaring on every hand, I went back through the jungled hills, Grom with me, until at dawn we came again to the high cliffs that loomed above the Valley of Broken Stones.

At the mouth of the valley I broke my spear, and I took all the unpoisoned shafts from my quiver, and snapped them. I painted my face and limbs as the Æsir painted themselves only when they went forth to certain doom, and I sang my death-song to the sun as it rose over the cliffs, my yellow mane blowing in the morning wind.

Then I went down into the valley, bow in hand.

Grom could not drive himself to follow me. He lay on his belly in the dust and howled like a dying dog.

I passed the lake and the silent camp where the pyre-ashes still smoldered, and came under the thickening trees beyond. About me the columns loomed, mere shapeless heaps from the ravages of staggering eons. The trees grew more dense, and under their vast leafy branches the very light was dusky and evil. As in twilight shadow I saw the ruined temple, cyclopean walls staggering up from masses of decaying masonry and fallen blocks of stone. About six hundred yards in front of it a great column reared up in an open glade, eighty or ninety feet in height. It was so worn and pitted by weather and time that any child of my tribe could have climbed it, and I marked it and changed my plan. I came to the ruins and saw huge crumbling walls upholding a domed roof from which many stones had fallen, so that it seemed like the lichen-grown ribs of some mythical monster's skeleton arching above me. Titanic columns flanked the open doorway through which ten elephants could have stalked abreast. Once there might have been inscriptions and hieroglyphics on the pillars and walls, but they were long worn away. Around the great room, on the inner side, ran columns in better state of preservation. On each of these columns was a flat pedestal and some dim instinctive memory vaguely resurrected a shadowy scene wherein black drums roared madly, and on these pedestals monstrous beings squatted loathsomely in inexplicable rituals rooted in the black dawn of the universe.

There was no altar – only the mouth of a great well-like shaft in the stone floor, with strange obscene carvings all about the rim. I tore great pieces of stone from the rotting floor and cast them down the shaft which slanted down into utter darkness. I heard them bound along the side, but I did not hear them strike bottom. I cast down stone after stone, each with a searing curse, and at last I heard a sound that was not the dwindling rumble of the falling stones. Up from the well floated a weird demon-piping that was a symphony of madness. Far down in the darkness I glimpsed the faint fearful glimmering of a vast white bulk.

I retreated slowly as the piping grew louder, falling back through the broad doorway. I heard a scratching, scrambling noise, and up from the shaft and out of the doorway between the colossal columns came a prancing incredible figure. It went erect like a man, but it was covered with fur, that was shaggiest where its face should have been. If it had ears, nose and a mouth I did not discover them. Only a pair of staring red eyes leered from the furry mask. Its misshapen hands held a strange set of pipes, on which it blew weirdly as it pranced toward me with many a grotesque caper and leap.

Behind it I heard a repulsive obscene noise as of a quaking unstable mass heaving up out of the well. Then I nocked an arrow, drew the cord and sent the shaft singing through the furry breast of the dancing monstrosity. It went down as though struck by a thunderbolt, but to my horror the piping continued, though the pipes had fallen from the malformed hands. Then I turned and ran fleetly to the column, up which I swarmed before I looked back. When I reached the pinnacle I looked, and because of the shock and surprise of what I saw, I almost fell from my dizzy perch.

Out of the temple the monstrous dweller in the darkness had come, and I, who had expected a horror yet cast in some terrestrial mold, looked on the spawn of nightmare. From what subterranean hell it crawled in the long ago I know not, nor what black age it represented. But it was not a beast, as humanity knows beasts. I call it a worm for lack of a better term. There is no earthly language which has a name for it. I can only say it looked somewhat more like a worm than it did an octopus, a serpent or a dinosaur.

It was white and pulpy, and drew its quaking bulk along the ground, worm-fashion. But it had wide flat tentacles, and fleshy feelers, and other adjuncts the use of which I am unable to explain. And it had a long proboscis which it curled and uncurled like an elephant's trunk. Its forty eyes, set in a horrific circle, were composed of thousands of facets of as many scintillant colors which changed and altered in never-ending transmutation. But through all interplay of hue and glint, they retained their evil intelligence – intelligence there was behind those flickering facets, not human nor yet bestial, but a night-born demoniac intelligence such as men in dreams vaguely sense throbbing titanically in the black gulfs outside our material universe. In size the monster was mountainous; its bulk would have dwarfed a mastodon.

But even as I shook with the cosmic horror of the thing, I drew a feathered shaft to my ear and arched it singing on its way. Grass and bushes were crushed flat as the monster came toward me like a moving mountain and shaft after shaft I sent with terrific force and deadly precision. I could not miss so huge a target. The arrows sank to the feathers or clear out of sight in the unstable bulk, each bearing enough poison to have stricken dead a bull elephant. Yet on it came, swiftly, appallingly, apparently heedless of both the shafts and the venom in which they were steeped. And all the time the hideous music played a maddening accompaniment, whining thinly from the pipes that lay untouched on the ground.

My confidence faded; even the poison of Satha was futile against this uncanny being. I drove my last shaft almost straight downward into the quaking white mountain, so close was the monster under my perch. Then suddenly its color altered. A wave of ghastly blue surged over it, and the vast bulk heaved in earthquake-like convulsions. With a terrible plunge it struck the lower part of the column, which crashed to falling shards of stone. But even with the impact, I leaped far out and fell through the empty air full upon the monster's back.

The spongy skin yielded and gave beneath my feet, and I drove my sword hilt deep, dragging it through the pulpy flesh, ripping a horrible yard-long wound, from which oozed a green slime. Then a flip of a cable-like tentacle flicked me from the titan's back and spun me three hundred feet through the air to crash among a cluster of giant trees.

The impact must have splintered half the bones in my frame, for when I sought to grasp my sword again and crawl anew to the combat, I could not move hand or foot, could only writhe helplessly with my broken back. But I could see the monster and I knew that I had won, even in defeat. The mountainous bulk was heaving and billowing, the tentacles were lashing madly, the antennae writhing and knotting, and the nauseous whiteness had changed to a pale and grisly green. It turned ponderously and lurched back toward the temple, rolling like a crippled ship in a heavy swell. Trees crashed and splintered as it lumbered against them.

I wept with pure fury because I could not catch up my sword and rush in to die glutting my berserk madness in mighty strokes. But the worm-god was death-stricken and needed not my futile sword. The demon pipes on the ground kept up their infernal tone, and it was like the fiend's death-dirge. Then as the monster veered and floundered, I saw it catch up the corpse of its hairy slave. For an instant the apish form dangled in mid-air, gripped round by the trunk-like proboscis, then was dashed against the temple wall with a force that reduced the hairy body to a mere shapeless pulp. At that the pipes screamed out horribly, and fell silent for ever.

The titan staggered on the brink of the shaft; then another change came over it – a frightful transfiguration the nature of which I can not yet describe. Even now when I try to think of it clearly, I am only chaotically conscious of a blasphemous, unnatural transmutation of form and substance, shocking and indescribable. Then the strangely altered bulk tumbled into the shaft to roll down into the ultimate darkness from whence it came, and I knew that it was dead. And as it vanished into the well with a rending, grinding groan the ruined walls quivered from dome to base. They bent inward and buckled with deafening reverberation, the column splintered, and with a cataclysmic crash the dome itself came thundering down. For an instant the air seemed veiled with flying debris and stone-dust, through which the tree-tops lashed madly as in a storm or an earthquake convulsion. Then all was clear again and I stared, shaking the blood from my eyes. Where the temple had stood there lay only a colossal pile of shattered masonry and broken stones, and every column in the valley had fallen, to lie in crumbling shards.

In the silence that followed I heard Grom wailing a dirge over me. I bade him lay my sword in my hand, and he did so, and bent close to hear what I had to say, for I was passing swiftly.

"Let my tribe remember," I said, speaking slowly. "Let the tale be told from village to village, from camp to camp, from tribe to tribe, so that men may know that not man nor beast nor devil may prey in safety on the golden-haired people of Asgard. Let them build me a cairn where I lie and lay me therein with my bow and sword at hand, to guard this valley for ever; so if the ghost of the god I slew comes up from below, my ghost will ever be ready to give it battle."

And while Grom howled and beat his hairy breast, death came to me in the Valley of the Worm.

SKULLFACE

I : THE FACE IN THE MIST

"We are no other than a moving row
Of Magic Shadow-shapes that come and go."
–OMAR KHAYYAM

The horror first took concrete form amid that most unconcrete of all things – a hashish dream. I was off on a timeless, spaceless journey through the strange lands that belong to this state of being, a million miles away from earth and all things earthly; yet I became cognizant that something was reaching across the unknown voids – something that tore ruthlessly at the separating curtains of my illusions and intruded itself into my visions.

I did not exactly return to ordinary waking life, yet I was conscious of a seeing and a recognizing that was unpleasant and seemed out of keeping with the dream I was at that time enjoying. To one who has never known the delights of hashish, my explanation must seem chaotic and impossible. Still, I was aware of a rending of mists and then the Face intruded itself into my sight. I thought at first it was merely a skull; then I saw that it was a hideous yellow instead of white, and was endowed with some horrid form of life. Eyes glimmered deep in the sockets and the jaws moved as if in speech. The body, except for the high, thin shoulders, was vague and indistinct, but the hands, which floated in the mists before and below the skull, were horribly vivid and filled me with crawling fears. They were like the hands of a mummy, long, lean and yellow, with knobby joints and cruel curving talons.

Then, to complete the vague horror which was swiftly taking possession of me, a voice spoke – imagine a man so long dead that his vocal organs had grown rusty and unaccustomed to speech. This was the thought which struck me and made my flesh crawl as I listened.

"A strong brute and one who might be useful somehow. See that he is given all the hashish he requires."

Then the face began to recede, even as I sensed that I was the subject of conversation, and the mists billowed and began to close again. Yet for a single instant a scene stood out with startling clarity. I gasped – or sought to. For over the high, strange shoulder of the apparition another face stood out clearly for an instant, as if the owner peered at me. Red lips, half parted, long dark eyelashes, shading vivid eyes, a shimmery cloud of hair. Over the shoulder of Horror, breath-taking beauty for an instant looked at me.

II : THE HASHISH SLAVE

"Up from Earth's center through the Seventh Gate
I rose, and on the Throne of Saturn sate."
–OMAR KHAYYAM

My dream of the skull-face was borne over that usually uncrossable gap that lies between hashish enchantment and humdrum reality. I sat cross-legged on a mat in Yun Shatu's Temple of Dreams and gathered the fading forces of my decaying brain to the task of remembering events and faces.

This last dream was so entirely different from any I had ever had before, that my waning interest was roused to the point of inquiring as to its origin. When I first began to experiment with hashish, I sought to find a physical or psychic basis for the wild flights of illusion pertaining thereto, but of late I had been content to enjoy without seeking cause and effect.

Whence this unaccountable sensation of familiarity in regard to that vision? I took my throbbing head between my hands and laboriously sought a clue. A living dead man and a girl of rare beauty who had looked over his shoulder. Then I remembered.

Back in the fog of days and nights which veils a hashish addict's memory, my money had given out. It seemed years or possibly centuries, but my stagnant reason told me that it had probably been only a few days. At any rate, I had presented myself at Yun Shatu's sordid dive as usual and had been thrown out by the great Negro Hassim when it was learned I had no more money.

My universe crashing to pieces about me, and my nerves humming like taut piano wires for the vital need that was mine, I crouched in the gutter and gibbered bestially, till Hassim swaggered out and stilled my yammerings with a blow that felled me, half stunned.

Then as I presently rose, staggeringly and with no thought save of the river which flowed with cool murmur so near me – as I rose, a light hand was laid like the touch of a rose on my arm. I turned with a frightened start, and stood spellbound before the vision of loveliness which met my gaze. Dark eyes limpid with pity surveyed me and the little hand on my ragged sleeve drew me toward the door of the Dream Temple. I shrank back, but a low voice, soft and musical, urged me, and filled with a trust that was strange, I shambled along with my beautiful guide.

At the door Hassim met us, cruel hands lifted and a dark scowl on his ape-like brow, but as I cowered there, expecting a blow, he halted before the girl's upraised hand and her word of command which had taken on an imperious note.

I did not understand what she said, but I saw dimly, as in a fog, that she gave the black man money, and she led me to a couch where she had me recline and arranged the cushions as if I were king of Egypt instead of a ragged, dirty renegade who lived only for hashish. Her slim hand was cool on my brow for a moment, and then she was gone and Yussef Ali came bearing the stuff for which my very soul shrieked – and soon I was wandering again through those strange and exotic countries that only a hashish slave knows.

Now as I sat on the mat and pondered the dream of the skull-face I wondered more. Since the unknown girl had led me back into the dive, I had come and gone as before, when I had plenty of money to pay Yun Shatu. Someone certainly was paying him for me, and while my subconscious mind had told me it was the girl, my rusty brain had failed to grasp the fact entirely, or to wonder why. What need of wondering? So someone paid and the vivid-hued dreams continued, what cared I? But now I wondered. For the girl who had protected me from Hassim and had brought the hashish for me was the same girl I had seen in the skull-face dream.

Through the soddenness of my degradation the lure of her struck like a knife piercing my heart and strangely revived the memories of the days when I was a man like other men – not yet a sullen, cringing slave of dreams. Far and dim they were, shimmery islands in the mist of years – and what a dark sea lay between!

I looked at my ragged sleeve and the dirty, claw-like hand protruding from it; I gazed through the hanging smoke which fogged the sordid room, at the low bunks along the wall whereon lay the blankly staring dreamers – slaves, like me, of hashish or of opium. I gazed at the slippered Chinamen gliding softly to and fro bearing pipes or roasting balls of concentrated purgatory over tiny flickering fires. I gazed at Hassim standing, arms folded, beside the door like a great statue of black basalt.

And I shuddered and hid my face in my hands because with the faint dawning of returning manhood, I knew that this last and most cruel dream was futile – I had crossed an ocean over which I could never return, had cut myself off from the world of normal men or women. Naught remained now but to drown this dream as I had drowned all my others – swiftly and with hope that I should soon attain that Ultimate Ocean which lies beyond all dreams.

So these fleeting moments of lucidity, of longing, that tear aside the veils of all dope slaves – unexplainable, without hope of attainment.

So I went back to my empty dreams, to my fantasmagoria of illusions; but sometimes, like a sword cleaving a mist, through the high lands and the low lands and seas of my visions floated, like half-forgotten music, the sheen of dark eyes and shimmery hair.

You ask how I, Stephen Costigan, American and a man of some attainments and culture, came to lie in a filthy dive of London's Limehouse? The answer is simple – no jaded debauchee, I, seeking new sensations in the mysteries of the Orient. I answer – Argonne! Heavens, what deeps and heights of horror lurk in that one word alone! Shell-shocked – shell-torn. Endless days and nights without end and roaring red hell over No Man's Land where I lay shot and bayoneted to shreds of gory flesh. My body recovered, how I know not; my mind never did.

And the leaping fires and shifting shadows in my tortured brain drove me down and down, along the stairs of degradation, uncaring until at last I found surcease in Yun Shatu's Temple of Dreams, where I slew my red dreams in other dreams – the dreams of hashish whereby a man may descend to the lower pits of the reddest hells or soar into those unnamable heights where the stars are diamond pinpoints beneath his feet.

Not the visions of the sot, the beast, were mine. I attained the unattainable, stood face to face with the unknown and in cosmic calmness knew the unguessable. And was content after a fashion, until the sight of burnished hair and scarlet lips swept away my dream-built universe and left me shuddering among its ruins.

III : THE MASTER OF DOOM

> *"And He that toss'd you down into the Field,*
> *He knows about it all – He knows! He knows!"*
> –OMAR KHAYYAM

A hand shook me roughly as I emerged languidly from my latest debauch.

"The Master wishes you! Up, swine!"

Hassim it was who shook me and who spoke.

"To hell with the Master!" I answered, for I hated Hassim and feared him.

"Up with you or you get no more hashish," was the brutal responses and I rose in trembling haste.

I followed the huge black man and he led the way to the rear of the building, stepping in and out among the wretched dreamers on the floor.

"Muster all hands on deck!" droned a sailor in a bunk. "All hands!"

Hassim flung open the door at the rear and motioned me to enter. I had never before passed through that door and had supposed it led into Yun Shatu's private quarters. But it was furnished only with a cot, a bronze idol of some sort before which incense burned, and a heavy table.

Hassim gave me a sinister glance and seized the table as if to spin it about. It turned as if it stood on a revolving platform and a section of the floor turned with it, revealing a hidden doorway in the floor. Steps led downward in the darkness.

Hassim lighted a candle and with a brusque gesture invited me to descend. I did so, with the sluggish obedience of the dope addict, and he followed, closing the door above us by means of an iron lever fastened to the under side of the floor. In the semi-darkness we went down the rickety steps, some nine or ten I should say, and then came upon a narrow corridor.

Here Hassim again took the lead, holding the candle high in front of him. I could scarcely see the sides of this cave-like passageway but knew that it was not wide. The flickering light showed it to be bare of an sort of furnishings save for a number of strange-looking chests which lined the walls – receptacles

224

containing opium and other dope, I thought.

A continuous scurrying and the occasional glint of small red eyes haunted the shadows, betraying the presence of vast numbers of the great rats which infest the Thames waterfront of that section.

Then more steps loomed out of the dark in front of us as the corridor came to an abrupt end. Hassim led the way up and at the top knocked four times against what seemed the underside of a floor. A hidden door opened and a flood of soft, illusive light streamed through.

Hassim hustled me up roughly and I stood blinking in such a setting as I had never seen in my wildest flights of vision. I stood in a jungle of palm-trees through which wriggled a million vivid-hued dragons! Then, as my startled eyes became accustomed to the light, I saw that I had not been suddenly transferred to some other planet, as I had at first thought. The palm-trees were there, and the dragons, but the trees were artificial and stood in great pots and the dragons writhed across heavy tapestries which hid the walls.

The room itself was a monstrous affair − inhumanly large, it seemed to me. A thick smoke, yellowish and tropical in suggestion, seemed to hang over all, veiling the ceiling and baffling upward glances. This smoke, I saw, emanated from an altar in front of the wall to my left. I started. Through the saffron, billowing fog two eyes, hideously large and vivid, glittered at me. The vague outlines of some bestial idol took indistinct shape. I flung an uneasy glance about, marking the Oriental divans and couches and the bizarre furnishings, and then my eyes halted and rested on a lacquer screen just in front of me.

I could not pierce it and no sound came from beyond it, yet I felt eyes searing into my consciousness through it, eyes that burned through my very soul. A strange aura of evil flowed from that strange screen with its weird carvings and unholy decorations.

Hassim salaamed profoundly before it and then, without speaking, stepped back and folded his arms, statue-like.

A voice suddenly broke the heavy and oppressive silence.

"You who are a swine, would you like to be a man again?"

I started. The tone was inhuman, cold − more, there was a suggestion of long disuse of the vocal organs − the voice I had heard in my dream!

"Yes," I replied, trance-like, "I would like to be a man again."

Silence ensued for a space; then the voice came again with a sinister whispering undertone at the back of its sound like bats flying through a cavern.

"I shall make you a man again because I am a friend to all broken men. Not for a price shall I do it, nor for gratitude. And I give you a sign to seal my promise and my vow. Thrust your hand through the screen."

At these strange and almost unintelligible words I stood perplexed, and then, as the unseen voice repeated the last command, I stepped forward and thrust my hand through a slit which opened silently in the screen. I felt my wrist seized in an iron grip and something seven times colder than ice touched the inside of my hand. Then my wrist was released, and drawing forth my hand I saw a strange symbol traced in blue close to the base of my thumb − a thing like a scorpion.

The voice spoke again in a sibilant language I did not understand, and Hassim stepped forward deferentially. He reached about the screen and then turned to me, holding a goblet of some amber-colored liquid which he proffered me with an ironical bow. I took it hesitatingly.

"Drink and fear not," said the unseen voice. "It is only an Egyptian wine with life-giving qualities."

So I raised the goblet and emptied it; the taste was not unpleasant, and even as I handed the beaker to Hassim again, I seemed to feel new life and vigor whip along my jaded veins.

"Remain at Yun Shatu's house," said the voice. "You will be given food and a bed until you are strong enough to work for yourself. You will use no hashish nor will you require any. Go!"

As in a daze, I followed Hassim back through the hidden door, down the steps, along the dark corridor and up through the other door that led us into the Temple of Dreams.

As we stepped from the rear chamber into the main room of the dreamers, I turned to the Negro wonderingly.

"Master? Master of what? Of Life?"

Hassim laughed, fiercely and sardonically.

"Master of Doom."

IV : THE SPIDER AND THE FLY

"There was the Door to which I found no Key;
There was the Veil through which I might not see."
–OMAR KHAYYAM

I sat on Yun Shatu's cushions and pondered with a clearness of mind new and strange to me. As for that, all my sensations were new and strange. I felt as if I had wakened from a monstrously long sleep, and though my thoughts were sluggish, I felt as though the cobwebs which had clogged them for so long had been partly brushed away.

I drew my hand across my brow, noting how it trembled. I was weak and shaky and felt the stirrings of hunger – not for dope but for food. What had been in the draft I had quenched in the chamber of mystery? And why had the "Master" chosen me, out of all the other wretches of Yun Shatu's, for regeneration?

And who was this Master? Somehow the word sounded vaguely familiar – I sought laboriously to remember. Yes I had heard it, lying half-waking in the bunks or on the floor – whispered sibilantly by Yun Shatu or by Hassim or by Yussef Ali, the Moor, muttered in their low-voiced conversations and mingled always with words I could not understand. Was not Yun Shatu, then, master of the Temple of Dreams? I had thought and the other addicts thought that the withered Chinaman held undisputed sway over this drab kingdom and that Hassim and Yussef Ali were his servants. And the four China boys who roasted opium with Yun Shatu and Yar Khan the Afghan, and Santiago the Haitian and Ganra Singh, the renegade Sikh – all in the pay of Yun Shatu, we supposed – bound to the opium lord by bonds of gold or fear.

For Yun Shatu was a power in London's Chinatown and I had heard that his tentacles reached across the seas into high places of mighty and mysterious tongues. Was that Yun Shatu behind the lacquer screen? No; I knew the Chinaman's voice and besides I had seen him puttering about in the front of the Temple just as I went through the back door.

Another thought came to me. Often, lying half torpid, in the late hours of night or in the early grayness of dawn, I had seen men and women steal into the Temple, whose dress and bearing were strangely out of place and incongruous. Tall, erect men, often in evening dress, with their hats drawn low about their brows, and fine ladies, veiled, in silks and furs. Never two of them came together, but always they came separately and, hiding their features, hurried to the rear door, where they entered and presently came forth again, hours later sometimes. Knowing that the lust for dope finds resting-place in high positions sometimes, I had never wondered overmuch, supposing that these were wealthy men and women of society who had fallen victims to the craving, and that somewhere in the back of the building there was a private chamber for such. Yet now I wondered sometimes these persons had remained only a few moments – was it always opium for which they came, or did they, too, traverse that strange corridor and converse with the One behind the screen?

My mind dallied with the idea of a great specialist to whom came all classes of people to find surcease from the dope habit. Yet it was strange that such a one should select a dope-joint from which to work – strange, too, that the owner of that house should apparently look on him with so much reverence.

I gave it up as my head began to hurt with the unwonted effort of thinking, and shouted for food. Yussef Ali brought it to me on a tray, with a promptness which was surprising. More, he salaamed as he departed, leaving me to ruminate on the strange shift of my status in the Temple of Dreams.

I ate, wondering what the One of the screen wanted with me. Not for an instant did I suppose that his actions had been prompted by the reasons he pretended; the life of the underworld had taught me that none of its denizens leaned toward philanthropy. And underworld the chamber of mystery had been, in spite of its elaborate and bizarre nature. And where could it be located? How far had I walked along the corridor? I shrugged my shoulders, wondering if it were not all a hashish-induced dream; then my eye fell upon my hand – and the scorpion traced thereon.

"Muster all hands!" droned the sailor in the bunk. "All hands!"

To tell in detail of the next few days would be boresome to any who have not tasted the dire slavery of dope. I waited for the craving to strike me again – waited with sure sardonic hopelessness. All day, all night – another day then the miracle was forced upon my doubting brain. Contrary to all theories

227

and supposed facts of science and common sense the craving had left me as suddenly and completely as a bad dream! At first I could not credit my senses but believed myself to be still in the grip of a dope nightmare. But it was true. From the time I quaffed the goblet in the room of mystery, I felt not the slightest desire for the stuff which had been life itself to me. This, I felt vaguely, was somehow unholy and certainly opposed to all rules of nature. If the dread being behind the screen had discovered the secret of breaking hashish's terrible power, what other monstrous secrets had he discovered and what unthinkable dominance was his? The suggestion of evil crawled serpent-like through my mind.

I remained at Yun Shatu's house, lounging in a bunk or on cushions spread upon the floor, eating and drinking at will, but now that I was becoming a normal man again, the atmosphere became most revolting to me and the sight of the wretches writhing in their dreams reminded me unpleasantly of what I myself had been, and it repelled, nauseated me.

So one day, when no one was watching me, I rose and went out on the street and walked along the waterfront. The air, burdened though it was with smoke and foul scents, filled my lungs with strange freshness and aroused new vigor in what had once been a powerful frame. I took new interest in the sounds of men living and working, and the sight of a vessel being unloaded at one of the wharfs actually thrilled me. The force of longshoremen was short, and presently I found myself heaving and lifting and carrying, and though the sweat coursed down my brow and my limbs trembled at the effort, I exulted in the thought that at last I was able to labor for myself again, no matter bow low or drab the work might be.

As I returned to the door of Yun Shatu's that evening hideously weary but with the renewed feeling of manhood that comes of honest toil – Hassim met me at the door.

"You been where?" he demanded roughly.

"I've been working on the docks," I answered shortly.

"You don't need to work on docks," he snarled. "The Master got work for you."

He led the way, and again I traversed the dark stairs and the corridor under the earth. This time my faculties were alert and I decided that the passageway could not be over thirty or forty feet in length. Again I stood before the lacquer screen and again I heard the inhuman voice of living death.

"I can give you work," said the voice. "Are you willing to work for me?"

I quickly assented. After all, in spite of the fear which the voice inspired, I was deeply indebted to the owner.

"Good. Take these."

As I started toward the screen a sharp command halted me and Hassim stepped forward and reaching behind took what was offered. This was a bundle of pictures and papers, apparently.

"Study these," said the One behind the screen, "and learn all you can about the man portrayed thereby. Yun Shatu will give you money; buy yourself such clothes as seamen wear and take a room at the front of the Temple. At the end of two days, Hassim will bring you to me again. Go!"

The last impression I had, as the hidden door closed above me, was that the eyes of the idol, blinking through the everlasting smoke, leered mockingly at me.

The front of the Temple of Dreams consisted of rooms for rent, masking the true purpose of the building under the guise of a waterfront boarding-house. The police had made several visits to Yun Shatu but had never got any incriminating evidence against him.

So in one of these rooms I took up my abode and set to work studying the material given me.

The pictures were all of one man, a large man, not unlike me in build and general facial outline, except that he wore a heavy beard and was inclined to blondness whereas I am dark. The name, as written on the accompanying papers, Was Major Fairlan Morley, special commissioner to Natal and the Transvaal. This office and title were new to me and I wondered at the connection between an African commissioner and an opium house on the Thames waterfront.

The papers consisted of extensive data evidently copied from authentic sources and all dealing with Major Morley, and a number of private documents considerably illuminating on the major's private life.

An exhaustive description was given of the man's personal appearance and habits, some of which seemed very trivial to me. I wondered what the purpose could be, and how the One behind the screen had come in possession of papers of such intimate nature.

I could find no clue in answer to this question but bent all my energies to the task set out for me. I owed a deep debt of gratitude to the unknown man who required this of me and I was determined to repay him to the best of my ability. Nothing, at this time, suggested a snare to me.

V : THE MAN ON THE COUCH

"What dam of lances sent thee forth to jest at dawn with Death?"
–KIPLING

At the expiration of two days, Hassim beckoned me as I stood in the opium room. I advanced with a springy, resilient tread, secure in the confidence that I had culled the Morley papers of all their worth. I was a new man; my mental swiftness and physical readiness surprised me – sometimes it seemed unnatural.

Hassim eyed me through narrowed lids and motioned me to follow, as usual. As we crossed the room, my gaze fell upon a man who lay on a couch close to the wall, smoking opium. There was nothing at all suspicious about his ragged, unkempt clothes, his dirty, bearded face or the blank stare, but my eyes, sharpened to an abnormal point, seemed to sense a certain incongruity in the clean-cut limbs which not even the slouchy garments could efface.

Hassim spoke impatiently and I turned away. We entered the rear room, and as he shut the door and turned to the table, it moved of itself and a figure bulked up through the hidden doorway. The Sikh, Ganra Singh, a lean sinister-eyed giant, emerged and proceeded to the door opening into the opium room, where he halted until we should have descended and closed the secret doorway.

Again I stood amid the billowing yellow smoke and listened to the hidden voice.

"Do you think you know enough about Major Morley to impersonate him successfully?"

Startled, I answered, "No doubt I could, unless I met someone who was intimate with him."

"I will take care of that. Follow me closely. Tomorrow you sail on the first boat for Calais. There you will meet an agent of mine who will accost you the instant you step upon the wharfs, and give you further instructions. You will sail second class and avoid all conversation with strangers or anyone. Take the papers with you. The agent will aid you in making up and your masquerade will start in Calais. That is all. Go!"

I departed, my wonder growing. All this rigmarole evidently had a meaning, but one which I could not fathom. Back in the opium room Hassim bade me be seated on some cushions to await his return. To my question he snarled that he was going forth as he had been ordered, to buy me a ticket on the Channel boat. He departed and I sat down, leaning my back against the wall. As I ruminated, it seemed suddenly that eyes were fixed on me so intensely as to disturb my sub-mind. I glanced up quickly but no one seemed to be looking at me. The smoke drifted through the hot atmosphere as usual; Yussef Ali and the Chinese glided back and forth tending to the wants of the sleepers.

Suddenly the door to the rear room opened and a strange and hideous figure came haltingly out. Not all of those who found entrance to Yun Shatu's back room were aristocrats and society members. This was one of the exceptions. and one whom I remembered as having often entered and emerged therefrom – a tall, gaunt figure, shapeless and ragged wrappings and nondescript garments, face entirely hidden. Better that the face be hidden, I thought, for without doubt the wrapping concealed a grisly sight. The man was a leper, who had somehow managed to escape the attention of the public guardians and who was occasionally seen haunting the lower and more mysterious regions of the East End – a mystery even to the lowest denizens of Limehouse.

Suddenly my supersensitive mind was aware of a swift tension in the air. The leper hobbled out the door, closed it behind him. My eyes instinctively sought the couch whereon lay the man who had aroused my suspicions earlier in the day. I could have sworn that cold steely eyes gleamed menacingly before they flickered shut. I crossed to the couch in one stride and bent over the prostrate man. Something about his face seemed unnatural – a healthy bronze seemed to underlie the pallor of complexion.

"Yun Shatu!" I shouted. "A spy is in the house!"

Things happened then with bewildering speed. The man on the couch with one tigerish movement leaped erect and a revolver gleamed in his hand. One sinewy arm flung me aside as I sought to grapple with him and a sharp decisive voice sounded over the babble which broke forth:

"You there! Halt! Halt!"

The pistol in the stranger's hand was leveled at the leper, who was making for the door in long strides!

All about was confusion; Yun Shatu was shrieking volubly in Chinese and the four China boys and Yussef Ali were rushing in from all sides, knives glittering in their hands.

All this I saw with unnatural clearness even as I marked the stranger's face. As the flying leper gave no evidence of halting, I saw the eyes harden to steely points of determination, sighting along the pistol barrel – the features set with the grim purpose of the slayer. The leper was almost to the outer door, but death would strike him down ere he could reach it.

And then, just as the finger of the stranger tightened on the trigger, I hurled myself forward and my right fist crashed against his chin, he went down as though struck by a trip-hammer, the revolver exploding harmlessly in the air.

In that instant, with the blinding flare of light that sometimes comes to one, I knew that the leper was none other than the Man Behind the Screen!

I bent over the fallen man, who though not entirely senseless had been rendered temporarily helpless by that terrific blow. He was struggling dazedly to rise but I shoved him roughly down again and seizing the false beard he wore, tore it away. A lean bronzed face was revealed, the strong lines of which not even the artificial dirt and grease paint could alter.

Yussef Ali leaned above him now, dagger in hand, eyes slits of murder. The brown sinewy hand went up – I caught the wrist.

"Not so fast, you black devil! What are you about to do?"

"This is John Gordon," he hissed, "the Master's greatest foe! He must die, curse you!"

John Gordon! The name was familiar somehow, and yet I did not seem to connect it with the London police nor account for the man's presence in Yun Shatu's dope-joint. However, on one point I was determined.

"You don't kill him, at any rate. Up with you!" This last to Gordon, who with my aid staggered up, still very dizzy.

"That punch would have dropped a bull," I said in wonderment; "I didn't know I had it in me."

The false leper had vanished. Yun Shatu stood gazing at me as immobile as an idol, hands in his wide sleeves, and Yussef Ali stood back, muttering murderously and thumbing his dagger edge, as I led Gordon out of the opium room and through the innocent-appearing bar which lay between that room and the street.

Out in the street I said to him: "I have no idea as to who you are or what you are doing here, but you see what an unhealthful place it is for you. Hereafter be advised by me and stay away."

His only answer was a searching glance, and then he turned and walked swiftly though somewhat unsteadily up the street.

VI : THE DREAM GIRL

"I have reached these lands but newly
From an ultimate dim Thule."
—POE

Outside my room sounded a light footstep. The doorknob turned cautiously and slowly; the door opened. I sprang erect with a gasp. Red lips, half parted, dark eyes like limpid seas of wonder, a mass of shimmering hair – framed in my drab doorway stood the girl of my dreams!

She entered, and half turning with a sinuous motion, closed the door. I sprang forward, my hands outstretched, then halted as she put a finger to her lips.

"You must not talk loudly," she almost whispered; "*He* did not say I could not come; yet–"

Her. voice was soft and musical, with just a touch of foreign accent which I found delightful. As for the girl herself, every intonation, every movement proclaimed the Orient. She was a fragrant breath from the East. From her night-black hair, piled high above her alabaster forehead, to her little feet, encased in high-heeled pointed slippers, she portrayed the highest ideal of Asiatic loveliness – an effect which was heightened rather than lessened by the English blouse and skirt which she wore.

"You are beautiful," I said dazedly. "Who are you?"

"I am Zuleika," she answered with a shy smile. "I – I am glad you like me. I am glad you no longer dream hashish dreams."

Strange that so small a thing should set my heart to leaping wildly!

"I owe it all to you, Zuleika." I said huskily. "Had not I dreamed of you every hour since you first lifted me from the gutter, I had lacked the power of even hoping to be freed from my curse."

She blushed prettily and intertwined her white fingers as if in nervousness.

"You leave England tomorrow?" she said suddenly.

"Yes. Hassim has not returned with my ticket–" I hesitated suddenly, remembering the command of silence.

"Yes, I know, I know!" she whispered swiftly, her eyes widening. "And John Gordon has been here! He saw you!"

"Yes!"

She came close to me with a quick lithe movement.

"You are to impersonate some man! Listen, while you are doing this, you must not ever let Gordon see you! He would know you, no matter what your disguise! He is a terrible man!"

232

"I don't understand," I said, completely bewildered. "How did the Master break me of my hashish craving? Who is this Gordon and why did be come here? Why does the Master go disguised as a leper – and who is he? Above all, why am I to impersonate a man I never saw or heard of?"

"I can not – I dare not tell you!" she whispered, her face paling. "I–"

Somewhere in the house sounded the faint tones of a Chinese gong. The girl started like a frightened gazelle.

"I must go! He summons me!"

She opened the door, darted through, halted a moment to electrify me with her passionate exclamation: "Oh, be careful, be very careful, sahib!"

Then she was gone.

VII : THE MAN OF THE SKULL

"What the hammer? what the chain?
In what furnace was thy brain?
What the anvil? what dread grasp
Dare its deadly terrors clasp?"
–BLAKE

Awhile after my beautiful and mysterious visitor had left, I sat in meditation. I believed that I had at last stumbled on to an explanation of a part of the enigma, at any rate. This was the conclusion I had reached: Yun Shatu, the opium lord, was simply the agent or servant of some organization or individual whose work was on a far larger scale than merely supplying dope addicts in the Temple of Dreams,. This man or these men needed co-workers among all classes of people; in other words, I was being let in with a group of opium smugglers on a gigantic scale. Gordon no doubt had been investigating the case, and his presence alone showed that it was no ordinary one, for I knew that he held a high position with the English government, though just what, I did not know.

Opium or not, I determined to carry out my obligation to the Master. My moral sense had been blunted by the dark ways I had traveled, and the thought of despicable crime did not enter my head. I was indeed hardened. More, the mere debt of gratitude was increased a thousandfold by the thought of the girl. To the Master I owed it that I was able to stand up on my feet and look into her clear eyes as a man should. So if he wished my services as a smuggler of dope, he should have them. No doubt I was to impersonate some man so high in governmental esteem that the usual actions of the customs officers would be deemed unnecessary; was I to bring some rare dream-producer into England?

These thoughts were in my mind as I went downstairs, but ever back of them hovered other and more alluring suppositions – what was the reason for the girl, here in this vile dive – a rose in a garbage-heap – and who was she?

As I entered the outer bar, Hassim came in, his brows set in a dark scowl of anger, and, I believed, fear. He carried a newspaper in his hand, folded.

"I told you to wait in opium room," he snarled.

"You were gone so long that I went up to my room. Have you the ticket?"

He merely grunted and pushed on past me into the opium room, and standing at the door I saw him cross the floor and disappear into the rear room. I stood there, my bewilderment increasing. For as Hassim had brushed past me, I had noted an item on the face of the paper, against which his black thumb was tightly pressed as if to mark that special column of news.

And with the unnatural celerity of action and judgment which seemed to be mine those days, I had in that fleeting instant read:

"African Special Commissioner Found Murdered!
The body of Major Fairlan Morley was yesterday discovered in a rotting ship's hold at Bordeaux..."

No more I saw of the details, but that alone was enough to make me think! The affair seemed to be taking on an ugly aspect. Yet–

Another day passed. To my inquiries, Hassim snarled that the plans had been changed and I was not to go to France. Then, late in the evening, he came to bid me once more to the room of mystery.

I stood before the lacquer screen, the yellow smoke acrid in my nostrils, the woven dragons writhing along the tapestries, the palm-trees rearing thick and oppressive.

"A change has come in our plans," said the hidden voice. "You will not sail as was decided before. But I have other work that you may do. Mayhap this will be more to your type of usefulness, for I admit you have somewhat disappointed me in regard to subtlety. You interfered the other day in such manner as will no doubt cause me great inconvenience in the future."

I said nothing, but a feeling of resentment began to stir in me.

"Even after the assurance of one of my most trusted servants," the toneless voice continued, with no mark of any emotion save a slightly rising note, "you insisted on releasing my most deadly enemy. Be more circumspect in the future."

"I saved your life!" I said angrily.

"And for that reason alone I overlook your mistake – this time!"

A slow fury suddenly surged up in me.

"This time! Make the bet of it this time, for I assure you there will be no next time. I owe you a greater debt than I can ever hope to pay, but that does not make me your slave. I have saved your life – the debt is as near paid as a man can pay it. Go your way and I go mine!"

A low, hideous laugh answered me, like a reptilian hiss.

"You fool! You will pay with your whole life's toil! You say you are not my slave? I say you are – just as black Hassim there beside you is my slave – just as the girl Zuleika is my slave, who had bewitched you with her beauty."

These words sent a wave of hot blood to my brain and I was conscious of a flood of fury which completely engulfed my reason for a second. Just as all my moods and senses seemed sharpened and exaggerated those days, so now this burst of rage transcended every moment of anger I had ever had before.

"Hell's fiends!" I shrieked. "You devil – who are you and what is your hold on me? I'll see you or die!"

Hassim sprang at me, but I hurled him backward and with one stride reached the screen and flung it aside with an incredible effort of strength. Then I shrank back, hands outflung, shrieking. A tall, gaunt figure stood before me, a figure arrayed grotesquely in a silk brocaded gown which fell to the floor.

From the sleeves of this gown protruded hands which filled me with crawling horror – long, predatory hands, with thin bony fingers and curved talons – withered skin of a parchment brownish-yellow, like the hands of a man long dead.

The hands – but, oh God, the face! A skull to which no vestige of flesh seemed to remain but on which taut brownish-yellow skin grew fast, etching out every detail of that terrible death's-head. The forehead was high and in a way magnificent, but the head was curiously narrow through the temples, and from under penthouse brows great eyes glimmered like pools of yellow fire. The nose was high-bridged and very thin; the mouth was a mere colorless gash between thin, cruel lips. A long, bony neck supported this frightful vision and completed the effect of a reptilian demon from some mediaeval hell.

I was face to face with the skull-faced man of my dreams!

VIII : BLACK WISDOM

"Thou canst not see my face;
for man shall not see me and live."
–EXODUS 33:20

The terrible spectacle drove for the instant all thoughts of rebellion from my mind. My very blood froze in my veins and I stood motionless. I heard Hassim laugh grimly behind me. The eyes in the cadaverous face blazed fiendishly at me and I blanched from the concentrated Satanic fury in them.

Then the horror laughed sibilantly.

"I do you a great honor, Mr. Costigan; among a very few, even of my own servants, you may say that you saw my face and lived. I think you will he more useful to me living than dead."

I was silent, completely unnerved. It was difficult to believe that this man lived, for his appearance certainly belied the thought. He seemed horribly like a mummy. Yet his lips moved when he spoke and his eyes flamed with hideous life.

"You will do as I say," he said abruptly, and his voice had taken on a note of command. "You doubtless know, or know of, Sir Haldred Frenton?"

"Yes."

Every man of culture in Europe and America was familiar with the travel books of Sir Haldred Frenton, author and soldier of fortune.

"You will go to Sir Haldred's estate tonight–"

"Yes?"

"And kill him!"

I staggered, literally. This order was incredible – unspeakable! I had sunk low, low enough to smuggle opium, but to deliberately murder a man I had never seen, a man noted for his kindly deeds! That was too monstrous even to contemplate.

"You do not refuse?"

The tone was as loathly and as mocking as the hiss of a serpent.

"Refuse?" I screamed, finding my voice at last. "Refuse? You incarnate devil! Of course I refuse! You–"

Something in the cold assurance of his manner halted me – froze me Into apprehensive silence.

"You fool!" he said calmly. "I broke the hashish chains – do you know how? Four minutes from now you will know and curse the day you were born! Have you not thought it strange the swiftness of brain, the resilience of body – the brain that should be rusty and slow, the body that should be weak and sluggish from years of abuse? That blow that felled John Gordon – have you not wondered at its might? The ease with which you mastered Major Morley's records – have you not wondered at that? You fool, you are bound to me by chains of steel and blood and fire! I have kept you alive and sane – I alone. Each day the life-saving elixir has been given you in your wine. You could not live and keep your reason without it. And I and only I know its secret!"

He glanced at a queer timepiece which stood on a table at his elbow.

"This time I had Yun Shatu leave the elixir out – I anticipated rebellion. The time is near – ha, it strikes!"

Something else he said, but I did not hear. I did not see, nor did I feel in the human sense of the word. I was writhing at his feet, screaming and gibbering in the flames of such hells as men have never dreamed of.

Aye, I knew now! He had simply given me a dope so much stronger that it drowned the hashish. My unnatural ability was explainable now – I had simply been acting under the stimulus of something which combined all the hells in its make-up which stimulated, something like heroin, but whose effect was unnoticed by the victim. What it was, I had no idea, nor did I believe anyone knew save that hellish being who stood watching me with grim amusement. But it had held my brain together, instilling into my system a need for it, and now my frightful craving tore my soul asunder.

Never, in my moments of worst shell-shock or my moments of hashish-craving, have I ever experienced anything like that. I burned with the heat of a thousand hells and froze with an iciness that was colder than any ice, a hundred times. I swept down to the deepest pits of torture and up to the highest crags of torment – a million yelling devils hemmed me in, shrieking and stabbing. Bone by bone, vein by vein, cell by cell I felt my body disintegrate and fly in bloody atoms all over the universe and each separate cell was an entire system of quivering, screaming nerves. And they gathered from far voids and reunited with a greater torment.

Through the fiery bloody mists I heard my own voice screaming, a monotonous yammering. Then with distended eyes I saw a golden goblet, held by a claw-like hand, swim into view – a goblet filled with an amber liquid.

With a bestial screech I seized it with both hands, being dimly aware that the metal stem gave beneath my fingers, and brought the brim to my lips. I drank in frenzied haste, the liquid slopping down onto my breast.

IX : KATHULOS OF EGYPT

"Night shall be thrice night over you.
And Heaven an iron cope."
–CHESTERTON

The Skull-faced One stood watching me critically as I sat panting on a couch, completely exhausted. He held in his hand the goblet and surveyed the golden stem, which was crushed out of all shape. This my maniac fingers had done in the instant of drinking.

"Superhuman strength, even for a man in your condition," he said with a sort of creaky pedantry. "I doubt if even Hassim here could equal it. Are you ready for your instructions now?"

I nodded, wordless. Already the hellish strength of the elixir was flowing through my veins, renewing my burnt-out force. I wondered how long a man could live as I lived being constantly burned out and artificially rebuilt.

"You will be given a disguise and will go alone to the Frenton estate. No one suspects any design against Sir Haldred and your entrance into the estate and the house itself should be a matter of comparative ease. You will not don the disguise – which will be of unique nature – until you are ready to enter the estate. You will then proceed to Sir Haldred's room and kill him, breaking his neck with your bare hands – this is essential–"

The voice droned on, giving its ghastly orders in a frightfully casual and matter-of-fact way. The cold sweat beaded my brow.

"You will then leave the estate, taking care to leave the imprint of your hand somewhere plainly visible, and the automobile, which will be waiting for you at some safe place nearby, will bring you back here, you having first removed the disguise. I have, in case of later complications, any amount of men who will swear that you spent the entire night in the Temple of Dreams and never left it. But there must be no detection! Go warily and perform your task surely, for you know the alternative."

I did not return to the opium house but was taken through winding corridors, hung with heavy tapestries, to a small room containing only an Oriental couch. Hassim gave me to understand that I was to remain there until after nightfall and then left me. The door was closed but I made no effort to discover if it was locked. The Skull-faced Master held me with stronger shackles than locks and bolts.

Seated upon the couch in the bizarre setting of a chamber which might have been a room in an Indian zenana, I faced fact squarely and fought out my battle. There was still in me some trace of manhood left – more than the fiend had reckoned, and added to this were black despair and desperation. I chose and determined on my only course.

Suddenly the door opened softly. Some intuition told me whom to expect, nor was I disappointed. Zuleika stood, a glorious vision before me – a vision which mocked me, made blacker my despair and yet thrilled me with wild yearning and reasonless joy.

She bore a tray of food which she set beside me, and then she seated herself on the couch, her large eyes fixed upon my face. A flower in a serpent den she was, and the beauty of her took hold of my heart.

"Steephen!" she whispered and I thrilled as she spoke my name for the first time.

Her luminous eyes suddenly shone with tears and she laid her little hand on my arm. I seized it in both my rough hands.

"They have set you a task which you fear and hate!" she faltered.

"Aye." I almost laughed, "but I'll fool them yet! Zuleika, tell me – what is the meaning of all this?"

She glanced fearfully around her.

"I do not know all" – she hesitated – "your plight is all my fault but I – I hoped – Steephen, I have watched you every time you came to Yun Shatu's for months. You did not see me but I saw you, and I saw in you, not the broken sot your rags proclaimed, but a wounded soul, a soul bruised terribly on the ramparts of life. And from my heart I pitied you. Then when Hassim abused you that day" – again tears started to her eyes – "I could not bear it and I knew how you suffered for want of hashish. So I paid Yun Shatu, and going to the Master I – I – oh, you will hate me for this!" she sobbed.

"No no – never–"

"I told him that you were a man who might be of use to him and begged him to have Yun Shatu supply you with what you needed. He had already noticed you, for his is the eye of the slaver and all the world is his slave market!

"So he bade Yun Shatu do as I asked; and now – better if you had remained as you were, my friend."

"No! No!" I exclaimed. "I have known a few days of regeneration, even if it was false! I have stood before you as a man, and that is worth all else!"

And all that I felt for her must have looked forth from my eyes, for she dropped hers and flushed. Ask me not how love comes to a man; but I knew that I loved Zuleika – had loved this mysterious Oriental girl since first I saw her and somehow I felt that she, in a measure, returned my affection. This realization made blacker and more barren the road I had chosen; yet – for pure love must ever strengthen a man – it nerved me to what I must do.

"Zuleika," I said, speaking hurriedly, "time flies and there are things I must learn; tell me – who are you and why do you remain in this den of Hades?"

"I am Zuleika – that is all I know. I am Circassian by blood and birth; when I was very little I was captured in a Turkish raid and raised in a Stamboul harem; while I was yet too young to marry, my master gave me as a present to – to *Him*."

"And who is he – this skull-faced man?"

"He is Kathulos of Egypt – that is all I know. My master."

"An Egyptian? Then what is he doing in London – why all this mystery?"

She intertwined her fingers nervously.

"Steephen, please speak lower; always there is someone listening everywhere. I do not know who the Master is or why he is here or why he does these things. I swear by Allah! If I knew I would tell you. Sometimes distinguished-looking men come here to the room where the Master receives them – not the room where you saw him – and he makes me dance before them and afterward flirt with them a little. And always I must repeat exactly what they say to me. That is what I must always do – in Turkey, in the Barbary States, in Egypt, in France and in England. The Master taught me French and English and educated me in many ways himself. He is the greatest sorcerer in all the world and knows all ancient magic and everything."

"Zuleika," I said, "my race is soon run, but let me get you out of this – come with me and I swear I'll get you away from this fiend!"

She shuddered and hid her face.

"No, no, I can not!"

"Zuleika," I asked gently, "what hold has he over you, child – dope also?"

"No, no!" she whimpered. "I do not know – I do not know – but I can not – I never can escape him!"

I sat, baffled for a few moments; then I asked, "Zuleika, where are we right now?"

"This building is a deserted storehouse back of the Temple of Silence."

"I thought so. What is in the chests in the tunnel?"

"I do not know."

Then suddenly she began weeping softly. "You too, a slave, like me – you who are so strong and kind – oh Steephen, I can not bear it!"

I smiled. "Lean closer, Zuleika, and I will tell you how I am going to fool this Kathulos."

She glanced apprehensively at the door.

"You will speak low. I will lie in your arms and while you pretend to caress me, whisper your words to me."

She glided into my embrace, and there on the dragon-worked couch in that house of horror I first knew the glory of Zuleika's slender form nestling in my arms – of Zuleika's soft cheek pressing my breast. The fragrance of her was in my nostrils, her hair in my eyes, and my senses reeled; then with my lips hidden by her silky hair I whispered, swiftly.

"I am going first to warn Sir Haldred Frenton – then to find John Gordon and tell him of this den. I will lead the police here and you must watch closely and be ready to hide from *Him* – until we can break through and kill or capture him. Then you will be free."

"But you!" she gasped, paling. "You must have the elixir, and only he–"

"I have a way of outdoing him, child," I answered.

She went pitifully white and her woman's intuition sprang at the right conclusion.

"You are going to kill yourself?"

And much as it hurt me to see her emotion, I yet felt a torturing thrill that she should feel so on my account. Her arms tightened about my neck.

"Don't, Steephen!" she begged. "It is better to live, even–"

"No, not at that price. Better to go out clean while I have the manhood left."

She stared at me wildly for an instant; then, pressing her red lips suddenly to mine, she sprang up and fled from the room. Strange, strange are the ways of love. Two stranded ships on the shores of life, we had drifted inevitably together, and though no word of love had passed between us, we knew each other's heart – through grime and rags; and through accoutrements of the slave, we knew each other's heart and from the first loved as naturally and as purely as it was intended from the beginning of Time.

The beginning of life now and the end for me, for as soon as I had completed my task, ere I felt again the torments of my curse, love and life and beauty and torture should be blotted out together in the stark finality of a pistol ball scattering my rotting brain. Better a clean death than–

The door opened again and Yussef Ali entered.

"The hour arrives for departure," he said briefly. "Rise and follow."

I had no idea, of course, as to the time. No window opened from the room I occupied – I had seen no outer window whatever. The rooms were lighted by tapers in censers swinging from the ceiling. As I rose the slim young Moor slanted a sinister glance in my direction.

"This lies between you and me," he said sibilantly. "Servants of the same Master we – but this concerns ourselves alone. Keep your distance from Zuleika – the Master has promised her to me in the days of the empire."

My eyes narrowed to slits as I looked into the frowning, handsome face of the Oriental, and such hate surged up in me as I have seldom known. My fingers involuntarily opened and closed, and the Moor, marking the action, stepped back, hand in his girdle.

"Not now – there is work for us both – later perhaps"; then in a sudden cold gust of hatred, "Swine! ape-man! when the Master is finished with you I shall quench my dagger in your heart!"

I laughed grimly.

"Make it soon, desert-snake, or I'll crush your spine between my hands."

X : THE DARK HOUSE

"Against all man-made shackles and a man-made Hell–
Alone – at last – unaided I rebel!"
–MUNDY

I followed Yussef Ali along the winding hallways, down the steps – Kathulos was not in the idol-room – and along the tunnel, then through the rooms of the Temple of Dreams and out into the street, where the street lamps gleamed drearily through the fogs and a slight drizzle. Across the street stood an automobile, curtains closely drawn.

"That is yours," said Hassim, who had joined us. "Saunter across natural-like. Don't act suspicious. The place may be watched. The driver knows what to do."

Then he and Yussef Ali drifted back into the bar and I took a single step toward the curb.

"Steephen!"

A voice that made my heart leap spoke my name! A white hand beckoned from the shadows of a doorway. I stepped quickly there.

"Zuleika!"

"Shhh!"

She clutched my arm, slipped something into my hand; I made out vaguely a small flask of gold.

"Hide this, quick!" came her urgent whisper. "Don't come back, go away and hide. This is full of elixir – I will try to get you some more before that is all gone. You must find a way of communicating with me."

"Yes, but how did you get this?" I asked amazedly.

"I stole it from the Master! Now please, I must go before he misses me."

And she sprang back into the doorway and vanished. I stood undecided. I was sure that she had risked nothing less than her life in doing this and I was torn by the fear of what Kathulos might do to her, were the theft discovered. But to return to the house of mystery would certainly invite suspicion, and I might carry out my plan and strike back before the Skull-faced One learned of his slave's duplicity.

So I crossed the street to the waiting automobile. The driver was a Negro whom I had never seen before, a lanky man of medium height. I stared hard at him, wondering how much he had seen. He gave no evidence of having seen anything, and I decided that even if he had noticed me step back into the shadows he could not have seen what passed there nor have been able to recognize the girl.

He merely nodded as I climbed in the back seat, and a moment later we were speeding away down the deserted and fog-haunted streets. A bundle beside me I concluded to be the disguise mentioned by the Egyptian.

To recapture the sensations I experienced as I rode through the rainy, misty night would be impossible. I felt as if I were already dead and the bare and dreary streets about me were the roads of death over which my ghost had been doomed to roam forever. A torturing joy was in my heart, and bleak despair the despair of a doomed man. Not that death itself was so repellent – a dope victim dies too many deaths to shrink from the last – but it was hard to go out just as love had entered my barren life. And I was still young.

A sardonic smile crossed my lips – they were young, too, the men who died beside me in No Man's Land. I drew back my sleeve and clenched my fists, tensing my muscles. There was no surplus weight on my frame, and much of the firm flesh had wasted away, but the cords of the great biceps still stood out like knots of iron, seeming to indicate massive strength. But I knew my might was false, that in reality I was a broken husk of a man, animated only by the artificial fire of the elixir, without which a frail girl might topple me over.

The automobile came to a halt among some trees. We were on the outskirts of an exclusive suburb and the hour was past midnight. Through the trees I saw a large house looming darkly against the distant flares of night-time London.

"This is where I wait," said the Negro. "No one can see the automobile from the road or from the house."

Holding a match so that its light could not be detected outside the car, I examined the "disguise" and was hard put to restrain an insane laugh. The disguise was the complete hide of a gorilla! Gathering the bundle under my arm I trudged toward the wall which surrounded the Frenton estate. A few steps and the trees where the Negro hid with the car merged into one dark mass. I did not believe he could see me, but for safety's sake I made, not for the high iron gate at the front but for the wall at the side where there was no gate.

No light showed in the house. Sir Haldred was a bachelor and I was sure that the servants were all in bed long ago. I negotiated the wall with ease and stole across the dark lawn to a side door, still carrying the grisly "disguise" under my arm. The door was locked, as I had anticipated, and I did not wish to arouse anyone until I was safely in the house, where the sound of voices would not carry to one who might have followed me. I took hold of the knob with both hands, and, exerting slowly the inhuman strength that was mine, began to twist. The shaft turned in my hands and the lock within shattered suddenly, with a noise that was like the crash of a cannon in the stillness. An instant more and I was inside and had closed the door behind me.

I took a single stride in the darkness in the direction I believed the stair to be, then halted as a beam of light flashed into my face. At the side of the beam I caught the glimmer of a pistol muzzle. Beyond a lean shadowy face floated.

"Stand where you are and put up your hands!" I lifted my hands, allowing the bundle to slip to the floor. I had heard that voice only once but I recognized it – knew instantly that the man who held that light was John Gordon. "How many are with you?" His voice was sharp, commanding. "I am alone," I answered. "Take me into a room where a light can not be seen from the outside and I'll tell you some things you want to know." He was silent; then, bidding me take up the bundle I had dropped, he stepped to one side and motioned me to precede him into the next room. There he directed me to a stairway and at the top landing opened a door and switched on lights. I found myself in a room whose curtains were closely drawn. During this journey Gordon's alertness had not relaxed, and now he stood, still covering me with his revolver. Clad in conventional garments, he stood revealed a tall, leanly but powerfully built man, taller than I but not so heavy – with steel-gray eyes and clean-cut features. Something about the man attracted me, even as I noted a bruise on his jawbone where my fist had struck in our last meeting. "I can not believe," he said crisply, "that this apparent clumsiness and lack of subtlety is real. Doubtless you have your own reasons for wishing me to be in a secluded room at this time, but Sir Haldred is efficiently protected even now. Stand still." Muzzle pressed against my chest, he ran his hand over my garments for concealed weapons, seeming slightly surprised when he found none. "Still," he murmured as if to himself, "a man who can burst an iron lock with his bare hands has scant need of weapons."

"You are wasting valuable time," I said impatiently. "I was sent here tonight to kill Sir Haldred Frenton–"

"By whom?" the question was shot at me. "By the man who sometimes goes disguised as a leper?"

He nodded, a gleam in his scintillant eyes. "My suspicions were correct, then."

"Doubtless. Listen to me closely – do you desire the death or arrest of that man?"

Gordon laughed grimly.

"To one who wears the mark of the scorpion on his hand, my answer would be superfluous."

"Then follow my directions and your wish shall be granted."

His eyes narrowed suspiciously.

"So that was the meaning of this open entry and non-resistance," he said slowly. "Does the dope which dilates your eyeballs so warp your mind that you think to lead me into ambush?"

I pressed my hands against my temples. Time was racing and every moment was precious – how could I convince this man of my honesty?

"Listen; my name is Stephen Costigan of America. I was a frequenter of Yun Shatu's dive and a hashish addict – as you have guessed, but just now a slave of stronger dope. By virtue of this slavery, the man you know as a false leper, whom Yun Shatu and his friends call "Master", gained dominance over me and sent me here to murder Sir Haldred – why, God only knows. But I have gained a space of respite by coming into possession of some of this dope which I must have in order to live, and I fear and hate this Master. Listen to me and I swear, by all things holy and unholy, that before the sun rises the false leper shall be in your power!"

I could tell that Gordon was impressed in spite of himself.

"Speak fast!" he rapped.

Still I could sense his disbelief and a wave of futility swept over me.

"If you will not act with me," I said, "let me go and somehow I'll find a way to get to the Master and kill him. My time is short – my hours are numbered and my vengeance is yet to be realized."

"Let me hear your plan, and talk fast," Gordon answered.

"It is simple enough. I will return to the Master's lair and tell him I have accomplished that which he sent me to do. You must follow closely with your men and while I engage the Master in conversation, surround the house. Then, at the signal, break in and kill or seize him."

Gordon frowned. "Where is this house?"

"The warehouse back of Yun Shatu's has been converted into a veritable Oriental palace."

"The warehouse!" he exclaimed. "How can that be? I had thought of that first, but I have carefully examined it from without. The windows are closely barred and spiders have built webs across them. The doors are nailed fast on the outside and the seals that mark the warehouse as deserted have never been broken or disturbed in any way."

"They tunneled up from beneath," I answered. "The Temple of Dreams is directly connected with the warehouse."

"I have traversed the alley between the two buildings," said Gordon, "and the doors of the warehouse opening into that alley are, as I have said, nailed shut from without just as the owners left them. There is apparently no rear exit of any kind from the Temple of Dreams."

"A tunnel connects the buildings, with one door in the rear room of Yun Shatu's and the other in the idol-room of the warehouse."

"I have been In Yun Shatu's back room and found no such door."

"The table rests upon it. You noted the heavy table in the center of the room? Had you turned it around the secret door would have opened in the floor. Now this is my plan: I will go in through the Temple of Dreams and meet the Master in the idol-room. You will have men secretly stationed in front of the warehouse and others upon the other street, in front of the Temple of Dreams. Yun Shatu's building, as you know, faces the waterfront, while the warehouse, fronting the opposite direction, faces a narrow street running parallel with the river. At the signal let the men in this street break open the front of the warehouse and rush in, while simultaneously those in front of Yun Shatu's make an invasion through the Temple of Dreams.

"Let these make for the rear room, shooting without mercy any who may seek to deter them, and there open the secret door as I have said. There being, to the best of my knowledge, no other exit from the Master's lair, he and his servants will necessarily seek to make their escape through the tunnel. Thus we will have them on both sides."

Gordon ruminated while I studied his face with breathless interest.

"This may be a snare," he muttered, "or an attempt to draw me away from Sir Haldred, but–"

I held my breath.

"I am a gambler by nature," he said slowly. "I am going to follow what you Americans call a hunch – but God help you if you are lying to me!"

I sprang erect.

"Thank God! Now aid me with this suit, for I must be wearing it when I return to the automobile waiting for me."

His eyes narrowed as I shook out the horrible masquerade and prepared to don it.

"This shows, as always, the touch of the master hand. You were doubtless instructed to leave marks of your hands, encased in those hideous gauntlets?"

"Yes – though I have no idea why."

"I think I have – the Master is famed for leaving no real clues to mark his crimes – a great ape escaped from a neighbouring zoo earlier in the evening and it seems too obvious for mere chance, in the light of this disguise. The ape would have gotten the blame for Sir Haldred's death."

The thing was easily gotten into and the illusion of reality it created was so perfect as to draw a shudder from me as I viewed myself in a mirror.

"It is now two o'clock," said Gordon. "Allowing for the time it will take you to get back to Limehouse and the time it will take me to get my men stationed, I promise you that at half-past four the house will be closely surrounded. Give me a start – wait here until I have left this house, so I will arrive at least as soon as you."

"Good!" I impulsively grasped his hand. "There will doubtless be a girl there who is in no way implicated with the Master's evil-doings, but only a victim of circumstances such as I have been. Deal gently with her."

"It shall be done. What signal shall I look for?"

"I have no way of signaling for you and I doubt if any sound in the house could be heard on the street. Let your men make their raid on the stroke of five."

I turned to go.

"A man is waiting for you with a car, I take it? Is he likely to suspect anything?"

"I have a way of finding out, and if he does," I replied grimly, "I will return alone to the Temple of Dreams."

XI : FOUR THIRTY-FOUR

"Doubting, dreaming dreams no
mortal ever dared to dream before."
–POE

The door closed softly behind me, the great dark house looming up more starkly than ever. Stooping, I crossed the wet lawn at a run, a grotesque and unholy figure, I doubt not, since any man had at a glance sworn me to be not a man but a giant ape. So craftily had the Master devised!

I clambered the wall, dropped to the earth beyond and made my way through the darkness and the drizzle to the group of trees which masked the automobile.

The Negro driver leaned out of the front seat. I was breathing hard and sought in various ways to simulate the actions of a man who has just murdered in cold blood and fled the scene of his crime.

"You heard nothing, no sound, no scream?" I hissed, gripping his arm.

"No noise except a slight crash when you first went in," he answered. "You did a good job – nobody passing along the road could have suspected anything."

"Have you remained in the car all the time?" I asked. And when he replied that he had, I seized his ankle and ran my hand over the soles of his shoe; it was perfectly dry, as was the cuff of his trouser leg. Satisfied, I climbed into the back seat. Had he taken a step on the earth, shoe and garment would have showed it by the telltale dampness.

I ordered him to refrain from starting the engine until I had removed the ape-skin, and then we sped through the night and I fell victim to doubts and uncertainties. Why should Gordon put any trust in the word of a stranger and a former ally of the Master's? Would he not put my tale down as the ravings of a dope-crazed addict, or a lie to ensnare or befool him? Still, if he had not believed me, why had he let me go?

I could but trust. At any rate, what Gordon did or did not do would scarcely affect my fortunes ultimately, even though Zuleika had furnished me with that which would merely extend the number of my days. My thought centered on her, and more than my hope of vengeance on Kathulos was the hope that Gordon might be able to save her from the clutches of the fiend. At any rate, I thought grimly, if Gordon failed me, I still had my hands and if I might lay them upon the bony frame of the Skull-faced One–

Abruptly I found myself thinking of Yussef Ali and his strange words, the import of which just occurred to me, *"The Master has promised her to me in the days of the empire!"*

The days of the empire – what could that mean?

The automobile at last drew up in front of the building which hid the Temple of Silence – now dark and still. The ride had seemed interminable and as I dismounted I glanced at the timepiece on the dashboard of the car. My heart leaped – it was four thirty-four, and unless my eyes tricked me I saw a movement in the shadows across the street, out of the flare of the street lamp. At this time of night it could mean only one of two things – some menial of the Master watching for my return or else Gordon had kept his word. The Negro drove away and I opened the door, crossed the deserted bar and entered the opium room. The bunks and the floor were littered with the dreamers, for such places as these know nothing of day or night as normal people know, but all lay deep in sottish slumber.

The lamps glimmered through the smoke and a silence hung mist-like over all.

XII : THE STROKE OF FIVE

"He saw gigantic tracks of death,
And many a shape of doom."
—CHESTERTON

Two of the China boys squatted among the smudge fires, staring at me unwinkingly as I threaded my way among the recumbent bodies and made my way to the rear door. For the first time I traversed the corridor alone and found time to wonder again as to the contents of the strange chests which lined the walls. Four raps on the under side of the floor, and a moment later I stood in the idol-room. I gasped in amazement — the fact that across a table from me sat Kathulos in all his horror was not the cause of my exclamation. Except for the table, the chair on which the Skull-face sat and the altar — now bare of incense — the room was perfectly bare. Drab, unlovely walls of the unused warehouse met my gaze instead of the costly tapestries I had become accustomed to. The palms, the idol, the lacquered screen — all were gone. "Ah, Mr. Costigan, you wonder, no doubt." The dead voice of the Master broke in on my thoughts. His serpent eyes glittered balefully. The long yellow fingers twined sinuously upon the table. "You thought me to be a trusting fool, no doubt!" he rapped suddenly. "Did you think I would not have you followed? You fool, Yussef Ali was at your heels every moment!"

An instant I stood speechless, frozen by the crash of these words against my brain; then as their import sank home, I launched myself forward with a roar. At the same instant; before my clutching fingers could close on the mocking horror on the other side of the table, men rushed from every side. I whirled, and with the clarity of hate, from the swirl of savage faces I singled out Yussef Ali, and crashed my right fist against his temple with every ounce of my strength. Even as he dropped, Hassim struck me to my knees and a Chinaman flung a man-net over my shoulders. I heaved erect, bursting the stout cords as if they were strings, and then a blackjack in the hands of Ganra Singh stretched me stunned and bleeding on the floor.

Lean sinewy hands seized and bound me with cords that cut cruelly into my flesh. Emerging from the mists of semi-unconsciousness, I found myself lying on the altar with the masked Kathulos towering over me like a gaunt ivory tower. About in a semi-circle stood Ganra Singh, Yar Khan, Yun Shatu and several others whom I knew as frequenters of the Temple of Dreams. Beyond them — and the sight cut me to the heart — I saw Zuleika crouching in a doorway, her face white and her hands pressed against her cheeks, in an attitude of abject terror.

"I did not fully trust you," said Kathulos sibilantly, "so I sent Yussef Ali to follow you. He reached the group of trees before you and following you into the estate heard your very interesting conversation with John Gordon — for he scaled the house-wall like a rat and clung to the window-ledge! Your driver delayed purposely so as to give Yussef Ali plenty of time to get back – I have decided to change my abode anyway. My furnishings are already on their way to another house, and as soon as we have disposed of the traitor – you! – we shall depart also, leaving a little surprise for your friend Gordon when he arrives at five-thirty."

My heart gave a sudden leap of hope. Yussef Ali had misunderstood, and Kathulos lingered here in false security while the London detective force had already silently surrounded the house. Over my shoulder I saw Zuleika vanish from the door.

I eyed Kathulos, absolutely unaware of what he was saying. It was not long until five – if he dallied longer – then I froze as the Egyptian spoke a word and Li Kung, a gaunt, cadaverous Chinaman, stepped from the silent semi-circle and drew from his sleeve a long thin dagger. My eyes sought the timepiece that still rested on the table and my heart sank. It was still ten minutes until five. My death did not matter so much, since it simply hastened the inevitable, but in my mind's eye I could see Kathulos and his murderers escaping while the police awaited the stroke of five.

The Skull-face halted in some harangue, and stood in a listening attitude. I believe his uncanny intuition warned him of danger. He spoke a quick staccato command to Li Kung and the Chinaman sprang forward, dagger lifted above my breast.

The air was suddenly supercharged with dynamic tension. The keen dagger-point hovered high above me – loud and clear sounded the skirl of a police whistle and on the heels of the sound there came a terrific crash from the front of the warehouse!

Kathulos leaped into frenzied activity. Hissing orders like a cat spitting, he sprang for the hidden door and the rest followed him. Things happened with the speed of a nightmare. Li Kung had followed the rest, but Kathulos flung a command over his shoulder and the Chinaman turned back and came rushing toward the altar where I lay, dagger high, desperation in his countenance.

A scream broke through the clamor and as I twisted desperately about to avoid the descending dagger, I caught a glimpse of Kathulos dragging Zuleika away. Then with a frenzied wrench I toppled from the altar just as Li Kung's dagger, grazing my breast, sank inches deep into the dark-stained surface and quivered there.

I had fallen on the side next to the wall and what was taking place in the room I could not see, but it seemed as if far away I could hear men screaming faintly and hideously. Then Li Kung wrenched his blade free and sprang, tigerishly, around the end of the altar. Simultaneously a revolver cracked from the doorway – the Chinaman spun clear around, the dagger flying from his hand – he slumped to the floor.

Gordon came running from the doorway where a few moments earlier Zuleika had stood, his pistol still smoking in his hand. At his heels were three rangy, clean-cut men in plain clothes. He cut my bonds and dragged me upright.

"Quick! Where have they gone?"

The room was empty of life save for myself, Gordon and his men, though two dead men lay on the floor.

I found the secret door and after a few seconds' search located the lever which opened it. Revolvers drawn, the men grouped about me and peered nervously into the dark stairway. Not a sound came up from the total darkness.

"This is uncanny!" muttered Gordon. "I suppose the Master and his servants went this way when they left the building as they are certainly not here now! – and Leary and his men should have stopped them either in the tunnel itself or in the rear room of Yun Shatu's. At any rate, in either event they should have communicated with us by this time."

"Look out, sir!" one of the men exclaimed suddenly, and Gordon, with an ejaculation, struck out with his pistol barrel and crushed the life from a huge snake which had crawled silently up the steps from the blackness beneath.

"Let us see into this matter," said he, straightening.

But before he could step onto the first stair, I halted him; for, flesh crawling, I began dimly to understand something of what had happened – I began to understand the silence in the tunnel, the absence of the detectives, the screams I had heard some minutes previously while I lay on the altar. Examining the lever which opened the door. I found another smaller lever – I began to believe I knew what those mysterious chests in the tunnel contained.

"Gordon," I said hoarsely, "have you an electric torch?"

One of the men produced a large one.

"Direct the light into the tunnel, but as you value your life, do not put a foot upon the steps."

The beam of light struck through the shadows, lighting the tunnel, etching out boldly a scene that will haunt my brain all the rest of my life. On the floor of the tunnel, between the chests which now gaped open, lay two men who were members of London's finest secret service. Limbs twisted and faces horribly distorted they lay, and above and about them writhed, in long glittering scaly shimmerings, scores of hideous reptiles.

The clock struck five.

XIII : THE BLIND BEGGAR WHO RODE

"He seemed a beggar such as lags
Looking for crusts and ale."
–CHESTERTON

The cold gray dawn was stealing over the river as we stood in the deserted bar of the Temple of Dreams. Gordon was questioning the two men who had remained on guard outside the building while their unfortunate companions went in to explore the tunnel.

"As soon as we heard the whistle, sir, Leary and Murken rushed the bar and broke into the opium room, while we waited here at the bar door according to orders. Right away several ragged dopers came tumbling out and we grabbed them. But no one else came out and we heard nothing from Leary and Murken; so we just waited until you came, sir."

"You saw nothing of a giant Negro, or of the Chinaman Yun Shatu?"

"No, Sir. After a while the patrolmen arrived and we threw a cordon around the house, but no one was seen."

Gordon shrugged his shoulders; a few cursory questions had satisfied him that the captives were harmless addicts and he had them released.

"You are sure no one else came out?"

"Yes, sir — no, wait a moment. A wretched old blind beggar did come out, all rags and dirt and with a ragged girl leading him. We stopped him but didn't hold him — a wretch like that couldn't be harmful."

"No?" Gordon jerked out. "Which way did he go?"

"The girl led him down the street to the next block and then an automobile stopped and they got in and drove off, sir."

Gordon glared at him.

"The stupidity of the London detective has rightfully become an international jest," he said acidly. "No doubt it never occurred to you as being strange that a Limehouse beggar should ride about in his own automobile."

Then impatiently waving aside the man, who sought to speak further, he turned to me and I saw the lines of weariness beneath his eyes.

"Mr. Costigan, if you will come to my apartment we may be able to clear up some new things."

XIV : THE BLACK EMPIRE

"Oh the new spears dipped in life-blood as
the woman shrieked in vain!
Oh the days before the English! When
will those days come again?"
—MUNDY

Gordon struck a match and absently allowed it to flicker and go out in his hand. His Turkish cigarette hung unlighted between his fingers.

"This is the most logical conclusion to be reached," he was saying. "The weak link in our chain was lack of men. But curse it, one can not round up an army at two o'clock in the morning, even with the aid of Scotland Yard. I went on to Limehouse, leaving orders for a number of patrolmen to follow me as quickly as they could be got together, and to throw a cordon about the house.

"They arrived too late to prevent the Master's servants slipping out of the side doors and windows, no doubt, as they could easily do with only Finnegan and Hansen on guard at the front of the building. However, they arrived in time to prevent the Master himself from slipping out in that way — no doubt he lingered to effect his disguise and was caught in that manner. He owes his escape to his craft and boldness and to the carelessness of Finnegan and Hansen. The girl who accompanied him—"

"She was Zuleika, without doubt."

I answered listlessly, wondering anew what shackles bound her to the Egyptian sorcerer.

"You owe your life to her," Gordon rapped, lighting another match. "We were standing in the shadows in front of the warehouse, waiting for the hour to strike, and of course ignorant as to what was going on in the house, when a girl appeared at one of the barred windows and begged us for God's sake to do something – that a man was being murdered. So we broke in at once. However, she was not to be seen when we entered."

"She returned to the room, no doubt," I muttered, "and was forced to accompany the Master. God grant he knows nothing of her trickery."

"I do not know," said Gordon, dropping the charred match stem, "whether she guessed at our true identity or whether she just made the appeal in desperation.

"However, the main point is this: evidence points to the fact that, on hearing the whistle, Leary and Murken invaded Yun Shatu's from the front at the same instant my three men and I made our attack on the warehouse front. As it took us some seconds to batter down the door, it is logical to suppose that they found the secret door and entered the tunnel before we effected an entrance into the warehouse.

"The Master, knowing our plans beforehand, and being aware that an invasion would be made through the tunnel and having long ago made preparations for such an exigency—"

An involuntary shudder shook me.

"—the Master worked the lever that opened the chests – the screams you heard as you lay upon the altar were the death shrieks of Leary and Murken. Then, leaving the Chinaman behind to finish you, the Master and the rest descended into the tunnel – incredible as it seems – and threading their way unharmed among the serpents, entered Yun Shatu's house and escaped therefrom as I have said."

"That seems impossible. Why should not the snakes turn on them?"

Gordon finally ignited his cigarette and puffed a few seconds before replying.

"The reptiles might still have been giving their full and hideous attention to the dying men, or else – I have on previous occasions been confronted with indisputable proof of the Master's dominance over beasts and reptiles of even the lowest or most dangerous orders. How he and his slaves passed unhurt among those scaly fiends must remain, at present, one of the many unsolved mysteries pertaining to that strange man."

I stirred restlessly in my chair. This brought up a point for the purpose of clearing up which I had come to Gordon's neat but bizarre apartments.

"You have not yet told me," I said abruptly, "who this man is and what is his mission."

"As to who he is, I can only say that he is known as you name him – the Master. I have never seen him unmasked, nor do I know his real name nor his nationality."

"I can enlighten you to an extent there," I broke in. "I have seen him unmasked and have heard the name his slaves call him."

Gordon's eyes blazed and he leaned forward.

"His name," I continued, "is Kathulos and he claims to be an Egyptian."

"Kathulos!" Gordon repeated. "You say he claims to be an Egyptian – have you any reason for doubting his claim of that nationality?"

"He may be of Egypt," I answered slowly, "but he is different, somehow, from any human I ever saw or hope to see. Great age might account for some of his peculiarities, but there are certain lineal differences that my anthropological studies tell me have been present since birth – features which would be abnormal to any other man but which are perfectly normal in Kathulos. That sounds paradoxical, I admit, but to appreciate fully the horrid inhumanness of the man, you would have to see him yourself."

Gordon sat all attention while I swiftly sketched the appearance of the Egyptian as I remembered him – and that appearance was indelibly etched on my brain forever.

As I finished he nodded.

"As I have said, I never saw Kathulos except when disguised as a beggar, a leper or some such thing – when he was fairly swathed in rags. Still, I too have been impressed with a strange difference about him – something that is not present in other men."

Gordon tapped his knee with his fingers – a habit of his when deeply engrossed by a problem of some sort.

"You have asked as to the mission of this man," he began slowly. "I will tell you all I know.

"My position with the British government is a unique and peculiar one. I hold what might be called a roving commission – an office created solely for the purpose of suiting my special needs. As a secret service official during the war, I convinced the powers of a need of such office and of my ability to fill it.

"Somewhat over seventeen months ago I was sent to South Africa to investigate the unrest which has been growing among the natives of the interior ever since the World War and which has of late assumed alarming proportions. There I first got on the track of this man Kathulos. I found, in roundabout ways, that Africa was a seething cauldron of rebellion from Morocco to Cape Town. The old, old vow had been made again – the Negroes and the Mohammedans, banded together, should drive the white men into the sea.

"This pact has been made before but always, hitherto, broken. Now, however, I sensed a giant intellect and a monstrous genius behind the veil, a genius powerful enough to accomplish this union and hold it together. Working entirely on hints and vague whispered clues, I followed the trail up through Central Africa and into Egypt. There, at last, I came upon definite evidence that such a man existed. The whispers hinted of a living dead man – a skull-faced man. I learned that this man was the high priest of the mysterious Scorpion society of northern Africa. He was spoken of variously as Skull-face, the Master, and the Scorpion.

"Following a trail of bribed officials and filched state secrets, I at last trailed him to Alexandria, where I had my first sight of him in a dive in the native quarter – disguised as a leper. I heard him distinctly addressed as "mighty Scorpion" by the natives, but he escaped me.

"All trace vanished then; the trail ran out entirely until rumors of strange happenings in London reached me and I came back to England to investigate an apparent leak in the War Office.

"As I thought, the Scorpion had preceded me. This man, whose education and craft transcend anything I ever met with, is simply the leader and instigator of a world-wide movement such as the world has never seen before. He plots, in a word, the overthrow of the white races!

"His ultimate aim is a black empire, with himself as emperor of the world! And to that end he has banded together in one monstrous conspiracy the black, the brown and the yellow."

"I understand now what Yussef Ali meant when he said 'the days of the empire'," I muttered.

"Exactly," Gordon rapped with suppressed excitement. "Kathulos' power is unlimited and unguessed. Like an octopus his tentacles stretch to the high places of civilization and the far corners of the world. And his main weapon is dope! He has flooded Europe and no doubt America with opium and hashish, and in spite of all effort it has been impossible to discover the break in the barriers through which the hellish stuff is coming. With this he ensnares and enslaves men and women.

"You have told me of the aristocratic men and women you saw coming to Yun Shatu's dive. Without doubt they were dope addicts – for, as I said, the habit lurks in high places – holders of governmental positions, no doubt, coming to trade for the stuff they craved and giving in return state secrets, inside information and promise of protection for the Master's crimes.

"Oh, he does not work haphazardly! Before ever the black flood breaks, he will be prepared; if he has his way, the governments of the white races will be honeycombs of corruption – the strongest men of the white races will be dead. The white men's secrets of war will be his. When it comes, I look for a simultaneous uprising against white supremacy, of all the colored races – races who, in the last war, learned the white men's way of battle, and who, led by such a man as Kathulos and armed with white men's finest weapons, will be almost invincible.

"A steady stream of rifles and ammunition has been pouring into East Africa and it was not until I discovered the source that it was stopped. I found that a staid and reliable Scotch firm was smuggling these arms among the natives and I found more: the manager of this firm was an opium slave. That was enough. I saw Kathulos' hand in the matter. The manager was arrested and committed suicide in his cell – that is only one of the many situations with which I am called upon to deal.

"Again, the case of Major Fairlan Morley. He, like myself, held a very flexible commission and had been sent to the Transvaal to work upon the same case. He sent to London a number of secret papers for safe-keeping. They arrived some weeks ago and were put in a bank vault. The letter accompanying them gave explicit instructions that they were to be delivered to no one but the Major himself, when he called for them in person, or in event of his death, to myself.

"As soon as I learned that he had sailed from Africa I sent trusted men to Bordeaux, where he intended to make his first landing in Europe. They did not succeed in saving the Major's life, but they certified his death, for they found his body in a deserted ship whose hulk was stranded on the beach. Efforts were made to keep the affair a secret but somehow it leaked into the papers with the result–"

"I begin to understand why I was to impersonate the unfortunate Major," I interrupted.

"Exactly. A false beard furnished you, and your black hair dyed blond, you would have presented yourself at the bank, received the papers from the banker, who knew Major Morley just intimately enough to be deceived by your appearance, and the papers would have then fallen into the hands of the Master.

"I can only guess at the contents of those papers, for events have been taking place too swiftly for me to call for and obtain them. But they must deal with subjects closely connected with the activities of Kathulos. How he learned of them and of the provisions of the letter accompanying them, I have no idea, but as I said, London is honeycombed with his spies.

"In my search for clues, I often frequented Limehouse disguised as you first saw me. I went often to the Temple of Dreams and even once managed to enter the back room, for I suspected some sort of rendezvous in the rear of the building. The absence of any exit baffled me and I had no time to search for secret doors before I was ejected by the giant black man Hassim, who had no suspicion of my true identity. I noticed that very often the leper entered or left Yun Shatu's, and finally it was borne on me that past a shadow of doubt this supposed leper was the Scorpion himself.

"That night you discovered me on the couch in the opium room, I had come there with no especial plan in mind. Seeing Kathulos leaving, I determined to rise and follow him, but you spoiled that."

He fingered his chin and laughed grimly.

"I was an amateur boxing champion in Oxford," said he, "but Tom Cribb himself could not have withstood that blow – or have dealt it."

"I regret it as I regret few things."

"No need to apologize. You saved my life immediately afterward – I was stunned, but not too much to know that that brown devil Yussef Ali was burning to cut out my heart."

"How did you come to be at Sir Haldred Frenton's estate? And how is it that you did not raid Yun Shatu's dive?"

"I did not have the place raided because I knew somehow Kathulos would be warned and our efforts would come to naught. I was at Sir Haldred's that night because I have contrived to spend at least part of each night with him since he returned from the Congo. I anticipated an attempt upon his life when I learned from his own lips that he was preparing, from the studies he made on this trip, a treatise on the secret native societies of West Africa. He hinted that the disclosures he intended to make therein might prove sensational, to say the least. Since it is to Kathulos' advantage to destroy such men as might be able to arouse the Western world to its danger, I knew that Sir Haldred was a marked man. Indeed, two distinct attempts were made upon his life on his journey to the coast from the African interior. So I put two trusted men on guard and they are at their post even now.

"Roaming about the darkened house, I heard the noise of your entry, and, warning my men, I stole down to intercept you. At the time of our conversation, Sir Haldred was sitting in his unlighted study, a Scotland Yard man with drawn pistol on each side of him. Their vigilance no doubt accounts for Yussef Ali's failure to attempt what you were sent to do.

"Something in your manner convinced me in spite of yourself," he meditated. "I will admit I had some bad moments of doubt as I waited in the darkness that precedes dawn, outside the warehouse."

Gordon rose suddenly and going to a strongbox which stood in a corner of the room, drew thence a thick envelope.

"Although Kathulos has check-mated me at almost every move," he said, "I have not been entirely idle. Noting the frequenters of Yun Shatu's, I have compiled a partial list of the Egyptian's right-hand men, and their records. What you have told me has enabled me to complete that list. As we know, his henchmen are scattered all over the world, and there are possibly hundreds of them here in London. However, this is a list of those I believe to be in his closest council, now with him in England. He told you himself that few even of his followers ever saw him unmasked."

We bent together over the list, which contained the following names: "Yun Shatu, Hong Kong Chinese, suspected opium smuggler – keeper of Temple of Dreams – resident of Limehouse seven years. Hassim, ex-Senegalese chief wanted in French Congo for murder. Santiago, Negro – fled from Haiti under suspicion of voodoo worship atrocities. Yar Khan, Afridi, record unknown. Yussef Ali, Moor, slave-dealer in Morocco – suspected of being a German spy in the World War – an instigator of the Fellaheen Rebellion on the upper Nile. Ganra Singh, Lahore, India, Sikh – smuggler of arms into Afghanistan took an active part in the Lahore and Delhi riots – suspected of murder on two occasions – a dangerous man. Stephen Costigan, American – resident in England since the war – hashish addict – man of remarkable strength. Li Kung, northern China, opium smuggler."

Lines were drawn significantly through three names – mine, Li Kung's and Yussef Ali's. Nothing was written next to mine, but following Li Kung's name was scrawled briefly in Gordon's rambling characters: "Shot by John Gordon during the raid on Yun Shatu's." And following the name of Yussef Ali: "Killed by Stephen Costigan during the Yun Shatu raid."

I laughed mirthlessly. Black empire or not, Yussef Ali would never hold Zuleika in his arms, for he had never risen from where I felled him.

"I know not," said Gordon somberly as he folded the list and replaced it in the envelope, "what power Kathulos has that draws together black men and yellow men to serve him – that unites world-old foes. Hindoo, Moslem and pagan are among his followers. And back in the mists of the East where mysterious and gigantic forces are at work, this uniting is culminating on a monstrous scale."

He glanced at his watch.

"It is nearly ten. Make yourself at home here, Mr. Costigan, while I visit Scotland Yard and see if any clue has been found as to Kathulos' new quarters. I believe that the webs are closing on him, and with your aid I promise you we will have the gang located within a week at most."

XV : THE MARK OF THE TULWAR

"The fed world curls by his drowsy mate
In a tight-trod earth; but the lean wolves wait."
–MUNDY

I sat alone in John Gordon's apartments and laughed mirthlessly. In spite of the elixir's stimulus, the strain of the previous night, with its loss of sleep and its heart-rending actions, was telling on me. My mind was a chaotic whirl wherein the faces of Gordon, Kathulos and Zuleika shifted with numbing swiftness. All the mass of information Gordon had given to me seemed jumbled and incoherent.

Through this state of being, one fact stood out boldly. I must find the latest hiding-place of the Egyptian and get Zuleika out of his hands – if indeed she still lived.

A week, Gordon had said – I laughed again – a week and I would be beyond aiding anyone. I had found the proper amount of elixir to use – knew the minimum amount my system required – and knew that I could make the flask last me four days at most. Four days! Four days in which to comb the rat-holes of Limehouse and Chinatown – four days in which to ferret out, somewhere in the mazes of East End, the lair of Kathulos.

I burned with impatience to begin, but nature rebelled, and staggering to a couch, I fell upon it and was asleep instantly.

Then someone was shaking me.

"Wake Up. Mr. Costigan!"

I sat up, blinking. Gordon stood over me, his face haggard.

"There's devil's work done, Costigan! The Scorpion has struck again!"

I sprang up, still half asleep and only partly realizing what he was saying. He helped me into my coat; thrust my hat at me, and then his firm grip on my arm was propelling me out of his door and down the stairs. The street lights were blazing; I had slept an incredible time.

"A logical victim!" I was aware that my companion was saying. "He should have notified me the instant of his arrival!"

"I don't understand—" I began dazedly.

We were at the curb now and Gordon hailed a taxi, giving the address of a small and unassuming hotel in a staid and prim section of the city.

"The Baron Rokoff," he rapped as we whirled along at reckless speed, "a Russian free-lance, connected with the War Office. He returned from Mongolia yesterday and apparently went into hiding. Undoubtedly he had learned something vital in regard to the slow waking of the East. He had not yet communicated with us, and I had no idea that he was in England until just now."

"And you learned—"

"The baron was found in his room, his dead body mutilated in a frightful manner!"

The respectable and conventional hotel which the doomed baron had chosen for his hiding-place was in a state of mild uproar, being suppressed by the police. The management had attempted to keep the matter quiet, but somehow the guests had learned of the atrocity and many were leaving in haste – or preparing to, as the police were planning to hold all for investigation.

The baron's room, which was on the top floor, was in a state to defy description. Not even in the Great War have I seen a more complete shambles. Nothing had been touched; all remained just as the chambermaid had found it a half-hour since. Tables and chairs lay shattered on the floor, and the furniture, floor and walls were spattered with blood. The baron, a tall, muscular man in life, lay in the middle of the room, a fearful spectacle. His skull had been cleft to the brows, a deep gash under his left armpit had shorn through his ribs, and his left arm hung by a shred of flesh. The cold bearded face was set in a look of indescribable horror.

"Some heavy, curved weapon must have been used," said Gordon, "something like a saber, wielded with terrific force. See where a chance blow sank inches deep into the windowsill. And again, the thick back of this heavy chair has been split like a shingle. A saber, surely."

"A tulwar," I muttered, somberly. "Do you not recognize the handiwork of the Central Asian butcher? Yar Khan has been here."

"The Afghan! He came across the roofs, of course, and descended to the window-ledge by means of a knotted rope made fast to something on the edge of the roof. About one-thirty the maid, passing the corridor, heard a terrific commotion in the baron's room – smashing of chairs and a sudden short shriek which died abruptly into a ghastly gurgle and then ceased – to the sound of heavy blows, curiously muffled, such as a sword might make when driven deep into human flesh. Then all noises stopped suddenly.

"She called the manager and they tried the door and, finding it locked, and receiving no answer to their shouts, opened it with the desk key. Only the corpse was there, but the window was open. This is strangely unlike Kathulos' usual procedure. It lacks subtlety. Often his victims have appeared to have died from natural causes. I scarcely understand."

"I see little difference in the outcome," I answered. "There is nothing that can be done to apprehend the murderer as it is."

"True," Gordon scowled. "We know who did it but there is no proof – not even a fingerprint. Even if we knew where the Afghan is hiding and arrested him, we could prove nothing – there would be a score of men to swear alibis for him. The baron returned only yesterday. Kathulos probably did not know of his arrival until tonight. He knew that on the morrow Rokoff would make known his presence to me and impart what he learned in northern Asia. The Egyptian knew he must strike quickly, and lacking time to prepare a safer and more elaborate form of murder, he sent the Afridi with his tulwar. There is nothing we can do, at least not until we discover the Scorpion's hiding-place; what the baron had learned in Mongolia, we shall never know, but that it dealt with the plans and aspirations of Kathulos, we may be sure."

We went down the stairs again and out on the street, accompanied by one of the Scotland Yard men, Hansen. Gordon suggested that we walk back to his apartment and I greeted the opportunity to let the cool night air blow some of the cobwebs out of my mazed brain.

As we walked along the deserted streets, Gordon suddenly cursed savagely.

"This is a veritable labyrinth we are following, leading nowhere! Here, in the very heart of civilization's metropolis, the direct enemy of that civilization commits crimes of the most outrageous nature and goes free! We are children, wandering in the night, struggling with an unseen evil – dealing with an incarnate devil, of whose true identity we know nothing and whose true ambitions we can only guess.

"Never have we managed to arrest one of the Egyptian's direct henchmen, and the few dupes and tools of his we have apprehended have died mysteriously before they could tell us anything. Again I repeat: what strange power has Kathulos that dominates these men of different creeds and races? The men in London with him are, of course, mostly renegades, slaves of dope, but his tentacles stretch all over the East. Some dominance is his: the power that sent the Chinaman, Li Kung, back to kill you, in the face of certain death; that sent Yar Khan the Moslem over the roofs of London to do murder; that holds Zuleika the Circassian in unseen bonds of slavery.

"Of course we know," he continued after a brooding silence, "that the East has secret societies which are behind and above all considerations of creeds. There are cults in Africa and the Orient whose origin dates back to Ophir and the fall of Atlantis. This man must be a power in some or possibly all of these societies. Why, outside the Jews, I know of no Oriental race which is so cordially despised by the other Eastern races, as the Egyptians! Yet here we have a man, an Egyptian by his own word, controlling the lives and destinies of orthodox

Moslems, Hindoos, Shintos and devil-worshippers. It's unnatural.

"Have you ever" – he turned to me abruptly – "heard the ocean mentioned in connection with Kathulos?"

"Never."

"There is a widespread superstition in northern Africa, based on a very ancient legend, that the great leader of the colored races would come out of the sea! And I once heard a Berber speak of the Scorpion as 'The Son of the Ocean'."

"That is a term of respect among that, tribe, is it not?"

"Yes; still I wonder sometimes."

XVI : THE MUMMY WHO LAUGHED

"Laughing as littered skulls that lie
After lost battles turn to the sky
An everlasting laugh."
–CHESTERTON

"A shop open this late," Gordon remarked suddenly.

A fog had descended on London and along the quiet street we were traversing the lights glimmered with the peculiar reddish haze characteristic of such atmospheric conditions. Our footfalls echoed drearily. Even in the heart of a great city, there are always sections which seem overlooked and forgotten. Such a street was this. Not even a policeman was in sight.

The shop which had attracted Gordon's attention was just in front of us, on the same side of the street. There was no sign over the door, merely some sort of emblem – something like a dragon. Light flowed from the open doorway and the small show windows on each side. As it was neither a café nor the entrance to a hotel we found ourselves idly speculating over its reason for being open. Ordinarily, I suppose, neither of us would have given the matter a thought, but our nerves were so keyed up that we found ourselves instinctively suspicious of anything out of the ordinary. Then something occurred which was distinctly out of the ordinary.

A very tall, very thin man, considerably stooped, suddenly loomed up out of the fog in front of us, and beyond the shop. I had only a glance of him – an impression of incredible gauntness, of worn, wrinkled garments, a high silk hat drawn close over the brows, a face entirely hidden by a muffler; then he turned aside and entered the shop. A cold wind whispered down the street, twisting the fog into wispy ghosts, but the coldness that came upon me transcended the wind's.

"Gordon?" I exclaimed in a fierce, low voice; "my senses are no longer reliable or else Kathulos himself has just gone into that house!"

Gordon's eyes blazed. We were now close to the shop, and lengthening his strides into a run he hurled himself into the door, the detective and I close upon his heels.

A weird assortment of merchandise met our eyes. Antique weapons covered the walls, and the floor was piled high with curious things. Maori idols shouldered Chinese josses, and suits of mediaeval armor bulked darkly against stacks of rare Oriental rugs and Latin-make shawls. The place was an antique shop. Of the figure who had aroused our interest we saw nothing.

An old man clad bizarrely in red fez, brocaded jacket and Turkish slippers came from the back of the shop; he was a Levantine of some sort.

"You wish something, sirs?"

"You keep open rather late," Gordon said abruptly, his eyes travelling swiftly over the shop for some secret hiding-place that might conceal the object of our search.

"Yes, sir. My customers number many eccentric professors and students who keep very irregular hours. Often the night boats unload special pieces for me and very often I have customers later than this. I remain open all night, sir."

"We are merely looking around," Gordon returned, and in an aside to Hansen: "Go to the back and stop anyone who tries to leave that way."

Hansen nodded and strolled casually to the rear of the shop. The back door was clearly visible to our view, through a vista of antique furniture and tarnished hangings strung up for exhibition. We had followed the Scorpion – if he it was – so closely that I did not believe he would have had time to traverse the full length of the shop and make his exit without our having seen him as we came in. For our eyes had been on the rear door ever since we had entered.

Gordon and I browsed around casually among the curios, handling and discussing some of them, but I have no idea as to their nature. The Levantine had seated himself cross-legged on a Moorish mat close to the center of the shop and apparently took only a polite interest in our explorations.

After a time Gordon whispered to me: "There is no advantage in keeping up this pretense. We have looked everywhere the Scorpion might be hiding, in the ordinary manner. I will make known my identity and authority and we will search the entire building openly."

Even as he spoke a truck drew up outside the door and two burly Negroes entered. The Levantine seemed to have expected them, for he merely waved them toward the back of the shop and they responded with a grunt of understanding.

Gordon and I watched them closely as they made their way to a large mummy-case which stood upright against the wall not far from the back. They lowered this to a level position and then started for the door, carrying it carefully between them.

"Halt!" Gordon stepped forward, raising his hand authoritatively.

"I represent Scotland Yard," he said swiftly, "and have sanction for anything I choose to do. Set that mummy down; nothing leaves this shop until we have thoroughly searched it."

The Negroes obeyed without a word and my friend turned to the Levantine; who, apparently not perturbed or even interested, sat smoking a

Turkish water-pipe.

"Who was that tall man who entered just before we did, and where did he go?"

"No one entered before you, sir. Or, if anyone did, I was at the back of the shop and did not see him. You are certainly at liberty to search my shop, sir."

And search it we did, with the combined craft of a secret service expert and a denizen of the underworld – while Hansen stood stolidly at his post, the two Negroes standing over the carved mummy-case watched us impassively and the Levantine sitting like a sphinx on his mat, puffing a fog of smoke into the air. The whole thing had a distinct effect of unreality.

At last, baffled, we returned to the mummy-case, which was certainly long enough to conceal even a man of Kathulos' height. The thing did not appear to be sealed as is the usual custom, and Gordon opened it without difficulty. A formless shape, swathed in moldering wrapping, met our eyes. Gordon parted some of the wrappings and revealed an inch or so of withered, brownish, leathery arm. He shuddered involuntarily as he touched it, as a man will do at the touch of a reptile or sonic inhumanly cold thing. Taking a small metal idol from a stand near by, he rapped on the shrunken breast and the arm. Each gave out a solid thumping, like some sort of wood.

Gordon shrugged his shoulders. "Dead for two thousand years anyway and I don't suppose I should risk destroying a valuable mummy simply to prove what we know to be true."

He closed the case again.

"The mummy may have crumbled some, even for this much exposure, but perhaps it did not."

This last was addressed to the Levantine who replied merely by a courteous gesture of his hand, and the Negroes once more lifted the case and carried it to the truck, where they loaded it on, and a moment later mummy, truck and Negroes had vanished in the fog.

Gordon still nosed about the shop, but I stood stock-still in the center of the floor. To my chaotic and dope-ridden brain I attributed it, but the sensation had been mine, that through the wrappings of the mummy's face, great eyes had burned into mine, eyes like pools of yellow fire, that seared my soul and froze me where I stood. And as the case had been carried through the door, I knew that the lifeless thing in it, dead, God only knows how many centuries, was *laughing*, hideously and silently.

XVII : THE DEAD MAN FROM THE SEA

"In my dream, a wind came up out of the sea and set the waves in turmoil. And this wind brought a human figure rising from the depths and as I watched, this man came flying with the clouds of heaven. Wherever he turned his eyes, everything that they fell on was seized with terror; and wherever the sound of his voice reached, all who heard it melted like wax at the touch of fire.
—ESDRAS 13:2–4

Gordon puffed savagely at his Turkish cigarette, staring abstractedly and unseeingly at Hansen, who sat opposite him.

"I suppose we must chalk up another failure against ourselves. That Levantine, Kamonos, is evidently a creature of the Egyptian's and the walls and floors of his shop are probably honeycombed with secret panels and doors which would baffle a magician."

Hansen made some answer but I said nothing. Since our return to Gordon's apartment, I had been conscious of a feeling of intense languor and sluggishness which not even my condition could account for. I knew that my system was full of elixir – but my mind seemed strangely slow and hard of comprehension in direct contrast with the average state of my mentality when stimulated by the hellish dope.

This condition was slowly leaving me, like mist floating from the surface of a lake, and I felt as if I were waking gradually from a long and unnaturally sound sleep.

Gordon was saying: "I would give a good deal to know if Kamonos is really one of Kathulos' slaves or if the Scorpion managed to make his escape through some natural exit as we entered."

"Kamonos is his servant, true enough," I found myself saying slowly, as if searching for the proper words. "As we left, I saw his gaze light upon the scorpion which is traced on my hand. His eyes narrowed, and as we were leaving he contrived to brush close against me – and to whisper in a quick low voice: 'Soho, 48'."

Gordon came erect like a loosened steel bow.

"Indeed!" he rapped. "Why did you not tell me at the time?"

"I don't know."

My friend eyed me sharply.

"I noticed you seemed like a man intoxicated all the way from the shop," said he. "I attributed it to some aftermath of hashish. But no. Kathulos is undoubtedly a masterful disciple of Mesmer – his power over venomous reptiles shows that, and I am beginning to believe it is the real source of his power over humans.

"Somehow, the Master caught you off your guard in that shop and partly asserted his dominance over your mind. From what hidden nook he sent his thought waves to shatter your brain, I do not know, but Kathulos was somewhere in that shop, I am sure."

"He was. He was in the mummy-case."

"The mummy-case!" Gordon exclaimed rather impatiently. "That is impossible! The mummy quite filled it and not even such a thin being as the Master could have found room there."

I shrugged my shoulders, unable to argue the point but somehow sure of the truth of my statement.

"Kamonos," Gordon continued, "doubtless is not a member of the inner circle and does not know of your change of allegiance. Seeing the mark of the scorpion, he undoubtedly supposed you to be a spy of the Master's. The whole thing may be a plot to ensnare us, but I feel that the man was sincere – Soho 48 can be nothing less than the Scorpion's new rendezvous."

I too felt that Gordon was right, though a suspicion lurked in my mind.

"I secured the papers of Major Morley yesterday," he continued, "and while you slept, I went over them. Mostly they but corroborated what I already knew – touched on the unrest of the natives and repeated the theory that one vast genius was behind all. But there was one matter which interested me greatly and which I think will interest you also."

From his strongbox he took a manuscript written in the close, neat characters of the unfortunate Major, and in a monotonous droning voice which betrayed little of his intense excitement he read the following nightmarish narrative:

"This matter I consider worth jotting down – as to whether it has any bearing on the case at hand, further developments will show. At Alexandria, where I spent some weeks seeking further clues as to the identity of the man known as the Scorpion, I made the acquaintance, through my friend Ahmed Shah, of the noted Egyptologist Professor Ezra Schuyler of New York. He verified the statement made by various laymen, concerning the legend of the "ocean-man". This myth, handed down from generation to generation, stretches back into the very mists of antiquity and is, briefly, that some day a man shall come up out of the sea and shall lead the people of Egypt to victory over all others. This legend has spread over the continent so that now all black races consider that it deals with the coming of a universal emperor. Professor Schuyler gave it as his opinion that the myth was somehow connected with the lost Atlantis, which, he maintains, was located between the African and South American continents and to whose inhabitants the ancestors of the Egyptians were tributary. The reasons for his connection are too lengthy and vague to note here, but following the line of his theory he told me a strange and fantastic tale. He said that a close friend of his, Von Lorfmon of Germany, a sort of free-lance scientist, now dead, was sailing off the coast of Senegal some years ago, for the purpose of investigating and classifying the rare specimens of sealife found there. He was using for his purpose a small trading-vessel, manned by a crew of Moors, Greeks and Negroes.

"Some days out of sight of land, something floating was sighted, and this object, being grappled and brought aboard, proved to be *a mummy-case of a most curious kind*. Professor Schuyler explained to me the features whereby it differed from the ordinary Egyptian style, but from his rather technical account I merely got the impression that it was a strangely shaped affair carved with characters neither cuneiform nor hieroglyphic. The case was heavily lacquered, being watertight and airtight, and Von Lorfmon had considerable difficulty in opening it. However, he managed to do so without damaging the case, and a most unusual mummy was revealed. Schuyler said that he never saw either the mummy or the case, but that from descriptions given him by the Greek skipper who was present at the opening of the case, the mummy differed as much from the ordinary man as the case differed from the conventional type.

"Examination proved that the subject had not undergone the usual procedure of mummification. All parts were intact just as in life, but the whole form was shrunk and hardened to a wood-like consistency. Cloth wrappings swathed the thing and they crumbled to dust and vanished the instant air was let in upon them.

"Von Lorfmon was impressed by the effect upon the crew. The Greeks showed no interest beyond that which would ordinarily be shown by any man, but the Moors, and even more the Negroes, seemed to be rendered temporarily insane! As the case was hoisted on board, they all fell prostrate on the deck and raised a sort of worshipful chant, and it was necessary to use force in order to exclude them from the cabin wherein the mummy was exposed. A number of fights broke out between them and the Greek element of the crew, and the skipper and Von Lorfmon thought best to put back to the nearest port in all haste. The skipper attributed it to the natural aversion of seamen toward having a corpse on board, but Von Lorfmon seemed to sense a deeper meaning.

"They made port in Lagos, and that very night Von Lorfmon was murdered in his stateroom and the mummy and its case vanished. All the Moor and Negro sailors deserted ship the same night. Schuyler said – and here the matter took on a most sinister and mysterious aspect – that immediately afterward this widespread unrest among the natives began to smolder and take tangible form; he connected it in some manner with the old legend.

"An aura of mystery, also, hung over Von Lorfmon's death. He had taken the mummy into his stateroom, and anticipating an attack from the fanatical crew, had carefully barred and bolted door and portholes. The skipper, a reliable man, swore that it was virtually impossible to effect an entrance from without. And what signs were present pointed to the fact that the locks had been worked from *within*. The scientist was killed by a dagger which formed part of his collection and which was left in his breast.

"As I have said, immediately afterward the African cauldron began to seethe. Schuyler said that in his opinion the natives considered the ancient prophecy fulfilled. The mummy was *the man from the sea*.

"Schuyler gave as his opinion that the thing was the work of Atlanteans and that the man in the mummy-case was a native of lost Atlantis. How the case came to float up through the fathoms of water which cover the forgotten land, he does not venture to offer a theory. He is sure that somewhere in the ghost-ridden mazes of the African jungles the mummy has been enthroned as a god, and, inspired by the dead thing, the black warriors are gathering for a wholesale massacre. He believes, also, that some crafty Moslem is the direct moving power of the threatened rebellion."

Gordon ceased and looked up at me.

"Mummies seem to weave a weird dance through the warp of the tale," he said. "The German scientist took several pictures of the mummy with his camera, and it was after seeing these – which strangely enough were not stolen along with the thing – that Major Morley began to think himself on the brink of some monstrous discovery. His diary reflects his state of mind and becomes incoherent – his condition seems to have bordered on insanity. What did he learn to unbalance him so? Do you suppose that the mesmeric spells of Kathulos were used against him?"

"These pictures–" I began.

"They fell into Schuyler's hands and he gave one to Morley. I found it among the manuscripts."

He handed the thing to me, watching me narrowly. I stared, then rose unsteadily and poured myself a tumbler of wine.

"Not a dead idol in a voodoo hut," I said shakily, "but a monster animated by fearsome life, roaming the world for victims. Morley had seen the Master – that is why his brain crumbled. Gordon, as I hope to live again, *that face is the face of Kathulos!*"

Gordon stared wordlessly at me.

"The Master hand, Gordon," I laughed. A certain grim enjoyment penetrated the mists of my horror, at the sight of the steel-nerved Englishman struck speechless, doubtless for the first time in his life.

He moistened his lips and said in a scarcely recognizable voice, "Then, in God's name, Costigan, nothing is stable or certain, and mankind hovers at the brink of untold abysses of nameless horror. If that dead monster found by Von Lorfmon be in truth the Scorpion, brought to life in some hideous fashion, what can mortal effort do against him?"

"The mummy at Kamonos's–" I began.

"Aye, the man whose flesh, hardened by a thousand years of non-existence – that must have been Kathulos himself! He would have just had time to strip, wrap himself in the linens and step into the case before we entered. You remember that the case, leaning upright against the wall, stood partly concealed by a large Burmese idol, which obstructed our view and doubtless gave him time to accomplish his purpose. My God, Costigan, with what horror of the prehistoric world are we dealing?"

"I have heard of Hindoo fakirs who could induce a condition closely resembling death," I began. "Is it not possible that Kathulos, a shrewd and crafty Oriental, could have placed himself in this state and his followers have placed the case in the ocean where it was sure to be found? And might not he have been in this shape tonight at Kamonos's?"

Gordon shook his head.

"No. I have seen these fakirs. None of them ever feigned death to the extent of becoming shriveled and hard – in a word, dried up. Morley, narrating in another place the description of the mummy-case as jotted down by Von Lorfmon and passed on to Schuyler, mentions the fact that large portions of seaweed adhered to it – seaweed of a kind found only at great depths, on the bottom of the ocean. The wood, too, was of a kind which Von Lorfmon failed to recognize or to classify, in spite of the fact that he was one of the greatest living authorities on flora. And his notes again and again emphasize the enormous *age* of the thing. He admitted that there was no way of telling how old the mummy was, but his hints intimate that he believed it to be, not thousands of years old, but millions of years!

"No. We must face the facts. Since you are positive that the picture of the mummy is the picture of Kathulos – and there is little room for fraud – one of two things is practically certain: the Scorpion was never dead but ages ago was placed in that mummy-case and his life preserved in some manner, or else – he was dead and has been brought to life! Either of these theories, viewed in the cold light of reason, is absolutely untenable. Are we all insane?"

"Had you ever walked the road to hashish land," I said somberly, "you could believe anything to be true. Had you ever gazed into the terrible reptilian eyes of Kathulos the sorcerer, you would not doubt that he was both dead and alive."

Gordon gazed out the window, his fine face haggard in the gray light which had begun to steal through them.

"At any rate," said he, "there are two places which I intend exploring thoroughly before the sun rises again – Kamonos' antique shop and Soho 48."

XVIII : THE GRIP OF THE SCORPION

"While from a proud tower in the town
Death looks gigantically down."
–POE

Hansen snored on the bed as I paced the room. Another day had passed over London and again the street lamps glimmered through the fog. Their lights affected me strangely. They seemed to beat, solid waves of energy, against my brain. They twisted the fog into strange sinister shapes. Footlights of the stage that is the streets of London, how many grisly scenes had they lighted? I pressed my hands hard against my throbbing temples, striving to bring my thoughts back from the chaotic labyrinth where they wandered.

Gordon I had not seen since dawn. Following the clue of "Soho 48" he had gone forth to arrange a raid upon the place and he thought it best that I should remain under cover. He anticipated an attempt upon my life, and again he feared that if I went searching among the dives I formerly frequented it would arouse suspicion.

Hansen snored on. I seated myself and began to study the Turkish shoes which clothed my feet. Zuleika had worn Turkish slippers – how she floated through my waking dreams, gilding prosaic things with her witchery! Her face smiled at me from the fog; her eyes shone from the flickering lamps: her phantom footfalls re-echoed through the misty chambers of my skull.

They beat an endless tattoo, luring and haunting till it seemed that these echoes found echoes in the hallway outside the room where I stood, soft and stealthy. A sudden rap at the door and I started.

Hansen slept on as I crossed the room and flung the door swiftly open. A swirling wisp of fog had invaded the corridor, and through it, like a silver veil, I saw her – Zuleika stood before me with her shimmering hair and her red lips parted and her great dark eyes.

Like a speechless fool I stood and she glanced quickly down the hallway and then stepped inside and closed the door.

"Gordon!" she whispered in a thrilling undertone. "Your friend! The Scorpion has him!"

Hansen had awakened and now sat gaping stupidly at the strange scene which met his eyes.

Zuleika did not heed him.

"And oh, Steephen!" she cried, and tears shone in her eyes, "I have tried so hard to secure some more elixir but I could not."

"Never mind that," I finally found my speech. "Tell me about Gordon."

"He went back to Kamonos's alone, and Hassim and Ganra Singh took him captive and brought him to the Master's house. Tonight assemble a great host of the people of the Scorpion for the sacrifice."

"Sacrifice!" A grisly thrill of horror coursed down my spine. Was there no limit to the ghastliness of this business?

"Quick, Zulelka, where is this house of the Master's?"

"Soho 48. You must summon the police and send many men to surround it, but you must not go yourself–"

Hansen sprang up quivering for action, but I turned to him. My brain was clear now, or seemed to be, and racing unnaturally.

"Wait!" I turned back to Zuleika. "When is this sacrifice to take place?"

"At the rising of the moon."

"That is only a few hours before dawn. Time to save him, but if we raid the house they'll kill him before we can reach them. And God only knows how many diabolical things guard all approaches."

"I do not know," Zuleika whimpered. "I must go now, or the Master will kill me."

Something gave way in my brain at that; something like a flood of wild and terrible exultation swept over me.

"The Master will kill no one!" I shouted, flinging my arms on high.

"Before ever the east turns red for dawn, the Master dies! By all things holy and unholy I swear it!"

Hansen stared wildly at me and Zuleika shrank back as I turned on her. To my dope-inspired brain had come a sudden burst of light, true and unerring.

I knew Kathulos was a mesmerist – that he understood fully the secret of dominating another's mind and soul. And I knew that at last I had hit upon the reason of his power over the girl. Mesmerism! As a snake fascinates and draws to him a bird, so the Master held Zuleika to him with unseen shackles. So absolute was his rule over her that it held even when she was out of his sight, working over great distances.

There was but one thing which would break that hold: the magnetic power of some other person whose control was stronger with her than Kathulos's. I laid my hands on her slim little shoulders and made her face me.

"Zuleika," I said commandingly, "here you are safe; you shall not return to Kathulos. There is no need of it. Now you are free."

But I knew I had failed before I ever started. Her eyes held a look of amazed, unreasoning fear and she twisted timidly in my grasp.

"Steephen, please let me go!" she begged. "I must – I must!"

I drew her over to the bed and asked Hansen for his handcuffs. He handed them to me, wonderingly, and I fastened one cuff to the bed-post and the other to her slim wrist. The girl whimpered but made no resistance, her limpid eyes seeking mine in mute appeal.

It cut me to the quick to enforce my will upon her in this apparently brutal manner but I steeled myself.

"Zuleika," I said tenderly. "you are now my prisoner. The Scorpion can not blame you for not returning to him when you are unable to do so – and before dawn you shall be free of his rule entirely."

I turned to Hansen and spoke in a tone which admitted of no argument.

"Remain here, just without the door, until I return. On no account allow any strangers to enter – that is, anyone whom you do not personally know. And I charge you, on your honor as a man, do not release this girl, no matter what she may say. If neither I nor Gordon have returned by ten o'clock tomorrow, take her to this address – that family once were friends of mine and will take care of a homeless girl. I am going to Scotland Yard."

"Steephen," Zuleika wailed, "you are going to the Master's lair? You will be killed. Send the police, do not go!"

I bent, drew her into my arms, felt her lips against mine, then tore myself away.

The fog plucked at me with ghostly fingers, cold as the hands of dead men, as I raced down the street. I had no plan, but one was forming in my mind, beginning to seethe in the stimulated cauldron that was my brain. I halted at the sight of a policeman pacing his beat, and beckoning him to me, scribbled a terse note on a piece of paper torn from a notebook and handed it to him.

"Get this to Scotland Yard; it's a matter of life and death and it has to do with the business of John Gordon."

At that name, a gloved hand came up in swift assent, but his assurance of haste died out behind me as I renewed my flight. The note stated briefly that Gordon was a prisoner at Soho 48 and advised an immediate raid in force – advised, nay, in Gordon's name, commanded it.

My reason for my actions was simple; I knew that the first noise of the raid sealed John Gordon's doom. Somehow I first must reach him and protect or free him before the police arrived.

The time seemed endless, but at last the grim gaunt outlines of the house that was Soho 48 rose up before me, a giant ghost in the fog. The hour grew late; few people dared the mists and the dampness as I came to a halt in the street before this forbidding building. No lights showed from the windows, either upstairs or down. It seemed deserted. But the lair of the scorpion often seems deserted until the silent death strikes suddenly.

Here I halted and a wild thought struck me. One way or another, the drama would be over by dawn. Tonight was the climax of my career, the ultimate top of life. Tonight I was the strongest link in the strange chain of events. Tomorrow it would not matter whether I lived or died. I drew the flask of elixir from my pocket and gazed at it. Enough for two more days if properly eked out. Two more days of life! Or – I needed stimulation as I never needed it before; the task in front of me was one no mere human could hope to accomplish. If I drank the entire remainder of the elixir, I had no idea as to the duration of its effect, but it would last the night through. And my legs were shaky; my mind had curious periods of utter vacuity; weakness of brain and body assailed me. I raised the flask and with one draft drained it.

For an instant I thought it was death. Never had I taken such an amount.

Sky and world reeled and I felt as if I would fly into a million vibrating fragments, like the bursting of a globe of brittle steel. Like fire, like hell-fire the elixir raced along my veins and I was a giant! a monster! a superman!

Turning, I strode to the menacing, shadowy doorway. I had no plan; I felt the need of none. As a drunken man walks blithely into danger, I strode to the lair of the Scorpion, magnificently aware of my superiority, imperially confident of my stimulation and sure as the unchanging stars that the way would open before me.

Oh, there never was a superman like that who knocked commandingly on the door of Soho 48 that night in the rain and the fog!

I knocked four times, the old signal that we slaves had used to be admitted into the idol-room at Yun Shatu's. An aperture opened in the center of the door and slanted eyes looked warily out. They slightly widened as the owner recognized me, then narrowed wickedly.

"You fool!" I said angrily. "Don't you see the mark?"

I held my hand to the aperture.

"Don't you recognize me? Let me in, curse you."

I think the very boldness of the trick made for its success. Surely by now all the Scorpion's slaves knew of Stephen Costigan's rebellion, knew that he was marked for death. And the very fact that I came there, inviting doom, confused the doorman.

The door opened and I entered. The man who had admitted me was a tall, lank Chinaman I had known as a servant of Kathulos. He closed the door behind me and I saw we stood in a sort of vestibule, lighted by a dim lamp whose glow could not be seen from the street for the reason that the windows were heavily curtained. The Chinaman glowered at me undecided. I looked at him, tensed. Then suspicion flared in his eyes and his hand flew to his sleeve. But at the instant I was on him and his lean neck broke like a rotten bough between my hands.

I eased his corpse to the thickly carpeted floor and listened. No sound broke the silence. Stepping as stealthily as a wolf, fingers spread like talons, I stole into the next room. This was furnished in Oriental style, with couches and rugs and gold-worked drapery, but was empty of human life. I crossed it and went into the next one. Light flowed softly from the censers which were swung from the ceiling, and the Eastern rugs deadened the sound of my footfalls: I seemed to be moving through a castle of enchantment.

Every moment I expected a rush of silent assassins from the doorways or from behind the curtains or screen with their writhing dragons. Utter silence, reigned. Room after room I explored and at last halted at the foot of the stairs. The inevitable censer shed an uncertain light, but most of the stairs were veiled in shadows. What horrors awaited me above?

But fear and the elixir are strangers and I mounted that stair of lurking terror as boldly as I had entered that house of terror. The upper rooms I found to be much like those below and with them they had this fact in common: they were empty of human life. I sought an attic but there seemed no door letting into one. Returning to the first floor, I made a search for an entrance into the basement, but again my, efforts were fruitless. The amazing truth was borne in upon me: except for myself and that dead man who lay sprawled so grotesquely in the outer vestibule, there were no men in that house, dead or living.

I could not understand It. Had the house been bare of furniture I should have reached the natural conclusion that Kathulos had fled – but no signs of flight met my eye. This was unnatural, uncanny. I stood in the great shadowy library and pondered. No, I had made no mistake in the house. Even if the broken corpse in the vestibule were not there to furnish mute testimony, everything in the room pointed toward the presence of the Master. There were the artificial palms, the lacquered screen, the tapestries, even the idol, though now no incense smoke rose before it. About the walls were ranged long shelves of books, bound in strange and costly fashion – books in every language in the world, I found from a swift examination, and on every subject – outré and bizarre, most of them.

Remembering the secret passage in the Temple of Dreams, I investigated the heavy mahogany table which stood in the center of the room. But nothing resulted. A sudden blaze of fury surged up in me, primitive and unreasoning. I snatched a statuette from the table and dashed it against the shelf-covered wall. The noise of its breaking would surely bring the gang from their hiding-place. But the result was much more startling than that!

The statuette struck the edge of a shelf and instantly the whole section of shelves with their load of books swung silently outward, revealing a narrow doorway! As in the other secret door, a row of steps led downward. At another time I would have shuddered at the thought of descending, with the horrors of the other tunnel fresh in my mind, but inflamed as I was by the elixir, I strode forward without an instant's hesitancy.

Since there was no one in the house, they must be somewhere in the tunnel or in whatever lair to which the tunnel led. I stepped through the doorway, leaving the door open; the police might find it that way and follow me, though somehow I felt as if mine would be a lone hand from the start to grim finish.

I went down a considerable distance and then the stair debouched into a level corridor some twenty feet wide – a remarkable thing. In spite of the width, the ceiling was rather low and from it hung small, curiously shaped lamps which flung a dim light. I stalked hurriedly along the corridor like old Death seeking victims, and as I went I noted the work of the thing. The floor was of great broad flags and the walls seemed to be of huge blocks of evenly set stone. This passage was clearly no work of modern days; the slaves of Kathulos never tunneled there. Some secret way of mediaeval times, I thought – and after all, who knows what catacombs lie below London, whose secrets are greater and darker than those of Babylon and Rome?

On and on I went, and now I knew that I must be far below the earth. The air was dank and heavy, and cold moisture dripped from the stones of walls and ceiling. From time to time I saw smaller passages leading away in the darkness but I determined to keep to the larger main one.

A ferocious impatience gripped me. I seemed to have been walking for hours and still only dank damp walls and bare flags and guttering lamps met my eyes. I kept a close watch for sinister-appearing chests or the like – saw no such things.

Then as I was about to burst into savage curses, another stair loomed up in the shadows in front of me.

XIX : DARK FURY

"The ringed wolf glared the circle round
Through baleful, blue-lit eye,
Not unforgetful of his debt.
Quoth he, 'I'll do some damage yet
Or ere my turn to die!'"
—MUNDY

Like a lean wolf I glided up the stairs. Some twenty feet up there was a sort of landing from which other corridors diverged, much like the lower one by which I had come. The thought came to me that the earth below London must be honeycombed with such secret passages, one above the other.

Some feet above this landing the step halted at a door, and here I hesitated, uncertain as to whether I should chance knocking or not. Even as I meditated, the door began to open. I shrank back against the wall, flattening myself out as much as possible. The door swung wide and a Moor came through. Only a glimpse I had of the room beyond, out of the corner of my eye, but my unnaturally alert senses registered the fact that the room was empty.

And on the instant, before he could turn, I smote the Moor a single deathly blow behind the angle of the jawbone and he toppled headlong down the stairs, to lie in a crumpled heap on the landing, his limbs tossed grotesquely about.

My left hand caught the door as it started to slam shut and in an instant I was through and standing in the room beyond. As I had thought, there was no occupant of this room. I crossed it swiftly and entered the next. These rooms were furnished in a manner before which the furnishings of the Soho house paled into insignificance. Barbaric, terrible, unholy – these words alone convey some slight idea of the ghastly sights which met my eyes. Skulls, bones and complete skeletons formed much of the decorations, if such they were. Mummies leered from their cases and mounted reptiles ranged the walls. Between these sinister relics hung African shields of hide and bamboo, crossed with assagais and war daggers. Here and there reared obscene idols, black and horrible.

And in between and scattered about among these evidences of savagery and barbarism were vases, screens, rugs and hangings of the highest Oriental workmanship: a strange and incongruous effect.

I had passed through two of these rooms without seeing a human being, when I came to stairs leading upward. Up these I went, several flights, until I came to a door in a ceiling. I wondered if I were still under the earth. Surely the first stairs had led into a house of some sort. I raised the door cautiously. Starlight met my eyes and I drew myself warily up and out. There I halted. A broad flat roof stretched away on all sides and beyond its rim on all sides glimmered the lights of London. Just what building I was on, I had no idea, but that it was a tall one I could tell, for I seemed to be above most of the lights

I saw. Then I saw that I was not alone.

Over against the shadows of the ledge that ran around the roof's edge, a great menacing form bulked in starlight. A pair of eyes glinted at me with a light not wholly sane; the starlight glanced silver from a curving length of steel. Yar Khan the Afghan killer fronted me in the silent shadows.

A fierce wild exultation surged over me. Now I could begin to pay the debt I owed Kathulos and all his hellish band! The dope fired my veins and sent waves of inhuman power and dark fury through me. A spring and I was on my feet in a silent, deathly rush.

Yar Khan was a giant, taller and bulkier than I. He held a tulwar, and from the instant I saw him I knew that he was full of the dope to the use of which he was addicted – heroin.

As I came in he swung his heavy weapon high in air, but ere he could strike I seized his sword wrist in an iron grip and with my free hand drove smashing blows into his midriff.

Of that hideous battle, fought in silence, above the sleeping city with only the stars to see, I remember little. I remember tumbling back and forth, locked in a death embrace. I remember the stiff beard rasping my flesh as his dope-fired eyes gazed wildly into mine. I remember the taste of hot blood in my mouth, the tang of fearful exultation in my soul, the onrushing and upsurging of inhuman strength and fury.

God, what a sight for a human eye, had anyone looked upon that grim roof where two human leopards, dope maniacs, tore each other to pieces!

I remember his arm breaking like rotten wood in my grip and the tulwar falling from his useless hand. Handicapped by a broken arm, the end was inevitable, and with one wild uproaring flood of might, I rushed him to the edge of the roof and bent him backward far out over the ledge. An instant we struggled there; then I tore loose his hold and hurled him over, and one single shriek came up as he hurtled into the darkness below.

I stood upright, arms hurled up toward the stars, a terrible statue of primordial triumph. And down my breast trickled streams of blood from the long wounds left by the Afghan's frantic nails, on neck and face.

Then I turned with the craft of the maniac. Had no one heard the sound of that battle? My eyes were on the door through which I had come, but a noise made me turn, and for the first time I noticed a small affair like a tower jutting up from the roof. There was no window there, but there was a door, and even as I looked that door opened and a huge black form framed itself in the light that streamed from within. Hassim!

He stepped out on the roof and closed the door, his shoulders hunched and neck out-thrust as he glanced this way and that. I struck him senseless to the roof with one hate-driven smash. I crouched over him, waiting some sign of returning consciousness; then away in the sky, close to the horizon, I saw a faint red tint. The rising of the moon!

Where in God's name was Gordon? Even as I stood undecided, a strange noise reached me. It was curiously like the droning of many bees.

Striding in the direction from which it seemed to come, I crossed the roof and leaned over the ledge. A sight nightmarish and incredible met my eyes.

Some twenty feet below the level of the roof on which I stood, there was another roof, of the same size and clearly a part of the same building. On one side it was bounded by the wall; on the other three sides a parapet several feet high took the place of a ledge.

A great throng of people stood, sat and squatted, close-packed on the roof – and without exception they were Negroes! There were hundreds of them, and it was their low-voiced conversation which I had heard. But what held my gaze was that upon which their eyes were fixed.

About the center of the roof rose a sort of teocalli some ten feet high, almost exactly like those found in Mexico and on which the priests of the Aztecs sacrificed human victims. This, allowing for its infinitely smaller scale, was an exact type of those sacrificial pyramids. On the flat top of it was a curiously carved altar, and beside it stood a lank, dusky form whom even the ghastly mask he wore could not disguise to my gaze – Santiago, the Haiti voodoo fetish man. On the altar lay John Gordon, stripped to the waist and bound hand and foot, but conscious.

I reeled back from the roof edge, rent in twain by indecision. Even the stimulus of the elixir was not equal to this. Then a sound brought me about to see Hassim struggling dizzily to his knees. I reached him with two long strides and ruthlessly smashed him down again. Then I noticed a queer sort of contrivance dangling from his girdle. I bent and examined it. It was a mask similar to that worn by Santiago. Then my mind leaped swift and sudden to a wild desperate plan, which to my dope-ridden brain seemed not at all wild or desperate. I stepped softly to the tower and, opening the door, peered inward. I saw no one who might need to be silenced, but I saw a long silken robe hanging upon a peg in the wall. The luck of the dope fiend! I snatched it and closed the door again. Hassim showed no signs of consciousness but I gave him another smash on the chin to make sure and, seizing his mask, hurried to the ledge.

A low guttural chant floated up to me, jangling, barbaric, with an undertone of maniacal blood-lust. The Negroes, men and women, were swaying back and forth to the wild rhythm of their death chant. On the teocalli Santiago stood like a statue of black basalt, facing the east, dagger held high – a wild and terrible sight, naked as he was save for a wide silken girdle and that inhuman mask on his face. The moon thrust a red rim above the eastern horizon and a faint breeze stirred the great black plumes which nodded above the voodoo man's mask. The chant of the worshippers dropped to a low, sinister whisper.

I hurriedly slipped on the death mask, gathered the robe close about me and prepared for the descent. I was prepared to drop the full distance, being sure in the superb confidence of my insanity that I would land unhurt, but as I climbed over the ledge I found a steel ladder leading down. Evidently Hassim, one of the voodoo priests, intended descending this way. So down I went, and in haste, for I knew that the instant the moon's lower rim cleared the city's skyline, that motionless dagger would descend into Gordon's breast.

Gathering the robe close about me so as to conceal my white skin, I stepped down upon the roof and strode forward through rows of black worshippers who shrank aside to let me through. To the foot of the teocalli I stalked and up the stairs that ran about it, until I stood beside the death altar and marked the dark red stains upon it. Gordon lay on his back, his eyes open, his face drawn and haggard, but his gaze dauntless and unflinching.

Santiago's eyes blazed at me through the slits of his mask, but I read no suspicion in his gaze until I reached forward and took the dagger from his hand. He was too much astonished to resist, and the black throng fell suddenly silent. That he saw my hand was not that of a Negro it is certain, but he was simply struck speechless with astonishment. Moving swiftly I cut Gordon's bonds and hauled him erect. Then Santiago with a shriek leaped upon me − shrieked again and, arms flung high, pitched headlong from the teocalli with his own digger buried to the hilt in his breast,

Then the black worshippers were on us with a screech and a roar − leaping on the steps of the teocalli like black leopards in the moonlight, knives flashing, eyes gleaming whitely.

I tore mask and robe from me and answered Gordon's exclamation with a wild laugh. I had hoped that by virtue of my disguise I might get us both safely away, but now I was content to die there at his side.

He tore a great metal ornament from the altar, and as the attackers came he wielded this. A moment we held them at bay and then they flowed over us like a black wave. This to me was Valhalla! Knives stung me and blackjacks smashed against me, but I laughed and drove my iron fists in straight, steam-hammer smashes that shattered flesh and bone. I saw Gordon's crude weapon rise and fall, and each time a man went down. Skulls shattered and blood splashed and the dark fury swept over me. Nightmare faces swirled about me and I was on my knees; up again and the faces crumpled before my blows. Through far mists I seemed to hear a hideous familiar voice raised in imperious command.

Gordon was swept away from me but from the sounds I knew that the work of death still went on. The stars reeled through fogs of blood, but hell's exaltation was on me and I reveled in the dark tides of fury until a darker deeper tide swept over me and I knew no more.

XX : ANCIENT HORROR

"Here now in his triumph where all things falter
Stretched out on the spoils that his own hand spread,
As a God self-slain on his own strange altar,
Death lies dead."
−SWINBURNE

Slowly I drifted back into life − slowly, slowly. A mist held me and in the mist I saw a Skull–

I lay in a steel cage like a captive wolf, and the bars were too strong, I saw, even for my strength. The cage seemed to be set in a sort of niche in the wall and I was looking into a large room. This room was under the earth, for the floor was of stone flags and the walls and ceiling were composed of gigantic blocks of the same material. Shelves ranged the walls, covered with weird appliances, apparently of a scientific nature, and more were on the great table that stood in the center of the room. Beside this sat Kathulos.

The Sorcerer was clad in a snaky yellow robe, and those hideous hands and that terrible head were more pronouncedly reptilian than ever. He turned his great yellow eyes toward me, like pools of livid fire, and his parchment-thin lips moved in what probably passed for a smile.

I staggered erect and gripped the bars, cursing.

"Gordon, curse you, where is Gordon?"

Kathulos took a test-tube from the table, eyed it closely and emptied it into another.

"Ah, my friend awakes," he murmured in his voice – the voice of a living dead man.

He thrust his hands into his long sleeves and turned fully to me.

"I think in you," he said distinctly, "I have created a Frankenstein monster. I made of you a superhuman creature to serve my wishes and you broke from me. You are the bane of my might, worse than Gordon even. You have killed valuable servants and interfered with my plans. However, your evil comes to an end tonight. Your friend Gordon broke away but he is being hunted through the tunnels and can not escape.

"You," he continued with the sincere interest of the scientist, "are a most interesting subject. Your brain must be formed differently from any other man that ever lived. I will make a close study of it and add it to my laboratory. How a man, with the apparent need of the elixir in his system, has managed to go on for two days still stimulated by the last draft is more than I can understand."

My heart leaped. With all his wisdom, little Zuleika had tricked him and he evidently did not know that she had filched a flask of the life-giving stuff from him.

"The last draft you had from me," he went on, "was sufficient only for some eight hours. I repeat, it has me puzzled. Can you offer any suggestion?"

I snarled wordlessly. He sighed.

"As always the barbarian. Truly the proverb speaks: 'Jest with the wounded tiger and warm the adder in your bosom before you seek to lift the savage from his savagery'."

He meditated awhile in silence. I watched him uneasily. There was about him a vague and curious difference – his long fingers emerging from the sleeves drummed on the chair arms and some hidden exultation strummed at the back of his voice, lending it unaccustomed vibrancy.

"And you might have been a king of the new regime," he said suddenly.

"Aye, the new – new and inhumanly old!"

I shuddered as his dry cackling laugh rasped out.

He bent his head as if listening. From far off seemed to come a hum of guttural voices. His lips writhed in a smile.

"My black children," he murmured. "They tear my enemy Gordon to pieces in the tunnels. They, Mr. Costigan, are my real henchmen – and it was for their edification tonight that I laid John Gordon on the sacrificial stone. I would have preferred to have made some experiments with him, based on certain scientific theories, but my children must be humored. Later under my tutelage they will outgrow their childish superstitions and throw aside their foolish customs, but now they must be led gently by the hand.

"How do you like these under-the-earth corridors, Mr. Costigan?" he switched suddenly. "You thought of them what? No doubt that the white savages of your Middle Ages built them? Faugh! These tunnels are older than your world. They were brought into being by mighty kings, too many eons ago for your mind to grasp, when an imperial city towered where now this crude village of London stands. All trace of that metropolis has crumbled to dust and vanished, but these corridors were built by more than human skill – ha ha! Of all the teeming thousands who move daily above them, none knows of their existence save my servants – and not all of them. Zuleika, for instance, does not know of them, for of late I have begun to doubt her loyalty and shall doubtless soon make of her an example."

At that I hurled myself blindly against the side of the cage, a red wave of hate and fury tossing me in its grip. I seized the bars and strained until the veins stood out on my forehead and the muscles bulged and crackled in my arms and shoulders. And the bars bent before my onslaught – a little but no more, and finally the power flowed from my limbs and I sank down trembling and weakened. Kathulos watched me imperturbably.

"The bars hold," he announced with something almost like relief in his tone. "Frankly, I prefer to be on the opposite side of them. You are a human ape if there was ever one."

He laughed suddenly and wildly.

"But why do you seek to oppose me?" he shrieked unexpectedly. "Why defy me, who am Kathulos, the Sorcerer, great even in the days of the old empire? Today, invincible! A magician, a scientist, among ignorant savages! Ha ha!"

I shuddered, and sudden blinding light broke in on me. Kathulos himself was an addict, and was fired by the stuff of his choice! What hellish concoction was strong enough, terrible enough to thrill the Master and inflame him, I do not know, nor do I wish to know. Of all the uncanny knowledge that was his, I, knowing the man as I did, count this the most weird and grisly.

"You, you paltry fool!" he was ranting, his face lit supernaturally. "Know you who I am? Kathulos of Egypt! Bah! They knew me in the old days! I reigned in the dim misty sea lands ages and ages before the sea rose and engulfed the land. I died, not as men die; the magic draft of life everlasting was ours! I drank deep and slept. Long I slept in my lacquered case! My flesh withered and grew hard; my blood dried in my veins. I became as one dead. But still within me burned the spirit of life, sleeping but anticipating the awakening. The great cities crumbled to dust. The sea drank the land. The tall shrines and the lofty spires sank beneath the green waves. All this I knew as I slept, as a man knows in dreams. Kathulos of Egypt? Faugh! *Kathulos of Atlantis!*"

I uttered a sudden involuntary cry. This was too grisly for sanity.

"Aye, the magician, the Sorcerer.

"And down the long years of savagery, through which the barbaric races struggled to rise without their masters, the legend came of the day of empire, when one of the Old Race would rise up from the sea. Aye, and lead to victory the black people who were our slaves in the old days.

"These brown and yellow people, what care I for them? The blacks were the slaves of my race, and I am their god today. They will obey me. The yellow and the brown peoples are fools – I make them my tools and the day will come when my black warriors will turn on them and slay at my word. And you, you white barbarians, whose ape-ancestors forever defied my race and me, your doom is at hand! And when I mount my universal throne the only whites shall be white slaves!

"The day came as prophesied, when my case, breaking free from the halls where it lay – where it had lain when Atlantis was still sovran of the world – where since her empery it had sunk into the green fathoms – when my case, I say, was smitten by the deep sea tides and moved and stirred, and thrust aside the clinging seaweed that masks temples and minarets, and came floating up past the lofty sapphire and golden spires, up through the green waters, to float upon the lazy waves of the sea.

"Then came a white fool carrying out the destiny of which he was not aware. The men on his ship, true believers, knew that the time had come. And I – the air entered my nostrils and I awoke from the long, long sleep. I stirred and moved and lived. And rising in the night, I slew the fool that had lifted me from the ocean, and my servants made obeisance to me and took me into Africa, where I abode awhile and learned new languages and new ways of a new world and became strong.

"The wisdom of your dreary world – ha ha! I who delved deeper in the mysteries of the old than any man dared go! All that men know today, I know, and my knowledge beside that which I have brought down the centuries is as a grain of sand beside a mountain! You should know something of that knowledge! By it I lifted you from one hell to plunge you into greater! You fool, here at my hand is that which would lift you from this! Aye, would strike from you the chains whereby I have bound you!"

He snatched up a golden vial and shook it before my gaze. I eyed it as men dying in the desert must eye the distant mirages. Kathulos fingered it meditatively. His unnatural excitement seemed to have passed suddenly, and when he spoke again it was in the passionless, measured tones of the scientist.

"That would indeed be an experiment worth while – to free you of the elixir habit and see if your dope-riddled body would sustain life. Nine times out of ten the victim, with the need and stimulus removed, would die – but you are such a giant of a brute–"

He sighed and set the vial down.

"The dreamer opposes the man of destiny. My time is not my own or I should choose to spend my life pent in my laboratories, carrying out my experiments. But now, as in the days of the old empire when kings sought my counsel, I must work and labor for the good of the race at large. Aye, I must toil and sow the seed of glory against the full coming of the imperial days when the seas give up all their living dead."

I shuddered. Kathulos laughed wildly again. His fingers began to drum his chair arms and his face gleamed with the unnatural light once more. The red visions had begun to seethe in his skull again.

"Under the green seas they lie, the ancient masters, in their lacquered cases. Dead as men reckon death, but only sleeping. Sleeping through the long ages as hours, awaiting the day of awakening! The old masters, the wise men, who foresaw the day when the sea would gulp the land, and who made ready. Made ready that they might rise again in the barbaric days to come. As did I . Sleeping they lie, ancient kings and grim wizards, who died as men die, before Atlantis sank. Who, sleeping, sank with her but who shall arise again!

"Mine the glory! I rose first. And I sought out the site of old cities, on shores that did not sink. Vanished, long vanished. The barbarian tide swept over them thousands of years ago as the green waters swept over their elder sister of the deeps. On some, the deserts stretch bare. Over some, as here, young barbarian cities rise–"

He halted suddenly. His eyes sought one of the dark openings that marked a corridor. I think his strange intuition warned him of some impending danger but I do not believe that he had any inkling of how dramatically our scene would be interrupted.

As he looked, swift footsteps sounded and a man appeared suddenly in the doorway – a man disheveled, tattered and bloody. *John Gordon!* Kathulos sprang erect with a cry, and Gordon, gasping as from superhuman exertion, brought down the revolver he held in his hand and fired point-blank.

Kathulos staggered, clapping his hand to his breast, and then, groping wildly, reeled to the wall and fell against it. A doorway opened and he reeled through, but as Gordon leaped fiercely across the chamber, a blank stone surface met his gaze, which yielded not to his savage hammerings.

He whirled and ran drunkenly to the table where lay a bunch of keys the Master had dropped there.

"The vial!" I shrieked. "Take the vial!" And he thrust it into his pocket.

Back along the corridor through which he had come sounded a faint clamor growing swiftly like a wolf-pack in full cry. A few precious seconds spent with fumbling for the right key, then the cage door swung open and I sprang out. A sight for the gods we were, the two of us! Slashed, bruised and cut, our garments hanging in tatters – my wounds had ceased to bleed, but now as I moved they began again, and from the stiffness of my hands I knew that my knuckles were shattered. As for Gordon, he was fairly drenched in blood from crown to foot.

We made off down a passage in the opposite direction from the menacing noise, which I knew to be the black servants of the Master in full pursuit of us. Neither of us was in good shape for running, but we did our best. Where we were going I had no idea. My superhuman strength had deserted me and I was going now on will-power alone. We switched off into another corridor and we had not gone twenty steps until, looking back, I saw the first of the black devils round the corner.

A desperate effort increased our lead a trifle. But they had seen us, were in full view now, and a yell of fury broke from them to be succeeded by a more sinister silence as they bent all efforts to overhauling us.

There a short distance in front of us we saw a stair loom suddenly in the gloom. If we might reach that – but we saw something else.

Against the ceiling, between us and the stairs, hung a huge thing like an iron grille, with great spikes along the bottom – a portcullis. And even as we looked, without halting in our panting strides, it began to move.

"They're lowering the portcullis!" Gordon croaked, his blood-streaked face a mask of exhaustion and will.

Now the blacks were only ten feet behind us – now the huge grate, gaining momentum, with a creak of rusty, unused mechanism, rushed downward. A final spurt, a gasping straining nightmare of effort – and Gordon, sweeping us both along in a wild burst of pure nerve-strength, hurled us under and through, and the grate crashed behind us!

A moment we lay gasping, not heeding the frenzied horde who raved and screamed on the other side of the grate. So close had that final leap been, that the great spikes in their descent had torn shreds from our clothing.

The blacks were thrusting at us with daggers through the bars, but we were out of reach and it seemed to me that I was content to lie there and die of exhaustion. But Gordon weaved unsteadily erect and hauled me with him.

"Got to get out," he croaked; "got to warn – Scotland Yard – honeycombs in heart of London – high explosives – arms ammunition."

We blundered up the steps, and in front of us I seemed to hear a sound of metal grating against metal. The stairs ended abruptly, on a landing that terminated in a blank wall. Gordon hammered against this and the inevitable secret doorway opened. Light streamed in, through the bars of a sort of grille. Men in the uniform of London police were sawing at these with hacksaws, and even as they greeted us, an opening was made through which we crawled.

"You're hurt, sir!" One of the men took Gordon's arm.

My companion shook him off.

"There's no time to lose! Out of here, as quick as we can go!"

I saw that we were in a basement of some sort. We hastened up the steps and out into the early dawn which was turning the east scarlet. Over the tops of smaller houses I saw in the distance a great gaunt building on the roof of which, I felt instinctively, that wild drama had been enacted the night before.

"That building was leased some months ago by a mysterious Chinaman," said Gordon, following my gaze. "Office building originally – the neighbourhood deteriorated and the building stood vacant for some time. The new tenant added several storeys to it but left it apparently empty. Had my eye on it for some time."

This was told in Gordon's jerky swift manner as we started hurriedly along the sidewalk. I listened mechanically, like a man in a trance. My vitality was ebbing fast and I knew that I was going to crumple at any moment.

"The people living in the vicinity had been reporting strange sights and noises. The man who owned the basement we just left heard queer sounds emanating from the wall of the basement and called the police. About that time I was racing back and forth among those cursed corridors like a hunted rat and I heard the police banging on the wall. I found the secret door and opened it but found it barred by a grating. It was while I was telling the astounded policemen to procure a hacksaw that the pursuing Negroes, whom I had eluded for the moment, came into sight and I was forced to shut the door and run for it again. By pure luck I found you and by pure luck managed to find the way back to the door.

"Now we must get to Scotland Yard. If we strike swiftly, we may capture the entire band of devils. Whether I killed Kathulos or not I do not know, or if he can be killed by mortal weapons. But to the best of my knowledge all of them are now in those subterranean corridors and–"

At that moment the world shook A brain-shattering roar seemed to break the sky with its incredible detonation; houses tottered and crashed to ruins; a mighty pillar of smoke and flame burst from the earth and on its wings great masses of debris soared skyward. A black fog of smoke and dust and falling timbers enveloped the world, a prolonged thunder seemed to rumble up from the center of the earth as of walls and ceilings falling, and amid the uproar and the screaming I sank down and knew no more.

XXI : THE BREAKING OF THE CHAIN

"And like a soul belated,
in heaven and hell unmated,
By cloud and mist abated,
Comes out of darkness morn."
—SWINBURNE

There is little need to linger on the scenes of horror of that terrible London morning. The world is familiar with and knows most of the details attendant to the great explosion which wiped out a tenth of that great city with a resultant loss of lives and property. For such a happening some reason must needs be given; the tale of the deserted building got out, and many wild stories were circulated.

Finally, to still the rumors, the report was unofficially given out that this building had been the rendezvous and secret stronghold of a gang of international anarchists, who had stored its basement full of high explosives and who had supposedly ignited these accidentally. In a way there was a good deal to this tale, as you know, but the threat that had lurked there far transcended any anarchist.

All this was told to me, for when I sank unconscious, Gordon, attributing my condition to exhaustion and a need of the hashish to the use of which he thought I was addicted, lifted me and with the aid of the stunned policemen got me to his rooms before returning to the scene of the explosion. At his rooms he found Hansen, and Zuleika handcuffed to the bed as I had left her. He released her and left her to tend to me, for all London was in a terrible turmoil and he was needed elsewhere.

When I came to myself at last, I looked up into her starry eyes and lay quiet, smiling up at her. She sank down upon my bosom, nestling my head in her arms and covering my face with her kisses.

"Steephen!" she sobbed over and over, as her tears splashed hot on my face.

I was scarcely strong enough to put my arms about her but I managed it, and we lay there for a space, in silence except for the girl's hard, racking sobs.

"Zuleika, I love you," I murmured.

"And love you, Steephen," she sobbed. "Oh, it is so hard to part now – but I'm going with you, Steephen; I can't live without you!"

"My dear child," said John Gordon, entering the room suddenly, "Costigan's not going to die. We will let him have enough hashish to tide him along, and when he is stronger we will take him off the habit slowly."

"You don't understand, sahib; it is not hashish Steephen must have. It is something which only the Master knew, and now that he is dead or is fled, Steephen can not get it and must die."

Gordon shot a quick, uncertain glance at me. His fine face was drawn and haggard, his clothes sooty and torn from his work among the debris of the explosion.

"She's right, Gordon," I said languidly. "I'm dying. Kathulos killed the hashish-craving with a concoction he called the elixir. I've been keeping myself alive on some of the stuff that Zuleika stole from him and gave me, but I drank it all last night."

I was aware of no craving of any kind, no physical or mental discomfort even. All my mechanism was slowing down fast; I had passed the stage where the need of the elixir would tear and rend me. I felt only a great lassitude and a desire to sleep. And I knew that the moment I closed my eyes, I would die.

"A strange dope, that elixir," I said with growing languor. "It burns and freezes and then at last the craving kills easily and without torment."

"Costigan, curse it," said Gordon desperately, "you can't go like this! That vial I took from the Egyptian's table – what was in it?"

"The Master swore it would free me of my curse and probably kill me also," I muttered. "I'd forgotten about it. Let me have it; it can no more than kill

282

me and I'm dying now."

"Yes, quick, let me have it!" exclaimed Zuleika fiercely, springing to Gordon's side, her hands passionately outstretched. She returned with the vial which he had taken from his pocket, and knelt beside me, holding it to my lips, while she murmured to me gently and soothingly in her own language.

I drank, draining the vial, but feeling little interest in the whole matter. My outlook was purely impersonal, at such a low ebb was my life, and I can not even remember how the stuff tasted. I only remember feeling a curious sluggish fire burn faintly along my veins, and the last thing I saw was Zuleika crouching over me, her great eyes fixed with a burning intensity on me. Her tense little hand rested inside her blouse, and remembering her vow to take her own life if I died I tried to lift a hand and disarm her, tried to tell Gordon to take away the dagger she had hidden in her garments. But speech and action failed me and I drifted away into a curious sea of unconsciousness.

Of that period I remember nothing. No sensation fired my sleeping brain to such an extent as to bridge the gulf over which I drifted. They say I lay like a dead man for hours, scarcely breathing, while Zuleika hovered over me, never leaving my side an instant, and fighting like a tigress when anyone tried to coax her away to rest. Her chain was broken.

As I carried the vision of her into that dim land of nothingness, so her dear eyes were the first thing which greeted my returning consciousness. I was aware of a greater weakness than I thought possible for a man to feel, as if I had been an invalid for months, but the life in me, faint though it was, was sound and normal, caused by no artificial stimulation. I smiled up at my girl and murmured weakly:

"Throw away your dagger, little Zuleika; I'm going to live."

She screamed and fell on her knees beside me, weeping and laughing at the same time. Women are strange beings, of mixed and powerful emotions, truly.

Gordon entered and grasped the hand which I could not lift from the bed.

"You're a case for an ordinary human physician now, Costigan," he said. "Even a layman like myself can tell that. For the first time since I've known you, the look in your eyes is entirely sane. You look like a man who has had a complete nervous breakdown, and needs about a year of rest and quiet. Great heavens, man, you've been through enough, outside your dope experience, to last you a lifetime."

"Tell me first," said I, "was Kathulos killed in the explosion?"

"I don't know," answered Gordon somberly. "Apparently the entire system of subterranean passages was destroyed. I know my last bullet – the last bullet that was in the revolver which I wrested from one of my attackers – found its mark in the Master's body, but whether he died from the wound, or whether a bullet can hurt him, I do not know. And whether in his death agonies he ignited the tons and tons of high explosives which were stored in the corridors, or whether the Negroes did it unintentionally, we shall never know.

"My God, Costigan, did you ever see such a honeycomb? And we know not how many miles in either direction the passages reached. Even now Scotland Yard men are combing the subways and basements of the town for secret openings. All known openings, such as the one through which we came and the one in Soho 48, were blocked by falling walls. The office building was simply blown to atoms."

"What about the men who raided Soho 48?"

"The door in the library wall had been closed. They found the Chinaman you killed, but searched the house without avail. Lucky for them, too, else they had doubtless been in the tunnels when the explosion came, and perished with the hundreds of Negroes who must have died then."

"Every Negro in London must have been there."

"I dare say. Most of them are voodoo worshippers at heart and the power the Master wielded was incredible. They died, but what of him? Was he blown to atoms by the stuff which he had secretly stored, or crushed when the stone walls crumbled and the ceilings came thundering down?"

"There is no way to search among those subterranean ruins, I suppose?"

"None whatever. When the walls caved in, the tons of earth upheld by the ceiling also came crashing down, filling the corridors with dirt and broken stone, blocking them forever. And on the surface of the earth, the houses which the vibration shook down were heaped high in utter ruins. What happened in those terrible corridors must remain forever a mystery."

My tale draws to a close. The months that followed passed uneventfully, except for the growing happiness which to me was paradise, but which would bore you were I to relate it. But one day Gordon and I again discussed the mysterious happenings that had had their being under the grim hand of the Master.

"Since that day," said Gordon, "the world has been quiet. Africa has subsided and the East seems to have returned to her ancient sleep. There can be but one answer – living or dead, Kathulos was destroyed that morning when his world crashed about him."

"Gordon," said I, "what is the answer to that greatest of all mysteries?"

My friend shrugged his shoulders.

"I have come to believe that mankind eternally hovers on the brinks of secret oceans of which it knows nothing. Races have lived and vanished before our race rose out of the slime of the primitive, and it is likely still others will live upon the earth after ours has vanished. Scientists have long upheld the theory that the Atlanteans possessed a higher civilization than our own, and on very different lines. Certainly Kathulos himself was proof that our boasted culture and knowledge were nothing beside that of whatever fearful civilization produced him.

"His dealings with you alone have puzzled all the scientific world, for none of them has been able to explain how he could remove the hashish craving, stimulate you with a drug so infinitely more powerful, and then produce another drug which entirely effaced the effects of the other."

"I have him to thank for two things," I said slowly; "the regaining of my lost manhood – and Zuleika. Kathulos, then, is dead, as far as any mortal thing can die. But what of those others – those 'ancient masters' who still sleep in the sea?"

Gordon shuddered.

"As I said, perhaps mankind loiters on the brink of unthinkable chasms of horror. But a fleet of gunboats is even now patrolling the oceans unobtrusively, with orders to destroy instantly any strange case that may be found floating – to destroy it and its contents. And if my word has any weight with the English government and the nations of the world, the seas will be so patrolled until doomsday shall let down the curtain on the races of today."

"At night I dream of them sometimes," I muttered, "sleeping in their lacquered cases, which drip with strange seaweed, far down among the green surges where unholy spires and strange towers rise in the dark ocean."

"We have been face to face with an ancient horror," said Gordon somberly, "with a fear too dark and mysterious for the human brain to cope with. Fortune has been with us; she may not again favor the sons of men. It is best that we be ever on our guard. The universe was not made for humanity alone; life takes strange phases and it is the first instinct of nature for the different species to destroy each other. No doubt we seemed as horrible to the Master as he did to us. We have scarcely tapped the chest of secrets which nature has stored, and I shudder to think of what that chest may hold for the human race."

"That's true," said I, inwardly rejoicing at the vigor which was beginning to course through my wasted veins. "But men will meet obstacles as they come, as men have always risen to meet them. Now, I am beginning to know the full worth of life and love, and not all the devils from all the abysses can hold me."

Gordon smiled.

"You have it coming to you, old comrade. The best thing is to forget all that dark interlude, for in that course lies light and happiness."

ROBERT ERVIN HOWARD : A MEMORIAM

BY H. P. LOVECRAFT

The sudden and unexpected death on June 11 (1936) of Robert Ervin Howard, author of fantastic tales of incomparable vividness, forms weird fiction's worst loss since the passing of Henry S. Whitehead four years ago.

Mr. Howard was born at Peaster, Texas, January 22, 19066, and was old enough to have seen the last phase of southwestern pioneering – the settlement of the great plains and the lower Rio Grande valley, and the spectacular rise of the oil Industry with its raucous boom towns. His father, who survives him, was one of the pioneer physicians of the region. The family has lived in South, East and West Texas, and western Oklahoma; for the last few years at Cross Plains, near Brownwood, Texas. Steeped in the frontier atmosphere, Mr. Howard early became a devotee of its virile Homeric traditions. His knowledge of its history and folkways was profound, and the descriptions and reminiscences contained in his private letters illustrate the eloquence and power with which he would have celebrated it in literature had he lived longer. Mr. Howard's family is of distinguished southern planter stock – of Scotch-Irish descent, with most ancestors settled in Georgia and North Carolina in the eighteenth century.

Beginning to write at fifteen, Mr. Howard placed his first story three years later while a student at Howard Payne College in Brownwood. This story, Spear and Fang, was published in Weird Tales for July, 1925. Wider fame came with the appearance of the novelette, *Wolfshead*, in the same magazine in April, 1926. In August, 1928, began the tales dealing with Solomon Kane, an English Puritan of relentless duelling and wrong-redressing practices whose adventures took him to strange parts of the world, including the shadow-haunted ruins of unknown and primordial cities in the African jungle. With these tales Mr. Howard struck what proved to be one of his most effective accomplishments – the description of vast megalithic cities of the elder world, around whose dark towers and labyrinthine nether vaults lingers – an aura of pre-human fear and necromancy which no other writer could duplicate. These tales also marked Mr. Howard's development of that skill and zest in depicting sanguinary conflict which became so typical of his work. 'Solomon Kane', like several other heroes of the author was conceived in boyhood long before incorporation in any story.

Always a keen student of Celtic antiquities and other phases of remote history, Mr. Howard began in 1929 – with "The Shadow Kingdom", in the August *Weird Tales* – that succession of tales of the prehistoric world for which he soon grew so famous. The earlier specimens described a very distant age in man's history – when Atlantis, Lemuria and Mu were above the waves; and when the shadows of pre-human reptile men rested upon the primal scene. Of these the central figure was king Kull of Valusia. In Weird Tales for December, 1932, appeared The Phoenix on the Sword first of those tales of King Conan the

Cimmerian, which introduced a later prehistoric world, a world of perhaps 15,000 years ago, just before the first glimmerings of recorded history. The elaborate extent and accurate self-consisting with which Mr. Howard developed this world of Conan in his later stories is well known to all fantasy readers. For his own guidance he prepared a detailed quasi-historical sketch of infinite cleverness and imaginative fertility.

Meanwhile, Mr. Howard had written many tales of the early Picts and Celts, including a notable series, revolving round the chieftain Bran Mak Morn. Few readers will ever forget the hideous and compelling power of that macabre masterpiece, Worms of the Earth, In Weird Tales for November, 1932. Other powerful fantasies lay outside the connected series – these included the memorable serial, Skull-Face, and a few distinctive tales with a modem setting such as Black Canaan, with its genuine, regional background and its clutchingly compelling picture of the horror that stalks through the moss-hung, shadow-cursed, serpent-ridden swamps of the American far south.

Outside the fantasy field Mr. Howard was surprisingly prolific and versatile. His strong interest in sports – a thing perhaps connected with his love of primitive conflict and strength – led him to create the prize-fighting hero, 'Sailor Steve Costigan', whose adventures in distant and curious parts delighted the readers of many magazines. His novelettes of oriental warfare displayed to the utmost his mastery of romantic swashbuckling, while his increasingly frequent tales of western life – such as the 'Breckinridge Elkins' series – showed his growing ability and inclination to reflect the backgrounds with which he was directly familiar.

Mr. Howard's poetry – weird, warlike, and adventurous was no less notable than his prose. It had the true spirit of the ballad and the epic, and was marked by a pulsing rhythm and potent imagery of the extreme distinctive cast. Much of it, in the form of supposed quotations from ancient writings, served to head the chapters of his novels. It is regrettable that no published collection of his has ever appeared, and one hopes that such a thing may be posthumously edited and issued.

The character and attainments of Mr. Howard were wholly unique. He was, above everything else, a lover of the simpler, older world of barbarian and pioneer days, when courage and strength took the place of subtlety and stratagem, and when a hardy, fearless race battled and bled, and asked no quarter from hostile nature. All his stories reflect this philosophy, and derive from it a vitality found in few of his contemporaries. No one could write more convincingly of violence and gore than he, and his battle passages reveal an Instinctive aptitude for military tactics which would have brought him distinction in times of war. His real gifts were even higher than the readers of his published works would suspect, and had he lived, would have helped him to make his mark in serious literature with some folk epic of his beloved southwest.

It is hard to describe precisely what made Mr. Howard's stories stand out so sharply; but the real secret is that he himself is In every one of them, whether they were ostensibly commercial or not. He was greater than any profit-making policy he could adopt – for even when he outwardly made concessions to Mammon-guided editors and commercial critics, he had an internal force and sincerity which broke through the surface and put the imprint of his personality on everything he wrote. Seldom, if ever, did he set down a lifeless stock character or situation and leave it as such. Before he concluded with it, it always took on some tinge of vitality and reality, in spite of popular editorial policy – always drew something from his own experience and knowledge of life instead of from the sterile herbarium of desiccated pulpish standbys. Not only did he excel in pictures of strife and slaughter, but he was almost alone in his ability to create real emotions of spectral fear and dread suspense. No author – even in the humblest fields – can truly excel unless he takes his work very seriously;. and Mr. Howard did just that even in cases where he consciously thought he did not. That such a genuine artist should perish while hundreds of insincere hacks continue to concoct spurious ghosts and vampires and spaceships and occult detectives is Indeed a sorry piece of cosmic irony!

Mr. Howard, familiar with many phases of southwestern life, lived with his parents in a semi-rural setting In the village of Cross Plains, Texas. Writing was his sole profession. His tastes In reading were wide and included historical research of notable depth in fields as dissimilar as the American southwest, prehistoric Great Britain, and Ireland, and the prehistoric Oriental and African world. In literature he preferred the virile to the subtle, and repudiated modernism with sweeping completeness. The late Jack London was one of his Idols. He was a liberal In politics, and a bitter foe of civic injustice in every form. His leading amusements were sports and travel – the latter always giving rise to delightful descriptive letters replete with historical reflections. Humor was not a specialty, though he had on the one hand a keen sense of irony, and on the other hand an abundant fund of heartiness, cordiality, and conviviality. Though having numerous friends, Mr. Howard belonged to no literary clique and abhorred all cults of 'arty' affection. His admirations ran toward strength of body and character rather than toward scholastic prowess. With his fellow authors in the fantasy field he corresponded interestingly and voluminously, but never met more than one of them – the gifted E. Hoffmann Price, whose varied attainments impressed him profoundly – in person.

Mr. Howard was nearly six feet in height, with the massive build of a born fighter. He was, save for Celtic blue eyes, very dark; and in later years his weight averaged around 195. Always a disciple of hearty and strenuous living, he suggested more than casually his own famous character – the intrepid warrior, adventurer, and seizer of thrones, Conan the Cimmerian. His loss at the age of thirty is a tragedy of the first magnitude, and a blow from which fantasy fiction will not soon recover. Mr. Howard's library has been presented to Howard Payne College, where it will form the nucleus of the Robert E. Howard Memorial Collection of books, manuscripts, and letters.